INTERGALACTIC FEAST

Also by Lavanya Lakshminarayan

The Ten Percent Thief
Interstellar MegaChef

PRAISE FOR
INTERGALACTIC FEAST

"Intensely compelling. A riveting story of food and politics and learning to be your authentic self no matter the cost."

K. B. Wagers, author of *A Pale Light in the Black*

"Fun and deliciously chaotic, crammed full of the flavours of life, each balanced to create an unforgettable journey."

Tashan Mehta, author of *Mad Sisters of Esi*

"Retains the subtle, complex flavours of *MegaChef*, and gives us new, explosive tastes to savour. A magnificent arrangement of voice, craft and concept."

Samit Basu, author of *The City Inside*

PRAISE FOR
INTERSTELLAR MEGACHEF

"A rich exploration of why we love food and how it connects us to memory and family."

The Washington Post

"An intelligent dissection of utopian societies and the insidious nature of cultural imperialism."

Locus

"A lot of fun."

New Scientist

"Both playful and serious… Hand to readers of Becky Chambers and Ryka Aoki."

Booklist

"A delicious, futuristic flight of fancy… rich and nuanced."

Publishers Weekly

"An engaging story that dives into themes about the appreciation of food, colonization, and xenophobia and features two morally gray queer women attempting to find their footing with each other."

***Library Journal*, starred review**

"A funny, smart dive into how much food habits can tell about people and cultures across the world(s)."

Indrapramit Das, author of *The Devourers*

PRAISE FOR LAVANYA LAKSHMINARAYAN

'Smart, vivid, engaging.'

The Guardian

'Impressive.'

SFX

'Bold and creative.'

Starburst Magazine

'Innovative.'

Strange Horizons

'A new masterpiece.'

SciFiNow

'Vivid and engaging.'

The Times of India

FLAVOUR HACKER BOOK TWO

LAVANYA LAKSHMINARAYAN

SOLARIS

First published 2026 by Solaris
an imprint of Rebellion Publishing Ltd,
Riverside House, Osney Mead,
Oxford, OX2 0ES, UK

www.solarisbooks.com

ISBN: 978-1-83786-682-3

10 9 8 7 6 5 4 3 2 1

A CIP catalogue record for this book is available from the British Library.

Designed & typeset by Rebellion Publishing

Printed in Denmark

To all your star-kissed memories on a plate transcending space-time with love.

Patches, Scamper and Tugger: Mangoes, gulab jamun and carrot cake will always bring me home to you.

A Brief History of the Nakshatrans

2301 CE 1 Anno Earth	Nationhood collapses on Earth, giving rise to a new, united human civilisation that calls itself One Nation Earth.
2325 CE 25 Anno Earth	The Nakshatran Programme is founded on Earth.
2350 CE 50 Anno Earth	The Nakshatran Charter is drafted and made public at the First Nakshatran Conference.
2361 CE 61 Anno Earth	The first Nakshatran spaceflight is launched, seeking a new planet for humans to call home.
2376 CE 76 Anno Earth	*Nakshatran One* lands on Primus. It is Year One of the Interstellar Era.

A perfect plate is where all beginnings and endings meet. And a perfect plate is naturally Primian. We honour the past, revel in the present, and tread lightly into the future, stepping gently into the continuum of our Nakshatran legacy.

—Grace Menmo,
Art and Culture in the Interstellar Era:
The Definitive Edition
2065 Anno Earth | 1990 Interstellar Era

Feast boggles the mind, delivers a sucker punch to the senses, and launches food into the far future. It blends rich, evocative memories with impossible dreams. Just add water!

—Saraswati Kaveri,
Press conference announcing Feast Inc.
2074 Anno Earth | 1999 Interstellar Era

…and this year, the Golden Knife goes to a chef who has pushed the boundaries of our understanding of elevated cuisine with a cultural twist. She has demonstrated that foods from all Protectorates on Earth are worthy of appreciation, open to innovation, and quite frankly, extraordinary.

Congratulations, Saraswati Godavari of Elé Oota!

—Ahana Shah, Presenter,
The Jury of the Golden Knife Awards
2073 Anno Earth | 1998 Interstellar Era

ONE

'I've never been happier to see *anyone* in all my thirty-one years alive!' I flung my arms around Starlight Fantastic, nearly knocking my favourite E'nemon off balance.

Starlight Fantastic's many-fold tentacles enveloped me, tinged purple. 'I'm so proud of you! You've been everywhere, giving the most wonderful stream-media interviews, dazzling your way across the Loop…'

'Thank you!' I beamed, squeezing them tight.

'Oh, stop!' said Boundless Baz, from where he lounged on the sofa. 'The last thing we need is *another* celebrity chef with a supersized ego.'

'You have Kili to thank for this reunion,' Starlight Fantastic continued.

'He streamed all of us,' XX-29 added.

'Since clearly we've been forgotten by a certain *famous chef*,' Boundless Baz persisted.

'Hey! I'm here, aren't I?' I argued.

'Yes, I'm so grateful to be spending time with you for the first time in a complete māsa.' Boundless Baz rolled his eyes. 'Let's all rearrange our lives around Saras's schedule. What do you think, 29? Shall we walk out of service at Nonpareil the next time Saras demands an audience?'

'I think that's a terrible idea, Baz,' XX-29 said seriously, xir globular being tinged with deep-green concern. Xe shrank within xir mechatronic frame.

'Yes, that's an awful idea, Baz,' I confirmed. 'As someone who used to work at Nonpareil, I think your employers would likely fire you.'

XX-29 quailed, xir deep green being now mottled with heightened anxiety.

'I was joking,' Boundless Baz clarified.

'He was joking.' I grinned at XX-29, wondering if I'd ever learn to translate human humour to a B'naar being, or to any other form of intelligent life in the Milky Way Galaxy, for that matter.

'Being fired doesn't seem very funny,' XX-29 burbled, confused.

'*Anyway,*' Courage Oslo said, cutting in. 'We're very glad to see you, Saras.'

I beamed at my hosts. We were gathered around Courage Oslo and Curiosity Zia's living room for the first time in what felt like an age. I'd briefly worked with them at their experimental restaurant, The New Palette, and I was glad our friendship extended beyond the walls of their kitchen.

'Thank you for giving me an excuse for me to cook over an open flame,' I said.

'Thank *Kili,*' Curiosity Zia asserted.

Sneaky. I stroked Kili's curves, and he ruffled his whirring mechanical wings like a little bird. _I needed this._

You're welcome, Kili said. _I could tell you needed some time off. Your schedule for Feast has been relentless._

I'd become the face of Feast after we'd won *Interstellar MegaChef: The Millennium Feast Special*.

I had multiple galaxy-wide food science patents, comprising my signature flavour continuums and flavour matrices. XP Inc.'s legal team had worked behind the scenes to ensure that *all* my intellectual property was protected. I'd been invited to the most elite social events on Primus, interviewed endlessly and thrown in front of the cam-drones by the XP Inc. publicity team, all of whom were delighted by my public persona as a rags-to-riches Earthling immigrant—a *refugee,* no less—who had risen to fame, and found success on Primus, the heart of culture and inclusivity in the Greater Human Collective.

Half the culinary pundits hailed me as "the face of the future of food" while the other half claimed I was the "harbinger of doom for a thousand-year-old food culture."

It was an incredible adrenaline rush to give voice to my ambitions. It was also incredibly exhausting.

Cooking! Open flame! Kili chirruped, whirring around.

On the kitchen counter, a small pressurised cook-pot beeped loudly. 'I'm not sure how well this will turn out…' I said, warily regarding the bright pink appliance.

'Saras, you *really* don't have to cook for us…' Starlight Fantastic waved a couple of their fronds to indicate the very busy countertop in front of me.

'She definitely *wants* to cook for us,' Curiosity Zia chimed in. 'At least, Kili says she does. He badgered us into disabling the smoke alarms all morning.'

'I'm in favour of Saras cooking,' Boundless Baz said lazily, settling into the cushions.

'I *definitely* want to cook you all lunch,' I confirmed, grinning.

'Saras, we miss you in the Nonpareil kitchen. Family has never been the same since you left.' Boundless Baz seemed to register the blank faces around him, and explained how I'd first been assigned to cooking meals before dinner service, for the Nonpareil chefs. 'She'd whip out these incredible Earth-inspired dishes. I have recent Earthling ancestry, so it reminded me of my grandparents…'

My insides welled up with warmth and contentment as I half listened to Boundless Baz's story, while diverting most of my attention to my cooking equipment. Kili had bullied me into visiting Curiosity Zia and Courage Oslo this morning, but he hadn't said anything about everyone else being there. He hadn't mentioned ordering ingredients for one of my favourite Earthling dishes, including sourcing locally grown substitutes for many Earthling ingredients that weren't available on Primus. My insides had lit up the moment I walked in to see a neatly laid out mise en place that hinted at the prospect of making khatti dal and steamed arasi… and over an open flame, at that.

The cheerful murmur of my friends' voices surrounded me, wrapping me up like a warm blanket.

I wish you had a larger frame, I streamed Kili.

Are you trying to bot-shame me?

I want to give you the biggest hug in the world and never let you go, I said, _and you're currently too small._

Huh.

And you squirm too much.

I can be still.

I laughed.

I'll prove it, he said, and settled on my shoulder, curling one of his small mechanical wings as far as it would go around the back of my neck.

See? Still. He whirred gently.

That tickles, I giggled.

I'm sorry I bothered to demonstrate affection, Kili sulked.

Thank you for this day, I said as I resumed my cook.

I'd pre-soaked some lentils that were a close approximation of toor dal for a couple of hours, letting them soften. They went into the pressure pot, along with some sliced matomatos (a Primian substitute for tomatoes, which were the size of cherry tomatoes back on Earth, except bright blue, bursting with just the right sourness for this dish). Coarsely ground dried red chillis and turmeric joined them. I could have used a spice blend extracted from ras, but these Earth flavours needed to be bold. I'd added some inji and garlic paste, poured water into the pot, and shut the lid, hoping the machine would replicate the same effect as a pressure cooker back home.

Primian cooking never used whole ingredients. Their culinary tradition relied on extracting ras from naturally grown, local ingredients, concentrating flavours through a number of processes, and infusing different gels, gelées, terrines and pâtés with their flavour profiles. It had its roots in the earliest days of settling the planet—the Nakshatrans who'd first travelled here from Earth had vowed to "tread lightly," and after spending decades living on molecularly constituted spaceflight foods, had developed a complete culinary philosophy around them. They took little from the land, even though the land had plenty to give, and stuck rigidly to cooking methods that honoured their origins.

Perhaps my Earthling ways didn't permit me to appreciate the deep roots of this culture; it seemed exceedingly minimalist, prioritising conservation—on a planet where resources were seemingly limitless—over flavour. And maybe that's why the Primians were so protective of their cuisine. After all, the Earth had exploited its once-limitless resources to the point of near extinction, although the planet had struggled to right itself and do better since.

I flipped open the lid on my pressure pot and heaved a sigh of relief.

The dal had taken on a beautiful consistency, and the scent of spice and sourness rose to fill the air.

'That smells heavenly,' Curiosity Zia said, drawing in a deep breath and closing her eyes.

'Done already?' Boundless Baz asked excitedly, shooting to his feet. 'I hope you've made enough for fourth helpings.'

'Not quite done,' I laughed, reaching for a masher, another piece of kitchen equipment that was ridiculously hard to find on this planet. Curiosity Zia and Courage Oslo were well-stocked for strange, bizarre, and often archaic cooking implements thanks to their travels across the galaxy, but most Primian kitchens were woefully underprepared for techniques that involved whole ingredients.

Shockingly violent, you must be a barbarian, Kili teased as I gently pounded the cooked dal.

I grinned. 'Such an *outdated, aggressive* technique,' I said, imitating Harmony Rhea's breathy, high-pitched voice from her practically feral judgment of me on *MegaChef.*

Curiosity Zia grabbed a potted caculent from the kaapi-table, and held it before her, like a microphone. 'Mashing,' she said, throwing her arms out wide. 'We haven't mashed food in decades in professional kitchens across Primus, have we? Such a fascinating, *quaint* way to cook!' It was a surprisingly accurate impression of Grace Aurelle, the head judge and "Chief Chef" on *MegaChef*. Curiosity Zia had her down pat, with the commanding voice that bit out each word, laced with venom and thinly veiled with dramatic flair.

I snorted. Boundless Baz and Courage Oslo collapsed into the couch cushions in peals of laughter, and Starlight Fantastic and XX-29 looked around at their human companions uncertainly, clearly unable to understand how reliving my first appearance on *Interstellar MegaChef*—complete with the judges' xenophobic, hostile barbs—could be funny. Curiosity Zia attempted to explain how laughter was a very human way to process trauma, to the further amusement of everyone in the room.

'But isn't it demeaning to revisit the tragic past like this?' Starlight Fantastic asked, their tentacles curled up and pulsing mottled teal with uncertainty. 'The first time Saras was on the show, it was a debacle. She was heartbroken. She redeemed herself on the special episode and showed those judges what's what, but—'

'Humour is a way to not let the sadness of the past overwhelm you,' Curiosity Zia explained patiently.

'But… but *laughter*? *Mocking* the experience?' XX-29's mechatronic frame shuddered. 'The B'naar have long communal thought-exchanges to comfort each other in hard times. The eldest, upon hearing a tragic tale, chooses a song of mourning and begins it. Each of us joins xir, in order of seniority in our clan, and we sing different parts together, giving into the overwhelming sadness. This can go on for days, and we are left undisturbed to commiserate.'

'Ah, we have a similar tradition,' Starlight Fantastic said sagely. 'But we meditate in silent frequencies, alone and still together, until the time of tragedy has passed.'

'*What?*' Boundless Baz said, shocked out of his hysterical laughter. 'Does that mean… all of you can sing? And all of you know every single part to every song? How many songs are there? How have we never heard B'naar music?'

'Our music is private, not commercial,' XX-29 said, the onus of patiently explaining native culture now squarely on xir shoulders. 'Each clan has their own songs. And then there are the coming together songs, across clans…'

I continued pounding the dal with a stupidly content smile on my face.

I built this life for myself, surrounded by my friends here and my team mates at XP Inc. And Serenity Ko.

I tamped down my nerves at the thought of seeing her at the XP Inc. picnic later that night. It was becoming impossible for me to forget the last time we'd been in the same room together. We'd kissed again—a spilling over of feelings that had expressed themselves after one jumpgate kick too many. I'd awkwardly shut it down and left in the middle of the night, as I'd done every so often in the three māsas that had passed since we'd first kissed in front of an interstellar audience.

And like all those times over those three māsas, she'd said precisely nothing about my reaction. It helped that we barely saw each other at work. She'd flung herself into the final touches of behind-the-scenes development at the office, and I turned up at so many soirees they made my head spin, all with a smile plastered across my face.

We'd agreed upon a complete split of our responsibilities on Feast, to make sure we weren't getting in each other's way—with the bonus of avoiding setting off our utterly doomed hormones.

Make food, I commanded myself.

Being in the warmth of the kitchen again, working to the murmur of conversation, reminded me of my restaurant back on Earth, the one I'd shut down in a hurry, paying my staff six months' severance and disappearing on a freighter to Primus. On lighter days at Elé Oota, when we were dishing out a familiar menu, Juno would often break into one of the fisherfolk songs that her parents taught her, her dance with the fires of the tandoor often flowing with its rhythms. And whenever we had a stressful service, with a new menu or celebrity diners, Kartikeya would mysteriously carve out an extra chunk of time on the dessert station, whipping out simple, tiny sweet treats to keep us going.

I missed them dearly.

'Speaking of music traditions, there's an Ibnis-viewing party at this shack in the Ur-sands next māsa. They're having a traditional madrigal chorus in honour of the Millennium Festival,' Curiosity Zia said. 'Saras, I'm letting you know so you can block your schedule in advance. It's late at night,' she added, turning to Boundless Baz and XX-29. 'You should be able to make it after service. Especially you, 29. It'll be something to stream home about.'

'I'll do my best,' I promised.

'If the celebrity marketing team doesn't double-book her that night,' Boundless Baz teased. 'If she doesn't forget all about us humble, *un*-famous, common-folk friends.'

'*I'll be there.*' I relented. 'I love having friends who guilt-trip me into hanging out.'

'Humble. *Un*-famous,' Boundless Baz repeated.

I rolled my eyes.

The pressure-pot started an automatic cleansing cycle as soon as I transferred my dal into a large pan. My fingers froze around the soaked tamarind I was about to squeeze into it.

I missed *real* cooking, working with whole ingredients and all the physicality of food: its texture beneath my fingertips, the scents rising from cook-pots and marinades, the sounds of dicing and slicing on a chopping board, and sizzling, bubbling, whistling, and popping over the crackle of an open flame; a rhapsody of sensations engulfing me at its centre, calling me to give into the beautiful rhythms of a cook, sometimes a gleeful frolic into the unknown, other times a measured, masterful waltz.

I inhaled, squeezing the tamarind juice into the pot and adding some cilantrino.

*When's the last time I cooked?* I asked Kili, suddenly in a panic.

Saras, you're really missing out on a fascinating explanation about B'naar music. Luckily, I've taken notes, Kili trilled enthusiastically.

That's fantastic, but when's the last time I cooked? I repeated.

Well, you've made yourself food at home in the Faith of the Light…

Right. But that's Primian verging on the extra-depressing because of the ingredient restrictions.

You've been cooking at the XP Inc. office to help them work out flavour matrices, he suggested helpfully.

Those have also been Primian foods. Ras infusions and concentrators, marbling gels and gelées and spheres… I'm talking about *real* food.

Open flame food?

Earth-style food.

Oh, māsas ago, he said breezily. _Saras, do you know that B'naar music is never recorded and never repeatable? They have this complex system that's an equivalent to our scales, but with *way* more notes…_

Some other time, Kili. Please? I said weakly.

I was light-headed. How had I gone so long without expressing my true self on a plate? I steamed the arasi—a starchy grain inspired by rice—in the pressure pot. While it was cooking, I lit the small campfire-sized stove that Courage Oslo and Curiosity Zia had smuggled onto Primus in the guise of scrap metal, and the sight of flames leaping merrily away filled me with joy… and just a hint of sadness at what I'd given up to be here.

I seasoned the dal, adding more spices, tasting frequently until I was sure the sharp tang of tamarind had achieved a round wholesomeness in harmony with the rest of the dish, and then prepared my tempering. My hands worked on autopilot, my thoughts far away.

I *knew* I'd taken several big risks developing Feast. I was fully aware that the expertise I lent to it came from my grasp of flavour, and the science of taste—not my ability to cook and plate it. As a food-sim delivering flavour and audio-visual experiences straight into the brain, the tech meant that there would be no cooking involved. And I'd leapt at the opportunity to spearhead it because of the sheer, insane scale of its ambition, to boldly go where no chef had gone before.

None of this is surprising, so why does it feel like such a rude shock?

When the tempering started to sputter, I added the blend of curry leaves, mustard and cumin seeds, and garlic cloves into the dal, and it sizzled and hissed, crisp, fragrant aromas stinging my eyes. As my tears escaped, running down my cheeks, a sharp sense of loss cracked open within me.

Stop it, I snapped at my own thoughts. *You've done something no other chef in the history of humanity across the galaxy can claim.*

And I had to succeed in order to escape my past.

It wasn't about validation anymore. I wanted to become too big to fail, a presence impossible to ignore on the galactic stage, so that even if my family found me, they wouldn't be able to disappear me without a fight.

'Are you done yet?' Boundless Baz moaned. 'My tummy's rumbling, and it's starting to feel cruel.'

The pressure pot pinged in response.

'Done!' I said extra brightly, trying to conceal the gloom descending upon me. 'Lunch is served! If you give me a moment, I'll get to plating…'

'We'll help ourselves, thanks,' Boundless Baz said, delighted, crossing the living room in a couple of strides. He grabbed a plate and hovered over the pot of dal, taking heavy, exaggerated breaths. 'It smells divine.'

'Stop salivating over our food,' Courage Oslo said.

'Nine Virtues, someone get him away from our lunch.' Curiosity Zia elbowed him in the ribs. '*I* will plate your food for you, Baz. You're looming over it like a gigant from a children's Ur-drama.'

I stood off to the side, watching them as if from light-years away. *This* is what I fell in love with food for—the experience of watching other people devour it. If I were being honest, that held true for Feast, as well. At least, it had looked like they were devouring it on the *MegaChef* special episode, when I watched it back later on. But if I was *completely* honest with myself, it just wasn't as fulfilling as creating something from scratch with physical ingredients, working with my hands...

'This is amazing, Saras!' Courage Oslo cut through my thoughts.

'Nine Virtues, it might be the best thing you've ever made!' Curiosity Zia said enthusiastically.

'Absolutely lovely flavours, Saras...' XX-29 burbled joyfully. A small globular appendage extended outward from xir mechatronic frame, and was slowly absorbing the food off xir plate.

'*This-is-sur-fucking-delicious,*' Boundless Baz moaned, shovelling his lunch into his mouth, multiple handfuls at a time.

'And *we're* supposed to be savages?' I quipped.

'I have Earthling origins,' he mumbled, then lost himself in his food again.

'Baz, you're not fresh off the freighter *and* an Earthling refugee, are you?' XX-29 chuckled. Everyone stopped eating at once and stared at XX-29 in horrified silence.

'What did I say?' XX-29 asked, frozen in fear and very confused.

'That... that was a bit insensitive,' Courage Oslo said slowly.

'It was Earthling humour?' XX-29 suggested with a small whine from xir globular person. 'Take a traumatic incident and make a joke?'

'Oh! Oh, no, XX-29, you might have misunderstood...' Curiosity Zia began.

Xe began to shrink into xirself within the cockpit of xir exoskeleton. A low howl sounded from within, and xir vox-box crackled in confusion, unable to translate xir words, if there were any.

'No, it's okay,' I said, forcing a laugh. 'It's been many māsas, we can laugh about it now.'

I omitted the bit where I was perfectly happy to laugh about it on account of how everything I'd told them about my past, including being a refugee, was an enormous lie.

The howl grew in intensity, and XX-29 rocked back and forth sadly.

'It's okay,' I insisted. 'Misunderstandings happen. I'm not offended. And there's no way to explain humour properly, is there?'

I looked around the room, willing someone else to join me in comforting XX-29. Boundless Baz picked up on what I was trying to do right away.

'It's okay, XX-29!' he said brightly, putting his plate down with a hint of regret. 'Look, if *I'd* said it, it might have been a bad idea, but you're still learning about humans, aren't you?'

'Stupid, stupid B'naar brain,' XX-29 whimpered morosely.

'There was the one time I tried to make humour,' Starlight Fantastic said lightly. 'I was at a trade show, and a storm set in. We were on a floating barge on Sagaricus, and as you all know, the planet is submerged by water, so there are always storms, but this trade show was woefully underprepared. So when the winds started whipping in, dragging the waves and rain, and all that soggy mess onto the barge, I changed shape to protect all the humans, like this...'

They fanned out their fronds and expanded, growing larger and larger until they resembled an enormous, many-tentacled monster from human legend. 'I began to cover as many of them as I could, and the humans started screaming. And to set them at ease, I said "*Thank goodness our peoples are no longer at war, yes?*"'

Starlight Fantastic adopted a sombre expression, which unfolded eerily across their stretched out being. 'Nobody found me funny.'

Goodness, Kili snorted, straining against the need to fly loop the loops with laughter.

Curiosity Zia's sides shook. I met her gaze and laughter

burst out of her, shrieking like a rocket. I cracked, and doubled over, too.

'D-d-did y-y-you get in-in t-t-t-rouble?' she gasped between wheezes.

'They called the authorities and I was fined,' Starlight Fantastic said moodily. 'I swore to never attempt human humour again.'

'Well, that's too bad.' Courage Oslo was losing his battle to keep a straight face.

Something between a snort and a sob escaped from Boundless Baz, who dropped his plate, moaned in sorrow, started to clean up, and then collapsed on the floor, holding his ribs.

'What is it? What's so funny?' Starlight Fantastic asked.

XX-29 whistled a cheery tune. 'My E'nemon friend, you are now four times your size, and your appearance is utterly terrifying. You're recounting a story about being perceived as a threat of war while taking on this appearance, and how sad it makes you to be misunderstood, but there's no way you were anything but monstrous at the time of the story. Except, you weren't aware of it. Perhaps this makes you funny to our human companions? I admit, this would be considered slightly comical even on B'naar…'

'You're *both* a riot,' Boundless Baz groaned from the floor. 'A full-fledged *riot*.'

'Maybe we can be the stars of your next Feast pop-up, Saras?' XX-29 tried again.

'Oh, no, oh, no,' Boundless Baz shrieked from the floor, now sobbing with laughter.

Kili gave up, zooming around the room shrieking with merriment. And I collapsed into Curiosity Zia. We crashed to the floor, arms around each other, laughing until we wept, all the world forgotten.

XP isn't an escape from reality. It's an enhancement to reality.

Our nano-pills mesh with your biocircuits, transmitting signals to your brain through our patented neural mesh technology. In turn, this syncs with our databases up on the Loop, bringing you into a whole range of sim experiences.

Your life is richer, brighter, happier...

—Grace Kube,
the launch of XP Inc.
2064 Anno Earth | 1989 Interstellar Era

TWO

PRIMUS WORE ITS sky like a shroud of mourning, a murky canopy of clouds scudding across its dome to obscure the stars from view. It was muggy and uncomfortably warm, threatening the worst storm in decades, and it was getting on Serenity Ko's nerves.

It was tediously humid, causing sweat to trickle down her back like tendrils tickling at her nonstop. She hadn't factored in the humidity when she'd agreed to take the XP Inc. team out on a midnight picnic in the Urswood. She also hadn't accounted for the fact that the Wanderers would be out en masse, performing some kind of rain shower ritual in a neighbouring glade.

Low chanting from the Wanderers reached her ears, mostly drowned out by her team's loud cheers and shouts of joy. They were revelling in their success at building Feast into a full product line in such a short timeframe. Flashes of light and movement spun between the trees, but they were dulled by the incandescence of Saraswati, who stood off to one side, surrounded by a crowd of admirers.

Serenity Ko experienced the unpleasant sensation of being dragged through a jumpgate, despite never having done so. Her entire being was overtaken by a kind of rubbery weightlessness, her vision swum, and her head pounded as if the Axian sky-dancers were performing an elaborate arachno-dance routine along the insides of her skull. *Looking* at Saraswati from afar was enough to set her off, unasked for feelings setting her imagination ablaze…

Serenity Ko sprawled out on the picnic blanket beneath her, and looked up at the distinct lack of starlight. Ibnis was a ghostly luminescent wheel in the sky, its lost moon impossible to spot. She'd harboured the hope that a night-time picnic would be a beautiful romantic cliché, stars, moon and all, even if their colleagues on Feast were all present (which made it a work outing, ergo casual, and therefore, the perfect time to ask Saraswati to go with her to a Legends of the Future gig in a couple of māsas—in a perfectly casual way, of course). Serenity Ko wasn't looking for a relationship, or anything of the sort. She just wanted excuses to be in the same room as Saraswati. And romantic clichés could only aid her cause.

The sky remained stubbornly obscured by clouds. The darkness wasn't complete in the way a clear night sky lends itself to infinite promise; rather, it was the kind of darkness that hinted at multitudes of almost-light. A gloom that could be interpreted as blossoming hope or fading dreams, guaranteeing nothing but deep thoughts leading to a splitting headache.

A weight flopped down beside Serenity Ko.

'You're surprisingly sober,' Courage Praia's voice said from somewhere above her.

'I'm pacing myself.'

'Pressure getting to you?'

'Surprisingly, no. I'm excited,' Serenity Ko said, and was surprised at how sincerely she meant it.

'Saras is a hit with the team,' Courage Praia said in a low voice. 'They hang on her every word.'

'For someone who keeps accusing me of having a crush on her, you sure seem to be keeping a close eye on her,' Serenity Ko said accusingly, pulling herself upright. She glowered at her closest friend and her second-in-command at XP Inc.

'Helping you out.' Courage Praia winked, a grin spreading across their face.

'You *know* all my reasons—'

'Yes, of course. I know you don't want a committed relationship—and haven't for years, now.' They continued, gently, 'I also know that you're worried about your work relationship impacting things with Feast—'

'So why are you here telling me about her?'

'There are tables laden with Feast cubes, and the whole team is partaking of them. The Ko I know would be flitting around user testing, making notes from their experiences. There's a whole bar with Boundless Ano serving custom cocktails. The Ko I know would be knocking them back. And then there's Saras, looking drop-dead gorgeous…'

Serenity Ko dared another glance at Saraswati. Her form-fitting dress clung to her curves in a manner wholly inappropriate for relationships fraught with unresolved sexual tension, and rather than sweating like she'd been dunked in a pool of water, she glowed in the dim flow-flora lights that illuminated the glade.

'The Ko I know would be hitting on her *right now*,' Courage Praia continued. 'Instead, I see Ko lying on a picnic blanket, relaxing. Or maybe brooding. It's… different. Maybe it's a good thing? It's a refreshing change.'

Serenity Ko's insides snapped to attention. She was consumed by a sudden wave of guilt. She'd stopped working, when there was so much left to do.

'I'm tired,' she said out loud, and then blanched.

Courage Praia's eyes widened in shock. 'That—that's surprisingly human of you, Ko!'

'Star-fuck me. I can't afford to be tired, not tonight!'

Tomorrow, they would debut Feast to an invitation-only few. Her product would leave the building and make its way out into the wider world, when they opened the doors to their first Feast pop-up restaurant. Forty of the biggest names in the stream-media would be invited in, and they would judge it firsthand, instead of speculating upon its promise.

After that, two dozen Feast pop-ups were scheduled going into their big launch at the Millennium Feast. A whole cross-section of the Primian population would test and taste the new product. They'd be studying their responses, identifying issues, racing round the clock to fix problems, anticipating the road map for emerging needs in the future, *all while building hype…*

Serenity Ko scrambled to her feet, tapping into her reserves of energy, newly resurrected and reanimated.

'Ko, I wasn't telling you to go be a workaholic,' Courage Praia said helplessly.

'Not going to work. Yet.'

'I'm sorry—'

'Thanks, Praia. Good talk. Needed the boost.'

The woodland glade was ringed by the silhouettes of trees, which far from being ominous and imposing, had the cheering disposition of solid, steady witnesses to a night of celebration. The grass was damp with dew, inviting one to wander around on it barefoot, digging one's toes in the earth. Somewhere in the distance, an owl hooted. The chants of the Wanderers rose and fell like waves against the beach.

Serenity Ko plunged herself into the deep end of the picnic, strutting up to the makeshift bar—a flowmetal picnic table with Boundless Ano on one side and Saraswati seated on a bench across from him. Kili hovered a few feet above Saras's head, a whirring little ball of chrome and green, eagerly recording Boundless Ano at work as he spun out cocktails.

A bouquet of scents filled her senses, now that she'd been jolted out of her reverie. There were decomposing leaves (a stark reminder that nothing lasts forever), damp soil (hinting at impending rain), and the ineffable fragrance of woodland that could only be described as "the great outdoors." And then, there was the overriding scent of Saraswati, who smelled like flowers blossoming against all odds in the dead of night, fresh-cut and herby despite the humidity doing its best to make them wilt.

'One nīlatini, please,' she said to Boundless Ano, by way of greeting.

'Hello, Ko,' Boundless Ano smiled.

Serenity Ko ignored him, directing all her attention to Saraswati, who eyed her with amusement. Kili dropped down and nuzzled her cheek fondly, and Serenity Ko stroked him absentmindedly, her gaze focused on Saraswati.

She turned to Boundless Ano. 'Make that *two* nīlatinis.'

Boundless Ano served her first drink, and she slid it across the bar towards Saraswati, who took a sip. 'Delicious!' she pronounced. 'That nīlafruit infusion is—'

'There's a Wanderer rain-dance ritual happening in the glade beside us,' Serenity Ko interrupted pointedly. 'We should go watch for a bit.'

'Sure—'

Boundless Ano laughed.

'What?' Serenity Ko scowled, despising the interruption.

'Ko, you can't just walk in on the Wanderers during a ceremony,' Boundless Ano said, dropping her given-name as he was wont to do. Serenity Ko didn't usually mind, seeing as they'd been to university together, and he'd been the closest thing to a friend back then. It irked her now, though, as he fiddled with a cocktail shaker in fancy ways, trampling all over her conversation with Saraswati, who seemed spellbound by his technique, her eyes following him intently. Naturally, this made Serenity Ko deeply jealous.

Boundless Ano continued to hold Saraswati's attention. 'This is typical Ko,' he explained. 'I once had to talk her out of interrupting a Vyāsr feasting ceremony—she was wasted and hungry, and they had an enormous peprino-basted roast beest—'

'I don't want to do anything offensive!' Saraswati said.

Serenity Ko's scowl deepened. 'Go on then, Ano. Tell us all about the Wanderers, with your *extensive* expertise.'

Boundless Ano rolled his eyes. 'See these? They're my rings, one for each time I've been Wandering,' he explained, holding up his right hand to reveal three stone-studded bands. 'If Serenity Ko had *bothered* to do her compulsory Wanderers service like practically everyone else on Primus, instead of being granted an official waiver for being a child prodigy and jumping straight into her job at XP Inc., she'd know that this isn't some savage rain-dance *ritual*.'

'What is it, then?' Saraswati asked, leaning forward.

'It's a combined Faith of the Light, Rumian and Vyāsr monk *ceremony* honouring the rain to come, and the Wanderers are merely present as *observers*.' Boundless Ano grinned. 'The Wanderers, as you know, are charged with monitoring the Arc, making sure all this unspoiled natural beauty we get to enjoy is healthy and thriving. And the other spiritual orders on Primus believe they're welcoming the rain, but also appeasing it so it doesn't destroy our world.'

'So… savages?' Serenity Ko tilted her head with a guileless smile.

'Typical Ur-sider,' Boundless Ano said, then turned to Saraswati. 'Ko has even less regard than most for the Wanderers.'

He placed a nīlatini before her, and Serenity Ko took a giant swig. 'And Ano has done more than his compulsory Wanderers service, so he's clearly got outdoorsy tendencies.'

Boundless Ano's lips twitched in amusement. 'All I'm saying, Saras, is don't let *Ko* be your guide to Primus!'

Saraswati laughed and turned to Serenity Ko, who nearly fell off the bench at the twinkle in her eyes.

'Right, let's not intrude on the ceremony,' she said decisively.

'People who don't want to be watched shouldn't perform in public spaces,' Serenity Ko grumbled, her plan to lead Saraswati off to a quiet corner now thwarted.

She glanced around. Grace Kube, Optimism Sah'r and Courage Na'vil were surrounded by a sea of faces, all hanging on to their every word as they recounted the story of how they'd founded XP Inc. Courage Praia and the ever-enthusiastic Curiosity Nenna were leading members of the Feast team in a spirited tasting session. In the absence of tranquility, quietude, and privacy of any sort, she decided to take the brazen approach.

'You're a Legends of the Future fan, aren't you?' Serenity Ko asked, without bothering to aspire to smoothness of any sort.

I have vids of her dancing around with a hairbrush, Kili streamed.

No, you don't! Saraswati said firmly.

'They're playing at the Stellar Arena as part of the Millennium Festival,' Serenity Ko blurted out.

'Who?' Saraswati asked.

'Legends. Of the Future,' Serenity Ko repeated slowly. 'Seriously, is the humidity broiling your ability to have a conversation?'

'D-did you just say *broiling*?' Saraswati giggled. 'Nine Virtues, Kili! Ko just used a *cooking* metaphor.'

Never thought I'd see the day, Kili laughed.

'I *listen* when you talk.' Serenity Ko pouted, secretly delighted at having made Saraswati laugh. 'Unlike *some* people.'

'Who, me?'

'Legends of the Future,' she said again, impatience rising to the surface as she tapped her fingers against her nīlatini. 'They're playing soon. Do you want to go with me?'

She hardly dared breathe as Saraswati considered the proposition for all of a few seconds that seemed to stretch out over a lifetime, busying herself with staring hard at the grass at her feet, acutely aware that Boundless Ano seemed to have disappeared with great purpose, to hunt around for ingredients in a haphazard collection of coolers, freezers and baskets behind the bar.

'Sure!' Saraswati said enthusiastically.

'Great!' Serenity Ko beamed. 'You could look more cheerful. They're pretty epic.'

'I know.'

'And don't worry, it's not a date.' She laughed, a little too loudly.

Saraswati smiled even more brightly at that.

'Saras, so sorry. I need a quick statement from you the night before the first Feast pop-up.' XP Inc.'s head of publicity appeared at her elbow, shattering the moment. Serenity Ko scowled at Optimism Tina momentarily, then decided that it was probably for the best that she'd interrupted things before they could devolve into an adult conversation about where she and Saraswati stood in their friendship-that-could-be-more-except-it-wasn't-for-reasons-they-never-seemed-to-discuss-openly.

She slipped away, delighted at her victory, now fully recharged to indulge her workaholic tendencies and continue tinkering with Feast. She walked over to the table groaning under the weight of all the nondescript, interchangeable Feast cubes, and stood off to one side as Courage Praia continued to encourage her Feast team to try everything and react as honestly as possible. She made hasty notes on the selections that were being made by her teammates.

In a buffet setting, the traditional small plates are preferred to the entrees, she recorded, *accounting for pre-existing familiarity with Feast, of course.*

She added an action item. *Must test a buffet-style pop-up to see how this plays out with strangers.*

Her intent was to simply hover on the fringes of all the conversations taking place around her, making copious notes while she watched people's reactions to Feast.

Then Saraswati appeared, bearing two Feast cubes on plates.

'Sorry about that,' she said. 'Optimism Tina needed a quote from me.'

'Of course!'

'Care to engage in a celebratory tasting?'

'With you? Always,' Serenity Ko said, then kicked herself for getting tongue-tied enough to be trading in clichéd responses.

They made their way to an unoccupied picnic blanket. Saraswati exhaled, dropping onto the ground. She looked at Serenity Ko, her cheeks bright pink. 'Thank you for all this, Ko. It's—it's more than I could have asked for, the evening before our big debut. I'm exhausted, but this feels like such a great way to unwind. Are midnight picnics a thing on Primus?'

'Yes,' Serenity Ko said, thinking back to the last time she'd been on one, when she was far too young to have developed an aversion to the outdoors.

'They're so charming. We never step outside after dark, back on Earth,' Saraswati said. 'Especially not into the wilderness.

It can be dangerous—abductions, muggings… A lot of what people say about the Earth is true, even if all Earthlings don't embody every stereotype.'

Serenity Ko nodded, at a loss for words. They lapsed into companionable silence, their Feast cubes untouched.

'I hope the pop-up turns out well tomorrow. But then again, it's success that really kills you in the end, isn't it?' Saraswati said cryptically.

'Wh-what?' Serenity Ko said.

'I was just thinking out loud,' Saraswati mused. 'You know, I never had the opportunity to experience my success properly on Earth. I have no practice handling this kind of pressure. I had to shut Elé Oota down, right after winning a Golden Knife, and flee the planet all because…'

Serenity Ko felt consumed by the overwhelming desire to kiss Saraswati, who was being devastatingly brooding, but also experienced a twinge of excitement that she'd said something about her past. 'Allie Otter?' she asked, stumbling on the unfamiliar words.

Saraswati paled.

'I'm not comfortable talking about it,' she said abruptly. 'Not tonight.'

'Okay.'

'I'm just grateful to be here. With you.'

'You deserve all this adulation and more,' Serenity Ko said, tamping down her confusion, filing the worlds "Allie Otter" away for later, but rushing headlong into the change of subject.

I concur, Kili said. _You deserve it too, Ko._

'Thanks, Kili.' Serenity Ko smiled.

Saraswati passed her one of the Feast cubes she'd been holding onto. 'Shall we?'

Their fingers grazed, and Serenity Ko bit down a gasp. The briefest brush of her skin was enough to set her nerves ablaze, her soul thrumming with yearning.

'Which one is it?' Serenity Ko asked, her voice higher pitched than usual.

'It's a surprise.'

Serenity Ko popped the Feast cube in her mouth.

The rich flavours of Berry-anna dance across her tongue. The pastry's slightly salted, foam isn't sweetened, and it's a nutty liqueur, to offset the fresh sweetness of the berry spheres. She's dancing through the Urswood, foraging for berries with her Ammamma, and grabs a rubus from a dense tangle of bushes, popping it in her mouth when Ammamma isn't looking. A burst of sourness douses her tastebuds, and she scrunches her eyes up at the sensation. When she opens them again and looks around her, the glade is filled with light and sweet birdsong, and their baskets are full.

The nutty liqueur sings upon the sides of her tongue, and in its initial intensity, she's taking shots at a bar on the night of her twenty-first birthday, but as it mellows to a warm bubbling haze, she's dancing with Appa in their living room, as Dad dances with Amma and Ammamma with Optimism Rihan and they're all flushed with joy—

The everberry bursts against her upper palate, flooding her with sweetness, and her lips are exploring Saraswati's, the fullness of her breasts pressed against her own, her arms encircling her waist, drawing her so close they might soon become inseparable, while all around them the live audience watching Interstellar MegaChef: The Millennium Feast Special *is drowned out in the urgency of the moment…*

Except when Serenity Ko remembers herself and pulls away, they're not on the set at all. They're in the Uru and Beyond Marketplace, and Saraswati is savouring a Berry-anna of her own, her head tilted back as she rolls it around upon her tongue. And when she opens her eyes, she looks Serenity Ko in the eye and says: 'Delicious.'

And they are kissing again as the last wave of flavours ebbs upon Serenity Ko's tongue…

Serenity Ko's eyes snapped open, her mind alight with a million thoughts about Feast unlocking secret desires, exploring the subconscious and blurring memories… and her heart racing. She glanced at Saraswati, and found that her gaze was locked upon her own.

Saraswati swallowed. 'The Berry-anna is smashing,' she said quietly.

'It's a clear winner,' Serenity Ko said, her mouth running on autopilot. She couldn't tear her eyes away from Saraswati, and a growing hunger gnawed at her. 'I—'

'Saraswati, there's someone I'd like you to meet!' Curiosity Nenna said brightly, stumbling into view.

'Sure, Nenna,' Saraswati said with a tight smile, rising to her feet. She cast an unreadable look back at Serenity Ko as she walked away. Serenity Ko pretended to be absorbed in retying the laces on her boots.

She avoided wandering off into any dark corners with Saraswati, unless they were firmly within her own mind.

Feast is a bastard child. A mutation of the Primian culinary tradition spearheaded by an Earthling. Nobody asked for it, and nobody wants it. Saraswati Kaveri is an opportunistic grifter.

—Good Cheer Chaangte,
Special guest on *Four Chefs*
2075 Anno Earth | 2000 Interstellar Era

Feast is a culinary masterpiece. We've never seen anything like it. Saraswati Kaveri is a genius.

—Pavi and Amol Khurshid,
Special guests on *Four Chefs*
2075 Anno Earth | 2000 Interstellar Era

THREE

'You're beautiful,' Serenity Ko said, her long billowing dress clinging to her hips.

'Thank you. You look great, too,' I said.

My cheeks felt warm, and I busied myself by ducking behind the counter and opening one of the chillers. Neat stacks of Feast cubes were piled within the freezer, resolutely unremarkable but now utterly fascinating as I struggled to shut her out. Prolonged eye contact with Serenity Ko was dangerous.

Serenity Ko stifled a sigh. She pulled out a chair and propped her feet on it, knocking a carefully folded serviette onto the floor in the process.

'One drama queen aside,' Courage Praia said, gesturing at Serenity Ko, 'we bring you some good stuff. XP Inc. managed to rent some replicas from the Museum of Primian History for tonight's pop-up.'

'Ooh, yes!' Courage Nenna squealed, producing a set of flowmetal packing cubes from her backpack. Some of them decompressed into larger boxes. She passed her palm over a scanner and they popped open with a rippling wave. ‘Tons of artefacts for interior décor—some flowmetal replicas, others made from less intelligent materials. Look—an ancient heating device off the spacecraft *Nakshatran One*,’ she said, holding it up. ‘Original seed trays from the early settler tents—with freshly planted saplings, of course,’ she proclaimed, pulling six of them out and adding clumps of dirt to the otherwise smooth ground. She proceeded to produce one fascinating piece of Primian history after another, arranging them on the floor haphazardly, like she was setting up shop as an interplanetary trader.

‘Oh, and you’ll love this!’ she announced. ‘May I interest you in a bejewelled goblet? This is supposed to be pre-Interstellar Era. Do you recognise it? Wait for it… it’s from *Earth!*’

She held the goblet up, and it smacked of all the wastefulness and opulence of my ancestors, the unbroken history of my home-world symbolised in its gilded, ruby-studded chalice. I blanched and took an involuntary step back.

‘No, no! I’m sorry, I didn’t mean to upset you.’ Curiosity Nenna rose to her feet and clapped her hands over her mouth.

‘Smooth,’ Serenity Ko said callously, though she swung her legs back to the ground, and leaned forward. I suppose she was concerned.

‘Are you okay?’ Courage Praia asked.

‘I—I forgot you’re a refugee…’ Curiosity Nenna’s voice came out as a squeak.

The need to perform the lie I’d been living since I got to Primus snapped me out of my sulk. ‘Oh! That’s okay, it’s just that I’ve had my Earth-origins probed into *all day* by the stream-media. Good Cheer Chaangte’s on a rampage, everyone hates me…’

Serenity Ko rolled her eyes. ‘We’ve heard it all, haven’t we?’ She turned to Kili, who now hovered beside her.

“I’m the most hated chef in all of chef-dom—” Kili said, aping me.

‘“They called me ‘a disgrace to the culinary arts’ today,”’ Serenity Ko continued.

“Chaangte said I’m ‘an opportunistic social climber from a Fringe planet.’”

'Have you guys been rehearsing?' I asked drily.

'No, and also fuck Chaangte,' Serenity Ko said, earnestly. 'Our pop-up debut is with the stream-media. They'll set public perception straight.'

'No pressure,' I sulked.

'They'll shut all of Chaangte's diatribes down—don't forget, *she* lost to *you* on the *Millennium Feast Special*. Everything she's done since has come across like sour grapes.'

True, Kili said.

'Fuck 'em, the star-fucked bastards,' Serenity Ko said cheerily. 'I'm around now, so if anyone so much as *breathes* about your origins…'

I flushed, and my breath came up short. I busied myself with prep, trying to ignore the flutterwings tumbling through my stomach at her words, and doing my best to push Serenity Ko out of my thoughts altogether.

Every once in a while, one of us would forget ourselves, and we'd have a really good time shooting the breeze. Until we gave into the electric current that filled the empty air between us, our hands brushing or our shoulders just a little too close for comfort… until our lips found each other's. And then I'd pull away, prompting a string of apologies from Serenity Ko and myself, awkwardly followed by a rapid change of subject to more work-related things. And the burgeoning electric field we somehow found ourselves trapped in would supercharge all over again…

Never mind that there was the ever-present risk that I'd unwittingly drop my secret history like a ray-bomb, revealing the fact that I was a Godavari runaway and not a Kaveri refugee, like I'd almost done last night. I was still kicking myself over that momentary lapse.

It was safest to shove Serenity Ko into the darkest back alleys of my mind, and not go looking for her.

I neatly organized the chillers in the order in which we'd be serving the Feast cubes within, which was the least prep I'd ever done in a professional kitchen.

We were debuting a set menu with five courses, each paired

with a beverage—with alcoholic and zero-proof options available. I'd handpicked the pairings, and the stringent quality bar to which I held the rest of the team had applied twice as severely to my own work.

Beside me, Boundless Ano was arranging his mise en place at the bar. He was incredibly easy to work with; he had a cheerful demeanour, but stayed focused upon his prep. And when our servers arrived, it only took a brief conversation to outline my plans for the evening with them.

One of the big benefits of Feast was the minimal kitchen equipment required to make and serve it. The XP Inc. publicity team had zeroed in on this, and chosen to have us host pop-up restaurants for their user-testing and pre-marketing initiatives. All they needed was a large tent, a couple of industrial chillers for the Feast cubes, fancy-looking plates and glasses, and a competent mixologist for the drinks.

And me.

Our diners for every pop-up were sent a complimentary nanopill packet with the internally tested, brand new Feast subscription. It was entirely portable, all plug and play.

Our weatherproof, climate-controlled tent had been set up at the Uru and Beyond Marketplace for this, our very first pop-up. At the very heart of its warrens and alleyways, with the scents and sounds of exotic foods and ingredients surrounding us, stalls pushing up against us on all sides, it was an entirely unremarkable structure, and intentionally so. The publicity folks at XP Inc. had opted for an understated introduction to Feast… all the way until our guests tried it for the first time, and it blew their minds.

Word had got round, though, and through the tent's transparent walls, I spotted several passersby peering curiously inside, and even stopping to ask what we were all about. Optimism Tina guarded the door possessively, unwilling to let anyone inside. A group of older women trilled excitedly when she patiently explained what we were doing, and left beaming. A happy family paused at the door, and then walked away looking distinctly less enthusiastic than when they'd arrived.

The tent's transparent walls and ceiling lent the illusion of being open to the elements, which, though ominous, were atmospheric in their drama. Minimalist decor, with tasteful flowmetal tables and chairs upon the bare ground, so as not to detract from the star attraction of the evening—the audiovisual and flavour experiences delivered by Feast. Artefacts paying tribute to Nakshatran and Primian history nestled unobtrusively along makeshift wall shelves. Serenity Ko and the gang had done a solid job adding decor to the inside of the tent while generally staying out of the kitchen. The space was everything I'd envisioned.

The open kitchen was warmly lit, its counters stacked with unassuming, pedestrian-looking Feast cubes, the only colour in the mise en place for the drinks. Outside, as the first diners made their way up the path, where fireflits fluttered like beacons, the twinkling lights in all the shops and stalls around us winked in and out as the wind rushed through the alleyways in violent gusts. The worst storm in decades wasn't upon us just yet, but it would arrive at our doorstep soon enough.

Serenity Ko threw me a reassuring smile before she receded to the annexe, from which she and her team were all set to watch tonight's tasting unfold. Optimism Tina hurried to the doorway to put on her best publicist face and usher our dinner guests in.

I recognised several of the faces from the stream-media. Boundless Sean, from *The Consummate Cuisinologist,* whom I'd met at half a dozen dinner parties—I owed him an interview soon. Harmony Selia from *The Gourmand Gossip*—she'd harassed me at the Uru and Beyond Marketplace with an army of cam-drones several māsas ago, only to warm up to me after our win on the special episode of *Interstellar MegaChef.* Serenity Ko referred to her as a "confirmed star-fucker," but I was just happy she wasn't coming after me.

There were the folks from the popular culinary stream, Four Chefs, all of whom gave me a big smile. They weren't sold on the concept of Feast, but they hadn't reacted to it in outrage, smearing it as a bastardisation of Primian cuisine amidst xenophobic attacks on my Earthling origins. Other familiar names flickered by as the space filled up, and I politely acknowledged each and every single one of them...

Until my heart skipped a beat.

It can't be.

It can't be! Kili gasped from his spot on my shoulder.

Who the fuck put Good Cheer Chaangte on the guest list?

She sashayed in dramatically, her blonde hair in a long braid, her eyes made up to dwarf the narrow bones of her face. And she flashed me an enormous smile that was the furthest thing from friendly, evidently delighted at what I realised was a look of dismay upon my face. She pointedly took her seat at a table that faced me, her smile widening at my open discomfort.

Chaangte's here, I streamed Serenity Ko.

_Oh, no._

Was it you?

Absolutely not, she said firmly. _Ask Tina._

I asked Optimism Tina, who promptly hurried to my side.

'I thought it would be an epic victory if you shut her up for good!' Optimism Tina whispered enthusiastically.

'And you didn't think to ask if I was *okay* with it?' I whispered back urgently.

'I didn't think it would matter.' Optimism Tina shrugged, her voice still low. 'You've already beaten her once in public, on the *MegaChef* special.'

'She's come after me with a *kitchen knife* since!'

'And now, you'll prove her wrong once and for all. She won't be able to deny the genius of Feast,' Optimism Tina said confidently. 'Trust me.'

'I trust *you*,' I said through gritted teeth. 'I don't trust *her*.'

Good Cheer Chaangte had made it her mission to make my life miserable. I'd first run into her when I was working at Nonpareil, the critically acclaimed Primian fine-dining restaurant run by Earthling immigrants Pavi and Amol Khurshid. She was their sous-chef drunk on power, and unafraid to show it. She'd verbally bullied me, roped Serenity Ko in to sabotage one of my dinner services, punched me in the face when I confronted her, attempted to compete against me on the special episode of *Interstellar MegaChef*, lost to me, and then come after Feast—by which I meant me—with every kitchen knife in her arsenal.

And far from coming across as a sore loser, she'd rallied half the culinary world to her side. She'd taken to being a public streamer, claiming to be the last bastion upholding Primian food and values. She'd drawn attention to my Earthling origins, alleged that I was obsessed with personal glory at the cost of all other chefs across the galaxy, furthering the Earthling philosophy of dominance and colonisation over the Nakshatran value to "tread lightly." She had millions of viewers, and had inspired thousands of streamers to take potshots at me in the same way.

She was also working with the former *MegaChef* judge, Courage Ab'dal, at Leaf and Bone—who, rumour had it, had quit the show in protest against Feast.

As the first round of aperitifs were served, I tamped down my nerves.

Everyone has opinions and is welcome to them, I told myself firmly. *And her opinions don't matter.*

'You call this an aperitif?' Good Cheer Chaangte's voice carried through the tent, loud and clear. 'It's so acidic I've lost my appetite!'

She sent it back to the kitchen, and beside me, Boundless Ano's face fell.

'Ano,' I hissed quietly. 'It's not true. Nobody else has reacted the same way.'

'But—'

'She just wants to make a scene. The best way to handle her is to give her no attention.'

I looked at his hands working frantically to make her another aperitif. 'And stop doing that!' I added sternly. 'We don't give into bullying.'

I spritzed water over the tiny Feast spheres meant to serve as the amuse-bouche. It was a play on a Primian dish called the Citric Crush, normally served in a thimble-sized, crystal clear glass. The traditional version consisted of a citrus-infused gelée, suspended like a miniature Suriya in a clear liquid, intended to be swallowed in a single shot.

The Feast version was a bright yellow sphere, no larger than a fingernail.

Upon my command, the lights within the tent were dimmed dramatically, but for the small flow-flora lamps adorning each table.

The Citric Crush was promptly served, an indiscriminate bubble of colour.

I held my breath.

A murmur rose, accompanied by titters and chuckles.

I glanced at Good Cheer Chaangte, eyeing the Feast sphere in disbelief, her face twitching between disgust and wonder. She picked it up and popped it into her mouth, along with the other diners.

The world seemed to shrink, then explode in the interminable seconds that followed…

There were gasps and cries of delight. Their eyes glazed over as they were transported into an array of sim experiences, their memories triggered, their flavour centres set alight, the XP Inc. databases kicking in to amplify every infinitesimal detail of what they were tasting.

As one, the entire room woke to reality, and thundered into applause.

'Bursting with all the traditional flavours!' I heard Boundless Sean exclaim. 'Sharper than simply lemon, more aromatic than the usual overpowering scent of lime… and that undercurrent of spice running counterpoint to it all.'

'The kaffir leaf and lemongrass! Nine Virtues!' one of the Four Chefs expostulated. 'The texture of that peprino-corn oil delivered just perfectly, a gentle tingling on the tastebuds…'

Harmony Selia openly wept. 'I grew up beside a lemon tree grove by the Urswood. We climbed those trees, my sisters and I… and I was there with them, right this very moment!'

Good Cheer Chaangte's expression was unreadable. Her face contorted as she struggled to control what she was conveying to her viewers while streaming the tasting, live. She seemed awestruck, then aghast, then utterly livid.

I stepped out from behind the kitchen counter, summoned up all my showmanship, and proceeded to make the speech I'd prepared for the occasion.

'I present to you the future of Primian food,' I said grandly. 'Combining cutting-edge tech courtesy of XP Inc. with the food supplement edibites, and my contributions to developing the science of flavour, our humble food experiment went on to win the *Interstellar MegaChef: Millennium Feast Special*, and our small team of intrepid culinary explorers will be catering the Millennium Feast a few māsas from now. It is an honour to serve you, discerning gourmands and esteemed members of the stream-media, with the future of food.

'Welcome to our pop-up, and may I present to you… a *Feast!*'

A mature, white cosmo-wine was instantly conveyed from the kitchens to the diners, the pairing for the first course of their dinner. As another round of applause rang out within the pop-up restaurant, I bowed and made my way back to prepare the first course—a Feast cube simulating a shrooming symphony.

'Just add water,' I muttered, grinning as Boundless Ano slapped me a high five beneath the counter.

You are brilliant, and I am star-fucking proud of you! Kili said, nuzzling my cheek fondly.

*I don't believe it! It's flawless! It's beautiful!* Serenity Ko shouted.

I spritzed each Feast cube with just enough water for it to puff up ever so slightly and change colour, and I savoured my victory over every single one of my detractors.

For the *MegaChef* special episode, our brief had been to take traditional Primian food into the future by innovating upon traditional recipes. We had all the tech we needed for a food-sim. We even had a substrate in the form of edibites. But our offering had a single flaw—it didn't involve any *actual* cooking. Until Curiosity Nenna had suggested a simple, brilliant idea, the hallmark of every packaged convenience food ever in the history of humanity: *Just add water.*

Who knew that was all it would take to win *Interstellar MegaChef*?

I sent out the first course. It was traditionally served as a velvety broth, infused with ras from over a dozen shroomings foraged in the Urswood and the wider Arc. All our sims were catered to replicate that sense of walking through the damp woods with a crisp autumn breeze…

And true to form, the tasting went off to wild shouts and the sharing of foraging memories—everyone had one from when they were a child, and several involved long-dead grandparents.

'And the flavour profile!' Boundless Sean effused. 'The silky smooth texture; the crunch of the noki-noki crackle!'

I glanced at Good Cheer Chaangte again, half daring her to disparage the first course, and was delighted to see the corners of her lips turned firmly downward as she struggled to process it.

I can't believe it's working! I said.

Oh, it's working… and how! Kili replied.

I couldn't wait for dinner service to be over, to take the team out for a well-deserved drink that was likely to turn into a rowdy party.

A vision of Serenity Ko popped into my head unbidden, her braid undone, looking down at me as she pinned me to her sofa cushions. Two navas ago, after one jumpgate kick too many, I'd looked into her eyes after an age spent exploring her lips with mine—an age that was far too short—and I'd lost myself within her, only to suddenly recognise that I had to escape her gravity, and fast.

I'd shut the moment down and fled.

Maybe tonight, I'll ask her to dance. That's safe, right?

I forced myself to focus on the second course—a meen crudo.

The Feast cubes went out, and the responses were symphonic. The fennelo-ras infusion this course evoked—the traditional accompaniment to a char-meen—was hitting all the right notes. Diners tearfully reminisced about vat-fishing, and thrilled with wonder at the experience of swimming with a wild char-meen in the rivers. I beamed with pride; that underwater sim experience had nothing to do with me, and everything to do with Serenity Ko.

They love you! I streamed her.

They love you more! she streamed back.

I wanted her to be mine, undeniably so. But I was being avoidant for a reason.

If I were being completely honest, I didn't care if we labelled our relationship or not, if we were exclusive or not—those were just excuses.

The truth was this: She didn't know anything about me. The *real* me. And it felt wrong to be so honest about my feelings for her, while being perfidious about everything else about myself.

I'd spent long, lonely nights refraining from streaming her, not wanting to regret the joyous things we might do when inebriated and jubilant all at once, which would inevitably lead to us being tangled up in her bed, ripping our clothes off each other. I ached for her, but I'd lied to her for nearly a year now.

I was *going* to tell her the truth about being a Godavari, right after the Millennium Feast. Until then, though…

I couldn't be vulnerable with her if it wasn't with all of me.

And it was really for the best if I kept her at arm's length—what if my family ever discovered where I was?

I needed to be free of my bloodthirsty, warmongering Godavari past. Serenity Ko didn't deserve to be sucked into its gory gravity.

Are you okay, Saras? Kili streamed.

I need to be free.

You are, aren't you?

I need Feast to succeed so my family can't touch me, even if they find me.

Ah, but Saras, Kili said gravely. _You do realise that the bigger your celebrity grows, the more likely they are to discover you?_

I've had nano-bleach skin procedures, changed my hair— I began.

Even so. They could discover you and come for you.

_And you choose to tell me now, after I've put my face on

every single stream-media outlet dealing with food out there?_ I snapped.

We've had this conversation before, Kili said patiently.

You're right, Kili, I conceded. _But I refuse to hide for the rest of my life._

I'm with you, Saras.

I sent out the beest carpaccio. Each of the diners lost their bearings the moment they popped the cubes in their mouths, receding into the manifold worlds of the sims they were being offered. Good Cheer Chaangte was doing her level best not to react to any of the sims, or the flavour experiences, and she was fighting a losing battle. Her face said it all.

Food, *flavour,* was a visceral experience, and you could never rationalise an argument with it.

So as much as she wanted to hate what I was serving at her table, as much as she loathed me for my Earthling origins, she was unable to lie about it, and her mask of deceit was slipping.

When I sent out the dessert—the Ur-Sand Pearls—I knew that I was on the verge of a triumph.

Ordinarily, this was served in the form of golden pearls infused with lemon ras, bursting with citric flavours, adorning a cloud of flash-frozen powdered sugar crystals, like fine sand on a beach. It was meant to evoke the infinite view when one was ocean-side, staring at the waves and contemplating the mysteries of the universe.

The diners in the room came undone, reflecting upon their deepest memories, and the unanswered questions of their lives. A hand slipped into mine and squeezed it, and it felt as if my heart would burst out of my chest.

'Magnificent,' Serenity Ko whispered, her breath warm against my ear.

I caught sight of Good Cheer Chaangte, tears trickling down her face, and my heart, still brimming with joy, sang with the viciousness of the vindicated. Her eyes met mine, and she gazed at me with unfettered hatred.

I looked back at her triumphant. This victory was all mine, and freedom would soon follow.

XP Inc. is the brainchild of Grace Kube, Courage Na'vil and Optimism Sah'r.

The org promises to deliver seamless sim experiences beamed straight into your brain, and it remains to be seen how successful they will be in time to come...

—Serenity Medi,
Primus: A New Hope for Humanity
2065 Anno Earth | 1990 Interstellar Era

FOUR

THE WALLFLOWER WAS the kind of bar that was just elevated enough to exist in Collective Four, but just dingy enough to supply patrons with dimly lit booths and covert corners to lurk in while they got to the bottom of various bottles and cocktail glasses to get them through a hard day's night.

Tonight was not a hard day's night. There was no lurking.

The party was in full swing. Their first Feast pop-up had been a stellar success.

Apart from one grouchy Good Cheer Chaangte, all the stream-media who had attended the tasting session were streaming rave reviews all over the Loop, and that meant it was the perfect opportunity for a blistering bash.

If Serenity Ko had paused to reflect, she might have wondered if the number of occasions she'd had to live it up over the past few māsas had rendered celebrations meaningless—all life was one epic, extraordinary victory march and she was unstoppable, rendering one night of carousing redundant.

Serenity Ko didn't pause to reflect; it wasn't her style.

Instead, she shimmied up on a bar table, shouting at Saraswati to come join her while a dizzying electrochord solo played over the speakers. Saraswati, for her part, buried her head in her hands and laughed until tears spilled down her cheeks, and that suited Serenity Ko just fine.

Her heart pounding as she jumped off the table, she ordered

a round of shots for everyone at their table. It was impossible for the server to discern just how many shots that was, seeing as folks kept dropping in and out of the impromptu XP Inc. party.

'Could you confirm the number, please?' the server asked hesitantly.

'Ask Praia!' Serenity Ko yelled. 'Oi, Praia!'

Now that business had been taken care of, Serenity Ko slid into a booth beside Saraswati. Perhaps it was the dim light that made her at least forty percent more attractive than she'd ever been, perhaps it was the alcohol, or the dopamine from the triumphant Feast pop-up, or perhaps she was just sur-fucking drop dead gorgeous… Serenity Ko wasn't bothered about the specifics as she propped her chin in her hand, beamed her biggest smile, and said, 'Hey.'

'Hey?' Saraswati giggled.

Serenity Ko cringed. That was the stupidest thing she'd ever said to anyone while trying to pick them up. Then again, Saraswati was giggling, and it was the most beautiful sound in the world.

'Remember me?' Serenity Ko said stupidly.

'You make it impossible to forget you.' Saraswati rolled her eyes. 'Especially dancing on tables.'

'It's part of the Serenity Ko package.'

I've saved it for all posterity, Kili chimed in, hovering beside Saraswati. _Footage forever._

'You're the best, Kili.' Saraswati beamed.

'You're the worst, Kili,' Serenity Ko said, but laughed.

She studied Saraswati over the top of her cocktail glass, whose contents were being rapidly depleted. 'Did you ever think we'd get here?' she asked, suddenly serious.

'To The Wallflower?' Saraswati teased.

'No, celebrating something we built together,' Serenity Ko clarified.

'We've been here before, you know…' Saraswati feigned struggling to concentrate, her brows knitting together. 'After the *MegaChef* special episode.'

Serenity Ko snorted. 'You know what I mean. We've come a

long way since then. We're actually building that thing into a complete product. That thing is now succeeding in the open market—well, not fully open market, yet, but it's killing it at user testing. That thing... *what the fuck is it called again?*'

'Feast?' Courage Praia suggested, appearing at the booth with a tray laden with shot glasses.

'That's the one!' Serenity Ko said, wondering if it was the alcohol or the incredibly attractive way Saraswati's curls framed her face that was getting her all tongue-tied. *Probably both,* she decided, grabbing a shot glass.

'I didn't think we'd make it,' Courage Praia said honestly. 'No offence, Ko, but you can't find your way around a kitchen to save your life. If Saras hadn't shown up right when she did, with all her fancy food jargon and flavour expertise, we'd have been sunk.'

'You're too ki—' Saraswati began, but Courage Praia cut her off.

'And if Saras hadn't *stayed* despite all your temper tantrums, and shenanigans, and working with a bunch of idiots like us who know our way around algorithms and databases but can't tap into the raw emotion of flavour...' They shook their head. 'We wouldn't be here tonight.'

'Hear, hear!' Grace Kube said, and Serenity Ko whirled around to see the Triumvirate had arrived.

Optimism Sah'r, who ran the team that wrote all their code, and Courage Na'vil, who was in charge of the neuropsych mesh, flanked him. The former was beautiful, as she always was—Serenity Ko had always had the tiniest crush on her, even though she was, for all practical purposes, one of the co-founders of XP Inc. and therefore her boss who was far older than her, but she could always appreciate blatant good looks and razor sharp intelligence from afar, couldn't she? The latter muttered something after his usual fashion, refusing to make eye contact with her.

'What was that, Na'vil?' she asked pointedly.

'Congratulations, Ko,' Courage Na'vil said wearily, as if the success of his org's latest sim experience was a personal affront. 'I'm glad this test went smoothly without raising any ethical concerns.'

Serenity Ko fought off a scowl. *There it is, the "ethical concerns" phrase. Again.*

Instead, she smiled sweetly and said, 'It's thanks to you, Na'vil. You've kept us on a short leash, after all.'

Everyone at the table laughed at that, and Courage Na'vil joined in, too. 'You know we exist on opposite ends of the org to make sure there's always balance, right?' he asked, with surprising sincerity. 'It's the tension that ensures we put the best sim experiences in the galaxy out there. Neither of us can function without the other.'

Serenity Ko flushed as the words hit home. 'I—I know that,' she said. 'All our heated arguments have only helped make this better.' She meant it, too, and was surprised to recognise that it made her feel lighter to express the thought out loud.

'Tonight we celebrate,' she added gruffly. 'Tomorrow, I'll go back to kicking your arse in meetings.'

'Deal.' Courage Na'vil smiled.

They raised their shot glasses, and Grace Kube made a toast. 'To immaculate teamwork!'

Saraswati sputtered as she knocked back the shot, and Serenity Ko was suddenly aware that the presence of all her teammates was cramping her style and getting in the way of some good-natured flirting. And while Serenity Ko wasn't sure what kind of relationship she wanted with Saraswati outside of work, she definitely knew that she wanted to be in bed with her, preferably not talking.

She found herself watching Saraswati's hands with an intensity that she was getting used to, but that was still alarming when she was entirely sober. A crystal clear memory of what those hands looked like when she was cooking, forearms taut and rippling, rose within her, at the same time as the memory of their first encounter swam into place—Serenity Ko was pretty certain that she'd insulted her at that chance meeting in a flowcab.

Her feelings had evolved from drunk and actively hostile

to professionally cordial if impatient to impulsive kissing in front of a galactic audience, and now friendship that promised more—in certain lighting, and after particular successes, prospectively fuelled by alcohol.

'More shots!' Serenity Ko cried.

Saraswati gave her a look of disbelief.

'Yes, really,' Serenity Ko said, as Curiosity Nenna scurried away to arrange the next round of drinks. 'It's our night. We deserve to live it up.'

Before she had a moment to wink, making it adequately clear where this conversation was heading, new faces appeared at the table. Serenity Ko stifled a groan.

'Saras!' Courage Oslo pulled her into an enormous hug, as his partner Curiosity Zia beamed at them, her face tats glowing neon.

'Congratulations!' Curiosity Zia said. 'You deserve this more than anyone I know.' She turned and looked at the rest of the XP Inc. team. '*All of you,*' she added hastily.

Boundless Baz swept in and dragged Saraswati out of the booth, thrusting a bira in her direction. 'Drink,' he commanded. 'Savour the victory.'

Saraswati drank.

The B'naar they all called XX-29 extended xir mechanical appendages and wrapped Saraswati up in a big hug. 'You are brilliant. Everything you've done is brilliant,' xe said emotionally, xir globular being thrumming along in high-pitched notes, chromatophores shimmering purple with pride.

Serenity Ko was desperate to interrupt, to pull Saraswati away from xir and keep her all to herself, but resisted.

Be a grown-up, she thought sternly. *Give her some space. These are her friends.*

As they ushered Saraswati towards the dance floor, Serenity Ko pouted. It was impossibly difficult to watch her walk away, a monumental challenge to tear her eyes away from the swaying of her hips. She looked around her. The greater part of her team were engrossed in a spirited game of bira-pong. Courage Praia and Curiosity Nenna were at the bar organising drinks. The Triumvirate had retired to a private table. She was suddenly alone.

And then, an unexpected presence—the last person she wanted to see, really—dropped into the booth beside her.

'Congrats, Ko,' Honour Aki said.

Serenity Ko groaned. Not inwardly, as would have been polite, but loudly, and intentionally rudely.

'Not you, Aki.'

'I just said congrats.' Honour Aki scowled. His eyes were deep and searching, and his auburn topknot glittered with gemstones. Serenity Ko couldn't deny that he was a good-looking man; she also couldn't deny that he was a pest.

'Why are you even here?' she asked rudely. 'You weren't invited.'

'Half of XP Inc. is here,' Honour Aki said.

Serenity Ko glanced around the bar again. It wasn't untrue. As the evening had progressed, the party had grown in size and raucousness, and was taking on all the classic signs of work-revelry entropy, all embodied by faces she'd seen at XP Inc., even if they didn't work on Feast, familiar nametags slipping by on her optics feed. Folks had taken over the dance floor, where they were proceeding to demonstrate that sim-building brilliance didn't necessarily translate to rhythmic coordination; the adrenosim-bros engaged in increasingly passionate debates about the best strategies in *OutCooked 6: Outwit, Outlast, Outcook!* (all of which would be vigorously denied in the morning, even as a few of them took over a visio-node that had been streaming a tripwicket game, and proceeded to demonstrate the perfect way to beat the popular cooking game); still others were paying court to the Triumvirate, no doubt hoping that their attempts to win over the notoriously immovable founders and bosses at XP Inc. with flattery and alcohol would reap rewards in the morning.

Saraswati and her friends had mysteriously disappeared.

Everyone was preoccupied, and Serenity Ko was alone at a table with Honour Aki. This was great, just fucking great. She'd consistently told him she'd only been interested in sleeping with him, and he'd ardently pursued her in hopes of a romantic relationship, for the better part of a year.

'Why don't you go join that half of XP Inc.?' Serenity Ko suggested weakly.

'I just want to tell you that my feelings for you haven't changed. And I'll always be here for you,' Honour Aki said, gazing deep into her eyes, his own brimming with tears.

'Oh, for fuck's sake, Aki.'

Serenity Ko rose to her feet and slid out the booth, practically running across the bar to where Curiosity Nenna and Courage Praia were arguing with the bartender about their latest drinks order.

'Hide me,' she pleaded.

Courage Praia grinned, and Curiosity Nenna pretended she had no idea what was happening, in the manner of high-performing interns all across the universe. Serenity Ko stood at the bar with them, taking an active, exaggerated interest in their lives and various drinks orders, saying hello to XP Inc. folks she wouldn't have looked twice at ordinarily, and generally hiding from Honour Aki's advances for the better part of an hour until someone tapped her on the shoulder.

'Aki, I said *no!*'

'It's me,' Saraswati said, and Serenity Ko whirled around to find her grinning.

Through some cosmic convergence of social physics, Saraswati had found her in the packed bar again. She was so lost in Saraswati's smile, and the flattering way her fitted top accentuated her curves, that she didn't notice when Courage Praia and Curiosity Nenna made themselves scarce, like clean water on a Fringe planet. The pair found themselves effectively alone at the bar, surrounded by empty glasses and a bartender who had made it a career goal to see what was happening right before his eyes without ever actually *looking*.

'I'm sorry,' Saraswati said. 'They all showed up for me.'

'Of course!' Serenity Ko said brightly, her heart thrumming with an invisible music only she could hear. 'Want to dance?' she asked abruptly, before anyone else could interrupt them.

'Let's go!'

Serenity Ko rose to her feet, about to hop up on the bar, but Saraswati grabbed her hand.

'Not here,' she said. 'There's a dance floor.'

'In that case... *Not* the dance floor,' Serenity Ko said. She led her past the bar, to an alcove that concealed a stairway.

'Well, this is shady, Ko.'

'It's *private*,' Serenity Ko said coolly, while every atom in her body felt as if it had been set on fire.

'If I didn't know you better, I'd say you have shady intentions.'

'Maybe,' Serenity Ko teased.

'Are we dancing or—'

'Dancing is just a socially acceptable excuse,' Serenity Ko said, before pushing Saraswati against the staircase railing and pressing her lips against hers.

All thought abandoned Serenity Ko in a moment, fleeting and free. Saraswati was kissing her back with a vengeance, hands tangling in the neat knots of her braid, her body taking over and giving into the kiss... Serenity Ko pulled her closer, like she never wanted to breathe again because this was sustenance enough...

Saraswati slid her hands down Serenity Ko's neck, tracing the curves of her breasts, and Serenity Ko moaned softly.

A door slammed and they broke apart. Someone walked down the staircase, and Serenity Ko stepped back, leaning against the wall behind her casually. Anyone with a functional pair of eyes would have been suspicious, but whoever walked by them was at least polite about it, opting to say nothing.

The space between them was already being filled by a supercharged tension.

'What was that?' Saraswati asked. 'What about our work relationship? And the fact that you "aren't looking for a relationship"?'

'I—I want you,' Serenity Ko said.

'That's the alcohol,' Saraswati teased.

'Yes. But also, I want you. And we're winning. We're succeeding. How bad can this go?' Serenity Ko hated the way her voice took on a slight whine.

A smile crept across Saraswati's face, and for some reason, Serenity Ko detected a hint of sadness in the curve of her lips. 'What's wrong?' she asked.

'I want you too, Ko,' Saraswati began. 'But we have to stay focused. For now. Maybe in the future—'

'Here you are!' Boundless Baz said brightly, stepping into the alcove, Kili whirring upon his shoulder. He took one look at the pair of them and quickly averted his gaze. 'Sorry, didn't mean to interrupt anything…'

'It's okay.' Saraswati smiled quickly. 'We'll be right out.'

'Oh, good!' Boundless Baz said hurriedly. 'Starlight Fantastic is stuck in traffic, but everyone else is waiting for you so we can turn this party up a notch.' He left in a hurry, clearly not wanting to linger.

'You left Kili with him?' Serenity Ko teased.

'I—I wanted to…'

'They want you outside,' Serenity Ko said, nodding to the main portion of the bar that lay beyond the alcove. Her head was a muddle of thoughts and unresolved feelings. She needed a drink.

After sampling Feast for the first time tonight, I can assure you all that it smacks of emotional manipulation. The kind Earthlings delight in...

—Good Cheer Chaangte,
The Prim and Proper Primian
2075 Anno Earth | 2000 Interstellar Era

FIVE

IT'S FUNNY HOW, no matter what you achieve in your chosen career, it's the bad days that stand out most clearly, stringing together to form the unflattering narrative of your life. But then, you live the good days, and the good days make everything you've ever been through completely worth it.

I was bone-tired as I made my way to the flowtram station, but my head spun with contentment, and the fact that I was mildly drunk.

The first Feast pop-up had been a resplendent success, and I was ready to bask in its afterglow as I crawled into bed for a well-earned rest. The adrenaline ebbed from me, and the pressure and uncertainty lifted, causing me to sway slightly as I walked. Or perhaps it was the lingering effect of one nīlatini too many, and not enough pushing Serenity Ko up against a wall and snogging her.

Serenity Ko had jumped me, and I'd never felt more alive, but then she'd downed an incredible number of shots for one human being, and Courage Praia had gently led her away to first throw up in the toilets, and then into a flowcab to take her back home—all before I'd even had the chance to think about whether I wanted to pursue that line of enquiry for the rest of the night.

'Before she starts a riot,' they'd grinned at me, by way of explanation.

'Let me at Saraswati,' Serenity Ko had slurred, and my heart had soared for a few seconds before she turned around and threw up in a shrubbery.

And that had been the end of that.

I must have cut a bedraggled, sorry figure on the tram, but that was as far from the truth as I was from my home-world. I rode back in triumph to the Faith of the Light commune. Solitude and the feeling of winning the universe don't often go hand in hand, but here I was, happy and content, overall.

Tough, not getting to be with Ko tonight, Kili said, slipping into my thoughts.

Maybe it's better this way. I smiled sadly. _A small part of me is relieved._

Why?

I don't want her to get too close. There are too many lies between us. All mine.

You could always come clean to her.

*After* the Millennium Feast, I said. _Once I'm too big to fail, beyond my family's reach, even if they were to find me._

Are you sure you want to go to Legends of the Future with her in a couple of māsas? he asked cautiously.

Yes, I said instantly, then added. _And no. I'm not sure where the evening would go._

You could always have an adult conversation if it goes anywhere.

I snorted. _Or have sex and pretend it never happened afterwards. I think that's Ko's style._ But I said it with fondness.

All the Loop was consumed by the folks we'd hosted tonight, raving about Feast and how it was going to take the culinary world by storm. A few relatively reserved reactions were the only dampener to all the exuberance. Good Cheer Chaangte had released a grouchy vid proclaiming all culinary critics on Primus to be "spineless sell-outs," but I knew what I'd seen. Good Cheer Chaangte had been floored by Feast, and then blown away, and she could stick all the knives in me she liked, but the human being beneath all the hatred had fallen to pieces. All thanks to Feast.

I stepped off the tram as its doors whooshed open. This was the last stop on the line, at the edge of the Forty-Second Collective.

The station's signboard was grafted from a bioluminescent plant, pulsing in neon blues and greens as it crept across an enormous trellis. The glowing creeper had been trained to spell out *Faith of the Light* in both Ur-speak and Vox. It must have taken sur-years to get it just right. I brushed a trickle of sweat off my nose as the weather encompassed me in a muggy haze, the build-up to the worst storm in decades still relentless. There were flashes of lightning off in the distance, accompanied by the loud chirping of crickets and other insects as the humidity continued to swell, even though the rain hadn't hit Uru yet. I swayed across the platform to where the Faith of the Light gardens began.

A sea of black spread out for miles around me. Only the presence of flow-flora lights illuminated it—a lighting tech developed by the chlorosapients, blending flowmetal with natural Primian plants to harvest bioluminescence and amplify it with flowmetal's intelligent sensors. Each streetlight took on the physiology of the plant it drew its luminescence from, some towering over my head in the form of incandescent spindle-trees, others barely reaching my knee in thickets of rouge-berry shrubs, still others twining around tall fences in knots of creepers I was yet to learn the names of, their shapes smearing, ghostly, shimmering foliaceous halos watching my passage as if I were a pioneer on an untouched planet. It reminded me of my parents' summer home in the Chik'malur district, back on Earth, and that *one* night in the unpredictable monsoon when the brahmatamaras would bloom amidst the kaapi shrubs.

On one such night, I'd crept out of bed and met Noura—one of my sister's palanquin bearers—in the rose garden. We'd held hands and exchanged furtive kisses beneath the shelter of a gazebo, until we were startled out of our adolescent explorations by a churlish snigger. I'd snapped my head around and spotted Jog Tunga—visiting from his exile at boarding school—running away into the woodland beyond, howling with laughter like a jackal. Noura had disappeared from existence the next day; Jog Tunga had been buoyant for the rest of his visit.

I scowled. *He* was the reason I'd moved to the Faith of the Light commune. The cruel youth I'd known as a child had grown up to be a crueller prince, the scion of an allied clan, betrothed to my odious sister. He'd managed to track me down at my last residence, under the pretext of bearing a message from my family. And I'd run, my thirst to stay hidden from my family absolute.

When I fled the Earth, I'd run away to escape my parents with a harebrained scheme I hadn't had the time to fully think through. Arguably, I hadn't done the brightest thing by going on a galactically-broadcast cooking competition, but I'd undergone extensive nano-bleach procedures and had hair mods woven in to change my appearance. I cringed as I revisited my first time on *Interstellar MegaChef*. The humiliation was still seared into every fibre of my being, like a physical injury that flared up each time I thought about it. I'd suffered it because I'd wanted freedom, to escape *them*, my family. I'd hidden all my past victories and struggles because of *them*.

I won a fucking Golden Knife, and nobody can know about it. Because of them.

It was the Earth's highest culinary honour. It was hard to draw the line in interviews, to stop myself from name-dropping my culinary credentials, to preserve my secret identity. I was a nobody Earthling chef on this planet, an unexpected outsider who'd come from nowhere to spearhead a culinary revolution, when the truth was, I'd been working on cutting-edge culinary practices all my life.

My restaurant Elé Oota had been the talk of the Daxina Protectorate.

The night I'd won the Golden Knife, instead of hosting a bash with my team of chefs, I'd been picked up by my sister, the Priestess Immaculate Narmada, and whisked away to my parents' palatial home. My family revealed that *they'd* provided the seed funding for my restaurant so they could use it as a money laundering front.

While nominally elected in a performance of democracy, the Godavari clan I belonged to were effectively gangsters running their version of paradise in the Daxina Protectorate, responsible for the subjugation of minorities, expansionist policies, rampant corruption, and the historic slaughter of their rival family, the Kaveris—whose name I'd stolen to bolster my claim to amnesty when I escaped.

It had been horrifying to learn that my restaurant was a front to turn their blood money clean. It had been debilitating to hear that they'd bought off a slate of food reviewers so my restaurant would become popular, pouring in clean profits they could skim off the top as its secret shareholders. It had been mortifying to learn that they wanted to shut the whole sham down so I could perform the duty I was raised for: marry into the Bhadra clan to form an alliance and maintain political balance in the Protectorate.

Too bad for me I only liked women. 'Keep a harem,' my mother had said.

I'd had no choice but to run.

My life was a story of rebellion and struggle. A story of hidden triumphs. A story of escape. And I could share none of it with anyone on this planet.

Tonight is about achievement.

I sped up as the commune's housing came into view in a haze of twinkling lights. Mud splashed across the bottoms of my leggings, splattering my boots with muck.

I'd made my way through three different interviews to earn my place at the Faith of the Light. A requirement for living at their commune was a belief in the teachings of the Faith of the Light, and I claimed that I was furthering the Nakshatran principle to "tread lightly" by helping design Feast. After all, Feast encompassed food-sim experiences that didn't rely upon natural resources, a philosophy held closely by the chlorosapients who lived at the commune. Their teachings envisioned a future of complete self-sustenance for all human beings. Most members had light-harvesting mods and chlorophyll implants, and partook of edibites—the nutritive substance we were using for Feast—instead of eating off the land. They believed the future of humanity lay in never taking from another plant or animal life form, ever again.

They'd bought into my earnest delivery of my very fake application. As Kili was fond of reminding me, my trail of lies ran long, and kept growing.

I drew closer to my space, which was on ground level, at the edge of the maccanut grove.

A light shone through my window, flickering in the rain.

Did we leave the lights on, Saras? Kili asked casually.

Nope. My heart stuttered. _I hope it isn't Ko,_ I lied, suddenly ardently wishing to find none other than Serenity Ko in my bedroom.

I passed my palm over a scanner and the flowmetal doors pulled apart.

Oh, dear—

Kili juddered violently and dove into my damp pockets without finishing his thought.

'Are you making a habit of housebreaking?' I asked coldly. My palms were clammy and damp, and not just from the humidity or the alcohol.

A slender, long-legged man stood in my living room, poking at a creeper woven into my flowmetal walls as if he wanted to rip it out just to hurt it. His face wore a cold, indifferent sneer and a bejewelled gold crown sat atop his head. He didn't bother turning to look at me.

'Took you long enough,' he said.

Jog Tunga sank a finger into the thick, verdant flesh of the creeper, watching with satisfaction as his nail left an imprint in its stem.

'Leave the plant alone. It's not mine; it belongs to the Faith,' I snapped.

'Testy,' he snickered. 'I thought you had a good day.'

'And while you're at it, you can see yourself out,' I said with far more courage than I felt. 'Don't try too hard to avoid the lightning strikes. Your crown should help.'

His head whipped around in a swift, reptilian movement, and his eyes glittered like cold gemstones. 'Watch your tone. You're speaking to a Prince of the Protectorate; fools have been killed for less.'

'If you were going to kill me, you'd have done so already,' I retorted, feigning indifference. 'Admit it: I'm valuable to you. That's why you keep stalking me and come crawling to me, hoping to make friends so I can help you out with whatever it is you want. That's why you haven't told my parents where I am yet…'

He grinned, his lips twisting into an expression positively feral. 'Those are a lot of assumptions. Do they help you sleep at night?'

A nasty, slimy feeling crawled through my gut. *What if he's told my parents, and they've sent him to collect me?*

'Whatever you want to say, spit it out and leave.'

'Maybe I will. Maybe I won't.'

I bit back a string of curses. 'If I promise to listen, will you tell me what you want?'

'Maybe.' He grinned. A long pause stretched between us, and a sense of deep unease grew within my gut.

'Please?' I said, desperate to get rid of him, hating that I had to beg.

'Ah. The magic words. Your court manners aren't forgotten.'

'Fuck off.'

'Right, so we have to work on those court manners,' he said. 'Some would say you're having a grand time. You're famous across the galaxy, your little pet project debuted tonight to rave reviews. Why so cranky, hmm?' He took a step forward. 'Is the thought that you can run and you can hide, but your past is always going to catch up to you making you paranoid?'

'What. The fuck. Do you want? *Please.*'

'I just came here for a civil conversation,' he drawled, collecting himself and assuming a smug, self-assured expression. He drew himself up to his full height and, with affected dignity, arranged himself into a tall-backed chair deeper inside my living room. He appeared every inch the monarch holding court, from the crown adorning his head down to his elegantly crossed legs, one arm resting on the armrest, the other at his chin.

I took a seat, throwing my legs over the side of my chair in an equally affected display of insolence, just to get under his skin.

It worked. He scowled momentarily before rearranging his face into a smooth mask.

We stared at each other in stony silence.

'Go on, be civil,' I said. 'Converse.'

'You're successful, Saraswati,' he said, his tone smooth as chocolate ganache. 'Your public perception was dubious for a while, but tonight… Tonight, you showed them what you're made of, everything you stand for. You might be doing a servant's job back on Earth, but here you're a connoisseur of taste and flavour, and everyone adores you. *For now*.'

He flicked his fingers together, and cast a dozen different windows of footage up across the visio-node in my wall, all of which played simultaneously, screaming into my living room. The voices mingled in indiscernible cacophony, but a quick scan revealed captions flashing across each stream.

Feast: A triumph of Earthling ingenuity accompanied footage from the pop-up.

The Four Chefs, ridiculously hatted and jacketed as always, sat around a table in deep debate while a montage of pics and vids featuring yours truly (in entirely benign environments), flashed in the top right corner. It was captioned: *Is Earthing-led tech the answer to the future of Primian food? We think so: YES!*

Earth's history of violence gives way to a future of innovation proclaimed another feed, where most of the visual was taken up by dated footage from an Earthling war a hundred years old, while pics and vids of me flashed every once in a while, holding the *Interstellar MegaChef: Millennium Feast Special* trophy.

Earthling chef behind Feast spotted with Primian tech-wizard at The Wallflower featured my galactically famous kiss with Serenity Ko, playing on loop on one half of the stream. The other half showed Serenity Ko and me kissing each other with abandon at The Wallflower from just a few hours ago. I balked.

And finally, one stream caught my attention because its

viewership was through the roof. It featured Good Cheer Chaangte in an exclusive interview with Harmony Selia. *Former Nonpareil chef reveals the truth behind Earthling savage Saraswati Kaveri…*

Mixed feelings rushed through me—pride at the positive reception Feast was receiving; revulsion at my privacy being invaded and cam-drones recording Serenity Ko and me at The Wallflower; a twinge of annoyance at Good Cheer Chaangte for stirring controversy, again, and at Harmony Selia for giving her a platform, despite what I'd seen of *both* of them at the pop-up. The latter was disingenuous in the extreme, and the former rather insanely obsessed with me.

'You're well loved, it appears,' Jog Tunga said. 'For the most part.'

'My *product* is well loved,' I said.

'Right. Except notice how many times they tack the word "Earthling" onto their stories? They've done this ever since your first misadventure on *MegaChef*,' he said calmly. 'And I thought that, as a friendly face, I'd point it out to you.'

'Kind of you.'

'In case you've forgotten, that word "Earthling" has been used in several contexts. First they hate you, then they question you, then they love you, but always find a way to make you prove yourself.'

'Thanks for recapping my last year on this planet for me.'

'I figured you'd need a friend, in case you've been blinded to their hatred and judgment by all the recent adulation. Or a misplaced sense of loyalty to this sur-fucked rock.'

I snorted. 'A friend?'

'Yes, isn't it nice to know that someone's on your side?'

'Stop talking in circles and tell me what you want, Jog.'

'*Earthling* is a double-edged sword,' he said. 'They're using it so that when things go wrong, they can turn around and wield it as a weapon against you.'

My blood ran cold at his words.

'You think you've made it now,' Jog Tunga continued. 'You think that just because forty guests at your little pop-up restaurant said you're a genius, the lot of them will let up and leave you be.'

'Forty extremely influential guests.'

He waved his hand dismissively. 'Their influence goes both ways.'

I gritted my teeth. 'I'm well aware of that.'

'Just because they're suddenly in favour of you and your… *alleged* genius today, doesn't mean that they're going to stay on your side. That's how Primians react to us, in case it's taking time to sink in. That's how they react to *all* outsiders, and in that pecking order, us *Earthlings* are the lowest of the low. We need to stick together.'

'Right. We're on the same team, then?' It was a sarcastic, rhetorical question.

'Exactly!' he carried on, misreading me. 'Why should *these people,* who treat you like dirt one day and worship you the next, who make you prove them wrong again and again—all because they start off treating you as *guilty* until proven *innocent*, inconstant in both their adulation and their derision, benefit from all your talent, Saraswati?'

Because at least they aren't corrupt, power-mongering, murderous maniacs, I thought, but didn't say out loud.

'Do you think they're going to let you tinker with your kitchen toys independently, forever? Everyone will try to use you, and you'll wind up with nothing,' he said.

'Unlike my family,' I replied.

'At least your family wants what's best for you.'

'All my family wants is what serves their own interests.'

'And you benefit directly from their interests,' Jog Tunga said slowly, his eyes widening in disbelief, as if he couldn't fathom that I hadn't worked this out for myself.

'I don't believe in my family's interests,' I said.

'You're every bit as slow as Narmada told me you were,' Jog Tunga snapped.

'You're every bit as vile as you ever were.'

Jog Tunga ignored the insult, and pressed on. 'I want to make you an offer. Seeing as you can't stand your family and never want to see them again, I'll convince your parents to leave you alone. On this sur-fucked planet. Or anywhere in the galaxy you end up running to when you realise what a snake pit this place is.'

'Oh, really? And how are you going to pull that off?'

He leaned forward, his princely demeanour slipping. 'At this moment, Feast is proprietary, top secret Primian tech. It's too powerful a tool for *one planet* in all the known universe to wield—surely you agree. And so, I want you to give it to me, to take back to Earth.'

'What?' I burst out laughing. It was absurd.

'Why should Primus control tech like this when it can be used to better the lives of people all across the galaxy? People on your *home-world*, on *Earth*.'

'Just wait in line and license it like all the rest.'

'And let Primus grow more powerful? Control the market for food tech? It already controls every part of human occupied space, however anti-empire it claims it is...'

'Stop trying to win me over with conspiracy theories, Jog,' I said.

'I'm trying to reason with you.'

'Okay, here's me reasoning with you. I don't know the first thing about how the tech works. Couldn't tell you if you tickled me to death. I only designed the tasting experiences. I've signed so much scrollwork swearing me to secrecy, that if I decided to hand it to you, I'd be a criminal,' I explained. It was impossible to believe that this conversation was actually taking place.

'And right now, they love you,' Jog Tunga said, sarcasm dripping off every word. 'Put a toe out of line and you'll become the Earthling savage again, but no, you'd rather believe that this *love* is sincere.'

'I can't steal Feast,' I said flatly.

He slammed his palm down on the armrest of his chair. 'I'm going the extra mile by promising you that your parents will never bother you again. So long as you help me out.'

'Your promises are worth no more than the blood of a Kaveri,' I said unthinkingly, then clapped my hand over my mouth in horror at how easily the Earthling slur I'd grown up hearing all the time returned to me.

His lips curled into a smile, evidently delighted. 'You talk a big game, lording your virtue and goodness over your family's history. But here's the truth: there's no escaping your Godavari blood, *princess.* You're steeped in bigotry and bloodshed, just like the rest of them.'

'Get the fuck out,' I said, exhausted.

'You know, it's been a long day. You've got a lot to process. A massive victory to revel in, and all that. Give it a nava or two, and you'll see how deeply these sur-fuckers are prejudiced against you,' Jog Tunga said, rising to his feet and stretching exaggeratedly. 'I'll let you think on it, shall I?'

'There's nothing to think about.'

'Sleep on it.' He brushed past me uncomfortably close, whispering in my ear as he passed. 'I'll be in touch.'

The Osmos Girdle encircles Suriya beyond the orbit of Chomo in the Suriyan System.

It's the star system's primary source for precious stones, and collective, sustainable mining practices are conducted with the cooperation of the governments of Primus, Chomo and Sagaricus in an effort to gather resources without defacing their own planets.

—After Earth:
A Comprehensive Encyclopaedia of Greater Human Space
2025 Anno Earth | 1950 Interstellar Era

SIX

In the late depths of the evening, as what was forecast to be the rainiest day in recent history drew near, a string of Loop notifs screamed their way across Optimism Mahd'vi's visual, prompting her to first disable all incoming comms with a twitch of her fingers, then quell her rising anxiety at the thought that the Millennium Festival preparations were going horribly wrong, and finally take a deep breath and summon up the courage to go see what all the fuss was about.

She half expected anxious streams incoming from her Festival Planning Committee—an attack on an independent *Nakshatranāma* performance, perhaps…

She beamed.

The first Feast pop-up had been a resounding success. And Saraswati Kaveri was being hailed as a prophet of a food revolution.

The troublesome Earthling had been a preoccupation of hers, ever since she'd first appeared and been humiliated on *Interstellar MegaChef*. She'd gone to ground, only to resurface all over the Primian culinary scene, popping up in the unlikeliest places—like the restaurant Nonpareil, run by her fellow Earth-origins chefs, Pavi and Amol Khurshid. She'd disappeared again, only to return to *Interstellar MegaChef* and win their

Millennium Feast special episode, backed by XP Inc. and paired with the most powerful food tech the galaxy had ever seen.

If this hadn't been enough, she'd been spotted in the company of Jog Tunga, the savage Earthling prince, who seemed to enjoy lingering far from home, specifically on Primian soil. But then again, his flashy lifestyle saw him spotted with *everyone,* from pleasure dens on Sagaricus to 'cule vacations featuring a slate of the planet's hottest Ur-drama stars, and even cosying up to the K'artri-tva.

It's a shame all forms of surveillance are illegal on Primus, she thought.

All concern for planetary security, and general paranoia for anything that involved not one, but *two* high-profile Earthlings on her planet aside, Optimism Mahd'vi had personal reasons for keeping an eye on Saraswati Kaveri. It had everything to do with the woman's last name.

Optimism Mahd'vi was a survivor.

One of the last of the Kaveri clan, she and her older brother had escaped the slaughter of their people, fleeing the bloody stranglehold of the ruling Godavari family in the Daxina Protectorate.

The pair of them had escaped Earth on a strange spacecraft, been left at an orphanage on Primus, adopted into a Primian family, and raised with the overarching Nakshatran philosophy to "tread lightly." And they'd assimilated into the culture, like the blank slates that children tend to be, developing impeccable Ur-speak accents in the absence of the bastard influence of any native tongue, revelling in being accepted without a second thought. They even had given-names, following the traditional custom at their coming of age at seventeen. Scrupulously chosen from one of the nine virtues encompassing the spirit of space exploration in the Nakshatran Charter, the given-name was a parting wish as one transitioned from the potential of childhood into the solidity of adulthood, a dream for the future.

And yet, Optimism Mahd'vi had always remained uncomfortable that she'd never known her Earthling parents, and had no memories of her childhood home.

She had never known of another Kaveri. Until Saraswati. She experienced a mixture of hope and suspicion whenever the Earthling crossed her radar. It was the reason she'd invited her brother over this evening, to discuss "her Kaveri problem," as he'd taken to calling it.

As if on cue, her AI housekeeper streamed her. _Courage Kiva at the door. Shall I let him in?_

Optimism Mahd'vi replied in the affirmative, then rose from where she'd been doing her best to recline on the sofa. It never came easy to her; her muscles seemed hardwired to stay stiff and alert, even in her own home.

She strode through her space and into the foyer, where her brother was peeling off boots slick with water, trailing wet mud all over the floor faster than the mini-vacs could clean them up. His tall, skinny frame stooped over as he shook out his umbrella. Even so, she had to stand on tiptoe to give him a peck on the cheek, and he smiled gently.

'Any chance I can drop this off in the courtyard? There's a thunderstorm off the coast, and it's making its way to us!' he proclaimed.

'Leave it be. The vacs will mop up the floor anyway.' Optimism Mahd'vi looked at him curiously. 'What were you doing off the coast?'

'Wanderer ship had trouble with its engines…'

'I thought you were on holiday?' Optimism Mahd'vi raised an eyebrow.

'Specialized engines, Mahd'vi. Not too many on this planet—they're geared for the Osmos Girdle's lack of atmosphere, so there's always trouble when they need to be optimised for planetary ops.' Courage Kiva grinned cheerfully.

'Right. And you're the *only* expert out here?'

Courage Kiva slicked back his damp hair, and his smile turned sheepish.

'Never mind dinner plans,' Optimism Mahd'vi teased. 'What's dinner with your only sister when there's an engine to reckon with?'

Optimism Kiva wrapped her in a damp hug, then stood

back and surveyed the room. 'Ah! I see the geode I brought you from Sintra has pride of place on your shelf!'

'It's a lovely piece of rock. Tell me, when did you get back? When are you off again?'

'A nava ago, and two navas hence. I was on the Islets helping the Wanderers…' Courage Kiva began, then trailed off and frowned at her. 'Come now, don't look so sad about it!'

Optimism Mahd'vi sighed. 'Kiva, here I thought you'd be around for a bit. You're the only person I can be mostly human around, don't you see?' She gestured at her flowing, self-patterned pyjamas and simple green tunic, unadorned but for a belt at the waist.

'You mean I'm the only person you dress down for!' Courage Kiva chuckled.

'Yes!' Optimism Mahd'vi exclaimed. 'And I mean it as a compliment. It's terrible having to *perform* all the time.'

'And you love it almost all the time,' Courage Kiva said knowingly. 'Or you wouldn't have stayed at the Secretariat for so long.'

'Don't remind me it's all my fault. But I get tired, too, you know? Sometimes.'

Courage Kiva produced a bottle from an oversized pocket in his overcoat, as he shrugged it off and hung it up. 'That's why I brought this.'

'Spiced osmo-gin!'

'The very best!'

'Let me pour us a drink.'

Optimism Mahd'vi led the way to the kitchen. As she prepared their drinks, she listened to her brother recount news from the Osmos Girdle. While she had pursued a career in the public eye, her far more introverted sibling had chosen a quiet life away from the heart of it all, working on experimental propulsion systems in the asteroid belt, where precious stones were mined. This time, his stories included a pirate fleet that had planned to raid Edwinia, expecting no security systems, only to wind up on Itrou, where they'd been routed.

In turn, she filled him in on the Millennium Festival plans—

her committee was a rich source of minor wrongdoings to rant about. She then moaned about the persistently irksome Courage Ilio, the Secretary for Trade, whom she'd finally persuaded to lift the Primian ban on cricket chips imported from Earth. And finally, she casually mentioned the burgeoning success of Feast, and dropped Saraswati Kaveri into the conversation in the bargain.

'Ah, Feast sounds wonderful! I'm delighted to hear it's doing well already. Speaking of food, I tried the most incredible stonefruit dessert on Itrou—' Courage Kiva said, offering a distraction.

Optimism Mahd'vi hadn't made a career in the Secretariat for nothing.

'Don't change the subject, Kiva,' she said, her voice holding a warning note. 'You knew I was going to bring her up.'

'I was hoping you'd bring her up and let her drop. Gently. "A leaf falling into a river. All the gale can't force it to make a sound; it ripples silently, touches everything but says nothing..."'

'Stop quoting poetry at me.'

Courage Kiva sighed, then tilted his glass forward. 'I'll hear you out.'

Optimism Mahd'vi refilled both their empty glasses, adding peprinocorn ras and a hint of thengai-nut infusion to the osmo-gin.

'I need to talk to her,' Optimism Mahd'vi said, attempting nonchalance, but unable to suppress the urgency that found its way into her words. 'How could she have survived? *We* barely made it out alive.'

'You don't know that,' Courage Kiva said gently. 'I don't either. Maybe our parents saw the massacre coming and had a contingency plan to ship us off-world, well in advance of the slaughter.'

'You're older than me,' Optimism Mahd'vi pressed. 'And you remember nothing?'

'Only by two years,' Courage Kiva reminded her. 'And as I've said all our lives, I have almost no memory of that time.

Our mother smelled of jasmine, our father is no more than a sense of warmth. We had no siblings. Our home… I don't remember anything other than a scummy pond outside, where the frogs would gather when it rained. And that wasn't often, or maybe I hadn't lived there long enough before we left. And that's all, Mahd'vi.'

'You're not sparing me any gory details?'

'For the billionth time, no. If you're picturing a slaughter from the Ur-dramas, I don't know if it happened. Nobody does. I'll bet the surviving Godavaris don't know how it all happened, either.'

'The fucking Godavaris,' Optimism Mahd'vi spat.

'How do you know *our* family wasn't just as evil?' Courage Kiva asked.

'They couldn't have been.'

'Because they died?' Courage Kiva persisted, cautiously. 'Mahd'vi, you can't hold onto a past you never knew.'

'I can if it comes back to haunt my future.'

'The Kaveri girl.' Courage Kiva sighed, passing a hand over his face and pushing his hair back.

Optimism Mahd'vi laid all her suspicions out before him. This was a safe space, in the comfort of her home with no prying eyes or ears about. 'The Earthling prince she was seen with is an ally of the Godavaris,' she said. 'What are they scheming together?'

'I thought surveillance was banned here.' Courage Kiva frowned. 'Mahd'vi, if you're bending the law…'

'I'm not watching her,' Optimism Mahd'vi said quickly. 'But the Earthling prince keeps attracting stream-media. He loves performing for the cam-drones. Debauchery at pleasure dens in our star system, public appearances with folks like the K'artri-tva, plus he's always hooking up with Ur-drama stars. And… he was spotted at the Kaveri girl's space a few māsas ago…'

'So?'

'And I ran into him at a pub across the way from where she was, once.'

'Were you following her personally?' Courage Kiva's eyebrows shot up in concern. 'Or *him*?'

Optimism Mahd'vi stared at him in pointed silence. Courage Kiva sighed.

'What if he's blackmailing her?' Courage Kiva suggested.

Optimism Mahd'vi snorted.

'No, don't dismiss it. If we're getting deeply obsessed and wildly speculative…'

'"Savages hunt in packs. Spare one, you feed them all,"' Optimism Mahd'vi hissed, her temper fraying.

'That proverb is from the second century!' Courage Kiva laughed. 'Come now, Mahd'vi, you can't be progressive and inclusive when it suits your office, and then turn around and quote archaic philosophy at home.'

Optimism Mahd'vi rose to her feet. 'I thought this was a safe space!'

'It is,' Courage Kiva said. 'But you're my sister, and my only living family. I owe it to you to listen, *and* to be honest when I think you're spiralling.'

'Hah!' Optimism Mahd'vi scoffed. 'You never know, the Kaveri girl could be your cousin!'

'Or maybe she's just a refugee running away from something, who picked her last name at random.'

'That makes her a grifter.'

'That makes her someone who might need compassion.'

'You are the very milk of human kindness,' Optimism Mahd'vi sneered.

'And you've been working too hard, Mahd'vi. You're seeing shadows where none likely insist.'

'That's my *job*.'

'Your job is Secretary for Culture and Heritage, not interstellar spy.'

'There's an Earthling threat to us. I feel it in my bones. Damn the United Human Cooperative's Trust Protocols!'

'Those Trust Protocols prevent our planets and space stations from competing in an arms race and spying on each other nonstop.'

Optimism Mahd'vi glowered at her brother, now an unwelcome presence in her home, though she recognised that she was being silly.

Courage Kiva met her gaze evenly. 'You know what?' he said at last. 'You should talk to her. The Kaveri girl. I think it'll make you feel better to seek closure. To know the truth, and if not, to know that you'll never know the truth about everything and that's all right.'

'I wasn't asking for your permission,' Optimism Mahd'vi said coldly.

'Perish the thought,' Courage Kiva said, eyes twinkling as he adopted a saintly expression.

'I don't need you to validate anything I do,' Optimism Mahd'vi continued.

'Wouldn't dream of it.'

Optimism Mahd'vi made her way to the refrigerator under the pretext of rustling up some dinner. She then turned around, a fillet of vat-grown meat intended for a beest carpaccio in her hands. 'Kiva, you forgot another thing about our past! What was it they taught you when you turned four? Tell me again. The secret Kaveri riddle…'

Everything that can go wrong, will.

—Ancient Earth Proverb

SEVEN

STORM CLOUDS SWEPT in across the Arc. They gathered over the city of Uru, like a squadron of floating choux pastries piped to bursting.

The contours of the ever-shifting intelligent city ebbed and flowed to a symphony conducted by the weather. Each of Uru's reservoirs drained into enormous groundwater collection tanks so they could receive the rain. Its flowmetal structures shimmered in and out of focus as it redesigned itself for the safety of its citizens, while pedestrians at ground level and motorists in their sky-lanes—taking no chances—dove for cover in anticipation of the worst thunderstorm of the decade. The city and its people appeared to draw a collective deep breath, waiting for the cloudburst to summon forth an exhalation.

Wanderers across the Arc hunkered down in their bases, all the voices in the Faith of the Light Cathedral were raised towards Suriya in an unceasing murmur of orison…

And here we were, in the middle of a fistfight at a Feast pop-up.

We were *supposed* to be hosting members of the elite Culinary Circle, a secret club of restaurant-goers who gained access to private events of the most discerning kind by *attending* private events of the most discerning kind—

Saras! Kili shrieked a warning.

I dropped to my knees, narrowly avoiding a tray of Feast cubes flung my way by an irate Wanderer. Kili attacked the everfeather ornaments woven through their hair. The tray went whizzing over my head, dribbling Feast goop on its way past. Lightning flashed all around us, illuminating the chaos in the tent with the surreal intensity of a fever dream.

Look, I'll get to the Culinary Circle later.

A dozen Wanderers faced off against my team from XP Inc., armed with every makeshift weapon a pop-up kitchen on Primus could offer. As lightning streaked through the ominous skies visible through the ceiling of our tent, the horrified faces of the evening's Culinary Circle guests—bedecked in their finest Primian attire for an evening so exclusive they'd expected to regale envious friends about it for all time to come—revealed that this was more than they'd bargained for.

All I can say is, I didn't throw the first punch. That was on Serenity Ko, whose penchant for starting riots remained strong.

'Oof,' she groaned, as a fist bearing an ornamental cup caught her in the stomach.

'Not the fine crockery!' Curiosity Nenna shrieked, her all-enthusiastic-intern energy pushed to dangerous extremes. She lunged for the wielder—a tall, lean man whose nametag flashed across the Loop in my peripheral vision. 'That's a replica of a replica of a priceless Nakshatran artefact, you star-fucked loon. It's on loan from the Museum!'

She grasped the cup. He threatened to knock her over the head with it. They grappled for it, fingers white-knuckle tight on its jewelled rim.

Saras, this is a nightmare, Kili said.

You think?

Courage Praia was pinned to a wall by a woman wielding a replica of an engraving from Nakshatran Rock. They held their hands up in helpless surrender, and the woman shoved them to the floor.

Optimism Tina whacked an ageing Wanderer over the head with a sheaf of papyro-scrolls—our feedback surveys were so top secret, we were collecting them in physical form. It was a good thing we hadn't handed them out to our diners, yet.

Boundless Ano was locked in struggle with an elderly Wanderer. The Wanderer tried to prise Boundless Ano's rings off his fingers, while he did his best to twist out of his attacker's grasp.

Still on my knees, I crawled past the debris of an upended table, shooting its erstwhile occupants a sympathetic look as they huddled behind it. If I found shelter behind the kitchen counters, maybe I could work out how to get us out of this mess.

Or, you know, hide.

Thunder rumbled overhead. As it echoed in my gut, I knew that things were somehow going to get even worse.

As if on cue, Serenity Ko climbed up onto a dinner table.

I groaned.

She grabbed a terrified guest's walking stick and launched herself off her perch with a snarl on her face, cane angled like a javelin.

Optimism Tina and the Wanderer she was fending off scrabbled for purchase on the papyro-scrolls they were fighting over, reducing them to shreds of depressed confetti which fluttered morosely to the floor. Curiosity Nenna was knocked off her feet, and the ornamental goblet she'd been trying to rescue went sailing through the air as its wielder lost his grip on it. The cup of contention crashed into a pressurised cook-pot, bounced off the lid and rolled away on the floor.

And the pot exploded.

The lid shot into the sky, carbonated beverage spewing into the air, taking the roof right off the tent, a howl screaming in its wake just as the skies cracked open, pouring all the rage of the evening onto us as rain.

I buried my face in the ground, even as it turned to slurry, wondering how it had come to this.

Not true; I knew exactly how it had come to this.

IT HAD BEGUN with just a few ill-placed words. Words can do that sort of thing if they're repeated often enough. Serenity Ko might have been the one who erupted, but I knew I was at the heart of it all.

While everyone was shocked into a temporary truce by the sudden deluge, the day spun through my mind.

I'd been midway through my seventh interview of the afternoon and I was cracking.

Despite the blistering success of our first pop-up with the stream-media, where Feast was tried, tested and tasted to unparallelled approval, I was being put through the wringer by the ever-supercilious Primian food and culture critics, many of whom had *already* given Feast rave reviews.

I forced a smile at Boundless Sean from *The Consummate Cuisinologist*. He'd been been blown away by Feast a nava ago, though one really couldn't tell from his condescending tone. I focused at a point beyond his shoulder, counting my breaths to make sure I didn't snap.

The climate-controlled tent I'd been in all day was portable and impressively large. More importantly, given the circling thunderclouds, it was waterproof.

Choose a nice outdoor venue, they said. Make it symbolic, they said. Check the weather, they hadn't.

The Harmony Knot was coming apart.

The famed botanical installation was grafted together from Primian and Earthling flora as a symbol of the continuum of civilisation. It was meant to honour humanity's Earth-origins, the Nakshatrans' first journey across the stars, and Primian philosophy. It had been chosen as the venue for tonight's pop-up for all these symbolic reasons, and more. And it was undergoing a stress test that was difficult to watch. The wind whipped its way through its coiling creepers and dense foliage, raking it apart. Bougainvillea bracts and astriana petals swirled past in violent cascades, twigs and leaves snapping and spiralling in wayward eddies. The intense scent of petrichor drifted in through an open doorway, and the cold damp set into my fingers. Bluebuls and sparrows flocked to the trees, taking roost early, and an overlarge crow flapped past the window, glumly cawing on its quest to find shelter.

If I were the superstitious sort, these would be omens. The kind that would send me straight back to Earth on the fastest warpcraft available, all thoughts of culinary ambition abandoned to the grim rumblings of thunder overhead.

Instead, I explained my role in the development of Feast to Boundless Sean for the billionth time since I'd met him.

'You tried it the other day, at our pop-up, and clearly loved it,' I reminded him, reading off the stream Kili sent my way. 'I quote: "Feast is one of the most nuanced tasting experiences ever developed, within a kitchen or without."'

I paused and looked at him pointedly. 'As you know, the substrate is edibite, the tech is all XP Inc., but the flavour journey? The "nuanced tasting experience" you loved? The science behind the food experience, itself? That's what *I* bring to the table.'

'Care to explain to our lay readers how that "science" works?' Boundless Sean smiled.

'Let's take the Berry-anna,' I said, then immediately regretted my choice of dish. I swallowed as I quashed the unasked for desires it had bubbled up for me at the XP Inc. picnic, when I was seated beside Serenity Ko…

Boundless Sean looked at me expectantly. I continued.

'The Berry-anna is a decadent dessert. Slightly salted pastry, unsweetened foam, spheres infused with fresh berry flavours—a blend of sourness and sweetness, depending on how you choose to incorporate them: rubus, fraise, everberry, and more… And underscoring it all is that delicious nutty liqueur. It's a dessert that delivers a different experience of flavour with every single bite.'

Boundless Sean nodded in understanding.

'I've designed that experience. The transition from highlighting sweet notes to salty ones, the balance of sourness, the way that transforms your palate in different proportions, over a span of time. *That's* what I call my "flavour curve." And it's all delivered in a single bite. The intensity with which your tastebuds are stimulated, for every given flavour in a dish—that comprises your "flavour matrix."' I checked them off on my fingers. 'And when the sim-experiences or memories are triggered, they depend on how each flavour is being received, nanosecond over nanosecond, to create a rich immersive experience. But those prompts that get them to kick in? They're all from the science of flavour, and that's my expertise.'

'*You* are a *fascinating* choice,' Boundless Sean gushed, his emphasis and choice of words not lost on me. 'After all, an *Earthling* rising to fame in the world of *Primian* cuisine is not something we see often. And by that, I mean *ever.* Would you—'

'Pavi and Amol Khurshid,' I said, cutting him off while trying to stay polite. 'Top-notch Primian chefs, judges on *MegaChef*. Even *your* colleagues have given their restaurant, Nonpareil, rave reviews…'

Boundless Sean waved his hand dismissively. 'They're *one* data point. But sure, noted. It was just a figure of speech.'

'A figure of speech that ignores facts.' I raised an eyebrow. I was no big fan of Pavi and Amol—they'd been complicit in a lot of the unfair judgement that had come my way since I landed on Primus—but erasing them did not sit well with me.

Saras, don't lose your cool. Kili, perched on my shoulder, whirred gently. _He's trying to get a rise out of you._

I wish I could show him what that looks like, I streamed back, seething silently.

Not worth it.

Boundless Sean smiled, and I couldn't tell whether it was in contrition or satisfaction at having got to me. 'It's evident that there are vast philosophical differences between *our* Primian food and your *native* Earthling food. So, what I want to know is this: Why you?' he asked.

'Why not?' I said lightly, hoping I was doing a good job masking my indignation.

Boundless Sean laughed, then looked at me expectantly. I stifled a groan.

Every single interview, Kili streamed sourly.

Tell us why *we're* at the centre of the universe. Again.

Remind us why *our* culture is so aspirational and vastly superior. Again.

Tell us why *you* are worthy of aspiring to it. Again.

I parroted the well-developed, politically correct lie I'd prepped with the publicity team at XP Inc. 'I was an ambitious, passionate cook back on Earth. I came here to compete on *Interstellar MegaChef.* That didn't work out for me the first time I was on the show. Setbacks are commonplace in the world of a professional chef,' I said airily. 'So, I found a job at the critically acclaimed Nonpareil, learning from Pavi and Amol. And then I stumbled upon Serenity Ko and her top secret food-sim project at XP Inc. We hit it off, and here we are!' I beamed, grinding my molars as quietly as possible.

'And how have your Earthling origins influenced Feast?'

'They haven't. My expertise, gained from years as a professional chef on Earth, has *informed* Feast, but the flavours and experiences are all Primian. You see, despite those *philosophical differences* between our food cultures that you've so *thoughtfully* mentioned, we share an overarching love for flavour, a universal connection to food that sparks emotion, unlocks memory, and inspires hope. Feast is an expression of that love.'

Don't crack, Kili reminded me.

'Ah, love,' Boundless Sean said, zeroing in on his most pressing question for the day. 'I'm glad you brought that up. Rumour has it that you and your partner in this latest offering—Serenity Ko—are a bit of a partnership outside work, as well? You were spotted at The Wallflower a few days ago...'

'Saraswati Kaveri will only be answering questions directly pertaining to Feast, Sean. We discussed this,' Optimism Tina cut in smoothly from where she was seated beside me. 'So if that's all you've got...'

Our head of publicity smiled politely but firmly, and I fought to keep my shoulders from slumping with relief.

'Ah, no, that will be all.' Boundless Sean nodded towards the darkening world outside. 'Still going ahead with it, are we? I'll be surprised if anyone turns up in this weather.'

'We're optimists,' Optimism Tina said without a trace of irony. 'Thank you, Sean.'

*Sur-fucked prick.* Kili streamed his disapproval. He buzzed off my shoulder, his green and chrome body zigzagging all the way to the entrance of the tent, sizing up the continued dismemberment of the Harmony Knot.

He's not wrong about the weather, though, he murmured thoughtfully.

It's grim, I acknowledged.

I wonder who'll make it…

We shall see, I said, rising to my feet as Optimism Tina returned.

'That's the last of them,' she said, rubbing my back reassuringly. 'You were splendid.'

'Ugh. I'm glad to hear it!' I stretched, easing the cramps in my shoulders, which had been tensed through the better part of the day. 'You've worked with Kube, yeah? How'd he get so good at managing the stream-media? Does it ever get easier?'

'Depends on how far you want to lean in,' Optimism Tina said. 'But you're doing well so far. Giving uninterrupted interviews in Ur-speak when you aren't a native speaker, too!'

I knew she intended it as a compliment, however badly phrased, but if one more person mentioned my Earth origins within my hearing range, just *one* more…

'Earth girl!'

I spun, a grin spreading across my face. So much for that.

Serenity Ko swanned into the tent, flanked by Courage Praia and Curiosity Nenna, who'd taken to tagging along with her everywhere. They were like an entourage straight out of an Ur-drama. Their eyes were both unfocused, lips murmuring rapidly, and I figured they were in separate meetings on the Loop. Serenity Ko, though, was beaming while she took in her surroundings.

'Ko! What're you doing here? I thought your day was packed with meetings!' My heart hammered an irregular staccato.

'I thought I'd swing by to help,' Serenity Ko said officiously. 'See if you needed a hand round the kitchen—'

'No,' I said firmly. 'The last time you were in a kitchen with me, it ended badly.'

Tragically, Kili chimed in, though he buzzed off my shoulder to nuzzle her cheek.

She patted him, then scowled at me. 'That was *one* time, Saras. I would never do it again.'

'The worst bit is, I think that dessert you destroyed would have turned out badly even if you *weren't* trying to pull a prank on me.'

'Forgive and forge friendships,' Courage Praia said sanctimoniously. They emerged from their hyper-reality meeting and hugged me tight.

'*Thank you!*' Serenity Ko said. 'It's a Nakshatran virtue, number seven on the list...'

'I thought it was one of our guiding principles,' Curiosity Nenna said, sliding out of the Loop, as well. She bit her lower lip, then threw a hasty glance at Serenity Ko. 'I could be wrong, of course.'

'No, you're right. You're all right. I'm useless. I know nothing. No reason for my being here.' Serenity Ko pouted.

Courage Praia rolled their eyes, and Curiosity Nenna assumed the expression of wide-eyed confusion expected of high-performing interns everywhere in the universe. They busied themselves with setting up the décor in the tent, as Serenity Ko appeared by my side.

'Don't. Touch. Anything,' I warned, but flashed her a teasing smile.

'I wasn't going to...' Serenity Ko hastily withdrew her hand from a transparent machine, within which an effervescent liquid bubbled furiously. She caught me eyeing her sternly, then shrugged sheepishly. 'Okay, I was. But the actual drink—or is it food?—is on the *inside* of this machine. I can't *possibly* hurt it. What is it, anyway?'

'We had to change some of our drinks to accommodate the weather,' I explained, picking up a train of wine glasses to move to the bar. 'Instead of a feathered ice wine for dessert, we're doing a frothed mullion-berry sherry...'

I watched carefully as her eyes immediately glazed over. 'Earth to Serenity Ko. It's a bit rude to check into the Loop when someone's talking, don't you think?'

'I wasn't in the Loop,' Serenity Ko said hastily.

'So you were just bored, then.'

'I was thinking about what an expert you are at this.' She knocked her fist upon the counter twice, then blushed.

I was consumed by the desire to kiss her. She was *such* a distraction in the kitchen.

Heat rose to my cheeks, and I looked away. Serenity Ko, in turn, looked down at her hands, which fidgeted uselessly by her sides.

'How did the stream-media treat you today?' she asked casually.

_Uh-oh,_ Kili broadcast.

Tell me that wasn't a bad move, Serenity Ko pleaded.

Involuntarily, my hands clenched around the edges of the tray of wine glasses in my hands. I handed it hurriedly to Boundless Ano. A surge of unexpected rage swept over me, drowning me in its ferocity.

'Terrible,' I said, choking on anger.

'I'm sorry,' Serenity Ko said.

'Just fucking terrible,' I repeated, hollow.

'I'm so fucking sorry,' Serenity Ko said again. 'Want to talk about it?' she offered weakly.

'Sure, we can talk about it.'

I steadied my hands against the kitchen counter. They trembled violently.

'So… it was bad?' Serenity Ko asked hopelessly.

Out of the corner of my eye, I registered Boundless Ano hastily moving himself, and the tray of wine glasses in his hands, out of reach, right as I exploded. 'It was star-fucking *unreal*. I've spent—what, close to a Primian year on this sur-fucked planet? And every time I think the people here can't get *any more* insufferable or condescending, a new one pops up to surprise me. I had a photographer this morning compliment me on my smile. I was about to thank her for it, too. And then: "Such good teeth, despite your Earth-origins," she said kindly. What the fuck does that even mean? Dentistry and dental cleanses have existed for millennia, and they *originated on Earth*. Just like humanity! She said she'd seen holoreels of—

what was it?' My voice rose shrilly, hurting my own ears, but I found I couldn't control it. '"Toothless savages in war zones all over the Earth and Fringe planets. Have you ever watched them swallow protein shakes?" Of all the *nerve*.

'And then there was the interviewer who spoke to me in Vox *the entire time,* even though I was replying in Ur-speak right through. And yes, I know my Ur-speak has traces of an Earth accent—I'm from another planet, for fuck's sake. Pardon *me* if my diphthongs are clipped instead of rounded. Also, um, people's Ur-speak accents are different all over Primus—the Wanderers tend to drawl, the chlorosapients are more lilting... Does nobody ever notice?'

I paused and exhaled. 'But you've heard the Vox rant before, on account of *it happens all the time!*

'And every single one of them, *every last one,* was obsessed with what made *me* the right person for this job. As if I have to somehow prove myself to them. Which I have, because half of them have already tasted Feast and given us rave reviews, including giving the *flavours* we designed rave reviews. And whose flavours are those? *Mine.*

'How does it even matter that I'm from Earth? Except it does, because *every last one of them* wasted at least twenty minutes of my time explaining Primian cooking to me, as if I could have built this product without learning all about it. But no, do go on, tell the savage how to flick a light switch.'

I watched as everyone in the room winced at the archaic expression. It was bandied about often in the older Ur-dramas.

'But the worst bit?' I choked. 'The worst bit was this unspoken, underlying expectation that I would be *grateful* for being included at all, for being given this *opportunity* to *prove myself* and win their approval. That's how my interviews went.'

Optimism Tina rose from her seat, papyro-scrolls sliding from her lap onto the floor unheeded. 'Saras, I didn't realise how badly they were getting to you. I'm so sorry! I thought they were a bit off colour, but you seemed to take it in your stride so well...'

'Thanks, Tina. No, I'm used to it—it's been this way ever since we won *MegaChef*. I think I just cracked a bit today...' I composed myself, rolling my shoulders to relax all my tensed muscles. 'It's the pressure.'

'If it's all right with you, I'm going to excuse myself and have a stern word with your interviewers,' Optimism Tina said brusquely.

Thunder crashed overhead. Everyone glanced up through the roof of the tent at a sky the colour of squid ink.

'Maybe do that later?' I suggested. 'It's okay. My injured pride will survive, and it's only the apocalypse outside.'

'Good thing we have a roof,' Boundless Ano said, his eyes fixed skyward.

'Waterproof all round, too,' Serenity Ko said cheerily.

THE WATER WAS streaming in now, soaking us all. The fighting resumed in the rain.

When they look to the skies of their imagination, we look to the ground beneath our feet. We are the roots that let them spread their branches into the realms of dream. We are their anchor, the voice of the planet that gives them sustenance.

—Wanderers' Code

1475 Anno Earth | 1400 Interstellar Era

EIGHT

SOME SITUATIONS DEMAND fading into the background, beaming proudly while your… friend-you-desperately-want-to-sleep-with (for the lack of a better word), and the better half of your revolutionary food tech project, takes centre stage, whipping up a culinary storm while a real storm threatens to rage on outside, charming diners with a smile and dazzling their palates with intricately crafted food-sim experiences.

Other situations demand punching someone in the face, food tech project be damned.

Serenity Ko had started off basking in the former and, true to her habitual blatant disregard for her given-name, effortlessly flung herself into the latter. She'd thrown that first punch—wholeheartedly justifiably (in her version of events)—and set off a veritable riot.

This hadn't been on her agenda for the day. She'd imagined watching Saraswati steer the pop-up to another unprecedented success, winning the hearts and palates of their distinguished Culinary Circle guests along the way, and then taking her out to a quiet dinner—perhaps even a romantic one: as mentioned, she desperately wanted to sleep with her, even if she wasn't sure she wanted a committed relationship.

That quiet dinner now seemed unlikely, and any thought of romance—or even just unleashing her hormones—had long since fled the room.

The roof exploded off the tent, rain cascaded upon its

inhabitants, and Serenity Ko skidded through the slush, wielding a stranger's walking stick like an icepick, trying to find purchase and stop her careening trajectory. She smacked into the wall of the tent, and found herself passing straight through the flowmetal barrier into the damp hedgerows lining the Harmony Knot outside. The walking stick made contact and splintered with a sickening crunch. Serenity Ko winced at the thought that her bones could have wound up the exact same way. It was enough to snap her out of the red haze.

'Sun-fuck me. What have I done?' she moaned, doubling over the bushes and panting.

The last few hours leading into the opening—and grand unveiling of Feast—had run entirely smoothly, until they hadn't.

SHE'D SHOWN UP with Courage Praia and Curiosity Nenna, and Saraswati had made it difficult for her to pay attention to the words coming out of her mouth—as opposed to her mouth itself, painted a dusky pink to go with the rosia-stone necklace that offset her severe black tunic. She found those lips irresistibly kissable… but Saraswati kept insisting they needed to prioritise their work relationship, and that was fair, so why did it seem so *un*fair?

She took in Saraswati striding around the kitchen with an air of calm efficiency, Kili hovering millimetres off her shoulder, registered Courage Praia and Curiosity Nenna arguing in hushed tones over the best placement for an unremarkable if historically valuable piece of rock, considered going over to Optimism Tina, who was in between Loop meetings, and then chose to lean forward on the counter and make shoptalk as charming as she could.

It had been disastrous.

But, all things considered, Saraswati had cheered up significantly after her outburst. The mood had shifted by a smidge, but it was enough for everyone to get on with the business of the evening. Serenity Ko kept a watchful eye on Saraswati, though, and gave the kitchen equipment a wide berth while she was at it.

There's no need to get tangled up in the... She paused, trying to name at least one device in the skeletal kitchen set-up, and couldn't. *Right, no need to mess with the... stuff.*

Such neatly manicured, short nails, and even if her hands are a bit clunky, she's so good with them...

Serenity Ko pushed the unsolicited thought away, even as she admired Saraswati's work ethic (among other things).

Through the many hostilities and uncertainties leading up to winning *MegaChef*, and the immense pressure that had come into play since, Saraswati had remained a *nice* person. Firm and assertive when she needed to be, but always polite and considerate.

And she has the most attractive forearms I've ever seen.

She tore her eyes away, and decided to chip in with the decor, far away from the kitchen counters, as requested.

Before anyone in the tent had noticed, the hours had slipped past, and Suriya had set—though this was indiscernible, given the thickening clouds massing overhead. Opening hour was upon them.

Serenity Ko stepped back from where she'd been affixing a Galactic System model from about a millennium ago to a flowmetal hook in the roof, its many star systems twinkling amidst the soothing ambient lighting, and caught Saraswati watching her. She nearly fell off her stepladder, caught herself before her clumsiness made itself evident, and flashed her a smile. Her stomach felt like it had been invaded by flutterwings.

'Go time,' Saraswati muttered, having reapplied her makeup and straightened out her tunic.

The folks from XP Inc., Serenity Ko included, retreated to the back of the house, into a small alcove beside the open kitchen. They were screened off from the dining area by a trellis, and muted from the outside world within a sound-bubble. Only Optimism Tina stayed outside to fuss over their incoming guests from the Culinary Circle, along with Boundless Ano, who was spinning out aperitifs at the bar.

The Culinary Circle had turned out in their finest Primian attire—high collars and intricate embroidered weaves; stones from the Osmos Girdle shimmering in tasteful hairbands and nose pins; long, elaborate braids. They sat at their tables, sipping on their drinks and apparently charming each other with eloquence and wit. The amuse-bouche was borne to their tables by the immaculate waitstaff, all adept at blending into the background unless required, when (before a request was even uttered) they were at a diner's elbow, suggesting alternatives from the wine list and refilling water tumblers, self-effacing smiles at the ready.

The servers barely exchanged a glance before raising the cloches in a swift, smooth movement. The nondescript Feast jellies wobbled upon their plates.

Conversation stilled in the manner of an abrupt death, the kind of unfortunate end that comes when a spaceship explodes without warning. And then chuckles and giggles filled the room.

The Citric Crush was served.

A person in shimmering black gasped at the sight of the sphere. Another snorted. A third swore. A woman in a white synth-silk dress prodded the sphere before her tentatively, shuddered, then broke into a grin. A man with a walking stick pushed his chair back, shaking his head in a mixture of shock and amusement.

The minutes passed. Not a single diner said a word to another while they ate, their eyes glazing as they allowed themselves to be whisked away on an experiential journey.

Serenity Ko glanced quickly at Saraswati on another visionode stream. Saras's hands shook as she spritzed the next course with water. Her own heart was on the edge of a cliff, where the drop could mean the difference between life and death for the food-sim's popularity.

And then, the lady in shimmering black smiled. The man with the walking stick had tears in his eyes. The room erupted in polite applause, and the joy on everyone's faces was palpable until she felt her own eyes blurring over.

'Bloody brilliant!' one of the younger diners cried, jumping to their feet. They ran up to Saraswati and shook her hand. 'What a masterpiece! My compliments to you, to your entire team!'

'I give you the future of Primian food,' Saraswati said grandly, rattling off the speech she'd memorised. 'Welcome to our pop-up, and may I present to you… a *Feast!*'

She spread her arms outward, grandly. To Serenity Ko, she resembled a goddess.

The wine pairing arrived, right on cue, followed swiftly by another round of Feast cubes.

Serenity Ko and Curiosity Praia exchanged a grin. It appeared tonight would be a success, too.

The forager herbed salad was a hit.

Snatches of conversation were relayed over the visio-nodes, little phrases being muttered. 'Such attention to detail…' and '… if you'd served me a *real* forager herbed salad, I'd scarcely have been able to tell the difference—they even captured the *texture!*'

Only a couple of faces appeared unconvinced, and there was time enough to win them over, over the next four courses.

Curiosity Nenna stifled a sob, and Serenity Ko hugged her tight. Warmth brimmed within the little alcove they occupied, spilling over from the kitchen. The air was crisp with anticipation, every diner's eyes upon the servers' trays as they came round with the second course. Never mind that lightning illuminated the heavy skies, or that thunder rolled with the intensity of a meteor strike; there was an unnameable, ineffable breeze blowing through the room.

Nothing can go wrong, Serenity Ko thought.

Do we have a soundtrack? Saraswati streamed, out of nowhere.

Nope, she shot back.

Has Optimism Tina invited *live musicians*?

Serenity Ko's heart stuttered. The sims had personalised auditory experiences, drawing upon people's memories and the XP Inc. database. This seemed absurd.

She tiptoed to the wall bounding the edge of the alcove.

'Where are you going, Ko?' Curiosity Nenna hissed.

'Something's wrong.'

A couple of diners emerged from their second courses, beaming. And then their smiles slid off their faces and they craned their necks, peering into the darkness beyond the doorway. Dull chanting reached Serenity Ko's ears.

A fog had descended, and it was too dark to see past ten metres outside. It wasn't until they were right on the doorstep that she made out the shapes of close to a dozen Wanderers, shouting at the top of their voices.

'*Sims do more harm than good!*'

'*Dreams are not bigger than reality!*'

'*No more lies!*'

Glass shattered as Boundless Ano dropped a shot measure.

Many of the diners tilted their chairs back, angling them to get a good view out the entrance to the tent, where the noise was escalating. One sombre-looking Wanderer, everfeather ornaments woven through her hair, sang a dirge-like melody, which was reminiscent of a hymn of mourning, except the words were neither in Vox nor in Ur-speak. The chanting continued all around her.

'I'm going to stop this,' Serenity Ko said, taking a purposeful step forward.

She caught sight of Boundless Ano calmly making his way to the assembled crowd, and paused.

Good, she thought. *He's a Wanderer, they should listen to him.*

But Optimism Tina, who until that moment had been smiling and making polite conversation with one of the diners, beat him to it. 'This is a private event,' she said brusquely. 'I'd like to request you to leave.'

'Request it all you want,' one of the Wanderers said rudely. 'We're not going anywhere.'

Boundless Ano stood by Optimism Tina's side. 'Maybe you could stand off to the side,' he suggested, in an ingratiatingly reasonable tone. 'There's shelter at that gazebo off by the Harmony Knot. If you wait until our guests have been served, we could give you some personal time with the XP Inc. team so you can air your concerns.'

Serenity Ko took another step forward, adrenaline pulsing in the small of her back.

'I'm sorry, are we inconveniencing your little marketing

scam, peddling your profiteering bag of lies and dreams?' the same Wanderer asked gruffly.

'As a matter of fact, yes,' Optimism Tina said coolly.

'Too bad. We're here with a peaceful protest,' he said, as the everfeather Wanderer's song reached more dolorous depths, 'and we're going to stay.'

'Listen, my friend,' Boundless Ano said, holding his hand up so his Wanderers' rings were clearly visible. 'I'm a Wanderer too, volunteered three times, and you have my word—'

The Wanderer shoved past him and into the room. 'Your word counts for nothing, sellout. Anyone who forsakes the natural world for this simulation sound-and-light show doesn't deserve respect. "Look to the ground for it shall free you to dream of the skies..." Have you forgotten the oath already?'

Serenity Ko cast a quick glance at Saraswati, who smiled at her faintly. She returned the smile, but then turned all her attention to the Wanderers instead. She rolled up her sleeves, unbearably exasperated.

_Ko,_ Saraswati streamed a warning. _Let's just call security._

She ignored the request.

'Someone call security!' Saraswati said out loud instead.

'We... we don't have any,' Optimism Tina said, as the Wanderers streamed in, their chanting filling the enclosed space.

'*What?*'

'This is Primus, not Earth,' Optimism Tina snapped, losing track of all political correctness in the moment. 'We don't *need* security. I mean *ever*...'

There's always a first time, Kili said grimly.

Then, to everyone's surprise, the chanting stopped. The Wanderers began a silent demonstration.

Serenity Ko had half been expecting them to loot the place and tear it down, but instead, they arranged themselves into some kind of tableau. The everfeather woman started humming a different melody, accenting it with a small, chiming instrument she produced from a pocket. And a performance began, which, if it hadn't been so utterly intrusive, and downright *rude*, might have been funny.

Three of the Wanderers, including the singing one, were draped in everfeather and greendust. They took their positions with their arms outstretched towards the sky.

Trees. Or some plant-like thing.

Three more Wanderers decked out in rich blue sky-silk robes lay themselves upon the floor, waving their arms sinuously.

The... ocean?

The rest playacted at walking through this symbolically idyllic scene, until one by one, with great exaggeration, their eyes glazed over, and they mimicked being lost in sims. The singing woman's pitch changed, and she set to wailing, while her companions mimed wandering blindly, stumbling into each other, before setting to attacking each other. The many-armed ocean of Wanderers on the floor stopped waving, the tree-Wanderers stooped and crouched, dramatically wilting into the floor.

Everyone in the room looked on in disbelief, and Serenity Ko felt an uncomfortable burning spreading through her chest. She was unable to place whether this was from just how terrible the performance had been (exquisitely terrible), or because the protesters had actually got through with their message (extraordinarily on the nose).

The sensation coursing through her began to hurt. It felt as if her ribs were on the verge of exploding, and all of her limbs shook uncontrollably.

Serenity Ko laughed. Loudly and hysterically.

'You are an embarrassment to the people of Primus,' the grouchy Wanderer who appeared to be their leader cried. He glowered at Serenity Ko from his spot playing an ocean wave on the floor.

Serenity Ko howled with mirth, unable to contain herself. Tears made the world blurry, but not so blurry that she couldn't see what happened next.

The irate Wanderer scrambled to his feet, and his gaze swept the room until it rested upon Saraswati.

He pointed an accusing finger.

'*You,*' he cried.

Serenity Ko's laughter died on her lips.

'*You* are everything that has destroyed humanity. *You and your* Earthling *ways will be the death of us all*. Of Primus, our Nakshatran way of life, *of the universe itself.* "All it takes is an Earthling in the room to start a war—"'

He never got to the end of his sentence.

There was a flash of movement.

Time slowed hideously, and Serenity Ko's clenched fist met his stubbled jaw, sending his head back with a crack.

It hurt.

The protesting-Wanderers-turned-hideous-theatre-ensemble charged. The folks from XP Inc. charged back.

SERENITYS KO'S FIST still hurt. If only she hadn't punched that Wanderer in the face. If only those sur-fucking Wanderers hadn't shown up with their idiotic demonstration in the first place.

The fighting carried on in the tent. Serenity Ko regained her bearings outside, the cold deluge shocking her back to her senses. She flexed the jagged half of the walking stick still in her hands, and readied herself to go back inside. This time, she would be a messenger of peace, and bring order back to the evening. She'd apologise to the Wanderer she'd clocked, and *she would not knock someone's lights out*.

A bejewelled fist appeared beside her in the gloom, and she ducked on instinct, spinning the splintered stick in a wide arc. Cane met soft flesh with a muffled thump.

'Ouch!'

'Back the fuck off!'

'Hold up, calm down!' Serenity Ko noticed that his Ur-speak carried a distinct drawl.

Ten jewelled rings coruscated on the fingers of a pair of outstretched hands, and a familiar looking man stepped into focus.

'Courage Anto. I saved you at a bar in the Ur-sands the last time you started a riot,' he said hurriedly. 'I'm here to save you from this one, too.'

All it takes is an Earthling in the room to start a war
All it takes is an Earthling to convince you
That it doesn't matter what you're fighting for
All the Earthlings want
Is to get their greedy grubby fingers on more...

—Primian Children's Rhyme

NINE

SERENITY KO STEPPED into the tent, her arms spread wide.

'Let's talk like *civilised people,* shall we?' she announced imperiously.

Nobody paid her any attention.

Optimism Tina yanked her soggy papyro-scolls so hard that they thwacked her in the face, streaking her makeup as her opponent stumbled backward into the mulch. Courage Praia slipped through the sludge, straight past the Wanderer who'd pinned them to the wall, performing a slick one-eighty turn straight out of an Ur-drama to take the woman's legs out from under her.

Curiosity Nenna and her Wanderer opponent eyed each other uncertainly, each waiting for the other to make the first move. The Wanderer grabbed a snifter from a diner, who'd been holding it halfway to their lips since the fighting began.

He flung its contents at Curiosity Nenna.

She stepped aside deftly.

The drink splashed all across the front of a woman in an expensive-looking dress. Golden brown OakBrew blossomed across a pristine white synth-silk gown.

The Culinary Circle joined the fray.

Serenity Ko winced. This would make it harder to explain to Grace Kube and the folks at XP Inc.

The Culinary Circle comprised the most elite aficionados of Primian cuisine. They didn't *work* in the culinary profession, in any of the thousand kitchens spread across the planet;

they were simply the most distinguished *eaters* of the finest foods imaginable, period. Fine diners who belonged to an underground, top-secret programme, who racked up invitations to exclusive culinary events, one fine-dining restaurant experience at a time. Or so Optimism Tina had informed them all, stressing the import of the evening.

To be a member, you had to consistently eat your way across the fine-dining landscape in Uru for years on end, stumble upon ways to tell the difference between high-end restaurants that counted and high-end restaurants that didn't, and eventually, catch the eye of an existing Culinary Circle member, who could choose to invite you (or not) to an interview, depending on which restaurant you might happen to be in, and what dishes you were observed ordering on that very day. And assuming you passed their membership test, which was known to be shrouded in secrecy, you then had to keep up appearances, slowly making your way through a slew of affiliations, all laid out like concentric rings, until you reached the innermost circle.

Tonight, their guests comprised the innermost circle of the inner circle. And at this moment, they were flinging mud, drinks, and sodden napkins at everyone in sight.

There was a blaze of light, klaxons filling the air. An army of drones and masked humans in bodysuits swarmed the tent, stun-sabres and riot shields at the ready. A thick voice called, '*Nobody move!*'

'What *they* said!' Serenity Ko echoed.

The leader of the Primian Guard contingent was not amused, it turned out, to recognise Serenity Ko among the rioters.

'Last I checked, *we* were in charge,' the woman leading the Guard said coldly.

'Just helping out,' Serenity Ko replied pompously.

'Repeat offenders don't get to do that,' the woman said.

By this time, Serenity Ko had had the good sense to scan the Guardsperson on the Loop. *Good Cheer Soraya, She/Her* was an *extensively* decorated officer. Her holo-medals and badges shimmered on her glossy black riot gear, and Serenity Ko took an involuntary step back.

'Er, right, I'll leave you to it,' she mumbled, doing her best to fade away.

'Making a habit of this, are we?' Good Cheer Soraya asked.

'Just arrived,' Serenity Ko lied on impulse.

The Primian Guard was evidently not impressed. They'd been summoned during the worst thunderstorm of the decade to break up a low-level fight between private individuals airing differences of opinion.

As a bonus, what *could* have been a healthy debate on the future of sim technology, requiring no Primian Guard involvement whatsoever, had turned into a skirmish that had invited the unwanted intrusion of every single stream-media channel in the galaxy.

One of the Culinary Circle members—the enthusiastic young man who'd run up to shake Saraswati's hand—had been publicly streaming since the evening began, right through the start of the altercation, and well into its escalation into a ruckus. Every stream-media channel had picked up on his feed, descending on the portable XP Inc. tent in a swarm of cam-drones.

Harried and hopeless, the Guard attempted to enforce a media embargo, but between the pouring rain, the jagged afterimages left by each streak of lightning, and the overall persistence of the cam-drones, it became impossible to stun every media drone with their own security drones. And so, the galaxy bore witness to the aftermath of the fight: its participants soaked to the bone, shivering, grouchy, and entirely unapologetic, unhurt but for bruised egos on all sides.

'*She* punched me!' accused the irate Wanderer whom Serenity Ko had, indeed, punched. The Loop revealed him as Boundless Lilo.

She threw him her filthiest look. 'Pardon me for having a zero-tolerance policy towards xenophobia,' she said archly.

'Everyone stop talking,' Good Cheer Soraya snapped. 'You're wasting our time and resources. We brought a unit—that's *fifteen* of us—to break up whatever this…' She glanced around the room, desperately searching for the right words, then snorted. 'To break up a *food fight*. Because someone called in a protest-turned-violent. "Riot" was the word used, if I recall correctly. Have any of you ever *seen* a riot?'

Serenity Ko opened her mouth to respond, but shut it just as quickly when the woman looked at her pointedly and said: 'Barring your in-house career rioter, that is.'

She seemed to take their silence as an invitation to go on. 'Because this is not it. We're drenched, we're armed to the teeth with riot gear, and we are underwhelmed. I want to wrap this up as soon as possible.'

She glared around the room, looking past its human inhabitants to the dense cloud of cam-drones recording and transmitting across the stars like an electronic swarm of bees. 'Is there a private space we can occupy? I'd like to have *some* of this happen discreetly.'

'We have an annexe at the back…' Serenity Ko said helpfully.

'Any chance it still has a roof?'

'No,' she said apologetically. 'The roof was lost in the, um, incident.'

Good Cheer Soraya exhaled, an audible hiss. 'It'll have to do. Good thing our gear is waterproof.' She then announced loudly. 'Let's sound-bubble it and cordon it off. If *any* stream-media follows us inside, we will have your station shut down and off the Loop until Suriya collapses into itself. Do I make myself clear?'

She strode off towards the alcove.

'Hang on,' one of the diners protested. 'You don't mean to keep us here in the rain all evening, do you?'

The speaker was a woman in a white dress, which clung to her soggily, splattered all over with some kind of hideous stain. Serenity Ko would have giggled if their Culinary Circle guests didn't look so angry, a sea of cold fury that mirrored the streaming skies above.

'Apologies,' Good Cheer Soraya said brusquely. 'I didn't realise you'd be idiot enough to step out on an evening like this without umbrellas.'

Serenity Ko smirked as the white dress lady opened and closed her mouth several times, soundlessly, like something from the bottom of a fish tank. The other Culinary Circle members looked deeply offended.

'If you have a problem with my attitude, take it up with my superiors,' Good Cheer Soraya said indifferently, then turned to one of her team and barked. 'Run a tarp across the top of this structure, will you? Better that than give this lot umbrellas to fight with.'

The Guardsperson so addressed scurried off, with two other members of their team, to fulfil this order.

Good Cheer Soraya stepped into the annexe, calling over her shoulder: 'I have one Optimism Tina who called this in. Whoever you are, I'd like to start with you.'

As Optimism Tina made her way in for questioning, Serenity Ko glanced around the room. Saraswati caught her eye and frowned.

She decided that she wanted to make Saraswati laugh, and being drenched and mud-spattered already, lost her footing and fell, raking muck all over her clothes, which caught on the edge of a chair and ripped, stopping her momentum.

'Nine Virtues, Ko!'

A number of voices called out at once, and Courage Praia was the first to get to her side.' Are you okay?' they asked, as they extended a hand to gently pull her up.

'Yes, all good,' Serenity Ko huffed, rising to her feet. It hadn't worked: Saraswati's face looked even grimmer than before, hands gripping the counter even tighter, if that were possible.

'Caution, everyone!' she announced, laughing falsely. 'Wet floor.'

Courage Praia shot her a funny look as they walked beside her.

The Wanderers were huddled in a tight knot, the grouchy man she'd punched looking around wildly as if caught in a trap. Courage Anto appeared to be murmuring softly to them. The everfeather lady of the awful chanting appeared upset, and the others looked down at the wet mud. Meanwhile, the Culinary Circle complained loudly as members of the Guard deployed a hive of drones to pin a tarp in place overhead. The woman in the stained white dress seemed particularly vicious; her repeated use of the word "savages" was accompanied by unsubtle gestures towards the Wanderers.

Serenity Ko supposed she was relieved. Their guests seemed to have forgotten all about Saraswati's presence in the room. Her friends from XP Inc. appeared to have deflated—Courage Praia seemed embarrassed, Curiosity Nenna stood by a shelf, outright horrified, and Boundless Ano, who was still by the door, kept shaking his head, muttering to himself. The Primian Guard monitored the uneasy peace silently, and cam-drones flickered in and out of her vision. Somewhere in the galaxy—*several* somewheres, going by the density of the swarms of recording equipment—several someones were running live commentary, speculating upon the hideous evening, while a spellbound audience, all shut in on Primus by the relentless rain, looked on in awe, judgment, and dismay. She shook off a shudder at the thought of what her grandmother would say about her role in the spectacle, the conversation she'd have to have with her parents and her do-gooder brother Optimism Rihan, and his even-more-do-gooder-if-that-were-possible fiancée Good Cheer Eria…

'Lucky you,' she muttered to Saraswati as she reached the kitchen. 'No family to speak of, to judge you for the evening's events.'

Saraswati flinched and stepped back from the counter. Courage Praia's jaw dropped. Serenity Ko registered that she'd said a terrible, awful thing.

'Oh, fuck, I'm so sorry. That didn't come out right. I'm so, *so* sorry, Saras.'

Kili streamed privately. _Not cool. Not cool at all._

I can't get anything right.

No you can't, the funny little piece of tech said, peeved.

'Saras, please forgive me for saying that.'

Saraswati glowered at her wordlessly.

A flurry of cam-drones closed in, delighted to have picked up on what appeared to be a lovers' spat in the latest episode of a relationship that had captured the public imagination. Ever since their galactically broadcast first kiss, Saraswati and Serenity Ko had found themselves a hot topic of stream-media conversation, mostly the "will they, won't they, are they, aren't they?" kind. Serenity Ko's Loop comms had been inundated by strangers alternately cheering her on, praising her for being progressive and open-minded enough to date a "barbarian," and calling her a traitor to Primus, a disgrace to her grandmother, and other, far filthier things.

It struck Serenity Ko that Saraswati must be on the receiving end of the same unflattering attention or worse, and she marvelled that they'd never taken a moment to talk about it. That seemed like it was on her, though maybe Saraswati was a private person who didn't like sharing her feelings? She knew so little about her, and that made her feel like a stalker, except she couldn't be a stalker if Saraswati seemed to like kissing her back…

A cam-drone landed on her shoulder, and Serenity Ko whirled around, waving her hands aggressively. 'Oh, fuck off, will you, and give us a moment?'

The cluster of cam-drones intensified.

Ko, stop making a scene and they'll go away, Saraswati streamed tonelessly.

Ko, the calmer you look, the less interested they're going to be, Courage Praia said sagely.

Ko, don't give them what they're looking for! Curiosity Nenna warned.

The barrage of notifs sliding across her visual was beginning to give her a headache, the kind that could only come from good sense that was stating the obvious.

*I heard you the first time,* she snapped at all of them.

Except, I really am sorry, she said to Saraswati. _That was heartless of me._

What was? Saraswati asked, staring at her coldly.

That comment… about family.

Oh, is that what you think I'm upset with you for?

What do you mean?

I don't want to have this conversation here, surrounded by all these people and the whole fucking galaxy, Ko, Saraswati said, and she sounded tired.

Let me help, Serenity Ko offered. She fished around the underside of the counter, and a loud beep rang out. A shimmer in the air enveloped a small space surrounding Saraswati. Serenity Ko said, 'Glitch fuzz.'

The space around Saraswati distorted and pixelated, encapsulated in a vertical column that extended from the ground to where the makeshift ceiling had been pinned in place. It appeared to everyone on the outside like a cylinder made from an old-fashioned screen on the fritz. Serenity Ko stepped into it, and was uncomfortably aware of being so close to Saraswati that she could smell her—an aroma like cinnamon and a touch of sweet perspiration, with overtones of something floral…

'Nice perfume,' Serenity Ko said, heat rising to her cheeks.

Saraswati scowled.

'We're in a sound-bubble with a distortion filter. Nothing on the outside gets in without being fried, and…' She glanced around, checking the ceilings and the floor. 'There's nothing on the inside except you and me. And Kili.'

She stepped forward to hug her, but Saraswati crossed her arms over her chest and raised an eyebrow. Kili mirrored her body language, shutting down all his lights, including his display, where he usually mimicked having a pair of eyes.

Serenity Ko braced herself, and wished she had liquid courage. 'What have I done? You're clearly angry with me.'

'Are you out of your sur-fucked mind?' Saraswati hissed. 'Every cam-drone out there is recording us in this little bubble, and every commentator broadcasting on their stream channels is wondering if we're fighting or making out?'

'Let them,' Serenity Ko said airily. 'It's none of their business.'

'You seem to want to *make* it their business,' Saraswati said frostily. 'I *said* we'd talk *later*.'

'You're seething. You were gripping that kitchen counter like you wanted to rip it out the floor and hurl it at the wall. And aggravating events beyond our control aside, I think I must have said or done something to add to the shittiness of the day. Shitty comments about your refugee status and absence of family aside, which I'm still sorry about—'

She stopped abruptly as a queer look crossed Saraswati's face.

'What is it?'

'Nothing. Nothing to do with my family, I mean.'

'So tell me.'

'You really want to hear this now?'

'At least they've fixed the roof to keep the rain out.'

Saraswati took a deep breath and drew herself up to her full height. Serenity Ko felt a sinking feeling in the pit of her stomach, dragging her spirit with it all the way to the tips of her toes and into the soggy ground below.

'What the sur-fuck were you thinking attacking that Wanderer, Ko?'

'What?'

'You punched the guy just because he was airing his opinions.'

'Oh, *that's* what you're mad about?' Serenity Ko's ears rang with disbelief. 'Nine Virtues, Saras! The man was implying all sorts of things, calling you a murderer, destroyer of worlds, et cetera.'

'So? I've heard worse.'

'And you expect me to just stand by and let my'—all the words that could possibly describe their relationship tumbled through Serenity Ko's mind, and she found she couldn't use any of them—'my galactically famous, brilliant, actually nice and wholesome *friend* be verbally abused by some nobody rural bumpkin? Who thinks he can run his mouth just because of the planet he was born on?'

Tears filled Saraswati's eyes.

'Oh, no! I've said the wrong thing again. Fucking idiot, Ko.' She tried to wipe her tears away, and Saraswati took a step back.

That hurt.

'Are those happy tears or sad tears?' she asked miserably.

'They're angry tears!' Saraswati said, struggling to keep her voice down, even though she didn't need to. Serenity Ko was relieved, though—she didn't think she could take yelling of any sort at such close quarters. 'Angry tears, Ko! I'm not such a nice, wholesome damsel in distress that I need you slugging someone in the face to *defend my honour,* or some star-fucked Ur-drama nonsense like that. I can take one irate old man being nasty to me.'

'Oh, yeah? Sure didn't look like that when you had your little meltdown after those interviews. When was that again? Oh yes, less than six hours ago!'

Bright red blotches appeared on Saraswati's cheeks. 'Do you know why I was upset? Those interviewers just assumed I was a savage. What do you think punching some guy in the face is going to tell the world about me?'

'I'm sorry, is *your* fist hurting from defending yourself?' Serenity Ko shot back.

'Do you really think anyone will care?' Saraswati's eyes narrowed, and her voice shook. 'All they'll see is that the *Earthling's girlfriend*—yes, *girlfriend* is what they're all going to label you, even though there's nothing going on between us—defended the *Earthling's honour* in a display of *Earthling savagery,* which surely must be the *Earthling's native influences* rubbing off on her. "Poor Primian child, ruined! What was she ever thinking, getting involved with someone like that? A teammate is bad enough, but a romantic relationship?"'

'A bit self-important, aren't we?' Serenity Ko remarked drily.

'Spend a day in my shoes, Ko! This is what they're saying, every minute, every hour.'

'That's not my fault.'

'No it isn't, but today's fistfight *is!* What were you *thinking?*' Saraswati threw her hands up in the air, her voice rising at last.

'I *wasn't* thinking!' Serenity Ko yelled back. 'I was trying to save *you* from pain and embarrassment.'

'Soon, the aunties will shake their heads sadly. "Perhaps she'll realise the error of her ways and move on." Move on from what, exactly? Nothing, of course! But they don't want to believe that. Just like they won't believe that I didn't tell you to hit that man,' Saraswati carried on.

'Nothing?' Serenity Ko's throat went dry. 'We're not n-nothing. I mean, we're not something, but... *nothing?*'

'We are now,' Saraswati said. 'Nothing.'

'Because *other people* are bullying you?'

'Because you're self-absorbed and you don't care about what it's like to be me. That's why.'

'Right, because I was a good friend who defended you,' Serenity Ko said coldly.

'*I don't need saving!*'

'*I've got the memo. Loud and clear.*'

Courage Praia chose that moment to duck their head into their private bubble. 'Sorry, ladies,' they said, studying the floor and trying to appear as unaware of the tension in the space as possible. 'Ko, the Guard captain wants to talk to you right away.'

'I'll be there,' Serenity Ko snapped. She then glowered at Saraswati. 'I hear you. I'm sorry. Can we move on?'

'I need some space.'

'Sure.'

'Leave the sound-bubble and this glitch thing going?'

'As long as you like.'

Serenity Ko looked into Saraswati's eyes, hoping to see a glimmer that would indicate that all was in the process of being forgiven, even though she still couldn't see exactly what needed forgiveness in the first place. It was like gazing at Nakshatran Rock, waiting for it to move.

'It wasn't my fault,' she said, somewhat whiny. 'It was the Wanderers'. I hope you see that someday.'

Saraswati stayed silent.

'Right, so I'll see you for dinner later?' Serenity Ko swung her arms awkwardly, attempting casual.

'Nope.'

'Cool.'

Her face twitched as she tried to rearrange it to appear neutral, perhaps even content or optimistic. The moment she stepped out of the sound-bubble, a swarm of cam-drones descended on her. Her hands shook, but she clenched them into fists at her sides. *No need to feed these scavengers anything.*

Optimism Tina was slumped over on a chair, sipping on something that looked suspiciously strong. She flashed Serenity Ko a wan smile, and tossed her drink back.

She steeled herself and stepped into the alcove, where Good Cheer Soraya regarded her impassively.

'There's a bigger fine for repeat offenders,' Good Cheer Soraya said. 'Do it again and it's community service.'

'I'm sorry, I lost my cool,' Serenity Ko said, doing her level best to visualise the woman as her grandmother, and thereby channel contrition.

'Clearly. What were you thinking?'

'I wasn't thinking,' she said. 'I lost my cool, yes. But I did it to stand up for my... *friend*.'

She couldn't tell if they were even friends anymore, and it hurt too much to think about it.

The Wanderers and chlorosapients share a close relationship. We are both primarily concerned with sustainable practices—the Wanderers through our maintenance of the planet, and the chlorosapients through the preservation of ourselves. We both seek evolution to self-sustenance that doesn't steal from the land.

—Courage Anto,
Wanderer Savant
2073 Anno Earth | 1998 Interstellar Era

TEN

I MANAGED TO fall asleep only in the wee hours of the morning.

I hadn't had dinner last night, or slept more than four hours, so in addition to an overwhelming sense of panic, some acid reflux was kicking in. I popped a dental cleanse, followed by an antacid, and then a hangover cleanse to take care of the headache that had set in at my temples.

Saras, go easy on that stuff. Kili whirred down onto my shoulder and tried to nuzzle against me.

They hate me, don't they? I asked miserably.

Who?

Everyone.

_No._

Don't *lie* to me! I yelled.

Kili flew several feet away, settling upon the mirror over the sink. Shame burned through me. He was only an outdated piece of Earth tech who happened to be my best friend, a sentient intelligence made from red, green and chrome bits of metal and circuitry all wired together, but from the way he held himself—wings shrunk down beside him, his whirring erratic and jerky—I could tell he was hurt. Worse still, I knew I'd scared him. I'd never, not once, ever lost my temper at him.

I'm sorry, I said sincerely, collecting myself. _I shouldn't have lost my cool. Fuck me to the sun and back, I'm losing my mind. Please forgive me._

Already done.

I looked up at him and could tell he was fibbing. _You can take your time, you know?_

I'm coded to love you, Saras.

Tears pricked at my eyes.

I love you too, Kili.

Washing my hands, I splashed cold water across my face and looked at myself in the mirror. Dishevelled hair and badly nano-bleached skin aside, I didn't recognise the face staring back at me. My eyes seemed distant, like they belonged to a different person, and I felt like I was a faded, floating piece of space debris, untethered and unidentifiable.

Sorry to interrupt, Saras—

"Sorry" is a banned word for the next forty-eight hours, Kili.

Right, I don't mean to interrupt—

I smiled without meaning to.

—but you've got a stream incoming from Good Cheer Eria. Shall I let her through?

I sighed, and rubbed my face. _Please do._

After last night's debacle, I'd turned off *all* my XP Inc. tech, disabling Loop notifs coming straight through to my brain, so I wouldn't have to deal with any of it, whatever it was—I wanted no part of it. But first, I'd streamed Good Cheer Eria and asked her to set up a meeting with the Wanderers. I wanted to clear the air. *Personally.*

Kili beamed Good Cheer Eria's face at me, up on the bathroom wall.

'Saras! How are you?' she asked.

'I'm not having the best day, Eria,' I said weakly, summoning a smile.

'I'm so sorry. It's awful for you,' she said earnestly.

My stomach clenched. This did not inspire confidence.

'Thanks, Eria.'

'The Wanderers will be at the Cathedral in about an hour. Are you sure you want to meet them so soon?'

'Yes. It's the right thing to do.'

'And… Ko?'

'I don't know about Ko,' I said shortly. 'I only know I owe them an explanation.'

'Alright!' Good Cheer Eria smiled encouragingly. 'I'll see you soon.'

I could have streamed Serenity Ko about this meeting, but I'd chosen not to. I wanted to put some distance between us. Perhaps it was selfish of me, but I wanted to make it clear that we weren't some kind of package deal that did things together at each other's bidding. The kind of thing that defined "being in a relationship" or at this point even "being friends."

Want to talk? Kili asked.

I'm taking stock of things, I grumbled.

What things?

Everyone who's after me right now.

It was a long list. I slid into the Loop and confronted my fears.

The stream-media were hysterical after last night's riot.

Until now, apart from being condescending, vaguely xenophobic star-fuckers, they'd mostly left me to my own devices, by which I meant that they'd stalked me relentlessly (often fixating on the nature of my relationship with Serenity Ko), talked down to me endlessly (every time Primian food or culture came up), and commented on Feast skeptically (which would have been disheartening but reasonable if that hadn't been laced with xenophobia). Now, they were going after my origins, my "Earthling tendencies," my destructive influence on innocent Primians, and generally showering me with uncharitable judgments.

For a so-called *civilised* part of space, Primus had its issues.

Their adulation after the first pop-up had turned to derision after last night's disaster, and the word "Earthling" was splattered across it all.

Deep down, a little voice whispered that Jog Tunga had called it.

I did my level best to quell that voice.

His demand that I steal Feast and hand it over to him was hysterically funny, or would have been if it didn't smack of some insidious purpose. I wasn't likely to steal the tech from my own project and hand it over to *him,* was I?

Was I?

It would confirm every assumption they'd ever made of my Earthling origins, justifying how they treated Earthlings like criminals.

But they're treating you like a criminal anyway. Last nava, you were the prophet of a new food future. Now, you're being blamed for inciting violence at a riot you didn't start. Maybe Jog Tunga has a point…

The persistent little voice grew louder, more insistent. I shuddered. When my thoughts started agreeing with Jog Tunga in any capacity, it was time to take a raincheck from thinking.

'*Alright!*' I said out loud, jumping to my feet and stretching.

Kili hovered in front of me, at eye level. _Are you okay?_

Yes! No. I don't know, but I'm fine! I said, swinging my arms.

Right, you're giving into a paranoid spiral, he said with unreasonable accuracy. _You're wondering if Jog Tunga has a valid argument._

My cheeks grew warm. _Don't read my mind and call me out._

Don't make it so obvious that you're considering taking that imbecile seriously.

I held my palms up, thoroughly embarrassed. _You got me._

I quickly applied some sur-screen to my skin, running a brush through my tangled curls, before I stepped outside.

Late afternoon sur-light illuminated the lush, verdant fields, glistening like the freshly piped kiwi, cilantro and aam panna icing we used on one of our signature desserts back at Elé Oota. I wondered what my old team was up to now, twenty-one jumpgates away on another world. Had any of them recognised me on *MegaChef*? Would any of them know me if they met me now? The view blurred to soft emeralds and jade, studded with blossoms like gemstones glittering at the throat of a new world. It struck me how stunted my vocabulary was; I could only ever frame all this living, breathing splendour in terms of my life in the kitchen, or the bejewelled wealth of my family back on Earth. I brushed the tears from my eyes.

The Faith of the Light gardens sprawled all the way to the tree line at the horizon, and grew wild; there were no human-imposed plots with neat labels telling the plants what they ought to be, and how tall and profuse and high-yielding. All things grew where their seeds fell, untethered, uninterrupted and free. Gayam bulbs nestled side by side with wild arrioses; a veritable sea of coleus—each whorl of leaves different from its neighbour—was only interrupted by a competing profusion of kaffee shrubs. Five-fingered clusters of ragi and millets rustled in the breeze, astrianas and climbing creepers of every kind wound their way around spindle-trees and sur-oak. All the garden resembled a wooded grove that seemed to celebrate confusion, tame in its wildness, exuberant in its expression.

I caught sight of a pair of familiar faces bent over a shrubbery, clipping withered leaves off the stems. I didn't know them, but they squinted at me in the sur-light, and I raised my hand and waved at them.

'Nasty business last night,' the first said. 'Harmony Mave, by the way. She/Her. We haven't been introduced, but I thought I'd let you know Optimism Sukran and I don't think it's your fault. The riot.'

'Nor do most of the folks here,' Optimism Sukran said, panting as the dead branch they were heaving at finally gave way. 'It's just a noisy handful.'

'Thank you,' I said, and meant it.

'Good Cheer Eria says the nicest things about you, and we take her at her word.' Harmony Mave nodded.

'Thanks again.' I smiled.

'She's at the Cathedral, in case you'd like to find her.'

'A spot of cast-rot,' I heard one of them say, as I walked away.

'Only way to deal with it is to stop the infection from spreading,' the other grunted, gripping a thick stem tight with their shears and ripping it out of the ground.

THE FAITH OF the Light Cathedral was where space-time came to rest; a point of singularity where the thrumming of bees harmonised with the susurrus of flutterwings, and gentle shafts of sur-light drizzled through gaps and breaks in the canopy onto the foliate woodland floor in a whispering of life. The ground was a tangle of roots and knots, belied by the rustling pink sheaf-grass that grew uninhibited, but for the smooth paving stones that led the way. Wildflowers bloomed where they found snatches of sur-light, powdering the ground in shades of delicate cornflower blue, rich poppy red, and the vibrant yellow of lilies, amidst a carpet of blossoms stirred up by the gentle wind, trailing down from the boughs that arched into each other above my head. Broad, strong trunks lined the path, timeless witnesses to an ancient planet. Shroomings of many hues nestled in hollows and crevices, their translucent heliotrope, deep burgundy, silken grey, blue-spotted, yellow-mottled caps and feathers appearing to undulate in a haze of light and shadows. I was struck, once again, by the sensation that I was an ancient space explorer trespassing upon virgin land. The few surviving woods and forests on Earth were the preserve of powerful families like mine, and even then, they seldom trilled with birdsong.

A fluting melody whistled overhead, and I looked towards the sound to discover a stout little bluebul spreading its wings, raising its crest as it performed some kind of mating dance. A distant, quavering warble—a deeper pitch, a more urgent flurry of song—underscored it, but I couldn't spot the owner of its call, even as another bird responded to it, their refrains running contrapuntally. Accentuating the symphony was a percussive, syncopated, metallic tapping, apparently coming from a beautiful, small green bird, its head tufted red, with distinctive yellow cheeks.

I found myself drawn into a trance, swallowed by the mysteries of the woodland, walking into the heart of the Cathedral. To look up was to invite a wave of dizziness. Broken only by pockets of cascading light, the boughs above me knitted together more closely with each step, branches entangling to form rough archways, held up by the sturdy trunks of trees. Creepers and vines trailed down their woody arms reaching for each other, dappled with innumerable blooms given to countless shades of pink, incandescent orange, and creamy white—I recognised only the astrianas, a flowering vine native to the Primian soil. The light faded to a dim glow, and I tread carefully, avoiding stepping off the pavers, which were the only chlorosapient intervention on this sacred ground, introduced to prevent visitors from stepping on the sheaf-grass.

I recalled my first week on Primus at the immigration camp, where I'd delighted in causing the sheaf-grass to retract from me as I raced through a thigh-high savannah, and experienced an unexpected stab of shame. I didn't believe in the Faith of the Light's teachings, but being in their woodland was as close as I'd ever come to a spiritual experience. It drew a hush over the rattling anxieties within my mind, inducing self-reflection, inviting me to exhale even as I heard the murmur of human voices that were likely discussing me right at the edge of my hearing, around the very next bend in the track.

This is unreal, I whispered, breaking the silence that had descended over us.

Yes.

I hadn't said a word to Kili since we stepped into the forest, and I could tell from his distant tone that he was every bit as awestruck as I. Bobbing beside me, his little chrome body whirred and swivelled as he took it all in.

We'd never get to experience anything like this on Earth, he said quietly. _And I'm glad I'm here with you._

_So am I._

No matter what brought us here and how this all turns out.

Yes.

I strolled up a gentle slope and turned the corner to find myself in darkness. As my eyes adjusted to the gloom, it took the shape of an amphitheatre, each row of steps carved from the side of a hill, covered in tussocks of grass and rising along a curving path to where I stood. The canopy was thickest here; the trees appeared to lean in towards each other, branches criss-crossing at great height, growing into each other in a tangle, forming a dome that blocked out the skies above. A raised plinth was set at the centre, and a single beam of unbroken sunlight broke through a perfectly round aperture, streaming into the shadows to light the Circle.

The Circle was the chlorosapient altar, and it took the shape of a wheel. A single human form, intricately detailed and sculpted from flowmetal, its muscles flexed and straining, eyes haunted by an expression of yearning, arched forward, as if reaching towards its destiny. A densely knotted, centuries-old creeper grew towards, over and around it, twisting grotesquely through the human's calves and thighs, ripping its way out of its chest, wreathing the figure in vines as if threatening to swallow it, and yet, achingly, inches away from the grasp of its fingertips.

Good Cheer Eria had explained its meaning to me the first time I'd attended a meditation at the Cathedral. It signified the chlorosapient belief that complete self-sustenance in the light of the stars was the only sustainable future for humanity; to harvest the light as a single source of all nourishment. It was the reason they honoured plant life above all else, why the altar was crafted to symbolise yearning, seeking to reunite with the way of the plants. A popular belief was that on the day humans achieved this self-sustenance, the wheel would finally close its circle, plant and human as one beneath the Suriyan light.

It was equal parts intriguing and horrifying. I was living at the commune and faking a certain degree of belief in their philosophies—even going so far as to make appearances at meditation sessions. The philosophy was unsettling and alien to me, but alluring nonetheless because it spoke of deeper mysteries than I'd ever considered, and opened my mind to a way of life I'd never encountered before.

Stranger still was the occasional sight of a living, breathing chlorosapient, usually approaching the end of their life, prostrate before the altar, hands outstretched, their light-harvesting mods shimmering dully as their last breath drew near. Entire families gathered around to keep vigil, undisturbed by other members of the Faith who might be present, in prayer or meditation. Burials occurred in a sunny glade right beyond the cool dimness of the Cathedral; the dead were said to nurture the Circle when they returned to the earth.

At the moment, Good Cheer Eria sat at the centre of the Cathedral, surrounded by around sixty Wanderers and chlorosapients. They sat on the lowest rung of seats, in a rough semicircle, speaking in mumbles and whispers, hallowed ground as it was. I strained to hear their words, until a tall, lean man caught sight of me.

'The Earthling is here.' He raised his voice and gestured at me, scowling.

Rude, Kili said.

Not the first or the last, I'm sure.

Gritting my teeth, I slipped into the Loop and ignored the barrage of comms notifs that flooded me. Instead, I let my HUD identify and tag the crowd I was going to come to an understanding with. I braced myself.

Good Cheer Eria flashed me a strained smile, then rushed forward to greet me as I walked down the steps.

Flow-flora lights were tastefully scattered through the bower, woven into the towering canopy, glimmering amidst copses, illuminating her face so she appeared more otherworldly than usual. She drew me into a quick hug.

I put on my most sincere smile as I regarded the others, whose nametags all collided on the Loop.

'My sincere apologies first,' I said in Ur-speak. I projected more courage than I felt, climbing down the last few stairs to the gathering. 'I'm sorry for the riot last night, although it wasn't my fault. I never intended for it to happen. I didn't ask my friend to punch the protestor. And I'm here to understand and discuss your concerns about Feast.'

My fingers twitched, and I fought to keep from curling my fists as the eye-rolling began.

'It's bad enough that we're constantly targeted by pop culture and the stream-media,' an elderly chlorosapient said mournfully. Her Loop tag read *Courage Sheri, She/Her*. It wasn't lost on me that she'd spoken in Vox. 'We're a very *private* community, you know?'

'I know,' I acknowledged in Ur-speak.

'We don't protest unless we feel the need to do so,' she said, continuing in Vox as if she hadn't heard me. 'Traditionally, balance on Primus is held between the Ur-siders and the Wanderers. And it is our inalienable right to question the people of Uru when we believe they are losing their way.'

'She's just hankering for attention,' someone tutted, and I couldn't tell who'd spoken. 'Such an *Earthling* trait.'

I ignored the comment.

'Could we please be our best selves?' Good Cheer Eria asked firmly. 'We know what it's like to be outsiders. As chlorosapients, we're constantly judged for our beliefs—'

'Yes, because people don't understand that *we* represent the way *forward* for humanity,' the same voice said, and then a young man rose to his feet. 'Earthlings represent the *past* we so urgently sought to escape, when the Nakshatrans fled the ugliness of their collapsing civilisation.'

Curiosity Ydris, He/Him glowered at me after this pronouncement, his voice laced with scorn.

'This isn't about *Earthlings* versus us,' Courage Sheri said dismissively. 'This is about *Feast*. And what happened at the protest.'

'No denying there was an *Earthling* in the room, though,' Curiosity Ydris persisted. 'We've *never* been attacked at a protest before.'

'Discrimination is never justifiable,' Good Cheer Eria insisted.

'Judgment cannot exist without action,' Curiosity Ydris shot back.

'The past is not prophecy,' Good Cheer Eria said calmly.

'Sleep with one eye open when the past catches up to the present,' Curiosity Ydris retorted.

'The past is a lesson that must not weigh down the present; the present is a free moment,' Good Cheer Eria replied.

'The present shapes the future, and what we choose to take with us,' Curiosity Ydris snapped.

A deep voice cleared their throat loudly. 'Could we stop trading cryptic quotes from the *Nakshatranāma*?'

I was relieved at the interruption. I understood the poetic, archaic Ur-speak, but the epic poem was notoriously layered, and for a moment there, I hadn't been able to tell what in all the star-fucked universe they'd been on about, except that it'd had something to do with my Earthling past.

'Sorry.' Good Cheer Eria smiled good-naturedly. 'Got carried away.'

Curiosity Ydris smirked. In the dim light, a man with a topknot rose to his feet, and I spotted ten glittering rings coruscating on all his fingers. I recognised him from the previous night—he was a Wanderer Savant, and he wore an unreadable smile.

'Before you throw us all off course, Courage Anto,' Curiosity Ydris said pompously, 'I want to state that I believe that an Earthling on Primus is a threat. Earth philosophy directly influences the shape of Feast.'

I gritted my teeth.

He continued. 'Personally, it's one thing to work on the food-sim; I believe in the tech. It aligns more closely with chlorosapient beliefs than traditional Primian food, even if it does rely on delivering traditional flavours as opposed to the purity of sustenance. It's a whole different matter when *she* sets off *riots,* though!'

'Especially when the fallout is lashing out at Wanderers and calling us savages, when it was clearly *her side* that started it,' the old woman named Courage Sheri said dolorously in Ur-speak, before turning to me and saying it again in Vox.

If she translates to Vox one more time… Kili said, wings whirring irritably.

I'm trying *so* hard not to react.

'They're coming after me, too,' I said out loud, choosing a polite tone, 'And regardless of what they're saying on streammedia, *I* didn't start last night's riot. I was only in the room where it happened.'

'And there you have it!' Curiosity Ydris was triumphant. 'All it takes is an Earthling in the room…'

'Ydris!' Good Cheer Eria said, aghast.

I grimaced, and Kili streamed a string of unrepeatable expletives in my native Daxina. We knew the rest of the saying well: *All it takes is an Earthling in the room to start a war.*

'She's right, you know. She didn't start it,' the Wanderer from the previous evening drawled. His name tag on the Loop read *Courage Anto*.

'We've all seen the footage. You weren't there, Anto.' A new voice shouted. 'You turned up afterwards.'

'If you've seen the footage, you know she didn't start it,' Courage Anto insisted.

'Besides,' Good Cheer Eria said, her perfectly even tone starting to crack. 'Since when have *we* taken to holding these kinds of meetings to target people? Saras only wanted to apologise and then hear you out, and all you're doing is attacking her.'

My heart soared at her words. It came crashing down when she continued.

'I'll remind you that Saraswati is a *refugee* from the Earth. She came to Primus with *nothing*, seeking a new life. All she receives is persecution and prejudice in one form or another. Are we *those* people? The kind to kick someone when they're down, to belittle them while they strive to make their way in the world? Have we become so petty, so self-absorbed and self-righteous, that we can't accept someone for who they are, and appreciate the purity of their intention, raise them up when they doubt, and support them when they fail?'

She glowered at everyone assembled before her, then rounded on Curiosity Ydris.

'Of *all* people, you should know what it feels like to be an *outsider.* To forsake the life you once knew to pursue your beliefs, and chase dreams into the unknown.'

Curiosity Ydris simply glowered.

'The Nakshatrans would be ashamed of our treatment of Saraswati. I say this not with pity, but with compassion for all she has endured, and all she has lost on her way here. I wish you would do the same,' Good Cheer Eria concluded, deflating sadly.

Coils of guilt snaked through me at the enormous deception that shrouded the kernel of truth at the heart of what she'd said. My tangled web of lies was too thick, too knotted to pull apart. And so, I stood there, my righteousness at having had nothing to do with last night's riot fading, my heart stuttering with how my simple untruth was spiralling out of my control.

In the wake of Good Cheer Eria's speech, the gathering had broken up into small pockets of conversation. *They're judging you for being an Earthling.*

I wanted to finish having my say before they came to any conclusions. 'Last night,' I began, 'I was accused by a protester of bringing my "Earthling violence" to this planet, of disrupting Primian culture and the natural order of this planet by daring to develop a new kind of food. As someone from the Earth, I am well aware of the culture of excess that precedes me every time I walk into a room. This does not mean I believe in it. So please tell me your concerns about Feast, and I'll do my best to have them heard by the folks at XP Inc.'

I was exhausted by the time I reached the end of this speech. It felt all too brief, but there wasn't anything else to say. There were a few nods of agreement, and a couple of encouraging smiles, but nearly everyone appeared vastly unimpressed. Good Cheer Eria gazed at me fondly but sadly.

Out of nowhere, the words poured out of them—the fears that "sound and light" simulations would replace connections with the natural world, and drown out the importance of food that was harvested off the land with perfect minimalism, thereby devaluing the land itself; the low numbers of Ursiders taking to being Wanderers, content to experience the natural world through experiences like Feast; the devaluation of the planet because simulated dreams could convey all the experiences anyone ever wanted with zero effort…

It was an incredibly long list, and while the chlorosapients backed the idea of Feast, it was clear that their closely allied Wanderers were skeptics who believed they'd been ignored.

'Saraswati,' Courage Anto said, when the voices died down. 'I'm sorry if I didn't say that right.'

'You were close.' I smiled.

'About last night…'

'Yes?'

'I apologise on behalf of the Wanderers. Those protestors—they don't represent all of us. Much like you don't represent all Earthlings.'

'Thank you,' I said, genuinely moved.

'But what you're building is going to destroy us all,' he said kindly. 'Even if it isn't your fault.'

The interweaving branches overhead closed in on me like a tomb, the dance of light and colour upon the forest floor was a fever dream, and the symphonic birdsong echoed eerily, a cacophony of madness as the shadows closed in.

Tail-chasing and satellite slinging are two of the most popular sports in the Suriyan System.

Originating on the planet Sagaricus, tail-chasing involves riding the momentum of a comet in its wake by "shadowing" it. Satellite slinging uses gravity somewhat differently...

—*A Lifestyle Guide to the Suriyan System*
2072 Anno Earth | 1997 Interstellar Era

ELEVEN

WHEN HER THERAPIST had suggested that she find new ways to let off steam, Serenity Ko had plunged into thc Loop with all the zeal of a Vyāsr monk at a banquet. Her enthusiasm knew no bounds. She'd zeroed in on three possible hobbies: finishing the Bloxxos she'd amassed over the years, gardening at the Faith of the Light, and satellite slinging.

The first seemed too close to home, and smacked of failure to commit to all her past projects. The second involved nauseating amounts of sur-light. Satellite slinging, though...

She'd taken a launch vehicle up to Primus's orbit, and gazed at the amateur racetrack in awe. A shimmering blue circuit appeared on her visual feed, ribboning off into the distance, wending its way around Primian satellites and space junk. Giving in to its shiny allure, she'd hopped into a meta-orbital cab to see it up close. And unable to help herself, she'd been drawn into a race simulator, crashed her racer within seconds, and decided that *this was it*.

She'd taken to satellite slinging like a fish to water (on a planet where the fish hadn't mutated and water was still relatively free of nuclear waste). Three māsas of relentless training later, she'd earned her amateur racing licence, poring over orbital physics theories, honing her reflexes through intense workouts, learning the ins and outs of basic racers, and throwing herself into mastering a new skill.

It was much like being in a *Formula Enthusiast* race-craft, except a whole lot more death defying. Satellite slinging delivered the illusion of control, which was a refreshing change from working like a maniac in the XP Inc. office while simultaneously marvelling at the food words coming out of Saraswati's mouth, like a tourist from a Fringe planet staring at the Unity River monument for the first time. Serenity Ko was still undecided as to whether it was an improvement on reaching the bottom of a cocktail glass (or a dozen), but she had to admit that it was refreshing to be lucid, her reactions walking a razor's edge, her breath controlled and her head in the zone.

A tiny voice in her head reminded her that this level of effort would serve her best if it were directed towards understanding the culinary arts, namely Primian food culture, but that line of thinking was fraught with pressure. It was an extension of her work on Feast, and she was already dangerously close to showering in the office. There was the fact that her grandmother, Grace Menmo, was a household name when it came to Primian food and its history. Also, her relationship with Saraswati had started over a Berry-anna tasting at the Uru and Beyond Marketplace… and what *was* that relationship now, anyway? She was livid that Saraswati was blaming her for the riot, and it brought her savage satisfaction to think she was putting distance between them.

Every time she so much as *thought* about food, she experienced a sense of loss, of being swallowed into an identity that didn't belong to her, that she'd created for herself in the pursuit of ambition. It was thrilling to boldly go where no cook had gone before, but Serenity Ko was no cook. She often wondered if her grandmother had been right, and if Feast simply wasn't *her* journey to embark upon.

Racing demanded utmost focus and precision. It closed her brain off to all distraction. So long as she forgot about those waivers she'd signed about risks to life and other unpleasant things.

Serenity Ko revelled in the momentary lull—that all-enveloping hush like being sealed into a vacuum, the tiny pop as her eardrums adjusted to hearing nothing but her heartbeat and her breathing—that always preceded the scream of her craft's engines, and the bone-rattling, gut-crunching momentum of being launched from the starting line. She almost felt serene, despite the anticipation building, her shoulders tensing, her eyes intensely focused on the course ahead of her, its pathway between the satellites marked by a pulsing beam of light rippling through the blackness of space.

The countdown beeped, and a timer appeared on her racer's HUD, ticking down.

… Five… Four… Three…

She revved her engines, hand poised over the throttle.

…Two… One…

An interminable pause, and then the lights went out. Her hand slammed down on the button and the launch vehicle flung her out into the void.

Hands steady, she banked her racer into the first sweeping turn, then readied herself to nudge the brakes going into the tight second corner. Even in the vastness of space, there was an optimal way to master this circuit, and Serenity Ko knew it like the back of her hand.

Her therapist had been skeptical when she'd announced her new hobby—all forms of courting death being questionable—but Serenity Ko insisted that alternately working on sharpening her reflexes and dulling them to numbness in alcoholic stupor framed her life in perfect balance.

She braked, then flipped her craft onto its edge to slide it through a curve before righting it, a manoeuvre she'd practised in sim-training a few hundred times over, and on the track about a dozen times.

Primus had recently opened their first amateur racetrack, carefully monitored by the racing authorities from Sagaricus, and thrill-seekers across the planet had been ecstatic. The *Formula Enthusiast* races were good fun, but they were conducted in the Primian atmosphere, where the sky-lanes were inevitably bounded by the law of gravity. Satellite slinging, on the other hand, held more interesting uses for the universe's weakest and most infinite force.

To her right, Serenity Ko spotted another craft nosing ahead of her and gritted her teeth. She'd lost ground on her flip; a nanosecond's distraction was all it took for errors to creep in. She needed to make it up, and spied the first satellite looming ahead of her. If she dipped to the right on her approach, she'd rub up against its gravity, and it would hurl her outward. All she needed to do was get her timing just right on her exit…

A notif popped up on the Loop right as she slipped into the satellite's pull.

'Kube, I'm busy,' she snapped. She looked through him on the stream that filled most of her optics feed, to the various counters on her HUD, displaying information about her velocity and attitude, options for braking points and thrust ratios, and more. Her brain raced through the math as she felt her craft decelerate, slipping sideways, being held by the gravity of the asteroid she was slingshotting around.

She dared a glance at her boss at XP Inc. and immediately regretted it. He did not appear amused.

'I've been trying to get through to you for hours, Ko.'

'I'm *trying* to go *missing*,' she said through gritted teeth. Her window for pulling off the perfect sling was coming upon her.

There were three possible options for her upcoming sling: the first would draw her closer to the asteroid, having her effectively hug its gravity before flinging her out wide with maximum velocity; the second was more conservative, and would save her a whole precious second on the rebound; while the third was a flat trajectory that would launch her into the lead immediately, but hamper her gains from its gravity field. She chose the aggressive long-term strategy with a flick of her haptics. It would also give her precious seconds to address Grace Kube, and hopefully get rid of him.

'Kube, there's supposed to be a comms fog while I'm racing,' she said tersely.

'Yes, lucky I have friends who know how to bypass those,' he said, as if bored.

'It's a safety risk.'

'Slow your craft down, throw the race, I don't care. You set off a riot. *Again*. We're covering the damages *again*—You're welcome, by the way. There are consequences, and you've got to face them.'

Serenity Ko was lining her craft up for the slingshot; twitchy little micro-movements of her wrist guiding it into position. She hissed as she drifted too far to the right, then flicked her wrist gently to return to her optimal path.

'Suspend me, fire me, dock my pay,' she said listlessly, her every intent focused on shifting into the highest gear.

Any moment now...

Now.

Her racer roared as it punched through the vacuum, engines screaming as she took a wide line across the course. She spotted *two* other craft ahead of her now—never mind, she'd catch up to them over time with the velocity she'd gained. There were still minutes left to the finish line.

She flicked her gaze back to Grace Kube, who watched her impassively. 'Done?'

'You've got half a minute before the next sling,' Serenity Ko said coolly, her fingers making micro-adjustments every so often, deftly dancing over the sensitive controls.

'The riot.'

'Trying not to think about it. Do your worst, et cetera. I'm busy just now.'

'Optimism Mahd'vi just got in touch,' Grace Kube said. 'She wants more government oversight. Now more than ever.'

'She's said this every nava since forever. We've discussed this every nava since forever. And like every nava since forever, she can fuck right off.'

'Cute. And if that was a challenge before, it's star-fucking near impossible now,' Grace Kube said.

'Because the Wanderers have their grass-stained knickers in a—'

'Don't care about the Wanderers and their knickers, thanks.' He held a scarred hand up in distaste. 'It's got nothing to do with the Wanderers, anyway.'

'Hang on, Kube.'

Serenity Ko angled her racer in towards the next satellite. She was going to approach it at a higher velocity to shorten her path around it, exiting at a flatter angle to gain ground on the track. This was always trickier than following the natural curve of space, and she needed focus, especially since she wasn't planning to hit the brakes too hard. The craft juddered as it was gripped by gravity, and she let it follow the satellite's trajectory—a far more irregularly shaped piece of machinery than the last somewhat smoother rock, a bumpy ride all the way through. She kept her hands steady on the controls, and as the HUD displayed her slinging options, she positioned herself, switched gears and shot out of orbit, engines shrieking. She was gaining on the craft in front of her.

'Impressive,' said Grace Kube, who looked anything but impressed.

'Can't your lecture wait another four and a half minutes?' Serenity Ko frowned.

'It can, but I thought interrupting your joyride would do a better job at impressing the *gravity* of the situation upon you. No pun intended.'

'Hah. Get it over with, then?'

Grace Kube looked down at his palms, then looked up at her, his movements gratingly slow. Serenity Ko *knew* he was trying to throw her off balance, and it didn't change a thing about how aggravating it was. Her fingers twitched with impatience, causing her racer to momentarily veer off course, costing her precious tenths of a second.

'Optimism Mahd'vi's concern is optics. Because Saras.'

'What about Saras?'

'She's an Earthling.'

'Right. So?'

'An Earthling who's being blamed for setting off a riot.'

'I'll make a statement, take the fall for it.'

'Heroic. Won't work.'

'It'll blow over in a nava.'

'It won't be enough. She wants us to double down on our political perspective.'

'It's a fucking *food-sim*, Kube.'

'She insists upon Secretariat approval for all our Feast sims, Ko—'

'Last I checked XP Inc. owned the tech.'

'A Primus-first approach—'

'All our products are Primian foods, right now.'

'A Primus-first approach that emphasises Primian *superiority*—'

'What are we, an empire from the dark ages?'

'—in the light of the violence that took place today—'

'It was hardly *violence*.'

'—to assert that we are aligned with Primian culture above all else.'

'Because using Primian tech, working on Primus, and releasing Primian food-sims aren't on the nose enough?'

'Yes.'

'Because we have *one* Earthling on our team?'

'Yes.'

'Mahd'vi can fuck off.'

Grace Kube sighed. It was evidently his turn to be exasperated, and Serenity Ko relished it.

'Back in a sec, Kube.'

A new satellite was drawing closer on her HUD. She was gaining on the racer in second place. One more perfectly timed sling would likely put her ahead, and in the chase for a race win. Not that it counted for anything other than pride—this was amateur hour in regulation rentable-by-the-hour, standard-issue racers, unlike the actual Galactic Championship stuff she'd taken to following.

A fireball blossomed to fill her HUD.

She slammed the brakes and veered violently to the right. Her craft shuddered as she urged it to disobey all the laws of physics and turn impossibly off course, fighting the momentum that was carrying it into the conflagration that had recently been the racer ahead of her. Nausea arose, and spots danced before her eyes as a slew of in-flight warnings shrieked at her, Kube shouting above them all to ask if she was okay.

An escape pod hurtled past, narrowly missing her, and she hoped to all the Nine Virtues that its occupant was all right. The dome of flame burned blindingly bright until the vacuum extinguished it in a heartbeat. Shrapnel ricocheted off her racer's shields, which were perfunctory at best. Serenity Ko threw her craft into a right-hand roll, trying to use her velocity to spiral away from the wreckage. Her head spun as if she'd had a jumpgate kick too many, and the seconds crawled by like molasses.

Race Control to Serenity Ko, came an urgent stream.

Huh?

Are you okay?

Yes.

You're well off course, and you can right your racer now.

Star-fuck me sideways, thank goodness, Serenity Ko moaned.

Please put your racer in power mode 2. I repeat, power mode 2.

She eased the thrusters and her racer continued on its erratic trajectory, gradually braking. She was sick to her stomach and her brain felt like it had been run through a blender. Her eyes were still squeezed firmly shut, in anticipation of a bone-shattering impact.

'Ko, are you all right?' Grace Kube said, and she heard the words as if they were from very far away.

'What do you think, Kube?' she shot back irritably.

'We'll just table this discussion for tomorrow, yes?'

'No, let's have it out now, Kube. *Consequences*, remember?'

'Ko—'

'Except give me a moment before you resume being a star-fucker.'

Race Control, this is Serenity Ko, she streamed. _Are they all right?_

Yes. Escaped in the nick of time.

What was it?

Engine fault. We are investigating. Please put your racer in power mode 2.

Already there.

Return to the parking bay. Autopilot. No manual controls, please.

Affirmative.

Serenity Ko plugged in the commands and slumped over, her face in her palms. She was shivering. She massaged her eyes gently and opened them, deciding that it was better to deny what had just happened altogether and save processing it for when she was in a safe space with her therapist.

Or never. Never sounded great.

'Where were we?' she asked, assuming an indifference her body didn't quite echo. 'Oh, yes, we were discussing how to sell out.'

'Tomorrow,' Grace Kube said firmly.

'I'm good.'

Grace Kube regarded her uncertainly. 'No, you aren't.'

'Craft's on autopilot, Kube. This is boring; it'll take ten whole minutes to dock.'

Her hands shook of their own accord.

'There's a meeting with Optimism Mahd'vi next nava. We'll get on the same page before we meet her. Later,' Grace Kube said conclusively, as if that resolved everything.

Serenity Ko stared at him in disbelief. '*You* interrupted *me* when I was flying this sur-fucking monster around satellites at seven hundred klicks an hour. *Consequences,* you said.'

'I shouldn't have done it.' A funny look crossed Grace Kube's face, his lips twitched and Serenity Ko observed that his deep brown skin was paler than usual. 'I had no idea…' He paused, seemed to collect himself, and continued. 'I think you should dock your racer, get back on Primian soil, and get a good night's sleep. Forget about everything. The riot, the accident you were in.'

He paused.

There was that strange expression again, and he exploded.

'*Sur-fuck me sideways, Ko,* I have no idea what happened, but it looked *terrible!* What the actual *fuck* are you doing racing, anyway? You're my most precious sim designer, *everyone* fucking loves you and would unquestioningly give you a kidney if you needed it—and no, a lifetime supply of kidneys is no reason to go blow yourself up in space. You're fucking brilliant and likeable and I'm sure your family loves you.'

Serenity Ko flinched at the ferocity of his words. 'What're you trying to say, Kube?'

'Why the fuck don't you pick a *safe* pastime? Attending the sinfonia, maybe, or reading epic poetry?' Grace Kube ran a hand over his bald, scarred head. '*Gardening.*'

It was so unexpected that she started to laugh; a mix of nerves, hysteria and surprise bursting out of her. 'Are—are you actually... Nine Virtues, Kube,' she giggled. 'Are you actually expressing *concern* for my well-being?'

He scowled. 'Last I checked we were friends. That's what friends do. Unless you'd rather we weren't. Friends, I mean.'

'No, I'm sorry...' She hiccupped. 'I didn't mean it that way.'

The hiccups came quick and fast, and Serenity Ko found that she was suddenly exhausted. All the adrenaline had drained from her system, and now she was facing a storm of feelings she'd been trying to run away from: an ache between her shoulders from long hours spent at work, guilt worming its way through her system for inciting violence at the Feast pop-up, the creeping, miserable possibility that Saraswati was having a far worse time of it, and that it was all her fault, the emptiness of the possibility that Saraswati had meant it when she said their not-relationship-but-lots-of-fun-making-out that had barely begun was over for good, and cold, *biting* cold fear from having just witnessed a racer blow up in front of her eyes. The world seemed to lurch, and she felt like she was coming untethered in the vastness of space, far from everything she'd ever known, infinitesimal and insignificant in the void... and hungry, too.

'Why don't I stay with you until you're back on the ground?' Grace Kube offered gently.

'No, thanks,' Serenity Ko said hotly, hideously embarrassed at the big, fat tears that were leaking down her cheeks.

'All right, Ko. You hang up when you want to.'

She didn't, not when she docked, stumbled out of the racer, threw up all over the vacuum-sealed docking station floor, caught the first cab back to Primian orbit, descended to its surface, crammed her face with leftovers from the fridge, and stumbled into bed. Neither of them said a word.

Serenity Ko was grateful to have company. It made the thought of *consequences* just that little bit less terrifying, even though she knew, as she drifted into unconsciousness safe in her bed, that she was going to have to wake up eventually, and face the day.

All life in Uru is balanced.

The Wanderers and Ur-siders exist in a constant push and pull of forces, each exerting their philosophies upon the other so preservation and progress walk hand in hand, neither overwhelming the other, towards the unknowable light of the future.

—Serenity Medi,
Primus: A New Hope for Humanity
2065 Anno Earth | 1990 Interstellar Era

TWELVE

Resounding applause met the end of Optimism Mahd'vi's speech. Humans and alt-beings from every walk of life picnicked in the rippling sheaf-grass in the Valley—happy families with baskets bursting with food, trying to keep an eye on their unruly children running wild; small groups of teenagers taking hits of MellO, or sipping biras, each trying to outdo their friends for coolness points; hundreds of Wanderers, their rings glittering in the dimming light; monks from both the monasteries, giving each other a wide berth but otherwise not proselytising their faiths to the ever-growing crowd… It seemed as if all of Primus had turned out in honour of the Millennium Festival, and Optimism Mahd'vi felt a thrill of pride in the good work she'd accomplished with her team over the māsas gone by.

She smiled at her audience and stepped off the raised dais to make her way backstage into a large tent. A sound-bubble enclosed the structure, and the Millennium Festival Planning Committee sat assembled within its walls.

They occupied the centre of the Valley, a swathe of unoccupied flowering grassland that was banked on all sides by the rocky slope of the Ursridge. Bound by the Urswood off to the northwest, and ringed by the cliffs trailing down to the Ur-sands, the long shadow of Nakshatran Rock receded gently across the unbroken stretch of green while Suriya descended below the horizon. The last dying embers of light kissed the ground with its warmth, Ibnis rising in a ghostly halo of cloud.

Boundless Tai's eyes flicked upwards as twinkling lights illuminated the darkening sky. Optimism Mahd'vi followed his gaze.

The drones for the cosmic ballet emerged in their positions across the clear, dark skies, their lights winking in and out as if they were shooting stars in synchronicity. A swell of music signalled the performance was about to begin, and Optimism Mahd'vi noted the smug grin creeping across Boundless Tai's face. As their expert on live performances, he'd arranged the evening's entertainment.

'Never seen such a turnout for the cosmic ballet,' Boundless Tai said, flicking an invisible strand of lint off the fine embroidery on his jacket. 'And to think we've found such a glorious moment in the weather, too…'

'Naturally, we're broadcasting across the galaxy,' Curiosity Ariam piped up, not to be outdone, running their hand through their fashionably dishevelled hair. 'We've got POV cams for each of the dancers—human and drone alike.'

Optimism Mahd'vi permitted herself to smile. 'A moment, Ariam, before you run away with streaming numbers.'

She turned to Boundless Tai. 'Congratulations, Tai! You've done a stellar job, and it was particularly clever of you to set this up in the Arc. There are hundreds of Wanderers in the audience.'

Boundless Tai had the good grace to appear embarrassed by the high praise. 'It was simple logic,' he said. 'We know the Wanderers have been agitated by the focus that Feast has been getting—they've never been fans of the whole sim world. Add endless Loop programming into the equation, and they aren't the happiest folks out there.' He directed a pointed glance at Curiosity Ariam, then continued in a hurry, before they could interject. 'I figured we could draw them in by hosting many of our large-scale, live performances in the Arc. Right next door to their Wandering Paths, after all. Unlike, say, the street music festival from last māsa, or the parade we have planned after the Millennium Feast. Or even the upcoming Legends of the Future concert…'

'Nine Virtues, Tai!' Curiosity Ariam said irritably, taking a pull from their MellO vape. 'Sure, you brought a bunch of Wanderers to this performance, but *I* did the rest. Sure, there were some very *analogue* promos, but Honour Fen managed to swing a lot of Loop and sim-marketing deals with Harmony Utra…'

At this, Honour Fen squeaked and knocked over a glass of water.

'Give credit where it's due,' Curiosity Ariam smiled. 'It was a stroke of genius—*my* genius—to get Boundless Nnika to take dance lessons with the cosmic ballet, even if I do say so myself.' The producer in charge of Primus's biggest Ur-dramas and Loop programming paused dramatically, then held a palm up in the air, feigning the bellowing voice of reality show hosts all across the galaxy. 'Multiple Drammy-winning mega-sensation, the biggest star of *Stars Unrivalled* herself… fucks up colossally while attempting to learn how to dance ballet.'

Curiosity Ariam laughed in delight at their own impression.

'One of the most popular streams we've ever had! Should have turned it into a full-on show…' They trailed off, disappointment crossing their face, and then brightened. 'Still not too late, is it? We'll wrap up all the Festival stuff and then maybe turn it into a competition. Have Ur-drama stars face off against each other in cosmic ballet lessons. They'll be terrible, and everyone will want to watch. It's never been done before! Could be a great replacement for *Uru: Origins,* whenever it's cancelled.'

They turned pointedly to Optimism Mahd'vi at that. 'Though I've got to say, your Excellency, our numbers are soaring thanks to the Festival. An upswing in loyalism to Primus and our origins, perhaps? And on that note, maybe we could write a few new seasons? It only makes logical sense—'

Optimism Mahd'vi slid into the Loop, mulling over the fracas at the latest Feast pop-up while Curiosity Ariam prattled on.

'*An innocuous Wanderer protest against insidious food-sim technology has turned ugly! One of our own—and we all know that Wanderers are the conscience, the unsung heroes of Primian culture, the flag bearers of Nakshatran philosophy—called out the unwarrantedly famous Earthling chef and known mischief-maker, Saraswati Kaveri, for threatening Primian culture with her new food invention,'* shrieked Good Cheer Chaangte, her eyes dramatically made up, eyebrows dancing furiously to punctuate her sentences. '*Live footage shows Saraswati Kaveri egging on her girlfriend (now turned bodyguard, it appears) as Serenity* Ko attacks *the innocent protestor. Has the savage's influence gone too far? Well,* I *certainly think so...*'

Optimism Mahd'vi slid it off her visual with her haptic controls, and proceeded to watch another half-dozen or so reports. The ones that didn't follow the same script were blaming the Wanderers, liberally referring to them as "savages out of the Primian wilderness," or "the less cultured side of Primus, attuned more to zealous conservation than urban social niceties." And then there were the shippers, diehard fans of Saraswati Kaveri and Serenity Ko, who were rooting for them to announce their engagement any moment.

'Ariam,' Optimism Mahd'vi interrupted, when the producer's incessant bragging had turned too tedious to ignore. 'This isn't supposed to be a monologue.'

'Sorry!' Curiosity Ariam said hurriedly. 'I just thought you'd be delighted with how things are going, your Excellency. Our slam poetry streams are achieving record viewership. We're about halfway through our list of poets, and it's quite a refreshing change from the stodgy old repetitive recitals of the *Nakshatranāma*—'

'*Hey.* That's unnecessary,' Boundless Tai interrupted, visibly annoyed.

Curiosity Ariam raised their voice, talking over him. 'Our slam poets are really getting younger generations, and interstellar viewers, into the Primian poetic tradition...'

'The Primian Palace of Performing Arts has been sold out night over night for the last three māsas,' Boundless Tai said, raising his voice in turn.

It was starting to grate on Optimism Mahd'vi's nerves. 'When I want my committee to behave like young children trying to impress mommy, I'll hire young children and give them art projects,' she said icily.

That put an end to the argument.

'Would you like that recorded in the minutes of the meeting?' Honour Fen asked hesitantly.

'Fen, you're a Savant, aren't you?' Curiosity Ariam snapped. 'Figure it out.'

'Ariam, that's enough. Well done on the slam poetry streams. Thanks for helping promote this cosmic ballet performance by getting Nnika to take dance lessons. We'll discuss the future of *other* programming *outside of this meeting*,' Optimism Mahd'vi said brusquely, then gestured at Boundless Tai. 'Tell me about the live performances, Tai.'

Boundless Tai resumed their report. The Primian Palace of Performing Arts was sold out for the entire run of the theatrical performance, *Nadira*, a reimagining of the life of Nadira D'Cruz, who'd first led the Nakshatrans to settle Primus. The sinfonia was bringing in record numbers for the span of its season. 'We haven't had the concert hall this packed since Legends of the Future performed their smash-sinfonia album there...'

The Hall of Song was similarly booked for māsas in advance, where Honour Bali and Courage Navaz took turns performing the *Nakshatranāma* the traditional way—the epic poem was split into nine parts, one performed each night, over the span of a nava.

'Naturally, we have to think of our strategy for performing the *Nakshatranāma* at the Millennium Feast,' Boundless Tai said.

'*If* it's performed at the Millennium Feast,' Curiosity Ariam said sourly.

'*When* it's performed,' Optimism Mahd'vi snapped. 'Non-negotiable.'

'We're prepping for our 360-degree stream of the upcoming Legends of the Future concert,' Curiosity Ariam offered, attempting to broker peace.

'I assume you're going to work together closely on this,' Optimism Mahd'vi said, glancing from Curiosity Ariam to Boundless Tai. 'I don't want to hear you wasting my time by fighting about it while I'm in the room.'

Both Curiosity Ariam and Boundless Tai appeared apologetic at her tone of censure.

'Fen,' Optimism Mahd'vi continued, somewhat more gently as she regarded her socially awkward intern, who turned white as a sheet at being addressed.

Genius when it comes to delivering good work, hopeless when it comes to presenting it to a wider audience.

'How are things looking with the Millennium Feast?' Optimism Mahd'vi inquired politely.

'We—we're working on identifying the ideal venue...' Honour Fen began, her voice barely louder than a whisper.

'We keep seeding footage from the *Interstellar MegaChef* special episode,' Curiosity Ariam piped up. 'It's all over the Loop, in as many innocuous spaces as one might be tempted to look. But I have extensive thoughts on XP Inc.'s development process so far. I talked to Grace Kube about giving us exclusive behind-the-scenes access, but he shut the idea down the moment I said it out loud...'

'I've been in conversation with Grace Kube since long before you had a given-name,' Optimism Mahd'vi said acerbically. 'Leave negotiating with XP Inc. to me.'

She paused, then regarded the producer in silence. 'Also, last I checked your name wasn't Honour Fen. Stop interrupting everyone all the time, Ariam. The planet doesn't revolve around you.'

Curiosity Ariam blanched. 'That's not what you say when you ask me to amp up the pro-Primian messages on my shows...'

'Enough!' Optimism Mahd'vi snapped. 'We're all in this together. And it's all for the greater glory of *Primus*.'

Curiosity Ariam's lips twisted mutinously, but they didn't respond. Boundless Tai became very preoccupied in studying the geometric patterns embroidered upon his silk jacket.

'Fen, continue,' Optimism Mahd'vi said imperiously.

'So far, most of the Feast committee is in favour of an off-world venue, somewhere in orbit,' Honour Fen whispered. 'To honour the Nakshatran arrival. They believe a slow descent into Primian orbit while experiencing Feast is the ideal way to commemorate them.'

'It's an excellent idea,' Optimism Mahd'vi said in approval.

'B-but I have another one,' Honour Fen mumbled.

'Yes?'

'We host it right here on Nakshatran Rock. We need to take the next step forward, after the Nakshatrans. We are Primians, looking outward, upward, to the stars and the universe that lies beyond.' Honour Fen's face turned redder the longer she spoke.

'Boring,' Curiosity Ariam said, dismissively.

Optimism Mahd'vi looked up at the cosmic ballet, gracefully pirouetting across the night sky. 'It's a thought worth exploring,' she said, surprised by how much the proposal resonated with her. 'I want an assessment of both options by the end of the māsa.'

'Th-thank you,' Honour Fen mumbled.

'This meeting is over,' Optimism Mahd'vi announced, her eyes on the principle dancers making their way across sub-orbital space. The cosmic ballet was truly marvellous. The troupe comprised dozens of anthropomorphic drones that were capable of flight, each carefully crafted, finely tuned dancer mapped to anatomical precision and mirroring a live human ballerina, whose every move was relayed to a pliant machine, capable of supreme movement in thin air. She'd personally picked tonight's performance from their extensive repertoire—a performance of *Ascent/Descent,* composed by the legendary sinfonist Boundless Lora over seven hundred years before, in honour of the Nakshatran arrival on Primus and the subsequent development of Primian civilisation. It was moving but dynamic, vibrant and poignant all at once… and it was exactly the kind of crowd-pleaser that would stir high emotions in viewers all around the galaxy.

It didn't take much to impress people, as Optimism Mahd'vi had learnt over the decades. When she was younger, and far greener, she'd tried to shine a light on more obscure, esoteric works of genius, attempting to ingrain them in the popular imagination. She'd been faced with more failure than success in those early attempts, and it had gradually dawned on her that the popular imagination was a simplistic one; most people enjoyed treading familiar patterns, where sensory pleasure was less driven by curiosity and the need for discovery than a sort of self-satisfied contentment that came with having recognised oneself in what one was consuming. She'd shelved her more ambitious plans for art and culture for discerning consumers, and had resorted to reiterating the populism of more tried and tested works.

This wasn't to say that *Ascent/Descent,* or anything else she'd endorsed, wasn't deserving of praise. It just pained her to think of how *easily* people were pleased.

The Millennium Feast was going to be an enormous win, despite the recent Feast riot. It played right into Optimism Mahd'vi's plans for the food-sim, though. She streamed Grace Kube to remind him that she expected complete creative control to be handed over to her immediately.

And then she mulled over the Kaveri riddle, as her brother had narrated it to her a few navas ago. A plan knit together, and she streamed Saraswati Kaveri.

*The media are vultures. Ignore them. Meet me at the sinfonia. My assistants will find a slot that works for both of us.*

She signed it with her name, omitting her title of office, determined to lull Saraswati Kaveri into a false sense of security so she could crack the mystery of her murky past wide open.

Road map for Feast:

Phase 1: Primian Staples—all the tradition you can get!

Phase 2: Primian Deep Cuts—for the true believer!

Phase 3: Experimental/off-world foods—for everyone else!

—Serenity Ko's Notes

2074 Anno Earth | 1999 Interstellar Era

THIRTEEN

SERENITY KO STEPPED into the XP Inc. office in downtown Uru, deep in thought. She had to admit that Grace Kube had had a valid point, all those māsas ago. She'd been a monster on SoundSpace, pushing her team far too hard, lording her self-proclaimed superiority over them and micromanaging the process. She'd been a waking horror when she'd set out to design Feast as well, determined to prove Grace Kube wrong when he'd denied her a promotion.

Instead, she'd achieved something unexpected, and discovered everything she thought she knew about herself to be false, a put-on to protect her own fragile, faltering ego.

The tunnel she was in was incandescent, doused in colour, the words *Experience Your Best Life!* shimmering upon its walls. She barely registered the visual as she reckoned with her thoughts.

When she'd first approached her grandmother, who just happened to be the all-intimidating, redoubtable culture critic Grace Menmo to everyone else, she'd badgered her into teaching her about Primian cuisine. Her Ammamma, in a rare lapse of professional judgment, had acquiesced out of fondness for her granddaughter, much to Serenity Ko's glee. In her hubris, Serenity Ko had intended to master everything about Primian cooking in a nava or two, then boss her team around until they created a food-sim that captured its flavours and experiences. She'd been defiant in the face of her grandmother's warning that she was taking on more than she was equipped to handle.

She cringed at the memory of her arrogance—the many ways she'd disrespected her Ammamma's friends in the culinary world, and the assumption that a two-thousand-year history of food could be reduced to two weeks' research by someone who couldn't cook to save her life, for a start—while the tunnel's holographic visuals glimmered and rearranged into a carefully curated audiovisual experience that told the story of XP Inc., playing over her visual feed.

A twenty-something Grace Kube, clean-shaven and already balding, his head scarred from modding, gives an acceptance speech at the Aesthete Guild; his first demonstration of XP Inc.'s proof of concept...

It was hideously embarrassing for her to look back at it all—the sheer vanity that had set her off on this project. And yet, it was also strangely liberating to have learnt to let go, to trust in other people's expertise. Humbling, even. She now saw her team's strengths in a whole new light—one that didn't involve her shining at its centre as if she were a star system all on her own, but where everyone shone together like a galaxy, like the universe itself, ever-expanding and infinite in possibility...

Working with Saraswati had opened her eyes to this new reality. Saras had seamlessly grasped the principles of Primian cuisine, despite being fresh off the Earth. Saras had deconstructed their food culture with such keen acumen that Serenity Ko had despised her for her expertise, even as she admired her, all while her foolish belief—that she'd be able to pull it off on her own—came crashing down.

As the team came together to build Feast, Serenity Ko had unconsciously let *Saras* take the lead on the project, gazing open-mouthed as she put together sensory matrices and flavour curves to build Feast into something beyond her wildest imaginings.

And here I am, fucking things up, as usual. She grimaced.

Serenity Ko tracked obstacles and people in the tunnel on her HUD. On the map, she caught sight of a small blip, labelled *Curiosity Nenna, She/Her*, who was gaining ground on her fast, flanked by *Courage Praia, They/Them*. It was as if her conscience were catching up to her, and a twinge of guilt wormed its way up her gut. Both her teammates had taken part in the fracas at the Feast pop-up, backing her even though they strongly disapproved of violence of all kinds. And in return, she'd abandoned them after her interrogation with the captain of the Primian Guard, leaving them to clean up her mess so she could go fling a space racer around satellites and try not to die.

She'd barely had time to process the racing incident. If this was really an amateur racing club, then why in all the fucking galaxy was it so dangerous?

'Had a good night, did we?' Courage Praia said, slipping in at Serenity Ko's elbow. Curiosity Nenna took her place on the other side, her eyes firmly fixed on her boots, which had a purple floral pattern running up her calves.

Serenity Ko shrugged. 'It was all right.'

'So, The Wallflower? Some shack in the Arc?' Courage Praia pressed, then carried on as if they'd read her guilty conscience. 'A nice place to hide while you ditched us with all the cleaning up after the riot?'

Serenity Ko flicked a glance their way. Their lips were downturned. They had a large, ugly bruise across their forehead, and a couple of long scrapes down their arm.

'Went straight home,' Serenity Ko lied. 'Alone.'

'So you wouldn't have to face us and be told off?'

'I don't see Nenna complaining,' Serenity Ko said irritably.

'Yes, Ko. Let's wait for the *intern* to confront her boss—three levels higher, am I right? Let's wait for the *intern* to ask her boss what the fuck she was thinking last night. I refer specifically to starting a riot and abandoning her team to clean up,' Courage Praia said coldly, then cast a quick glance at Curiosity Nenna. 'No offence, Nenna.'

Curiosity Nenna mumbled inaudibly.

'Last I remember, *you* couldn't even defend the team vision to Na'vil and the neuros,' Serenity Ko shot back.

'I've had some time to grow. We all have. Or so I thought.' Courage Praia scowled.

Serenity Ko huffed, then grabbed Courage Praia and Curiosity Nenna by the arms, dragging them off the walkway that made its way straight through the XP Inc. headquarters, into the nearest alcove on the right.

A transparent flowmetal dome arched overhead, and orchids bloomed with a violent profusion all around them. Serenity Ko cast a quick look around the brightly coloured picnic tables lining the space and made a beeline for the elaborately decorated kaapi bar and snack counter at the far side.

Boundless Ano nearly dropped the glass he was cleaning when she slammed her palm down on the counter in front of him.

'All of you clearly have words, so say them,' Serenity Ko demanded.

'Well, good morning to you, too, Ko,' Boundless Ano said faintly.

Serenity Ko placed her hands on her hips and glared around at her teammates—or were they friends, by now?—in open challenge. Curiosity Nenna was still absorbed in her shoes, but Courage Praia returned her gaze evenly.

'You shouldn't have punched the Wanderer, Ko,' they said firmly.

'I have nothing but regrets,' Serenity Ko said, placing two fingers over her chest in an exaggerated symbol of interstellar peace.

'You shouldn't have left us to deal with the fallout,' Courage Praia continued.

'*That* I'm genuinely sorry for, but I couldn't stick around,' Serenity Ko said more sincerely, then hated herself as her voice reached a grating whine. 'Especially not after Saras…'

She paused, and the heat rose to her cheeks. 'Saras and I had an argument. About the Wanderer. About many things, really, but especially that, and—'

'And you shouldn't have left *Saras* alone!' Courage Praia snapped. 'I don't want to interfere in whatever it is you have going on—*believe me,* been there, done that, no thanks! But as a *friend*, it was fucking selfish of you.'

'She told me she didn't want to get dinner, that she needed space…'

The same whine. Sometimes, Serenity Ko wanted to sew her lips shut.

'Friends say things they don't always mean when they're angry. *You,* of all people, should know that. She looked heartbroken when she left,' Courage Praia said, then shot a filthy look at Boundless Ano. '*Right?*'

'It's true,' Boundless Ano replied. 'She looked tragic.'

Courage Praia stepped on Curiosity Nenna's foot, and the intern squeaked. 'She seemed unhappy,' she said hurriedly.

'I'll make it up to her,' Serenity Ko said, wishing the floor would crack open and swallow her whole. 'And to you. Thank you for cleaning up. It was all my fault. And I'm sorry.'

Courage Praia exhaled audibly, and their shoulders sagged. 'All right, thank you. Here endeth the lecture.'

It wasn't apparent on the surface, but Serenity Ko's insides were in turmoil, squirming as her guilt went to war with her convictions, righteous justifications rising to be quelled, while gut-churning visions of a sad and broken Saraswati trudging home in the rain grew larger than life, and the thought of facing her again grew more fraught with each passing second.

Serenity Ko knew *exactly* how the galaxy was reacting to what she'd done. She'd awoken to a firestorm on her streams; every channel from the ever-professional Four Chefs to Good Cheer Chaangte's personal rant space speculating upon how things had gone wrong. And this was fine; it had been their grand plan to have *everyone* talking about Feast—after all, all publicity was good publicity, wasn't it? What Serenity Ko *should* have anticipated was that all publicity wasn't necessarily good for *Saras,* regardless of who fucked up. Because Saraswati was an Earthling.

Serenity Ko, once blissfully unaware of the seething xenophobia that underscored the picture-perfect life on Primus, formerly hideously prone to inherent biases that crept their way into her vocabulary, had witnessed firsthand how all the nastiness of stereotypes, cultural superiority, and straight up bigotry were levelled at Saraswati. The way Good Cheer Chaangte had bullied her at Nonpareil, or the way people insisted on speaking to her in Vox, as if she didn't possess perfect Ur-speak; the sympathy and disbelief that tumbled across most Primian faces when they brought up her Earth-origins, and even just the language used to allude to the Earth itself.

All the while, everyone was quick to reassure Saraswati that of course, *she* was different, and why, she barely even had an Ur-speak accent…

What was I thinking? That I'd *take the fall?*

Even now, her self-centred narrative, her naiveté born of a sheltered, privileged life seemed to lead her astray. And it was plain unfair—she'd gone to work on herself over these māsas, reconnecting with her therapist, addressing her tendency to drown her sorrows at the bar, and being kinder to everyone around her regardless of the circumstances.

Nine Virtues, I even have a gratitude log on the Loop!

It was frustrating, to say the least.

And while the consequences of the riot were being directed at Saraswati, they were setting her road map for Feast on fire, as well.

'Kaapi for everyone?' Serenity Ko offered.

Without waiting for a response, Boundless Ano was whipping up their preferred beverages, and Serenity Ko filled them in on her last conversation with Grace Kube.

'It's unacceptable,' Courage Praia said, crossing their arms over their chest. 'We can't give the Secretariat control of Feast.'

'It's unfair to all the other humans out there. And the alt-beings too.' Curiosity Nenna worried at her lower lip.

'It's star-fucked *bullshit* is what it is!' Serenity Ko exploded. 'It's one thing to release Primian food first as a marketing strategy—we're *on* fucking Primus, the market is *right* here. It makes business sense. But to brand things *superior*, give Optimism Mahd'vi final approval on our experiences… That's where I draw the line.'

'Primus *isn't* an empire; we're supposed to be *anti*-empire. It's in the Nakshatran Charter. There's no way we can assert Primian superiority without breaking our founding principles,' Boundless Ano added.

'Right? That's what I told Kube. Told him to fuck right off.' Serenity Ko sipped on her frothball aggressively, and snorted as some of the micro-foam went straight up her nose.

'I'm sure he's taking you seriously,' Boundless Ano said drily, while Courage Praia thumped her on the back.

'I see Mahd'vi's point, though,' Curiosity Nenna piped up in a small, hesitant voice.

Everyone whirled to look at her, disbelief written across their faces as clear as day.

'You're *kidding*.'

'I don't *agree* with it,' Curiosity Nenna ventured hesitantly. 'But Saras is an Earthling. She's the public face of Feast. And the riot… while it wasn't her fault—' She broke off, looking at the purple-tipped toes of her sneakers for an excruciatingly long moment. 'While it wasn't her fault,' she repeated, refusing to look at Serenity Ko, 'she was in the room, and the riot was set off in response to something the Wanderer said to *her*. It might be better if…'

She mumbled her last words so inaudibly that Serenity Ko found herself leaning forward on tiptoe, straining to hear.

'Say that again?'

Curiosity Nenna turned as red as a rougeberry sphere. 'If she… *werendl elendoll*.'

'Spit it *out*, Nenna. I *promise* none of us will *bite*,' Serenity Ko snapped, which was not reassuring.

'It might be better if she weren't around at all,' Curiosity Nenna whispered, then clapped her hands over her mouth in horror, her eyes wide.

'You're right,' Serenity Ko said, feeling empty. 'Of course you are. We've known this from the start. What we're doing is infinitely more complicated because we've got Saras at the front, leading our project, facing the public, convincing them to try it…'

Her hands shook at her sides, and micro-foam kaapi sloshed over the side of her cup.

'And they *should!* It's a food revolution in a package. And Primians don't like challenges to tradition, sure… but this? This level of scrutiny is all because she's an Earthling, which is *ridiculous*. She knows *everything* about food. It would have been *impossible* to build Feast without her—well, maybe not absolutely impossible. We could have always hired a Primian chef to help us. But we didn't, did we? We found an *Earthling*. And I have *no regrets*. Do *you?*'

She paused, casting a withering stare at them all.

'Of course not,' Courage Praia snorted.

'Um, no,' Boundless Ano echoed.

'None whatsoever!' Curiosity Nenna squeaked.

'Where are you going with this, Ko?' Courage Praia asked cautiously, unsure of whether their friend was about to deliver some kind of revolutionary speech, or was on the verge of a spiralling meltdown.

Serenity Ko stormed out the pantry without a backward glance, and stepped on the walkway in the tunnel again.

'I'm going to go to those star-fuckers—Kube and Mahd'vi, the whole lot of them—and tell them we *refuse*. Outright, flat out refuse. And if they *try* and interfere with what we're doing, *try* and make us say Feast embodies Primian *superiority*, I will quit.'

'Whoa, Ko!' Courage Praia said, catching up to her. Curiosity Nenna was some distance away, panting as she struggled to make up lost ground. 'Easy there.'

'I'm going to grab some xurriotles off my desk first, and fling them at Kube when I meet him,' Serenity Ko said, her jaws clenched in determination. 'Let him try those sur-fucking divine Chomian biscuits and tell me Primian food is *superior*. I dare him, I really do.'

Serenity Ko stomped off the walkway and into the bay where the Feast team had taken up residence.

Packaged foods from all across the galaxy littered every single table: wheels of Axian cheeses, Chomian xurriotles, cream rolls from half a dozen bakers in the Copernican System, a whole shelf filled with Solar packaged foods, from

Earth-style stir fries and curries to Lunar puddings, and the ever-popular, recently unbanned cricket chips. A fully outfitted team of designers and engineers were working on what she'd determined would be Phase 3 of the Feast rollout—an expanded range of foods that went beyond Primian cuisine.

Meanwhile, the pod that was working on the current tasting menu for the Feast pop-up series occupied an entire bay on the floor, another pod working on its rollout at the Millennium Festival had taken over row upon row of workspaces, and every single visio-node reflected the chaos of the complexity of their work: readouts from tastings, feedback scrolls, flavour curve hypotheses for different recipes, lines of edibite integration code, neuropsych and neuro-dev mesh maps, databases of sim experiences under review…

The minute Serenity Ko popped into view, at least two dozen of her Feast teammates rose from their seats in unison, to accost her for help solving problems.

'Folks!' she bellowed. 'I don't mean to be a star-fucker, but I've got an urgent meeting with Kube. I will be back *right after,* and I'm double-booked on all my meeting slots for the day, but if you've got something that's *seriously high priority,* send me a stream, and I'll try and move things around.'

She experienced instant regret as her Loop notifs began to buzz like her brain was being rattled around in a blender.

'*Thank you for being the best!*' she called, rushing to her work station to grab the xurriotles.

And then she stopped, dead in her tracks.

'Star-fuck me sideways,' she swore.

At her workspace was a painstakingly woven basket, its agony apparent in the strange way the reeds were twisted together and its lopsided handles wilted. It was filled with heaps of flowers, and woven into its side was a misshapen heart, worked through the reed knots with the kind of care that made Serenity Ko want to throw up. At the bottom right corner, impossible to miss, was the signature of her not-so-secret admirer:

Always, Honour Aki

Courage Praia burst out laughing and Serenity Ko elbowed her in the ribs, but a grin spread across her face despite herself. 'I don't believe this is still happening,' she said, collapsing into her chair with a groan, all thoughts of her attack on Grace Kube and Optimism Mahd'vi momentarily forgotten. Even Curiosity Nenna managed to overcome her nervousness for long enough to laugh out loud, before appearing stricken at what she'd dared to do.

'Ko… you'd better talk to Kube… and Mahd'vi… quick… before Aki sabotages Saraswati… for you,' Courage Praia gasped between peals of laughter. They doubled over, moaning with pain. 'I spy a… jealous… ex…'

Amidst the throng of people and the buzz on the floor came a loud sob, and an auburn topknot rushed away from behind a large rack of mithai that had been specially imported from the Earth.

'Fuck Aki,' Serenity Ko said passionately. 'And fuck Kube and Mahd'vi, too. We've got Saras's back, and we won't let her down.'

So long as I don't fuck things up any further, she thought, but didn't say out loud.

Savages beget savagery, and that savagery is all over Feast.

—Good Cheer Chaangte,
Special guest on *Four Chefs*
2075 Anno Earth | 2000 Interstellar Era

If Chaangte wants to talk, I'm here to have a civilised conversation.

—Saraswati Kaveri,
Special guest on *Four Chefs*
2075 Anno Earth | 2000 Interstellar Era

FOURTEEN

I BRUSHED A stray curl off my face and beamed at my guests for the afternoon. *Another day, another Feast pop-up in an exotic destination in Uru.*

I'd been hosting pop-ups all nava, and to my utter relief, none of them had gone the way of the Culinary Circle.

Optimism Tina was doing her very best to reschedule the botched attempt to win over the Circle, in the hope that we might be able to impress them enough for them to say nice things the second time round. But in the meantime, we were still testing Feast with regular Primians chosen by lottery. The user-testing folks at XP Inc. had organised applicants into different cohorts so we'd get data to analyse based on hundreds—if not thousands—of user testing cases, all of which Serenity Ko and her team had identified and turned into some kind of complex matrix that was permanently holorayed across the office floor.

We'd organised a pop-up in the Urswood featuring the "artistic folks" cohort, and Feast had inspired outbursts of spontaneous poetry all across the pop-up floor. The versifying got a little competitive towards the end, with the slam poets all vying to outdo each other with their cleverness and wit. Allusions to the *Nakshatranāma* took a turn for the acerbic, and it was with a twinge of regret that I served the kaapi-blast bundt cake dessert. The "artistic folks" came unhinged then, and we had to escort a host of babbling poets with wild eyes—still declaiming visions of beauty and proclaiming undying loves long lost while absolutely nobody was listening—out the tent.

Serenity Ko hadn't been there in person—the XP Inc. publicity team was taking no chances with further riots—but she'd clearly caught the whole thing on a stream. She slid into my comms, sending me visions of happy faces bouncing around a padded cell, streaming tears of mirth and joy. I pointedly ignored her.

She then shared her notes with me:

- *Tunc down intensity of sims when artistic leanings are detected in biochemistry?*
- *Tune down intensity of sims overall? But then, we break immersion for the less "artistically minded"?*
- *Ban poets?*

I snorted, but I wouldn't give her the satisfaction of a response. I was still mad at her for starting that riot.

The next few pop-ups were uneventful, featuring more "regular people," as Serenity Ko classified them. They responded to Feast well overall, but I had no idea what Serenity Ko was making of the findings, since she hadn't tried discussing them with me.

Instead, she apologised. Repeatedly. And I stone-cold ignored her. Repeatedly.

My gut clenched, and I pushed all thought of her away. This nava had felt like a decade, and it seemed that things wouldn't let up, even over my nava-end. I had to wrap up this pop-up, preferably without incident, then attend the sinfonia with Optimism Mahd'vi tomorrow, after which I'd promised to meet my friends at an Ibnis-viewing party at the Ur-sands.

The smile on my face nearly slid right off as I glanced at the tables we were serving. Our demographic for the day was particularly awful—happy couples and 'cules. And to drive the saccharine symbolism home, we were at the Unity River monument, which had nothing to do with romance, except that the publicity folks had latched onto the word "unity" as the theme of the evening.

If you asked me, our guests for the evening could stand to be a little less *united*.

Everyone was very evidently *madly* in love, from the two men who couldn't stop rubbing noses between soft, tender kisses, to the quartet of men and women who all kept swapping places with each other so they could get equal amounts of time cuddling with each other while making intense eye contact.

Put it this way, Saras, Kili said gently, nuzzling my cheek. _These folks are so happy, anything you do can only make them even *happier.*_

Unless it involves a riot.

Look at them go, Kili giggled, directing my attention to a man and woman who had quite forgotten they were in public, and were snogging with merry abandon.

I felt a stab of jealousy as I imagined Serenity Ko and I doing the exact same thing. _Why do I have to take the moral high ground about snogging Ko, again?_

Because you're sensible, Kili said firmly. _You want to be honest with her about everything. And now is not the best time to do so. Besides, she's a bit of an impulsive juggernaut who keeps trying to do what she thinks is best for you without checking with you first. She started a riot—_

Right. Enough reasons.

Outside the tent, the gravity-defying sculpture involved the Unity River flowing in ways that should have been impossible according to the laws of physics. Throngs of tourists surrounded it, awestruck by its magnificence, and our little pop-up tent faded into the background, which suited me just fine.

Beside me, Boundless Ano's intricate beverages were being whisked away by our immaculately professional servers. They were impeccable, managing to serve all the drinks without interrupting a single kiss. It was time for me to get my game face on and send the amuse-bouche out.

I spritzed each Feast cube with just enough water for it to puff up ever so slightly and change colour, resolutely trying not to think about the last time I'd seen a Feast Berry-anna. Stifling all memory of Serenity Ko, I alerted the head server to ready their team, and stepped out from behind my kitchen counter.

'I present to you the future of Primian food,' I said grandly, rattling off the same speech I made every single time. 'Welcome to our pop-up, and may I present to you… a *Feast!*'

To their credit, the happily-in-love guests before me disentangled themselves from their partners and applauded politely. I spread my arms out grandly, feeling foolish the whole time. Identical cloches were placed before our diners, and then lifted to reveal indiscriminate, gelatinous Feast cubes.

'Enjoy!' I said, forcing myself to be enthusiastic, before retreating.

'They're… quite intense, aren't they?' Boundless Ano beamed.

'It's… overwhelming.'

'Serenity Ko told me they're a key demographic—she wants to see how romance and Feast interact with each other,' Boundless Ano explained. 'She suspects there's likely to be a positive bias impacting how people in love respond to Feast, and that it might elicit more powerful responses.'

'Fascinating!' I said, as an unasked for memory bubbled up to the surface. It absolutely confirmed Serenity Ko's hypothesis.

When I was booted off *Interstellar MegaChef* after my first appearance, I found myself fleeing a mob of cam-drones at the Uru and Beyond Marketplace. Serenity Ko had come to my rescue in a dark alleyway. Her grandmother—the terrifying food critic and gourmand Grace Menmo—had challenged her to taste three different Berry-annas and create flavour profiles for all of them. I helped her navigate what must have been an impossible challenge for her, and she'd clearly been impressed by my palate. Shortly afterwards, she'd shown up at Nonpareil, where I was beginning my career as a chef on Primus, and asked me to help her build Feast. But really, the Berry-anna tasting was where everything had begun…

And then, at the XP Inc. midnight picnic, I'd tasted the

Berry-anna Feast cube for the first time… and it had blown my mind with a tangle of memories, setting my heart racing as I relived every ecstatic moment of kissing Serenity Ko.

I looked around the tent. Our amuse bouche was triggering all the pheromones. We usually cycled between the Citric Crush, the Nakshatran Gelato, and the Berry-anna, and it was clear that the last one on our list was an epic hit. Romance was in the air.

It was enough to make one sick.

As the room recovered and burst into delighted applause, a drop dead gorgeous man walked up to Boundless Ano. He wore his deep brown hair in a high braid, his eyes were limned with kohl, and his muscles rippled excessively beneath his far-too-tight shirt. I'm completely indifferent to men, but even I couldn't stop myself from staring. He lowered his voice. 'I'm asking my girlfriend to marry me today,' he whispered conspiratorially. His name tag read *Harmony Faiz, He/Him*.

'What, here?' Boundless Ano asked, evidently surprised.

'Biggest culinary occasion of our lives!' Harmony Faiz whispered animatedly. 'I need your help with the nose-pin, though.'

He discreetly passed a small box to Boundless Ano, holding it unsubtly open. Within it, an enormous nose-pin glittered opulently. 'You have bubble-wine, I take it?' he asked.

'Naturally,' Boundless Ano said casually, if a little breathlessly.

'I'll place an order for an extra round of bubbly with the third course. Would you drop the nose-pin in her glass?'

'Of course!' Boundless Ano said, delighted. 'And would you like me to bring it over?'

'No, I'd love it if *you* could do that,' Harmony Faiz said, turning to me and smiling. 'She's your *biggest* fan.'

'I—I don't want to intrude.'

'No! She'll *love* it!' His large green eyes were beseeching. 'Please. She's the love of my life. And she really is your biggest fan. Always defending you—hates the way people come after you for being an Earthling. Had a huge fight with her best friend after the riot—insisted it wasn't your fault. Thinks you're a culinary revolutionary, a complete inspiration to women, chefs, immigrants, the marginalised…' He ticked them off his fingers. 'A complete inspiration to people everywhere.'

'Okay,' I agreed, hesitantly. 'Congratulations in advance!'

He beamed at me, and turned and walked away. Boundless Ano fanned himself with a toasted cracker he'd been intending to place in the drink he was making. 'Yummy,' he said.

'Delicious to behold,' I agreed. 'And I don't even *like* men.'

I added water to the next course—a meen crudo—and sent the Feast cubes out. I resolved to pay close attention to the responses, but the more pop-ups I hosted, the more monotonous it became to stand behind the counter, doing absolutely no cooking whatsoever other than "just add water"—as I repeatedly reminded our audience everywhere.

My fingers itched to dice whole ingredients, julienne fruits and vegetables, throw them together in a dish and sauté, blanch, baste, stir-fry, tadka, reduce, bubble, stew, deep fry things together in absurd combinations—experimental, boldly flavoured and completely unpredictable in a saucepan. The mathematical precision of Feast, its ease and simplicity, was beginning to feel like a sweater that had shrunk in the wash, now sitting too tightly upon my skin. It didn't help that I had this endless free time standing around, a smile plastered across my face, my jaws aching, watching the same overwhelmed and emotional responses to the memories dredged up by Feast—carefully calibrated, scientifically determined to manipulate memory centres in the brain and trigger audio-visual sensations based on absolutely nothing of substance.

I wanted a *real kitchen*. Like the one I'd left behind at Elé Oota. I constantly wondered what all my friends back on Earth were doing.

I'd settle for the kitchen I'd worked in with Courage Oslo and Curiosity Zia.

Or even just their little contraband stovetop in their living room, whipping up snacks for my little circle of friends…

But I couldn't ignore the draw of Feast, its scale and ambition. The meen crudo was a hit. All around me, happily-in-love partnerships were suddenly planning fishing trips, reminiscing about off-world oceans and the tang of salt bearing the taste of Sagaricus's foreign seas …

I created this.

The surge of pride swelling within me wrapped me up like a warm hug.

I created this new way for people to come together and relive their pasts, swap stories, imagine their future, all based on taste and flavour.

I never imagined I'd ever achieve anything like this back on Earth. To think of only cooking for my friends—for the sake of cooking itself—was selling my ability short.

This is my destiny.

Are you okay, Saras? Kili asked. _You look a bit peaky._

Fine, just fine. I grinned.

You look positively unhealthy… Kili said uncertainly, voice pinched with concern.

Never been better!

Okay, good, Kili continued, evidently unconvinced. _Because you're up._

Boundless Ano dropped the ceremonial nose-pin in a flute of bubble-wine, and placed it on a tray, along with a second glass. The rest of the bottle—now on the house, with compliments to the happy couple—sat in a cart, on ice. One of the servers followed me with it as I wended my way through the tables, to where the man named Harmony Faiz sat with his equally lovely girlfriend. His eyes widened when he saw me, and he hurriedly tried to wave me away, but it was too late.

His girlfriend—*Courage Hasha, She/Her*—had caught sight of me.

I smiled right as her face crumpled, and it hit me that something was horribly wrong.

'You're proposing?' the woman wailed.

Her voice cut through the murmur of conversation, which didn't just fall away, but took a nosedive off the Ursridge.

Abort? Kili said enquiringly.

Abort, I confirmed, making an about turn.

'Why? Why are you proposing?' she said hysterically.

It being somewhat too late to pretend none of this had ever happened, I stepped forward confidently and held the tray out to Harmony Faiz, who took the upsetting glass of bubbly containing the ceremonial nose-pin within it, and proffered it to his girlfriend hesitantly. 'I love you, Hasha,' he said, his voice fraught with uncertainty.

I held my breath, glancing around the restaurant, unsurprised that all eyes in the room were intently focused on this one specific table.

In response, Courage Hasha shrieked and batted the glass of bubble-wine away. It went flying out of Harmony Faiz's hand, splashing its contents all across the ground, then fell to the earth and shattered. The ceremonial nose-pin rolled away.

'I—I—' she wailed. Then, to my horror, she buried her head in her hands and sobbed.

I swallowed, backing away quietly to give them some space.

She twisted her napkin in her hands, then flung it on the floor. 'I didn't know it until just now...' she howled miserably. 'But I'm still in love with Xerx!'

'*What?*' Harmony Faiz pushed back his chair, aghast.

She snivelled inconsolably, snot running down her nose, distorting her perfect face. 'I never should have broken up with him! It's just... the shroom-broth reminded me of foraging with him, the meen crudo of the rivers in the Urswood...'

'You're kidding!' Harmony Faiz whispered, his face ashen. 'I thought you told me you hated all that outdoorsy Wanderers crap! Star-fuck me, we've spent the *last six years* together visiting the most *expensive cities* in the galaxy.'

'I know... *I know!*' she moaned. 'It was the only way I could forget him!'

My heart unspooled as I anticipated the publicity nightmare this was going to bring on. I knew in an instant that *everyone* in the room was streaming this meltdown live, with me standing at its very heart. I considered running.

Don't run, Kili said. _This isn't your fault. Stand your ground._

Just a quick dash...

I stood my ground, though, as the hitherto happy couple escalated their disastrous break-up.

'I never meant for this to happen…' the woman continued, blubbering as her mascara trailed down her face in dark smudges. 'I even told him, the last time I saw him—'

'Six years ago. *Right?*' Harmony Faiz asked sharply.

She looked at him tragically. 'Fifteen minutes ago, when we were making love in the sim—'

'Star-fuck me sideways,' Harmony Faiz swore.

XP Inc.'s new privately hired security team—a staple after the riot—chose that moment to intervene, and led the wretched couple away.

I tried to conceal my feelings behind a smooth, expressionless mask. My shaking hands knotted in the folds of the long, silk jacket I was wearing. I was aware of everyone's eyes on me as I walked back to the counter, holding my back ramrod straight and betraying none of my dismay.

I'm sorry, Saras, Kili streamed.

That'll be all over the streams already, I said, resigned.

'Free bubbly, on the house, for everybody!' Boundless Ano announced from the bar, giving me a concerned look.

I half-heartedly got through the rest of service, and as we sent out the dessert course, I slid into the Loop.

Don't look! Kili warned.

I looked.

'*Saraswati Kaveri is now behind a dramatic break-up, all thanks to her divisive, devastating tech: Feast!*' Good Cheer Chaangte crowed shrilly. '*Was this secretly planned so that Saraswati could win that gorgeous hunk away from his fiancée? Or have things gone wrong, and has Saraswati revealed her plan to break up couples all across Primus by playing her hand too soon? We've got it all for you, right here…*'

I was sick to my stomach. All I wanted to do was dissolve into the floor of my home at the Faith of the Light until the universe collapsed.

Unfortunately, you can't always get what you want.

A Primian wedding banquet is a delicate affair. Tradition trumps innovation because tradition is all the things a marriage stands for—that which is eternal.

—Grace Menmo,
Art and Culture in the Interstellar Era: The Definitive Edition
2065 Anno Earth | 1990 Interstellar Era

FIFTEEN

THE END OF the nava came as a relief to Serenity Ko. If it hadn't arrived right when it did, she'd have cracked, dropped off the grid, escaped on holiday to somewhere quiet and tranquil—one of those dead rocks with artificial hot springs in the Osmos Girdle, maybe—and let the noise in her mind swallow her whole. Or not. She simply couldn't afford to go on vacation at this moment; Feast was in turmoil, and even as things appeared to be going smoothly on the surface, there were endless knotty little details that had to be utterly *perfect* before they hosted their next pop-up. Infinitesimal departures from the ideal experience stuck to the existing prototype like so many fine grains of sand, and the prototype itself was beginning to resemble a beached whale.

They hadn't got through the tasting with the Culinary Circle, on account of her starting a riot, but there were still reams of data to go on. A delay of a millisecond on one of the sims had to be ironed out—it was incremental, and kept adding up, further delaying the onset of the memory triggers that had been built into the neuropsych mesh. Optimism Sah'r was working on perfecting its performance, but this meant stripping back the complexity of the sim, and Serenity Ko was reluctant to make compromises.

'The whole dish is a feast of shroomings,' she insisted. 'This sim is all about discovering them in the woods, and the dust motes in the light streaming down through the leaves is an *essential* detail. It elevates the fullness of the experience.

Without it, we're stuck with a mundane walk through the forest, picking shroomings, who cares.'

'Because you're an expert on foraging, and love walking in the woods?' Optimism Sah'r asked wryly.

'Because I'm an expert on identifying what *other* people like about the fucking woods,' Serenity Ko shot back.

'Ko, all I'm suggesting is a reduction in the frequency of the dust motes. We can still keep the cascading light,' Optimism Sah'r reasoned.

Serenity Ko made a face to emphasise her thoughts on the proposition. 'I want to meet you halfway, Sah'r, but this is not halfway.'

Stalemate after stalemate—that was every single conversation around Feast. On a slightly less microcosmic level, Optimism Tina kept filling her in with unnecessary updates about redoing the pop-up with the Culinary Circle.

'I think I'm on the verge of a breakthrough with the junior undersecretary, who really enjoyed the first Feast dish. She's willing to talk to the senior undersecretary, though that could take a few days…'

Serenity Ko zoned out as Optimism Tina narrated the finer details of the Culinary Circle's grand pecking order, responding to a minor and entirely unforeseen Phase 3 disaster taking place in the Feast bay. Off-world foods were producing strange allergies, and one of her team members was currently mottled in shades of green thanks to a run in with an Axian cheese during an experimental tasting.

And her meeting with Grace Kube had been a minor disaster. She'd flung the xurriotles from Chomo upon his workspace triumphantly, dared him to declare them inferior to Primian cooking, and had been swallowed up in an enormous bear hug in response.

'I'm so glad you're alive, Ko,' Grace Kube had said, voice thick with emotion. 'I can't believe how close we came to losing you.'

'I… er, Kube… are you all right?'

'Why in all the star-fucked universe have you taken to

satellite slinging, Ko? Of *all* the fucking *depraved* hobbies someone could pursue—'

Serenity Ko had started off reassuring him that it was perfectly safe, and had ended up wiping her eyes on the edge of her sleeve, with no idea when the floodgates had opened, or why she was reliving the terrifying incident. She tried valiantly to rally.

'Kube, I'm here to discuss the Mahd'vi situation.'

'Later. I think you need to take the day off.'

'What?'

'Go. Rest. Recover...' He'd risen to his feet, placed a hand gently between her shoulder blades, and steered her out of his office.

Days had passed since the riot, and Saraswati hadn't responded to any of her streams. Serenity Ko, in turn, was becoming hideously aware of what life must be like for Honour Aki, who had persisted in pursuing her attentions. He'd rebounded from her dismissal of his handwoven basket bearing flowers, and was now adopting a wholly different approach to winning her over. A distastefully luminous hair ornament had appeared at her workspace the day after, as if highlighting the ominous silence from Saraswati.

So, Serenity Ko welcomed the end of the nava like an old friend, waking late in the day, feeling the aches and pains in her bones cracking as she stretched, and relishing the prospect of gloriously free time during which she could nurse her wounds and do her level best *not* to think of Saraswati and the tangle of feelings that rose to strangle her like a seven-part Sagarican sailing knot stuck in her throat.

And then she remembered she was running late for lunch with Optimism Rihan and Good Cheer Eria.

'Ah fuck,' she swore, throwing herself into the shower.

Collective Four was unrecognisable in sur-light. Serenity Ko had a hazy memory of lanterns strung between buildings, bobbing up and down like an ocean of incandescence as the flowmetal city shifted and swivelled near-imperceptibly, adapting to its surroundings, its mycelial intelligence synchronising with the wider world in perfect harmony.

Her preferred optics dimmed the bright blue afternoon sky, but she was unused to the relative silence of the food and nightlife district during the day. No throbbing rhythms all around her, a noticeable absence of large holo-signs proclaiming the names of award-winning restaurants and their award-winning chefs (which she usually ignored for the twinkling holo-signs proclaiming the names of award-winning cocktail bars and their mixologists). Throngs of people of a different kind from those she was accustomed to surrounded her—instead of constantly teetering off the cliffs of insobriety, they comprised happy families and tourists, filming their experiences on a variety of tech, and she experienced a vague childhood memory about nava-end luncheons being a tradition… Somewhere in this maze of streets was a little garden that had the best carrot pastry anywhere in the universe.

The second *best carrot pastry after Ammamma's,* she thought, her brain instantly smacking her with a heady cocktail of loyalty laced with guilt. She hadn't spent much time with Ammamma of late. Arguments about Feast inevitably worked their way into their conversations, in the manner of beginning them and ending them in fireworks, Serenity Ko storming off like a five-year-old throwing a tantrum. It was most unbecoming.

She was honestly surprised that Optimism Rihan and Good Cheer Eria had invited her, and *not* Ammamma, to help pick a caterer for their upcoming wedding. She passed through the doors of The Bespoke Nakshatran, and found them seated at a large, circular table, a glass of oak sherry in front of her brother, and a glass of water before his chlorosapient fiancée.

Serenity Ko waved cheerily, hoping the big smile on her face would compensate for being over an hour late. Instead, Good Cheer Eria clapped her hand to her mouth in horror, and Optimism Rihan scowled deeply.

'Ordinarily, I'd say it's great to see you, but you're an hour late and you've got a bruise the size of Ibnis on your face. It looks worse than the footage of the riot,' Optimism Rihan said, clucking his tongue. He drew his sister into a hug, and she winced.

'The right arm's a bit sore, Rihan,' Serenity Ko said casually. 'But I'm otherwise all right.'

He held her at arm's length, and Serenity Ko tapped her foot impatiently as he surveyed her, as if looking for other dents and cracks. 'Are you done yet?'

'Nine Virtues, Ko! Have you been eating... at all?' Optimism Rihan cried in dismay.

'Yes, of course!' Serenity Ko snapped. 'Why is everyone always commenting on my weight?'

'Forgive us for caring about your nutritional needs because we know you can't cook and we hardly ever see you,' Optimism Rihan said. 'Our parents send their love, and would like me to remind you where they live.'

'Such *drama*.' Serenity Ko rolled her eyes, while her insides squirmed at the thought of the last four family dinners, all of which she'd missed. 'I'm always a stream away.'

'Right,' Optimism Rihan said skeptically, while Serenity Ko turned to hug Good Cheer Eria.

'How are you, Eria?' Serenity Ko asked. 'Things all right over at the Faith of the Light?'

Her reply was cut off when a tall blond man strode in through a door. His black chef's jacket stretched at the seams where it rippled across his bulging biceps. 'Straggler's here at last?' he asked, his gaze smouldering in the general direction of Serenity Ko.

'She is, finally!' Optimism Rihan grinned back. 'Ko, meet my friend Courage Firdoz. We called him Dozer back in school because he was always inexplicably wide awake; the last person to leave a party, the first person in class the next day... Dozer, this is my sister, Serenity Ko.'

'Nice to meet you, Dozer,' Serenity Ko said, her voice coming out huskier than she'd expected.

'Ko, can I get you a drink?' Dozer asked in his deep voice.

'A nīlatini, please,' Serenity Ko said demurely, flashing him her most charming smile. It was her first drink that nava, and she reckoned she deserved a reward, given how things were going.

'Right away!' Dozer said, spinning on his heel and striding off.

'Nine Virtues, pull yourself together, Ko.' Optimism Rihan snorted.

'I'm just appreciating a gorgeous man!' Serenity Ko protested.

'And inviting high drama to our wedding by making eyes at our prospective caterer while you're head over heels in love with Saraswati,' Optimism Rihan smirked.

'I'm not in love,' Serenity Ko snapped, now overwhelmingly ashamed.

'Right.'

Serenity Ko rapidly changed the subject. 'You're getting someone who *isn't* Ammamma's friend to cater the wedding?'

Optimism Rihan's smooth, deep brown skin flushed scarlet. 'I'm just tasting. Keeping our options open,' he said defensively. 'It can't hurt, can it? I mean, I'll still do tastings with Ammamma's recommendations, of course. And pick the best one, according to both of us. Dozer's got a bit of a reputation for his sustainable food practices…'

Serenity Ko grinned slyly. 'Striking out on your own when food is involved is a dangerous game, Rihan. Ammamma will *not* be amused. If even a single ras infusion is out of place…' She let the threat hover.

Optimism Rihan cast a worried glance at Good Cheer Eria. 'Surely, we can't go *that* wrong on our own.'

'This is positively *rebellion,'* Serenity Ko gloated, her smile widening when her brother winced at her choice of word. 'What next, Rihan? Will you be serving *cocktails*? Streaming your honeymoon at the pleasure dens in Sagaricus?'

Optimism Rihan licked his lips nervously, and took a sip of his sherry.

Good Cheer Eria's eyes widened, and she seemed positively aghast. 'Rihan, I thought you said your grandmother knew about this! I don't want to cause any friction in your beautiful family…'

Optimism Rihan took Good Cheer Eria's hand and squeezed it, then scowled at his sister. 'It'll be fine, Eria. Ammamma *knows* we're here.'

'*Cocktails,*' Serenity Ko crowed, now teasing her brother mercilessly. 'Rebellion!'

'At your service!' Dozer said, placing a nīlatini down before her with a flourish. 'Who's rebelling?'

Serenity Ko caught a whiff of vanilla and musk, and her stomach did somersaults while her mouth ran dry and her brain blanked out. *This* was why she needed to fix things with Saraswati, so the charms of complete strangers wouldn't catch her off-guard like this, and she could go back to struggling to navigate Saraswati's charms instead.

'We're all rebels,' Optimism Rihan said smoothly. 'In our own small ways, every act of living is a rebellion.'

'All too true!' Dozer said enthusiastically, then turned his attention to Serenity Ko, his deep green eyes twinkling. 'Care to take a sip? I promise it's the best in town.'

Aware of the heat rising to her cheeks, Serenity Ko took a large swig of the neon blue drink. It took every ounce of willpower in her arsenal not to spit it out. She choked it down, forcing herself not to gag, and smiled brightly. 'It's like nothing I've ever had before!' she announced. And it was true. She'd never, not once, *ever* in her nearly thirty years of existence, ever tasted anything so vile.

Dozer was positively brimming with delight, bouncing on the balls of his feet. All sense of vague attraction Serenity Ko had experienced fizzled away as the words tumbled out of his mouth in his resonant, deep voice. 'I substituted the stone-gin with a sustainable alcohol I brewed myself, from the discarded pods of stonefruit—tonnes go to waste every year!'

With good reason, Serenity Ko thought sourly, wishing she could pick up her serviette and scrub her tongue with it. Dozer continued. 'It's been distilled with notes of imli-ras and gayam-skin, which gives it its distinct spiced flavour. And that's just scratching the surface.' He had somehow attained even greater buoyancy, bobbing up and down with every other word. 'I've been brewing my own citrine bitters—but from the seeds! Such a distinct bite to them. And as for the nīlafruit infusion… why don't you taste it and tell me how you think I made it?'

'Why don't you just tell me?' Serenity Ko asked, struggling to stay polite.

'Why don't you guess?' He winked, clearly misreading her expression.

'Why don't you tell me first, so I can savour it later?' Serenity Ko said, leaning forward and running her fingers over the rim of her cocktail glass. 'Feels selfish to keep this drink all to myself.'

'Why don't you have a go, and I'll tell you all about it at the same time?'

Optimism Rihan and Good Cheer Eria were watching this exchange with alarm, and Serenity Ko realised that Optimism Rihan, who knew her far better than his innocent fiancée, was terrified that their conversation was some kind of advanced flirting.

'I think Rihan should taste its genius,' she said, struck by a wicked idea. She passed the drink to him. 'We *all* should.'

Dozer seemed crestfallen for a moment, but recovered immediately. '*Excellent* idea!'

Optimism Rihan shot Serenity Ko a filthy look, instantly suspicious. His fingers twitched on the stem of the glass, and he took a hesitant sip. Serenity Ko tapped her foot violently on the floor, the laughter writhing within her as her brother's eyes widened in horror, and he swallowed hurriedly.

'My turn!' Good Cheer Eria said enthusiastically. 'If it's sustainably made, it aligns with my chlorosapient principles.' She beamed. Optimism Rihan looked on helplessly, unable to stop her without creating a scene, and Serenity Ko's ribs began to ache.

Good Cheer Eria took a much larger sip, clearly oblivious to the dynamic in the room, and sputtered. 'Oh!'

A hacking cough overcame her, and tears leaked down her face. 'I'm so sorry, must have gone down the wrong way,' Optimism Rihan said loudly, rubbing her back.

'Ah, well, this happens,' Dozer said, evidently disappointed to have lost the opportunity for a dramatic reveal. 'I substituted the nīlafruit with—'

'Perhaps we could continue with the tasting?' Optimism Rihan asked, cutting him off.

'Of course, of course! I get carried away… it's so exciting to be appreciated as an artist,' Dozer said as he walked back towards his kitchen. 'Doesn't happen every day!'

'I'll bet it doesn't,' Serenity Ko sniggered once he was out of sight. 'This is the one, Rihan! I approve. Ammamma approves. I approve on Ammamma's *behalf*.'

Optimism Rihan scowled at her. 'That was just *one* drink. The rest of his tasting menu is bound to be better.'

It was not.

Canapés made from things that should not belong together on a menu, let alone on the same plate, were paraded before them. Beautifully cubed vat-grown salmon was served with a caviar infused with ras extracts from twigs of all sorts.

'Usually discarded by even the most discerning ras harvester!' Dozer crowed.

Crumbling pastry castoffs were reassembled together, bearing small gelées infused with ras drawn from citrus pips, overripe berry spheres, and cheeses well past their use-by date.

'Only the most Nakshatran palates will appreciate the zero-waste philosophy of these deconstructed pastries!' Dozer announced.

In place of vat-grown sirloin, the beest carpaccio was made from reconstituted weeds.

Good Cheer Eria, whose chlorosapient beliefs prevented her from eating most foods that weren't edibites, appeared to be turning a deeper shade of green than her usual chlorosapient makeup.

'All right, I can't do this any more,' Serenity Ko announced when Dozer made his way back to the kitchen to produce another monstrosity.

'Ko, he's a *friend*,' Optimism Rihan warned, though he didn't try and dissuade her.

'Follow my lead,' Serenity Ko hissed. 'I'm going to give you the perfect excuse to leave. Meet me round the corner at Faro's.'

As the kitchen door swung open, she wailed, flinging her arms up in despair. 'I can't do this any more, Rihan! It's too much to take!'

'There, there,' Optimism Rihan said uncertainly.

'All this wedding talk, this *delicious* food, reminds me of all that could have been!' Serenity Ko howled.

'It must be so difficult,' Optimism Rihan suggested.

'Bad time?' Dozer inquired politely.

'It's too soon! *Too soon!*' Serenity Ko bawled. 'We were supposed to be married by now! And he called it off without a second thought!'

And then she got to her feet and rushed from the room, bursting out into the sur-light, committing to her heartbreak and hysteria until she turned the corner and pulled up short. She caught her breath and leaned back against the wall, arms crossed at her chest.

She grinned when she caught sight of Optimism Rihan and Good Cheer Eria making their way to her.

'You're welcome.'

'That was *bold,*' Good Cheer Eria said appreciatively, then clasped Optimism Rihan's hand, squeezing it tight. 'I'm sorry, my love, but I've never eaten such terrible food in my life.'

Optimism Rihan shook his head in disbelief. 'We always knew he wasn't the brightest, but this was…'

'*Inedible,*' Serenity Ko said firmly.

'*You* were all over him until that cocktail arrived.'

'Single people have rights,' Serenity Ko pouted.

'You really expect me to believe you're not all over Saras?' Optimism Rihan teased.

'She's not talking to me right now.'

'Ah, the riot.' Optimism Rihan nodded sagely.

'I'm sorry, Ko,' Good Cheer Eria said sincerely.

'Great strategy, hooking up with other people instead of talking through your issues with the person you're in love with. Very adult.' Optimism Rihan snorted.

The truth in his words hit her hard, and she paled.

'I should stream her. No, I should just call her. Right?' She looked helplessly from her brother to his fiancée, her brain a cascade of freewheeling thoughts.

'I saw her at the commune this morning. She's meeting Optimism Mahd'vi at the sinfonia today,' Good Cheer Eria said hesitantly.

'I've got to go. I'll find her there. Beg for forgiveness,' Serenity Ko moaned.

'That is a *terrible* idea,' Optimism Rihan said.

'Yes, join us for our next tasting…' Good Cheer Eria suggested, exchanging a glance with Optimism Rihan.

'That might not be the best idea—' Optimism Rihan began.

'Excellent idea, I think I shall,' Serenity Ko said conclusively. 'It'll keep my mind off things.' And then she sighed, sagging against the wall. 'Sur-fuck me; it's all my fault.'

'Don't swear,' snapped a familiar voice. 'And stand up straight.'

Serenity Ko jolted out of her pity party, and found herself face to face with her Ammamma.

Why is sinfonia an exclusively Primian art form?

Because nobody else will willingly listen to it.

—Chari Charleston,
Earthling stand-up comedian
2065 Anno Earth | 1990 Interstellar Era

SIXTEEN

The Primian Sinfonia was performing Honour Xaro's "Opus No. 1: Nakshatrans Outside Time." Despite her composed, dignified demeanour, and her deep appreciation for Primian classical music, Optimism Mahd'vi found herself unable to enjoy the moving performance. Being face to face with the Kaveri girl, observing her up close, set off too many spirals of thought that refused to be swayed by the exquisite orchestra on stage. She'd carefully noted everything about the Earthling savage from the moment of her arrival at the Sinfonia Theatre. She'd appreciated the arresting deep purple luminoweave dress—wholly appropriate for the evening, and a surprisingly tasteful choice for an Earthling. The Kaveri girl had only given her savage origins away when, mouth agape from her first glimpse of the Theatre's flowmetal splendour, she'd uttered an entirely pedestrian, banal "Wow."

Optimism Mahd'vi had done her best not to smirk at the Earthling's provincial expression. The Sinfonia Theatre was marvellous, even by Primian architecture's high standards. It was shaped like a waveform in the sea of aesthetically astounding flowmetal structures that lined the streets of Collective Two, and it was sinuously spectacular. The building resembled an audio wave, and as the rest of the flowmetal city swivelled and reoriented itself ever so slowly, the Sinfonia Theatre's peaks and troughs rose and fell with a rhythm of its own.

'Rumour has it that the building keeps tempo with the music being played inside,' Optimism Mahd'vi had explained. 'I'm not its architect, so I can't say for sure. It's about five hundred years old.'

'It's incredible,' the Kaveri girl had gasped, like every Fringe-planet bumpkin Optimism Mahd'vi had encountered over the course of her long diplomatic career.

Optimism Mahd'vi made mental notes to be gentle but firm with her. She needed the Earthling to warm up to her, but didn't need to mollycoddle her while she was at it. 'It must far outclass anything you have on Earth.'

The girl's pale cheeks turned bright red, and she mumbled something inaudible. Her sallow skin was definitely the product of a skin-bleach procedure, Optimism Mahd'vi decided. Only the human settlers on Sagaricus were this lacking in melanin, because they were largely underwater and seldom exposed to the direct light of the stars.

'I'm sorry, I didn't catch that,' Optimism Mahd'vi said politely, trying to push her.

'The Earth's palaces are spectacular in their own way,' the Kaveri girl said boldly.

Her directness was barbaric. But then again, if the Kaveri girl really was a survivor, then she couldn't be judged for being a little rough around the edges, could she? The Earthling dignitaries she'd met had always been shockingly rude, and those were the *educated* ones, so the Kaveri girl couldn't be faulted for embodying her planet's culture—or lack thereof.

I should really start thinking of her as Saraswati, Optimism Mahd'vi had mused as they took their seats. *If I humanise her in my mind's eye, I'll be able to look straight into her heart and see what lies within*. It was an archaic piece of Nakshatran philosophy; seldom quoted, but often referred to in deeper philosophical debates on diplomacy.

The orchestra tuned their instruments, and a hush fell upon the audience, waiting in anticipation for the performance to begin.

The violoncellist played a long, quavering note, followed by a profound silence. And then a sweeping passage of exposition burst into the quietude, the violoncellos playing seemingly disparate scores, opening the first movement of the Opus, a meditation on freedom. The first violoncellist played long, drawn-out phrases at the upper end of their instrument's register, a wail of a melody contrasted by the urgency and choppiness of the musicians accompanying them. Through nuanced harmonies, the diverging voices of all the instruments would slowly tend to musical resolution, symbolising the eternal peace of the unknowable future, but it would take around forty minutes to arrive at the calm. Beside her, Optimism Mahd'vi noticed Saraswati wince, rigidly stiff at the edge of her seat.

The rhythmic plucking of a chordophone aggressively rose in tempo and volume, and stole the limelight from the violoncellist, its player seated cross-legged in sweeping robes upon the stage, plucking multiple strings in simultaneity. The two instruments engaged in a gloriously dissonant conversation, and a duet of flutes played in counterpoint. The string section created a low, droning hum in the background. Every now and again, a spotlight caught a lone woman on stage, who sang dizzying snatches of an aria, while a triangle chimed an accompaniment and a theremin created a soundscape that shouldn't have been.

'Excerpts from the *Nakshatranāma* in its original language,' Optimism Mahd'vi whispered to her guest, eyeing Saraswati Kaveri's wide-eyed startle each time the vocalist began to sing. Some of her vocal melodies were polyphonic, an eerie experience even for those accustomed to the sound, and Saraswati Kaveri evidently wasn't.

There was a crescendo towards tumultuous, impossibly high notes, and the piece ended on a single discordant note held across all instruments.

Optimism Mahd'vi caught sight of Saraswati's fingernails digging into her seat. 'Breathtaking, isn't it?'

'Yes,' Saraswati replied, smiling weakly.

The second movement began with the percussion section playing in polyrhythms. Optimism Mahd'vi knew this was popular with young children—it was often used to introduce them to the idea of the sinfonia—and she grimaced when she observed her barbarian guest tapping her foot to snatches of the beat.

'This must be very alien to you,' Optimism Mahd'vi suggested. 'After all, Earth music isn't quite as… what's the right word?' She paused, pretending to think about it, and then continued in Vox as an intentional insult. 'Not quite as *sophisticated*.'

Saraswati's cheeks turned a furious red, as her mouth twitched soundlessly. *Really, these Earthlings are all so easy to read.*

'It's not as *experimental,*' Saraswati Kaveri said, practically hissing the last word in Ur-speak. 'And there's no telling if an experiment is working or not, is there?'

Optimism Mahd'vi was amused by the barb—it hinted at slightly higher intelligence than she'd presumed. *Must be the Kaveri genes,* she thought immediately, before catching herself. *Assuming the Kaveri identity is true.*

After the third movement was played, Optimism Mahd'vi invited Saraswati to a closed off refreshments booth. Once they were served their cups of starfruit wine, she studied the Earthling woman across the table from her. An effective rule of any negotiation was to say as little as possible, encouraging the other person to spill all their secrets, play all their bargaining chips, and be eager to please—anything to fill the dreaded, awkward, burgeoning silence. Optimism Mahd'vi was a masterful player of this game, and she sought to draw Saraswati's secrets out of her by wielding the power of dead air.

'Thank you so much for having me as your guest, Secretary,' Saraswati said politely, breaking the silence as expected. 'This has been an enriching experience, and I look forward to the second half of the performance. I humbly express my gratitude to you for sharing your culture with me.'

She raised her glass in a toast. It was a ridiculously trite diplomatic speech, and Optimism Mahd'vi countered with a contrived toast of her own. 'Ah, young Earthling. Thank you for doing me the honour of suffering an old woman's presence, and for being open to having a conversation with her. A government official is always only ever lonely.'

They tapped glasses, then exchanged them, in the Primian tradition for unofficial but formal meetings between strangers.

Each sipped from the other's glass, waiting for the silence to be broken.

'That's delicious!' Saraswati Kaveri exclaimed. 'Rich, fruity body, a hint of mineral undertones…' The smile that broke across her face was genuine; Optimism Mahd'vi detected a chink in her facade and let her carry on. 'And are those upper notes spiced?'

'You're the culinary prodigy,' Optimism Mahd'vi said flatteringly.

'You're too kind. I detect some nutmeg and… black pepper? I'm sorry, it's equivalent on Primus is the peprino-corn?'

'An astute palate if I ever saw one.' Optimism Mahd'vi flashed an approving smile. 'I find it astonishing that someone with no cooking credentials has found their way into shaping the future of galactic cuisine. You must be tremendously gifted.'

'Ah, I'm merely passionate about food,' Saraswati said demurely.

'The mastery of *our* techniques you demonstrated on the *MegaChef* special, coupled with the innovations to *our* cuisine, necessitate a culinary background, hmm? Primian cooking doesn't come easily to most people.'

'I-I worked as a line cook in a small restaurant on Earth,' Saraswati said hurriedly. Optimism Mahd'vi made note of the slight stutter.

'Indeed, all while concealing your identity from those persecuting you.'

'Yes, a *very small* restaurant.' The words tumbling out of her mouth now. 'So small as to escape any official attention.'

'Brave.'

'I couldn't just hide, waiting for them to come for me,' Saraswati said boldly.

Far too boldly, Optimism Mahd'vi thought. *Especially if you had knowledge of the massacre of our clan.*

'I applaud your courage as a Kauvery,' she said out loud, intentionally mispronouncing the name to distance herself from it. 'The Kauvery were a very persecuted family.'

'Yes, but I wasn't even born when they were hunted down.'

Optimism Mahd'vi leaned forward. 'Your parents survived?'

She thought she detected a nervous swallow, and a bead of sweat broke upon Saraswati's brow. 'M-my mother was a distant member of the family. Through marriage. She escaped to Protectorate Paradiso…' Saraswati paused. 'Ah, but you're probably unfamiliar with Earth-politics. And I ramble on. This starfruit wine is really most excellent.'

'So you grew up in Protectorate Paradiso?'

'I was born there. I studied there, too. At a culinary school.'

'And they protected your identity?'

Saraswati took a sip of her wine. 'Until recently, yes. I had no idea I was being tracked by the Daxina Protectorate until recently, when my life came under threat. That's why I had to escape.'

'Such a tragedy.' Optimism Mahd'vi tutted sympathetically. 'To flee from the life you've painstakingly built from nothing.'

'It was a difficult decision that had to be made,' Saraswati said haltingly.

'Your audition video for *Interstellar MegaChef* was particularly devastating,' Optimism Mahd'vi said, shaking her head sadly. 'It looked like your kitchen was tumbling down all around you. An attack of that scale in a neighbouring Protectorate—Paradiso, you say?—surely constitutes an act of war…'

'That happened in Daxina,' Saraswati said softly. 'Where I was born…'

'You returned?'

'With a false identity.'

'Why?'

'To see where I came from.'

'At immense risk to your own life?'

Saraswati stared at her in unreadable silence.

'I'm sorry, talking about my past makes me uncomfortable,' she finally said.

'Of course, forgive me. I don't mean to be insensitive,' Optimism Mahd'vi said placatingly. 'I just find your story so remarkable; a true tale of resilience and courage against all odds, a fable of rebirth on Primus…'

'Thank you.'

'Naturally, I want to know how we might best help you. Especially given recent unpleasant events.'

'You're most generous.'

'Not at all. Primus opens its skies to all who seek refuge. We wish to help you rebuild.'

'Thank you.'

Optimism Mahd'vi sipped on her wine, her mind racing in a multitude of directions. Saraswati's story was far too convenient, and quite simply didn't add up. Then again, her own survival story—being spirited away to an entirely different planet with her twin brother—was equally remarkable. But Saraswati had been spotted in the company of an Earthling prince who—historically, at least—should have been an enormous threat to her life and livelihood. Jog Tunga was allied to the Godavari clan, and the Godavaris had murdered the Kaveris and their followers in cold blood...

Optimism Mahd'vi decided on one of the many tactics she'd prepared for this meeting.

'I wanted to speak to you, directly—woman to woman, if you will,' she began gently. 'Personally, I'm horrified by the Primians who are attempting to smear your reputation. It appals me, and it's against everything we stand for as a culture. I'm sorry.'

'You are most kind. If there's one thing I've learnt, it's that every culture has its bad eggs,' Saraswati replied.

'Indeed. And on that note, forgive me for being so direct about this, but someone who *could* be a threat to your life has been spotted multiple times on this planet. An Earthling prince named Jog Tunga. An *ally* to the Godavari clan, responsible for the murders of so many of ou—' She caught herself in time, and corrected herself. 'Of so many of *your* people.'

Saraswati's eyes were glassy and expressionless. She stared at Optimism Mahd'vi evenly, and Optimism Mahd'vi met her gaze with one of deep concern, even leaning forward and patting her hand awkwardly, as if to reassure her. She wielded the dead air like a subtle knife. Saraswati matched her, her defences seemingly uncrackable. But her lack of reaction, the expressionless eyes and the resolute set of her jaw told Optimism Mahd'vi everything she needed to know.

Optimism Mahd'vi's heart raced faster the longer the silence stretched on. All her very worst suspicions were likely true. The Earthling prince and this Kaveri pretender—for *surely* she was a confirmed pretender now—were clearly colluding on something that would be to the detriment of Primus, perhaps all the galaxy. She removed her hand from where it lay on Saraswati's and nonchalantly sipped on the last of her starfruit wine, weighing her options.

She could have Saraswati taken away and interrogated—she'd figure out how to fill out the scrollwork justifying it later. She could say nothing at all, and instead build their relationship on the off chance that she might be able to trap Saraswati. It was clear the young woman didn't trust her, though trust was a relative thing, entirely dependent on how hostile she made the circumstances around her.

And then, there was the crushing disappointment welling up within her, brought on by her growing certainty that Saraswati was not "the Kaveri girl," or a Kaveri at all. It was accompanied by bitterness at being hoodwinked, taken in by her own desperate need to find a link to her lost origins.

Did she even need to use the Kaveri test, the riddle she'd had her brother, Harmony Sukran, remind her of over dinner the other day?

Once, a river sage was passing through an Earthling village. They were looking for new disciples, to pass on their philosophy so they might rule the world. Each of the village's clans sent their smartest children to pass the river sage's test. Each child was to present them with a riddle that they couldn't solve—

An explosion rocked the ground.

Optimism Mahd'vi fell to the floor. The table crashed down upon her, pinning her in place. Her ears ringing, her vision blurry, the last thing she registered was Saraswati hovering over her, her face a stricken mask, before her phalanx of security drones closed around the Earthling and the world faded to black.

Honour Olive: Grace Menmo has been ominously silent about Feast
Boundless Xan: Ah, but it is her granddaughter's brainchild, after all...
Curiosity Lev: NO!
Honour Olive: You heard right!
Serenity Aya: We'll get into all the details. But first... Grace Menmo, we love you!

—*Four Chefs*, Season 3, Episode 3
2075 Anno Earth | 2000 Interstellar Era

SEVENTEEN

'MY FAVOURITE AND *only* granddaughter has taken to ignoring her grandmother.'

Ammamma affected a slouch, raised a quivering hand to her face, and pretended to wipe a tear from her eye, her lips scrunched up, the wrinkles lining them standing out starkly pitiful despite the dim, soothing light at their chef's table. Good Cheer Eria appeared to be on the verge of tears herself, and Optimism Rihan tutted sympathetically, encouraging the old woman. Serenity Ko scowled at them all.

'I haven't been ignoring you. I've been busy,' she said crossly.

'Too busy for your only surviving grandmother. I gave you your first bath when you were a baby. I cooked your first solid meal—it was rasam grain-pulp, and I added an extra dollop of ghee-spheres in the bowl, a labour of love...' Her voice wobbled as she trailed off.

Good Cheer Eria's eyes shone, and she reached out and held Ammamma's hand, giving Serenity Ko a disappointed frown.

'All I ask is that my streams be returned—one in every *five* will do. Is that too much to ask?' Ammamma said pathetically.

'I'm sorry,' Serenity Ko said insincerely. Her grandmother was trying to guilt her into a vulnerable headspace so she could sink her fangs into her—as Grace Menmo—and take a bite out of her.

Ammamma sighed dramatically. 'And with my favourite grandson's wedding right around the corner, too. This is a time for *family,* and instead, my favourite granddaughter is off chasing flights of fancy—'

'I *said* I'm sorry.'

'What a pleasure it is to seat *the* Grace Menmo at my chef's table this evening!'

Ammamma stiffened, her back ramrod straight, all trace of weakness leaving her in an instant. An elegant smile transformed her from a pathetic, neglected old woman into a formidable and discerning—yet polite—authority on Primian culture, especially Primian cooking.

'Why, Boundless Evi,' she said, her voice strong and commanding. She turned to greet the Executive Chef of Transformateur as she arrived at their table and bent down to plant air kisses on the old woman's cheeks. 'It's a pleasure to see you, my dear.'

Serenity Ko did her best to hide, sinking into the plush cushions of the small booth that enclosed them and attempting to hide her face behind a large, very transparent carafe of impeccably crystal clear water. She dropped her napkin when it became apparent that she was still very much in plain sight, then took the excuse to duck under the table, only to thwack her head on it.

'Ah, and it's lovely to host you again, Serenity Ko,' Boundless Evi said politely, her smile frosting over somewhat.

Serenity Ko couldn't blame her. The last time she'd eaten at Transformateur, she'd been on the prowl for sim ideas to inspire Feast, and while the restaurant had sparked a ton of them, she'd been left hungry by the minimalist portions on the tasting menu. She'd embarrassed herself—and her grandmother—by asking Boundless Evi if there was anything *more* she could eat after the dessert course had been served. *That was the* old *Ko,* she reminded herself severely. *The* new *Ko is* nice.

'It's wonderful to be here again,' Serenity Ko said. 'Really loved it the last time round.'

'Glad to hear it,' Boundless Evi said disbelievingly, then proceeded to address the table. 'Honour Les will be your server for this evening's wedding tasting menus. If there's anything specific you need from me, any special requests at all, just let them know and they'll find me at the pass.'

'One of our brightest and best,' Ammamma declared as Boundless Evi strode away.

Honour Les beamed when they heard the compliment directed at their boss, and attentively walked them through the tasting menu. 'We have three menus, each recommended for a different type of wedding theme. Each has substitutes for our honoured chlorosapient guests, including the beautiful bride herself. Congratulations to the happy couple! We'll be presenting you with five dishes from each menu, for you to judge—and hopefully delight in—and all paired with wines hand-selected from the cellars.

'Naturally, we don't do *cocktails*,' Honour Les laughed in conclusion. 'Or sims.'

'*Certainly* not for a wedding, that would be most inappropriate,' Ammamma said, beaming in approval as Honour Les walked away to arrange their set of first courses. 'Especially the sims.'

Serenity Ko scowled at the barb. And her heart sank at the thought of no cocktails, but she felt a vicious spike of joy when she saw Optimism Rihan's face fall, too. She smiled at him innocently. 'But we tried cocktails at our earlier tasting—'

'What earlier tasting?' Ammamma hissed, rounding on Optimism Rihan.

'What tasting?' Optimism Rihan enquired benignly. 'We only had lunch together.'

'*What*. Earlier. Tasting?' Ammamma repeated, eyeing Good Cheer Eria sternly.

She didn't have a chance. Few did, under Ammamma's gaze. Serenity Ko's heart *almost* went out to her as she tripped and stumbled through their disastrous experimental food experience at The Bespoke Nakshatran. Ammamma's eyes grew round as saucers as Good Cheer Eria described the food they'd been offered, and then twinkled with mirth by the time she recounted how Serenity Ko had planned their escape. She laughed merrily at the end, and Optimism Rihan, evidently believing that the old lady had let them off the hook, joined in.

'Really, what was Dozer thinking?' he asked, chuckling.

'What was *Dozer* thinking?' Ammamma snapped. 'What were *you* thinking?'

Optimism Rihan quailed. Serenity Ko revelled in her nice guy brother being the subject of unfriendly scrutiny for a change. He muttered something that sounded like "mimsy-whimsy-toodle."

'Speak up, Rihan.'

Right then, the first course appeared with Honour Les, a broad smile upon their face. They placed four beautiful plates before the family—each segmented into three parts, featuring a wildly minimalist dish—and proceeded to walk them through each one.

'For the first, a filigreed forever knot—very traditional, made from honey-froth and thyme-ras…'

A sudden emptiness lurched within Serenity Ko, and it wasn't hunger. It was an aching, yawning hole inside her where she missed Saraswati with every fibre of her being. She'd have been right at home at this table. She'd have understood all the fancy food words being spoken. But Saras had ignored every single stream she'd sent her since the riot, and it did not bode well.

Serenity Ko had attempted every line of argument there was, beginning with a simple, straightforward—and admittedly insincere—apology. When that hadn't worked, she'd switched to pointing out that they *had* to talk if they wanted to maintain a functioning professional relationship. She'd tried to make her laugh by mocking their Feast pop-up diners. She'd even streamed Saras with wholehearted sympathy, only to be stonewalled with silence.

The nagging, shameful feeling of resorting to Honour Aki-esque persistence gnawed at Serenity Ko's insides, with a far more unasked for twinge of *sympathy* for the man. *It must feel terrible to be him, whenever I'm around,* she thought uncomfortably, only to then spiral into arguments in her defence—after all, she'd made her feelings for him, or lack thereof, crystal clear. *Repeatedly.*

In her case, Saraswati hadn't, not really…

The smell of something both sweet and spiced wafted up to her from her plate, and she unconsciously reached for what had been described as the forever knot. She picked it up and, still lost in her thoughts, shovelled it into her mouth, letting the golden sugary sweetness of the honey-froth dance across her tongue, while the thyme-ras-infused pastry crackled against the roof of her mouth, and a burst of sour cherry exploded against her palate.

'Ohmygoodness,' she leaned her head back against the cushions, suddenly reminded of eating Berry-annas with Saraswati. It was gone in barely a swallow.

'So, Ko approves,' Optimism Rihan said.

'Overpowering.' Ammamma tutted.

'What do you mean? It's *bursting* with flavour,' Serenity Ko argued.

'Too much for the first course at a wedding. Everything at a wedding has to be delicate, precise…' Ammamma said condescendingly. She took a sip of the recommended wine pairing and blanched. 'Too fruity.'

'Right, of course,' Optimism Rihan said, tossing Serenity Ko a warning look and smoothing over their disagreement.

'It's only *your* big day of course,' Ammamma said, glancing from Optimism Rihan to Good Cheer Eria. 'If you want to take chances with it, then by all means, go ask your friend to cater the feast. Or, you know, listen to *Ko's* opinions on food…'

'Unfair,' Serenity Ko muttered.

'*This* is far more to my liking,' Ammama said, completely ignoring her. She popped a delicate, flaky white morsel into her mouth. 'Thengai-nut pastry surrounding a molten chilli jam mousse at the centre. Perfect for piquing the appetite.'

Serenity Ko scooped it up off her plate and tasted it, and had to grudgingly admit that her grandmother was right.

'Eria, which of your terrines do you like?' she asked,

including her in the conversation before Ammamma could make any snide remarks at her or her brother's expense again.

'The thengai-milk infused one,' Good Cheer Eria said softly. 'It's very subtly flavoured.'

'Excellent, we don't even need to taste the last one. It's decided,' Ammamma said imperiously, waving Honour Les over. She took a sip of the wine pairing. 'Would it be possible to have a more earthy wine to accompany this?' she asked politely.

'Of course,' Honour Les smiled. 'I'll see what our sommelier can recommend.'

'If you give me your wine list, I'm sure I'll be able to find something,' Ammamma offered.

'Naturally, we'd be delighted.'

'Lovely. We've settled on the ten thousand forevers millefeuille for the first course,' Ammamma announced as the plates were cleared away.

Good Cheer Eria paled beneath her vibrant green makeup. She threw her fiancé a despairing glance.

Optimism Rihan cleared his throat. 'Um, Ammamma…'

'Yes?'

'Well, we… um, we really appreciate your bringing us here, and introducing us to Boundless Evi's food—I mean, it's spectacular, isn't it, Eria?'

'Yes, absolutely lovely,' she said in a strained voice.

Serenity Ko looked on in glee, wondering what pronouncement Optimism Rihan was about to make, likely to her grandmother's growing ire. It was pleasant to have Ammamma's vexations directed away from herself, for a change.

'What're you trying to say, Rihan?'

'We… we're just not sure we want Transformateur to cater our wedding. It's *such* fancy food, and really, we're very regular people…'

Ammamma smiled gently. 'Oh, Rihan. Don't worry, we'll go try Optimism Gon's kitchen if you aren't happy with this.'

'And lick the walls?' Serenity Ko snorted.

Ammamma glowered at her.

'His restaurant only opens once every nava, and the whole

thing is edible—' She explained for Optimism Rihan's benefit. 'You can lick it all—'

'We're very happy with this,' Optimism Rihan said loudly.

'What's the problem, then?' Ammamma asked waspishly.

'It just feels excessive, don't you think? Fine dining at a wedding feast instead of home-style food…'

'You're *Grace Menmo's grandson,*' Ammamma said sharply.

Serenity Ko quaffed the wine remaining in the tasting glass before her, slyly reaching out for one of her brother's cups and knocking it back as well. This was getting good.

'I know,' Optimism Rihan practically whimpered.

'*Several* of my friends from the *industry* will be at your wedding,' Ammamma continued like a steamroller.

'I know. It's just…'

'It's me,' Good Cheer Eria said lightly. 'As a chlorosapient, my beliefs forbid excess when it comes to what we eat.'

'Of course, dearie, but Evi's got an entire menu that caters to your needs,' Ammamma said dismissively.

'It's not just what *I* eat,' Good Cheer Eria said, an insistent smile on her face. 'It's what *we* project, the future I'm symbolically supporting through this union…'

Her voice trailed off as a frown swept across Ammamma's face.

'For the second course,' Honour Les cut in, swiftly placing plates before them all. 'We have—'

'Honour Les, darling, we all need a minute,' Ammamma said, wearing a charmingly false smile. 'I'll handle the explanations; they're all on the Loop menu, aren't they?'

'Y-yes, of course.'

Honour Les retreated, clearly very embarrassed at having interrupted some kind of private family moment. Serenity Ko knocked back one of the fresh cups of wine that had been placed before her—pairing be damned—and watched the deep lines etch themselves into Ammamma's forehead again. *Oh, this is really good.*

'Are you telling me that you'd rather have experimental food—or Nine Virtues forbid, off-world food—at your wedding?'

Her voice was ominously low, and Serenity Ko flinched, even though the question wasn't directed at her.

'Are you telling me that you're going to disregard the culinary offerings of this *fine* restaurant, at the very cutting edge of all Primian expression, to serve the guests at your wedding *slop* cobbled together at some… marketplace, or *street food stall?*' Ammamma seemed to swell as her voice dropped even lower.

'No, of course not. We're just not certain that we've found the perfect caterer yet, that's all,' Optimism Rihan whispered, quailing under the intensity of the old lady's questioning.

'Oh, good, then we can proceed with the tasting,' Ammamma said benignly. 'I thought you were going to betray me, too, Rihan. Forgive me. Just because one grandchild chooses to stick a knife in my back in ingratitude and hubris, doesn't mean my other grandchild will, too.' She laughed airily, and then looked daggers at Serenity Ko, who gulped.

Ammamma picked up something wrapped in a carefully constructed hollow sphere, glowing in rainbow colours from within. 'Ah, this must be the broth suspension.' She tasted, chewed, swallowed. 'Evokes the earthiness of the woods; some lovely shrooming ras in there, Eria, darling. Very evocative of the Faith of the Light.'

Good Cheer Eria tasted the equivalent pâté on her plate and delightedly agreed, her bright tones only slightly strained. 'Delicious.'

'Now I'm not sure what my granddaughter is doing at this tasting, Rihan. She's repeatedly demonstrated scant regard or respect for our food culture, wouldn't you agree?'

'I—'

'Going so far as to create food that *isn't* food, that's a *sim* playing out in the mind, while diners chew on processed, edible cardboard. No offence to Harmony Li, Eria dear, but surely, surviving on edibites is a *choice*.'

'Consuming Feast is a choice, too,' Serenity Ko said tersely.

'Of course it is. And yet, you choose to ignore me, refuse to engage in conversation with me...'

'You've already made your views clear, Ammmama,'

Serenity Ko responded coolly. 'You disapprove of it because I've invented the future of food, while all you've done with our cuisine is try and maintain its past.'

'Ah, how stunted of me, to preserve a thousand-year-old cultural tradition.' Ammamma's tone dripped hostility.

Don't engage, she's goading you into sniping at her, Serenity Ko thought. She tried to focus on soothing visuals, like the sight of empty space when she went slinging, the neon blue glow of a nilatini done right, the soft rouge moue of Saraswati's lips...

'I understand that you were trying to be charitable to that Earthling. And you know me, I'm no xenophobe, so if you want to pursue a romantic relationship with her, then be my guest... but inviting her into our kitchens, using the food knowledge that *I* blessed you with, all to destroy our heritage—'

'*You* did nothing but belittle me all through our time together,' Serenity Ko snapped. 'I *tried* to learn from you, but Saras is the only one who didn't treat me like an idiot.'

'I didn't treat you like an idiot, Ko,' Ammamma said firmly. 'I only showed a little tough love, and tried to set realistic expectations.'

'Enjoying the second course?' Honour Les asked, continuing their habit of appearing at inopportune moments.

'*Yes!*' everyone chorused around the table in near unison.

'The port is absolutely perfect to pair with the broth of moss and memory,' Ammamma said cheerily, giving nothing about the ongoing disagreement away. Serenity Ko had to hand it to her—the old dragon had an immaculate poker face.

'Ah, that's one of our signature dishes,' Honour Les said with pride. 'We always hear the loveliest things about it. The shroomings are freshly sourced from the Arc each nava, and steeped in a vine-leaf vinegar for up to seven navas before they're deemed ready for ras extraction. The broth itself is agitated in our ice centrifuge—a novel technology that we've been using...'

Ammamma listened to Honour Les prattle on with the appearance of undivided attention.

Optimism Rihan gently kicked Serenity Ko beneath the table, and right as she was about to kick him back—a good ten times harder—he streamed: _What are you *doing?*_

What is *she* doing?

She's being Ammamma.

She's being awful.

You *know* how touchy she is about food, Ko.

*You* put her in a bad mood by turning down her favourite restaurant as your wedding caterer.

I didn't turn it down.

Ah, so you're going to cave. Typical.

I haven't caved yet, either.

*Yet,* Rihan. Oh so very typical, Serenity Ko sulked. _You'll do the nice guy, people pleasing thing eventually, and then she'll go back to picking on me._

She's not picking on you, Ko, Rihan said patiently. _She just wants to talk to you. And in typical fashion, you've been ignoring her._

I know what she wants to say, Serenity Ko snapped. _She wants to criticise Feast._

Have a conversation with her. Hear her out. She's old, Ko. Sometimes old folks just want to be heard.

Serenity Ko's cheeks burned with shame then. She'd been behaving like a petulant child, when really, she owed her grandmother a conversation. Perhaps not an explanation, but a conversation.

'I'm sorry for ignoring you, Ammamma,' she bit out, as soon as Honour Les had left their table to bring them the next course.

'What? Speak up, child.'

Serenity Ko could have sworn she'd heard her just fine, but she repeated herself.

'It's fine,' Ammamma said haughtily. 'I forgive you. You're just afraid I'll poke holes in your pet project.'

'Am not.'

'I just want to have a conversation with you.'

'Let's schedule something,' Serenity Ko said brusquely.

'That sounds agreeable to me.'

They glared at each other across the dinner table.

'I suppose it could be worse,' Ammamma laughed, breaking the silence. 'At least Rihan and Eria haven't asked you to cater their wedding.'

A wicked thought struck Serenity Ko, and she grinned. 'Rihan. Eria,' she began brightly. 'How would you like Feast to cater your wedding? It's on the house,' she added for good measure.

Optimism Rihan's jaw dropped, and Good Cheer Eria clapped her hands over her mouth.

'Oh, come on. It isn't the worst idea in the world…' Serenity Ko carried on.

Ammamma dropped her wineglass.

'Now that's just rude, Ammamma.'

And then a notification popped up on Serenity Ko's Loop feed right as sirens began to ring out. A flashing red exclamation point surrounded by a bright red circle occupied her field of vision.

URGENT: Explosion at the Sinfonia Theatre. All Primian citizens in the first ten Collectives to return to their homes *immediately*. Follow the security force's instructions. No exceptions.

Serenity Ko's mouth went dry. 'Where's Saras?'

United Human Cooperative-occupied space has been demilitarised following the Trust Protocol.

Suspected exceptions are the Fringe Planets, most notably those in the Solar System...

—*After Earth:*
A Comprehensive Encyclopaedia of Greater Human Space
2025 Anno Earth | 1950 Interstellar Era

EIGHTEEN

THE ROAR OF a million engines drowned my senses.

The floor wobbled. The walls around me rocked frenetically. My ears rang with a high-pitched keening.

Optimism Mahd'vi's chair was flung out from under her. She crashed to the floor, the table crashing down upon her. I lunged to grab her and a hailstorm of flying drones slammed into me. I dropped to the floor, frozen in place by their deadweight.

Saras! Kili hollered, struggling to free himself from my pocket, where I lay on top of him.

Stay, I commanded, willing him not to roll out. I struggled to free myself.

A gaping hole had ripped into the wall beside me, and the flowmetal structure dripped into it as if it were melting through a hatch into the vacuum of space, unspooling like a ribbon against all rules of planetary gravity.

My fingers twitched in panic. I was immobilised, my mind a flurry of fragmented thoughts like so much shrapnel.

Optimism Mahd'vi had been circling like a hawk, impaling my fabricated Earth-origins story with her questions about my being a Kaveri. *Why?*

And now she was on the ground... *Is she dead?*

There'd been the sound like a thunderclap. *A quake?*

My stomach twisted inside out as I slid along the floor. The drones pinning me in place scrabbled for purchase, gouging holes in the ground from the effort, shrieking across the flowmetal so loud they drowned the ringing in my ears. They snapped off the surface like buttons. I slid, racing towards the ever-widening void in the wall, my vision partially obscured by my halo of curls.

Fuck, the grav-management must be out.

‘Fuck—’

Something slammed into my middle, knocking the breath out of me, right as I reached the edge of the wall and caught a glimpse of what was a long way down, sideways, into a rupture in the side of the theatre that extended all the way into the next building, and the next one…

A large mechanical claw was wrapped around my torso. I wriggled my head around and saw an entire platoon of the Primian Guard behind me. They’d secured Optimism Mahd’vi to some kind of stretcher, which was bearing her out of the wrecked room, through a large rent in the ceiling. One of the Guard pointed beyond me, and aimed a large lightning launcher…

I spun my head around.

‘Kili!’ I screamed. ‘They’re going to fire at you.’

He must have been knocked out of my pocket!

I’ll find you, he said, racing away from me. _They think I’m a weapo—_

A burst of light slammed into him. He was knocked off course, plummeting towards the unknowable far end of the chasm. My breath hitched, then stopped altogether. My chest felt like it was about to burst.

*Kili? Kili!*

The silence that replied was numbing. I shoved against the flowmetal wall, all thought of my safety damned all the way to the Earth and back again, propelling myself through it, and found the claw’s grip on me unbreakable. I heard nothing but the ringing in my ears, and a deafening stillness where Kili should have been.

‘We know your target was Optimism Mahd’vi, *Earthling*,’ the new nameless interrogator pronounced. ‘We know you were either directly responsible for the explosion, or that you helped the *savage* who was.'

I glowered at them in stony silence. My heart was a hole where Kili was meant to be.

I was terrified that I was going to be condemned for it all and deported. My hands shook so violently—and had been shaking nonstop for an age since I'd been here—that I clenched them into fists, and my wrists were beginning to lose all feeling. I was doing my best to be bold and brazen, to adopt the kind of stance that would evade any kind of suspicion. I knew my scrollwork was good, fake though my proclaimed identity was. I'd spent most of my life savings to ensure all traces of my past were erased off the Loop. Any way to connect Saraswati *Kaveri* with Saraswati *Godavari* would be impossible to find…

There are always loopholes, said a dark voice. I shoved it away.

'Here's how this is going to go down,' the interrogator said, repeating all the official threats that had been delivered to me over what had felt like days. There was no way to tell how much time had passed. I was in a windowless room, my Loop access was blocked, and my head hurt. I could hear again, but that was as far as the good news went.

'You will confess to your involvement and tell us which of the barbarians put you up to it. We will see if we can go easy on you, and maybe even cut a deal on your sentencing. A steady job in exile, mining on a space station, sounds pretty reasonable given the carnage, doesn't it? It'll even be a level up from life on Earth.'

'I know my rights,' I shot back, repeating myself for the umpteenth time. 'I'm entitled to say nothing, and to legal counsel. As a refugee, I'm protected by the character referral codes—they're in your own laws, look them up? I can produce multiple Primian citizens who will vouch for my character. And I'm entitled to request comms to *all* of them. I'm also entitled to press charges against you for the *destruction of my personal tech* with no probable cause, namely my *Winger,* whom one of your imbecile units shot *despite* not having established *any* threat whatsoever.'

I willed myself not to stumble over my words, or give into the yawning ache within me that threatened to burst out of me in a flood of tears at the thought of Kili.

'Also, your xenophobic slurs are being noted. I will be raising those to the authorities, too. So,' I concluded. 'You either adopt a more civil tone, and politely let me out of your very dramatic dungeon, or I will make your lives incredibly miserable.'

'Is that a threat?' The interrogator twisted the end of a rather fraying moustache.

I sighed. I was glad that part of my diplomacy training on Earth had been a firm grounding in negotiation, and on immigration bylaws. And one of the first rules was to never lose one's temper, which was proving incredibly hard to do.

'It's not a threat. It's an indication of my intention to pursue recourse for the mental and emotional damage done to me.'

'Indeed,' Moustache said. 'And what about the mental and emotional damage *you* and *your lot* have inflicted upon the friends and families of the innocent Primian citizens who were present at the sinfonia this evening? Two hundred and one civilians seriously injured, with another three hundred moderately injured or in shock, with still more cases being reported by the hour. The ruins of a bomb twisted around the foundations of the grav-management hydraulics in the building, woven into the very flowmetal fabric itself. A bomb with aural sensitivity, charged by sound frequencies in the air. No fire, just sonic destruction. That's *off-world* tech.'

'Earthlings love fire,' I muttered.

'Hah! Is that a confession?' Moustache pointed a finger at me dramatically.

'Look, I come from the planet Earth. I ran away from it—check my scrollwork. I'm a *refugee,*' I insisted. Going on the offensive and daring them to pull up my records again was the only thing standing in the way of a complete investigation into my origins. And I *knew* my Loop credentials were clear. They *had* to be if I'd gotten this far already…

'I've witnessed wars on Earth,' I carried on. 'Ran away, as

I've said already. Lots of things blowing up, sparks and flames. A sonic bomb isn't an Earthling weapon.'

'So you confess familiarity with Earthling weapons?'

'Watch a news-stream. *Everyone* knows how they work.'

'Do you confess you know how they work?' Moustache asked excitedly.

'Start fire, make boom,' I said drily. 'I thought you said this was a sonic bomb. That's Martian tech.'

'Aha! You confess knowledge of *their* tech, then?'

'Mars and Earth fought a hundred-year war. The sonic bombs devastated thousands of Earthling lives. It's history,' I said. 'The kind of history that *every* Earthling *child* knows.'

Moustache zoned out, tugging at their facial hair intensely, and it was evident that they were looking it up on the Loop. Their ignorance was typical; I'd found that folks on Primus seldom concerned themselves with any history that didn't directly place them front and centre.

'You're right, Earthlings don't like subtlety...' Moustache trailed off, lost in thought. 'Your weapon of choice was the ray bomb.'

'Listen, do I look like I could build a bomb? I can barely use a sim.'

'You're a cook. You're good with your hands.' Moustache sniffed, then muttered. 'Just like every off-worlder from a Fringe planet. "Can't fire up an algorithm, will set fire to your house."'

I laughed humourlessly. 'Are you actually quoting an Ur-drama slur? Do you think that will get to me?'

'Listen, my friend,' Moustache said, evidently coming to a slew of illogical conclusions and leaning forward. 'You're one of only forty *off-worlders* who were in the Collective at the time of the incident. And one of *only three* from the Fringe planets, the *only one* from the Solar System ...'

'Are you saying only off-worlders are capable of violence?'

'Aren't they?'

'Aren't *you*?'

'You were the *only one* in close proximity to Optimism Mahd'vi.'

'*She* invited me to the sinfonia as her guest,' I said firmly before I could fly off the handle. 'How's she doing?'

'Are you expecting me to tell you if your plan worked?'

I ignored the question.

'I'll play it straight with you,' Moustache continued. 'You're an Earthling. And a refugee. You mysteriously showed up on this planet nearly a year ago.'

'With *legal* scrollwork,' I insisted. My scrollwork was perfectly legitimate; it was my *identity* that was completely false. I continued on, talking very slowly, repeating myself. 'With legal scrollwork. To take part in a *cooking show*.'

'Spies assume all sorts of covers.'

My insides churned, my gorge rising, as a wave of fear nearly drowned me. My lips twitched involuntarily. I urged them still.

Moustache grinned. 'We've tracked your movements and behaviours. Erratic, frequent changes of occupation—'

'Because most of the people on this planet are sur-fucked assholes who are impossible to work with—'

'A sudden change of living space—'

'I discovered the Faith—' I lied, but was cut off again.

'Destroying traditional Primian food on the *MegaChef* special aired across the galaxy—'

'*It was a dramatic way to present Feast on the plate!*'

'So you deny all involvement in the assassination attempt on Optimism Mahd'vi? You deny that you're a spy?'

'I flat out deny that I'm a spy. I'm outraged that you could even suggest it.'

Moustache left the room, interminable minutes ticked by, a new nameless interrogator took their place, and we began again. I steadied my shaking hands. I willed myself to stay calm, to betray nothing. I begged and pleaded with the cold, unforgiving universe to make sure I wasn't discovered or deported.

All the while, I blocked all thoughts of Kili from my mind.

* * *

In sequence: I'd spoken to the Loud One, who'd yelled at me. Then there was the Rude One, who threw every Earthling slur they had in the books at me—from the relatively benign "sun-fucker" to the outright insulting "dirt-licker." The Hostile One threatened me with every consequence including being spaced, which I knew had been illegal for the past few hundred years but didn't let on about. The Sugary One tried to sweet-talk me into implicating myself by offering me Primian pastries and kaapi.

I'd thought my time on Primus, facing constant hostile stream-media scrutiny, would have prepared me for this level of accusation and xenophobia.

I was wrong.

And I was exhausted.

They'd cycled through in the same order a second time, then sent in Moustache, whom I was beginning to think of as the Incompetent One. Every once in a while, the Tin-Foil-Hat One would step into the room to interrupt these one-sided conversations with a visio-cube, projecting conspiracy theories on the wall.

'Around the time of your arrival on Primus, Optimism Mahd'vi was insulted by an Earthling prince named Jog Tunga at an official dinner,' they said. 'Ever heard of him?'

I flinched. In exhaustion and exasperation, I considered telling them that he was stalking and harassing me, but as quickly as the last-ditch thought surfaced, I shoved it down into a dark, deep corner. Far from believing me, they'd probably shut me up in a shuttle and dump me on the nearest mining asteroid before they investigated.

'He's only allied with the family that murdered all of mine back on Earth,' I said, sticking to my tactic of going on the offensive.

'We believe he's personally invested in destabilising Primus and the UHC. Attacking Optimism Mahd'vi was his attempt to send a message.'

'Wouldn't put it past him, but like I said, their family likes killing mine. We're not meant to be allies.'

'Ever met him?'

'No.'

'We think you're lying.'

'Why?' My heart pounded. Of course I was lying, and I was hoping they didn't find out. It was immaterial that our meetings were forced upon me very much against my will. If my trail was discovered, they'd have ample reason to deport me. If my identity were discovered, they could send me back to my family...

'"Earthling tends to Earthling, united in destruction,"' they said sanctimoniously.

'You're fucking kidding. That's from a poem that was banned a thousand years ago,' I snapped.

'Doesn't mean it isn't true.'

'You'll be surprised to know that Earthlings can be good people, too.'

'Surprised? I'd be shocked.'

My favourite conspiracy theory, though, was even more far-fetched.

'You came here to Primus to win *Interstellar MegaChef*, yes?'

'That's correct.'

'Instead, you were humiliated on the show.'

'Yes.'

'You returned to the *MegaChef* special to destroy traditional Primian cuisine with Feast, symbolically smashing it on the plate before presenting the judges with Feast cubes. It was a warning of what you'd do to our culture.'

'I—*what*?'

'You acted alone to assassinate Optimism Mahd'vi, to destroy the personification of our culture.'

'No.'

'I don't believe you.'

'Shocking.' I rolled my eyes, drawing on all my reserves of energy to keep me going.

I was dizzy and beginning to feel faint. I hadn't eaten in an age. I had no idea how much time had passed. I was disorientated and didn't even know where I was—it could have been a spaceship, a bunker, there was no way to tell. My thoughts were beginning to slide around incoherently, my defiance beaten down, my innocence irrelevant.

Every accusation, every pronunciation of *Earthling* spat out as if it were contaminated water, every bizarre theory wilder than the last was giving me a pounding headache. And I was alone, entirely alone.

Fuck me, I'm going to die here alone.

I tried to keep my back straight, my posture relaxed, my tone nonchalant—as they'd taught me in my diplomatic training on Earth. I denied everything they threw my way, sticking to my assumed Kaveri identity like a life raft. I made myself arrogant, projected indefatigable self-assurance, and my insides crumbled, the words tumbling out of me like a script, repeating myself until I was hoarse…

When the uniformed officer from the Primian Guard walked in, I immediately labelled them the Military One and wondered if this was where they switched things up and introduced physical threats. That's how the military were used back on Earth—by my family, at least. My insides turned to mush and I braced myself.

'Optimism Mahd'vi sends her sincere apologies,' they said.

'What?'

'I'm Good Cheer Soraya. We met at the… unfortunate incident at the Feast pop-up.'

'Oh.'

'Optimism Mahd'vi's ordered your immediate release. She apologises for the incompetence of the investigators, for holding you against your will with no just cause, for any remarks made that might have been insensitive or insulting, for your general treatment in the wake of the incident. She wishes she could do so in person.'

'Oh.' My insides lurched. 'How is she?'

Good Cheer Soraya gave me a searching look. 'Unhurt. Shaken, a little bruised, but otherwise whole.'

'Thank the Nine Virtues!'

Good Cheer Soraya smiled. 'Indeed. If you'll follow me, I'm to drop you off wherever you'd like to go.'

Good Cheer Soraya led me through a deserted maze of corridors, and when we reached the surface, I doubled over, sagging against a trellis and gasping in deep lungfuls of fresh air. Stars dotted the night sky, and for the first time since arriving on Primus, I didn't give a fuck about their beauty and myriad mysteries. She patted my back awkwardly.

'The Cells will do that to anyone,' she said kindly.

'Are they used often?' I asked, horrified.

'I'm not at liberty to say,' she replied, thereby confirming my suspicions. 'Before we leave, you're going to need to turn your location public on the Loop,' she added tonelessly.

'What? That's an invasion of privacy.'

'New rule.' She shrugged. 'They're announcing it any moment. All off-worlders have to have their location live on the Loop at all times.'

My insides cringed. 'But… but they haven't even proved that an off-worlder was behind the explosion …'

We stepped into a flow-craft that was parked nearby, and she engaged its thrusters. I watched the world drop away from me, and recognised that we'd been in a nondescript building somewhere in Collective Fourteen.

'Are you saying you had something to do with it?' she asked. I glanced at her uncertainly and caught her eyes twinkling. 'You want the truth? Nobody had anything to do with it.'

'What do you mean?'

'It was an accident.'

'You're fucking kidding me.'

'They thought it was a sonic bomb, but it was the flowmetal tech that causes the Sinfonia Theatre to keep tempo with the music.'

'You're *fucking joking.*'

I leaned my head against the ship's transparent wall. I was exhausted, but hot, unfettered rage welled up within me.

'A circuit blew. It was misidentified in the wreckage as a bomb.' Good Cheer Soraya tensed visibly, keeping me clearly in her sights. 'Took them hours to find the architect's plans for the building, and everyone was very embarrassed afterwards.'

'Embarrassed,' I echoed in disbelief.

'Embarrassed,' Good Cheer Soraya affirmed. 'The investigating team has been suspended, pending investigation, which is quite funny if you think about it.'

'Funny.'

'Wrong choice of word. Sorry.'

'But off-worlders still have to broadcast their location live?' I asked, incredulous.

'I'm sorry. I don't make the rules,' she said. 'I'm sure it's only temporary.'

I lapsed into silence, turning this over in my mind, wondering what new changes were going to disrupt my life on this planet even though absolutely nothing that had happened in the last twenty-eight hours had been my fault.

'I went through *all that* for *nothing*?' I croaked.

'Optimism Mahd'vi sends her deepest apologies,' she said evenly.

'I don't want her fucking apologies. I want… I want fucking *nothing* to do with this planet. I want to leave and never come back. I'm done. I'm through with *all of you!*' The words exploded out of me before I knew they were coming. My breath came in jagged gasps. 'And most of all… most of all I want *Kili,*' I sobbed, curling up despite the harness holding me in place in my jump seat.

Good Cheer Soraya listened in silence. 'Would Kili be your Winger?' she asked gently. 'I saw it at the pop-up, curious little machine…'

'Yes,' I snapped, white hot rage surging through me. 'You or one of yours destroyed him. He… I can't believe he's *dead*.'

The last word came out as a whisper, anguish ripping through my rage and shredding my heart with it.

'I'm sorry,' Good Cheer Soraya said quietly. 'I'll alert the Guard to look for it.'

'*Him,*' I snarled.

'Sorry?'

'Tell your people to look for *him*.'

'Him. Of course.'

We rode the rest of the way in silence, my vision blurring from raw emotion. Good Cheer Soraya had empathy enough to leave me to my thoughts, which were an incoherent muddle.

'Where would you like to go?' she asked at last.

'I—my friends, I think some of them might be at the Ursands,' I said, suddenly recollecting the Ibnis-viewing party I was supposed to be at several hours ago, assuming we were still living the same day.

'I'll set you down there.'

I slid into the Loop and found dozens of frantic streams from Serenity Ko, and a slew of pics featuring Courage Oslo and Curiosity Zia with their arms wrapped around none other than Starlight Fantastic. Boundless Baz and XX-29 stood beside them. My heart leapt for joy at the thought of seeing them again. I couldn't think of anyone else who could make this terrible day better, except for Kili, and I couldn't bring myself to think of him just then.

On my way. See you soon, I streamed them.

And then, I flicked through Serenity Ko's frantic spurt of messages and dashed off a quick. _I'm okay._

'There's a small shack on the beach and it's fully automated. You can get some food, and you won't have to talk to a soul until you're ready to meet your friends,' Good Cheer Soraya said kindly. 'In case you need some time…'

'Thanks,' I mumbled. 'That works.'

'I'll have my people look for your Winger. We have folks who can restore any kind of tech. If we find him, I promise you we'll do our best,' she offered.

'Thanks again,' I whispered, swallowing a new wave of grief that was threatening to overwhelm me.

I stepped out of the ship and its lines blurred immediately as she flew it out into the night sky. I collapsed onto the sand, my throat parched, nearly blinded by a headache. I'd lost my closest friend in all the star-fucked universe.

I longed to walk out into the ocean and disappear.

A man with a golden crown upon his head drew into view.

Preserving our cultural traditions is a selfless act of service in honour of our ancestors. It's a powerful symbol that progress is not an arrow, unlike time.

—Grace Menmo,
Art and Culture in the Interstellar Era: The Definitive Edition
2065 Anno Earth | 1990 Interstellar Era

NINETEEN

'I GIVE YOU "Pacing: A new Primian pastime!"' Serenity Ko said dramatically, verging on the feral, as she stomped back and forth across her family's space.

'I'm sure she's fine, Ko,' Optimism Rihan said, slumping back against the couch cushions.

'Oh, *you're* sure she's fine. Then she *must* be fine, *mustn't* she?' Serenity Ko smiled brightly, baring her teeth.

'The reports say there are no fatalities,' Good Cheer Eria volunteered uncertainly.

'Well, that's a *relief.* Maybe she's just suffered a ton of broken bones or a skull fracture. *What. Good. News.*'

'She streamed you to say she's okay,' Optimism Rihan offered rationally.

'Yes, such helpful information. What the fuck does "I'm okay" mean? Why isn't she swinging by right now? Where is she? Is it the hospital?'

'She said she's okay—' Optimism Rihan repeated, then shut his mouth when Serenity Ko glowered at him.

'*What's she doing that's so important that she isn't here with me?*' Serenity Ko practically howled. 'Nine Virtues, maybe she's at my space. I should go home …'

She resumed pacing.

'What if they deport her? She's an Earthling. They'll go after her because they can!'

Serenity Ko streamed Saraswati again, demanding

information. She checked all her comms and then groaned when she saw half a dozen panic-stricken messages from Honour Aki checking in on her. In a flash of empathy, she realised she was behaving the same way with Saraswati, and felt an uneasy stirring of guilt within the pit of her stomach for ghosting him. She dashed off a quick *I'm okay. I hope you are, too* and slid out of her comms, ignoring the immediate flurry of replies he sent her way, though she cringed as she resumed obsessing over Saraswati.

'You don't own her, Ko,' Good Cheer Eria said softly, refusing to wilt under Serenity Ko's glare. 'Maybe she's busy, or she's exhausted and needs some space.'

'I'll give her space! She just needs to come here, I'll give her tons of blankets and all the space she wants. And I'll even make her hot xocolat… I mean, I'll get Dad to make her hot xocolat.'

She whirled around to where the rest of her family were seated at the dinner table, watching her outburst in silence that was a mix of amusement and concern. 'You'll make her hot xocolat, won't you, Dad?'

'Why don't I make *you* some hot xocolat, Ko?' Dad offered, smiling kindly.

'Ugh, kill me with kindness already.' Serenity Ko made a face, then spun on her heel, resuming her pacing.

'Ko, sit down,' her mother said, rising from her chair and approaching her daughter as if she were attempting to lure a cat into a wicker basket, wary of its claws. Serenity Ko hissed in return.

'This is very bad behaviour.' Her mother tutted.

'I'm sorry, Amma. I'm losing my mind. Do you know what I'm doing while I'm pacing and having this utterly inane conversation with all of you?'

Serenity Ko flung stream after stream across the visio-nodes embedded on the far wall, between two large sets of planters bearing her grandmother's herb garden. 'Do we have no other fucking visio-nodes in this space?' she snapped.

'Tch, don't swear,' Ammamma muttered.

'They're all fucking blaming her for it! Look at them go!' Serenity Ko practically howled, turning up the volume on a dozen streams all at once. A hideous blur of voices collided in cacophony, all echoing similar sentiments.

'*Spotted entering the sinfonia together were our Secretary for Culture and Heritage, Optimism Mahd'vi, and the Earthling chef Saraswati Kaveri, one of the minds behind the Feast project. Do we suspect foul play?*' clashed with '*...hot on the heels of starting a riot, as witnessed by over a dozen Culinary Circle members, Saraswati Kaveri is now at the heart of an explosion...*' and '*...could Earthling violence be behind the Sinfonia Theater explosion? Saraswati Kaveri, of Feast and Earthling notoriety, was at the occasion...*'

'What the fuck do they mean "Earthling notoriety"?' Serenity Ko growled. 'What the sur-fucking hells is fucking wrong with these fucked sideways fucking people? This isn't the fucking news, it's fucking speculation, *fuck me*.'

'I said, don't swear,' Ammamma said more firmly.

Serenity Ko opened her mouth to argue, but shut it again as Ammamma continued. 'We know this is horribly upsetting, Ko. And I'm sorry, I really am. But Optimism Mahd'vi seems to be just fine. Look at what they're saying now.'

Serenity Ko looked.

'The subtitles read: "Optimism Mahd'vi was stunned, but is unhurt, and will be making a statement soon,"' Ammamma said.

'I can read.'

'I wasn't sure if that red haze had blinded you or not.'

'Enough, Ma!' Dad said, throwing his mother-in-law a warning glance.

'I don't care about Optimism Mahd'vi,' Serenity Ko said, hating the tremor in her voice. 'I only care about Saras.'

'And your friend streamed to tell you she's okay,' Ammamma said slowly, as if reasoning with a petulant toddler. 'I don't know why we're all being subjected to this Ko tantrum. It's been a while since she was three-years-old and it was actually cute.'

'Ma, why don't we step into the garden?' Serenity Ko's mother said, gently placing a hand on Ammamma's shoulder. 'I have some trouble with my astrianas…'

'Right now? Just because she isn't adorable any more doesn't mean this isn't entertaining! If I didn't know better, I'd say Ko was *madly in love.*'

Serenity Ko's heart stuttered. '*What?*'

'Merely the ramblings of an old woman,' Ammamma said airily. 'Surely, Ko can't be in love. She's beyond human, after all.'

'*I am not in love with her.*'

Am I? The thought was unbidden, and entirely terrifying.

Dad rose from his seat and walked up to her. He held her by the shoulders as she shook, and looked into her eyes. 'Ko. Saras was Optimism Mahd'vi's guest. If Mahd'vi's fine, I'm sure Saras is, too. They can't have been too far away from each other during the incident.'

'Plus, she literally streamed you and said "I'm okay,"' Optimism Rihan groaned.

'There's no use living a thousand deaths before you die, my love,' Appa said soothingly.

'It feels like I'm dying already.' Serenity Ko's voice cracked.

'Shh, kiddo, it's okay,' Dad said, wrapping his arms around Serenity Ko, who felt the air rush out of her in something that wasn't quite a gasp but wasn't quite a sob, either.

'Why hasn't she sent me more intel?' Serenity Ko insisted. 'I can't get through to her, *or* to Kili anymore.'

From over her Dad's shoulder, she caught Appa and Amma exchange a look.

'What?' she asked, steeling herself and pulling away from her father's arms.

'Nothing.'

'We said nothing.'

'You *looked* at each other. It was one of *those looks.* The "should-we-tell-the-kids-about-sex?" kind.'

Appa ran his fingers through his peppery beard. 'Ah, well…'

'Appa,' Serenity Ko wheedled.

'Um, well, kiddo… This kind of thing hasn't happened since you were six years old and there was an Axian protest that turned into a riot. A lot of the Secretariat was banged up and, um, it went badly for the Axians after that.'

Serenity Ko sputtered. 'Your point?'

'What your father's trying to say and failing at—and I mean really, Madhu, you could do better,' Ammamma said, shooting Appa a dirty look. 'What your father's trying to say is that Primian security forces don't take threats to their soil, or members of the Secretariat, lightly. They've probably rounded up everyone at the venue and taken them in for questioning. Especially all the off-worlders, which is sad, but you can never be too careful.'

'*What?*' Serenity Ko snapped.

'Oh, come on. The Primian Guard showed up to question all of *you* after your recent riot, Primian and otherwise…' Ammamma rolled her eyes. 'It really isn't that different. Probably some extra security screening in the case of your friend, is all.'

'You mean harassment,' Serenity Ko said coldly.

'I *do not* mean harassment, Ko,' Ammamma said, her patience audibly wearing thin. 'I mean regular security protocols followed every time there's a breach of said security, like when there's a massive explosion at the heart of Uru and nobody knows the cause yet.'

Serenity Ko's eyes widened, and she spun around to pay attention to the dense cluster of voices still streaming across the visio-nodes.

'This isn't a big deal, Ko,' Ammamma said, exhaling. 'Your friend is a cook—'

'*Chef.*'

'Right, she's a chef. I'm sure she has nothing to do with it. She'll be *fine*. They'll let her go once they cross-check her scrollwork and verify her innocence.'

'*…continuing questions surround the presence of Saraswati Kaveri, the fire starter Earthling with a quick temper at the sinfonia…*'

‘*Earthlings don’t know a thing about sinfonia! Her presence there is an anomaly.*’

‘*…all I’m saying is, “where there’s Earth, there’s fire.”*’

‘Do you hear this garbage? It doesn’t matter if they let her go. *These* vultures are going to go after her regardless!’

‘It absolutely matters if they let her go,’ Ammamma said quietly.

‘But they’ll make her life miserable first, and that’s okay?’ Serenity Ko demanded. ‘*How do I know they won’t deport her?*’

Nobody met her gaze or answered her question.

Exhausted, she slumped into an armchair and slid into the Loop. A frustrating barrage of desperation from Honour Aki popped up on her comms.

I’ll save you from the treacherous Earthling, Ko. Don’t you worry, he said, followed by: _I’m looking her up on the Loop, and she has such a sketchy past before she burst onto *MegaChef*. I’m looking into her identity._

Don’t be a fuckwit, Aki, Serenity Ko streamed angrily.

‘It’ll die down as soon as the next controversy rolls around, I promise,’ said Dad, brushing Serenity Ko’s hair gently.

‘Oh, yes, I’ll just go start another riot or blow something else up as a distraction,’ Serenity Ko said.

‘I think it’s community service for third-time riot starters,’ Ammamma said drily.

‘Ammamma, if you have something to say to me, why don’t you just come out with it?’ Serenity Ko snapped.

‘I’ve been trying for the last three māsas, except my only granddaughter refuses to return my comms or be in the same room as me,’ Ammamma said tartly.

‘Go on, then. Come at me!’ Serenity Ko said, thumping her chest.

Optimism Rihan groaned and buried his head in a cushion. ‘I’m sorry you have to see this, Eria,’ he muttered.

‘*I’ll deal with you later,*’ Serenity Ko spat at her brother. ‘But you first. Go on, Ammamma.’

Her grandmother sighed, then with what appeared to be a

great effort, she rose to her feet, resting her hands palm down on the dinner table before her.

'Are you sure now is the best time for this?' Appa said, looking from his mother-in-law to his daughter uncertainly.

'Yes,' Serenity Ko said coldly.

'Yes,' Ammamma echoed, shifting into her Grace Menmo avatar.

'Come on, Madhu. It'll give her a distraction,' Dad said. 'Let's go check on those pastries.'

'Yes, let's leave the children to it,' Appa said, rising from the table.

'Are you sure you don't want to give me advice on my astrianas?' Amma tried again, frantically appealing to the old woman's better sense.

'No,' Grace Menmo said, ice edging her monosyllabic response.

'Auntie, I can help!' Good Cheer Eria practically cried, rising from the sofa and rushing into the garden. Optimism Rihan mumbled something unintelligible and followed his fiancée out the door.

'So,' Serenity Ko said.

'So.'

'Say what you want to say.'

'You've already heard it all. The culinary world is in an uproar over Feast. You've disrupted everything,' Grace Menmo said bitterly.

'There's always resistance to the future.'

'You're *dividing* people. *Our* people. It used to be Primian culture versus all the rest, and we needed to be vigilant, bringing people into the fold, encouraging them to embrace our ways as the only true path to being better as humanity…'

'You should start a cult,' Serenity Ko said.

'Stupid, foolish girl. The only hope for humanity lies in unity. It's bad enough that we've always been divided within the UHC, regardless of the feel-good-let's-all-hold-hands-and-play-together rubbish they feed us. Primus versus the Fringe planets, planets versus the space stations, planets and space stations against the asteroids, the asteroids against the moons… it's all nonsensical! And Primian culture—*our* ways, the ways of our Nakshatran ancestors who gave humanity a *second chance* at a good life—sought to unite everyone under its banner.'

'By erasing all differences,' Serenity Ko said hotly.

'Don't pretend you care about any of this, Ko,' Grace Menmo said wearily. 'Six māsas ago you'd have been shocked if you met someone from Luna, or a backwater like Io, who didn't know who Chloriana was.'

'Times have changed,' Serenity Ko sniffed, while cringing inwardly at how right her grandmother's observation was.

'You've created something that's dividing Primians. There are now traditionalists and futurists fighting over food, and you can bet that fight is going to expand to encompass everything. All the old ways will be challenged by something new, and new things aren't always for the better,' Grace Menmo said.

'Ammamma, it's *just food*,' Serenity Ko said, throwing her hands up in exasperation. '*Just. Food*. It's all a gimmick—every sim is, that's why we have to keep coming up with new ones all the time. In—I don't know, three years?—Feast will fade, and everyone will go back to enjoying their stupid traditionally made Nakshatran gelatos or shroom-broths that they labour over for hours on end.'

'And until then?'

'What about until then?'

'Do you accept the consequences—the chaos—that you might unleash with food tech like this?'

'Chefs slinging mud at each other on streams? Sure.'

'Do you realise this will start a food security arms race?'

'I understood none of those words.'

'Every planet out there is going to want this tech.'

'Yes, licensing deals. It's all in my road map for Feast.' Serenity Ko smiled smugly.

'And our own Secretariat…' Ammamma's voice trailed off.

'What about them?'

'They'll want to control it.'

Serenity Ko's heart skipped a beat. Ammamma was hideously spot on. She considered confiding in her about Optimism Mahd'vi's persistence in gaining Secretariat approval, about how this was already happening…

'Are you saying you don't trust our Secretariat?' she probed cautiously.

'I trust nobody in power,' Ammamma snapped. 'Not even myself. Why do you think I retired?'

Serenity Ko's curiosity was piqued by that, all thought of Optimism Mahd'vi extinguished. 'Why *did* you retire?'

'You know when they hero-worship you for decades, and you find yourself at the centre of a whole universe that's constantly hanging onto your every word, it gets hard to tell friend from foe, to discern right from wrong. It distorts your perspective of yourself, and of the world around you. I felt like a hollowed out shell. It had to stop,' Ammamma said simply.

Serenity Ko took a step back in amazement. 'That… was entirely genuine. No word games or cryptic messages.'

Ammamma sighed and sank back into her chair. 'Ko. You're too young to understand any of this. You think you have power, but it's only because someone is permitting you to live within that illusion. There's always someone pulling the strings, and it's only ever to their own advantage. Quid pro quo until you're no longer useful. I got out while I was ahead. I want the same for you.'

'What did you just say?'

Serenity Ko was struck by an idea, the powerful, insistent kind.

'I care for you, and I don't want to see you lose who you are in the process of short-term ambitions…'

'No, no, before that.'

'Quid pro quo?'

'That. Thanks, Ammama! Good talk.'

'You're going to do something foolish, aren't you?'

'Yes.'

'Idiot child.' Ammamma sank her head in her hands. 'You'll never learn.'

'You're the best, Ammamma,' Serenity Ko said, pecking her grandmother on the cheek before rushing up to her room.

Honour Aki had streamed her again.

Look, I'm sorry she's used and manipulated you and brainwashed you. But *nobody* has such a ghost-like presence on the Loop. I promise, I'll save you.

Aki, she said coldly. _Go fuck yourself._

A cascade of messages flooded her comms, but she ignored them. She stepped lithely over the Bloxxos on the floor, then sat at her work station.

Urgent. Let's negotiate.

She waited for Optimism Mahd'vi to respond, idly fiddling with the strap on her old *Formula Enthusiast* race helmet.

Urgent. Willing to concede Feast to you.

A notification loomed over her visual—an incoming call from Optimism Mahd'vi. Serenity Ko accepted it immediately.

'I hope you're all right, Secretary,' Serenity Ko said politely.

'Yes. Fine.'

In the background, Serenity Ko heard singing, the murmur of voices, a shout of laughter. She creased her brow. 'Where are you?'

'I'm streaming planet-wide from an Ibnis-viewing party in three minutes,' Optimism Mahd'vi snapped. 'Which you'd have discovered yourself… in three minutes.'

'Where's Saras?'

'Safe,' Optimism Mahd'vi said. 'For now,' she added ominously.

'What do you mean?' Serenity Ko's heart pounded.

'What do you think I mean?' Optimism Mahd'vi said. 'You've got two minutes now.'

'I'll keep it quick. You and I both know Saras had nothing to do with tonight's incident,' Serenity Ko said, cutting to the chase. 'She can't have. I mean, she's only a chef…'

'I've had her released from questioning.'

Serenity Ko bit back a sigh of relief. 'I'll give you what you want if you do something for me in return.'

Optimism Mahd'vi's lips turned upward in the shadow of a

smile. 'And what could *you* possibly have that *I* want?'

'Feast. Creative control. I'll let you weigh in on our programming, all our content—the sights, sounds, memory triggers, scents, everything. Final approval. Primian superiority. The works.'

'Why are we being so generous?' Optimism Mahd'vi's voice dripped with sarcasm.

'I know you're about to make a public address about the explosion,' Serenity Ko said hurriedly. 'All I ask is that you defend Saras, and say she had nothing to do with it. She and her Earthling origins are innocent.'

Optimism Mahd'vi laughed. 'Wait, you're willing to sell your product to me in exchange for a *speech*?'

'Yes.'

'Why?' A curious expression crossed Optimism Mahd'vi's face.

'Because Saras is innocent. She's a good person. And the stream-media is going after her with a vengeance. All because she's an Earthling...'

Optimism Mahd'vi regarded her coolly. 'Again. You're telling me that if I say nice things about her in public, you'll let me turn Feast into my vision?'

'Yes.'

'It's a good thing you don't work in politics,' Optimism Mahd'vi said drily. 'That's a terrible bargain.'

'I don't care about the bargain,' Serenity Ko said, tamping down her impatience. 'I just care about Saras. She doesn't deserve this just because of her origins—'

'And what do you know about her origins?' Optimism Mahd'vi asked sharply.

'Oh, come on, she's just a refugee! She ran away from a war, and all we've done on this sur-fucked planet is treat her like shit because of her home-world. What happens on Earth is not her fault. She is not her people.'

'What people would those be?' Optimism Mahd'vi's voice was laced with suspicion.

'*Earthlings!*' Serenity Ko snapped, before correcting her tone. 'Earthlings. Your Excellency.'

Optimism Mahd'vi's gaze lingered, and Serenity Ko felt herself dithering, confronted by those slate grey eyes.

'You want me to defend her in public? Is that all?' Optimism Mahd'vi asked.

'Yes, just get the stream-media off her back. She's been through enough.'

'And in exchange, I get final approval on all your Feast sims?'

'A deal's a deal.'

'Even if it's horribly one-sided and you're filled with regret later because I've short-changed you?'

Serenity Ko swallowed. 'Yes.'

'Done. I'll declare your friend's virtuousness on the streams, but remember…' Optimism Mahd'vi said cryptically. 'All our lies find our way back to Earth.'

'And from all our lies, our stories are woven,' Serenity Ko said automatically, quoting the *Nakshatranāma*.

'Clever girl,' Optimism Mahd'vi said. 'Watch your back with your little Earth friend.'

'What does that mean?' Serenity Ko frowned, but Optimism Mahd'vi was gone.

In her wake, there were only questions, and Serenity Ko took to pacing her room again.

The Godavari clan possesses a reputation for power-mongering through expansionist policies in the Daxina Protectorate on Earth. Their closest allies are the Tunga and the Bhadra clans...

—After Earth:
A Comprehensive Encyclopaedia of Greater Human Space
2025 Anno Earth | 1950 Interstellar Era

TWENTY

'WHAT DO *YOU* want?'

I blinked back my tears furiously. I was exhausted. My shoulders drooped and I forced them back, scrambling to my knees as the sand got all over my beautiful, brand new, now decrepit luminoweave dress. The fabric shimmered purple and mud in the dim light, rips and tears from the explosion streaking it ashen grey. It was enough to make me weep, except that Jog Tunga was standing right before me.

The Sagarra Sea was infinite behind his tall, lean shadow, and I yearned for it to sweep in with the tide and swallow him into its depths. Gentle waves lapped against the white sand beach, and the stars above us shimmered as if all the universe was mocking me, showing my desolate, irrational hopes their place in its grand scheme of things, which was evidently focused on fucking things up for me.

Jog Tunga cocked his head. 'Bad day?' he asked, showcasing his penchant for scripted villainy. Ordinarily, I might have found it slightly amusing, but in this moment, it just grated on my nerves.

'*Now* it is.'

I missed the slight weight in my pocket where Kili was supposed to be, and it sent a stab of pain through my gut.

'How did you find me?'

'Thanks to your favourite Primian people, your location on the Loop is now live all the time,' he grinned.

'Fuck me.'

'Tragic.' He feigned sympathy.

'Your being here, yeah.'

'I was talking about you.' He bent until he was in a half crouch, looking down at me. He was so close that his overpowering sandalwood cologne drowned out the tang of salt in the air.

'If you aren't fucking off, could you at least get to the point?'

He stretched an arm out lazily towards me. 'Need a hand? I'm not used to kneeling in the dirt.'

'Don't touch me!' I hissed, scrabbling backwards and falling over.

'Shh,' he whispered, then proceeded to make the aggravating chirruping sound people unsuccessfully used to beckon cats across the galaxy.

'I won't hurt you,' he said, attempting a soothing tone. It came off like a kitchen knife shearing scales off a fish. 'I'm on your side.'

My insides clenched. I shot to my feet, placing my weight firmly on the ground once more. I was no fighter, but if he was going to try and kill me, I wasn't going to make it easy.

'That's better,' he said, straightening up. He looked at my slight crouch, my fists balled up at my sides, and smirked. 'I'm not going to hurt you, you can drop the fists. Not that they'll do you much good.'

'Can never be too prepared with a mass murderer,' I growled.

'See, you're confusing me with your parents again.' He tutted. 'They send their regards, by the way.'

'They can take their regards and—'

'I'd choose my next words carefully,' he snapped. '*I* might tolerate your insulting lack of court manners, but they certainly won't.'

'Are you going to run home and tell on me?'

'No. Not yet, anyway.' He smiled, and it spread across his face like a threat. 'It all depends on what you do next.'

The wind shifted. The sound of laughter and the dull echoes of music drifted towards me and I shifted slightly to see if there was somewhere I could run to. Behind me was an outcrop of rocks, dark against the glimmering sands. They formed the base of a low line of bluffs, the cliff's edge lined with glowing lanterns. Another shout of laughter reached me, and I cast my gaze around, looking for a path, or any way up to where there was evidently a party in progress.

It must be the Ibnis-viewing ceremony. My friends are there.

If I could just spin on my heel and catch him off-guard, I'd be able to—

'Don't even think about it.'

His voice cracked through my illusions of escape, shattering them.

'What're you going to gain by running, Saras? I'll just find you again.' He yawned. 'You make this so *boring.* All the chasing, the sneaking around, pretending any of it makes a difference. It's a *tiny fucking planet*.'

My hands shook. He wasn't wrong.

'Make it quick,' I said, keeping the tremor from my voice.

'Finally, she's coming around.'

I regarded him in icy silence.

'Have you given any thought to the generous, no-strings-attached offer I made you?' Jog Tunga asked.

I froze, running our last conversation over in my head. Other than the fact that I didn't trust him any more than I trusted Good Cheer Chaangte with a knife, I hadn't given the lunatic proposition a moment's thought. At least, not seriously.

'Nope. Don't feel like stealing Feast for you, sorry,' I said. 'Not sure I trust you, not with powerful new technology, and not with getting my parents to fuck off and leave me alone—you can't even do that *yourself*.'

His face twisted momentarily, and he quickly smoothed over his expression. 'I understand you've been busy,' he said. 'It must be so hard. The fall. First they love you: a visionary, a food revolutionary. Then they blame you for a riot you didn't start, just because you're an Earthling. Point fingers at you for everything that goes wrong with Feast … because, you know, Earthling.'

He ticked off the mounting tally of shit experiences Primian xenophobia had subjected me to on his fingers while he spoke. 'They haul you in for questioning after an explosion at the sinfonia. See: Earthling… How did *that* go, by the way?' He grinned. 'I've never been in a prison cell on another planet. Must be a life-enriching experience, hmm? Something for the biopic, for sure. Did they give you kaapi and pastries, and politely ask you if you set off a bomb?'

It made me livid, how easily he pushed my buttons. I hated that he knew *everything* I'd been subjected to since we'd last met, I hated that he was choosing to manipulate me with it, and I *absolutely hated* that anything that he was saying at all was making me upset.

'No, wait, they reserve the kaapi and cookies for folks who aren't savages,' Jog Tunga said snidely, tilting his head. 'And that doesn't include you. *Earthling*.'

'As a matter of fact, there were kaapi and pastries,' I said frostily. 'Not that it's any of your business.'

'Ah, rolling out the interrogation red carpet, how lovely!'

'Are you here just to mock me?'

'I'm here because I *care* about you, Saras. That's just the kind of person I am.' He took a step forward, pretending to study me. 'It hurts me to see my future sister-in-law—a daughter of the *Godavari* clan, no less—treated like dirt on this cold, distant rock, so far away from her home-world. All I want is what's best for you.'

'If you were to fuck off and leave me the fuck alone for the rest of my life, that would be amazing, really, the maximum best for me,' I said, smiling sweetly.

'You know that's not going to happen,' he said, returning my smile, though it resembled a feral snarl on him. 'Not so long as you have something I want, and I believe you do. You're going to give it to me.'

'No.'

'I bet they threw you in a windowless cell. Someone probably played good cop, bad cop, homicidal maniac cop with you, threatened you with deportation, accused you of bombing this city, assassinating the Secretariat, et cetera. It's the kind of thing I'd do if I wanted to get an inconvenience out of my way. And *you*, Earthling, are an inconvenience to them.' He nodded at me. 'They hate immigrants, and they hate immigrants from the Fringes extra.'

He ran his eyes over me and I shivered.

'Surely you know this by now. It must be devastating. Need a hug?'

I blanched. 'No thanks.'

'All right, no hug. But here's the thing, Saraswati: They don't want you here. They don't *need* you here.' He shrugged. 'And look: You want to forgive them, play the victim or the martyr or whatever this is you have going on…? Be my guest. But *you owe these people nothing*.'

'I owe you nothing, either.'

He shot forward at an alarming speed and grabbed me by the wrist, pulling me close. 'You wretched ingrate. You owe me the last nine māsas of your life, if not more. I'm the only person who's been on your team right from the start.'

I laughed. 'You? On *my* team?'

'I haven't told your parents where you are. They're *desperate* for you to come back home, though only the river gods know why. I haven't breathed a word of your little adventures on this sur-fucked lump. And all I'm asking for in return—and for my continued silence, by the way—is a little help.'

'Let go of my wrist. You're hurting me.'

He twisted my arm and squeezed my wrist harder. 'I said, *all I want is a little help*.'

'No. I will not steal Feast's tech for you,' I spat, spelling it out for him.

'I'm offering you a way out,' he said, his voice silky smooth like butter. 'You have my terms. I'm sending you my contact. Dead drop by the Harmony Knot—the yellow park bench beneath the wisteria. Let me know when it's done. You've got two navas. I'm the only chance you've got.'

He shoved me, and I toppled over backwards into the sand. I scrambled to my feet.

'No.' I was getting tired of saying the word.

'You have no idea what you're doing here!' he spat. 'That piece of tech is one of the most powerful things ever built, and you're giving *them* exclusive control over it. The same people who just locked you up in a cell and threatened you.'

'I walked out, didn't I?'

'For now.'

'I'm the face of Feast,' I hissed.

'For now. Do you think they'd let you go if they didn't have a use for you?' Jog Tunga laughed, a scraping chuckle. 'I wouldn't.'

'Right, so what happens when I fulfil my use to *you*?' I shot back. 'I steal Feast for you, and then you stab me and call it quits.'

'You really are dim, aren't you?' Jog Tunga said, his eyes widening in disbelief. 'I have *nothing* to gain by bumping you off. No advantage. I mean, sure, maybe I could kidnap you and hold you hostage, ransom you to your parents until they declare me their heir to the Daxina Protectorate, a de facto Godavari…'

My blood ran cold as he worked through a barrage of lunatic schemes for power, using me as leverage.

'Maybe I could out your identity to the Primian authorities in exchange for favourable trade treaties for Earth. Or I could create a hostage crisis using you, currently one of the most famous people in the galaxy, to ensure we get access to Feast, or to all of Primus's resources, or the mines on the Osmos Girdle…' His eyes glazed over, practically glowing as he lived through one fantasy after another. And then his attention snapped back to me. 'But I'm doing none of the above. I'm being reasonable. I'm giving you a *choice. Agency.*'

He was circling me as he spoke. 'Do you know how lucky you are, Saras? To have Prince Jog Tunga give you a *choice*?'

'You're deranged.'

'You're obstinate,' he snapped, the sneer sliding off his face. 'Just fucking steal Feast and you will never see me, or your parents, or even *hear* from us again.'

I stepped forward, matching him pace for pace.

'See, here's my problem, fucko,' I said. 'I don't like you and I don't trust you. Even with something as benign as a food-sim. Never have, never will. I don't trust you lunatics to *not* blow up the universe. I don't trust you psychopaths to *not* come after me, abduct me, marry me off to one of the rival clans, sell me to a brothel moon for better trade deals on cricket chips, the whole shebang.'

'And you trust the *Primians?*' His voice was sharp with disbelief.

I flinched, and he flashed a victorious smile.

I wasn't sure if I trusted anyone at this point. The Primians hadn't been galactic aggressors in centuries, but that didn't mean they couldn't be in the future. XP Inc. was developing Feast for entertainment, but that didn't mean the Secretariat wouldn't use it for propaganda. Or sell their principles and license it to nefarious markets across the galaxy for the right price. I'd hosted over a dozen pop-ups now, and the overwhelming power of Feast—to transform experiences, evoke memories, inspire the imagination—thrummed through the room at each tasting.

Whoever controlled Feast had the power to control minds, and it was dawning on me that that power wouldn't always be used for the betterment of humanity.

To my abject shame, I realised my *own* reasons weren't only for the greater good. I'd looked behind the carefully maintained façade of Primian civilisation, and experienced their xenophobia and hostility firsthand. Every single time something related to Feast went wrong, I was blamed for it. And now, I was certain I'd have to take a firestorm of flak for the explosion at the sinfonia. Even Serenity Ko didn't understand me—she kept rising to my defence without my asking her to, and fucking things up for me in completely avoidable, unasked for ways.

'Your silence says it all, you know,' Jog Tunga mocked. 'Because not so deep down, Saraswati—just beneath your nano-bleach and badly permed hair—you're a Godavari. You can pretend you aren't all you like. Travel by your falsified Kaveri name, lie to all the authorities across the galaxy, tell your friends you ran away from the big bad dictatorship on your home-world, boo-hoo! But when it comes down to it, you think like us. You can see circles of power stalking each other, slipping into the cracks, moving closer, closer… ever so closer…'

And then he stood right before me, mere inches separating us. 'You can see everyone trying to gain absolute power, all around you. All the time. You can smell it, taste it… It's in your blood. And it's up to you to pick a side.'

'No.'

'You're bathed in the scent of power right now.' I flinched as he leaned forward, sniffing my hair loudly. 'It's the stench of blood on you. You reek of the crimes of your family, of their *power. Of the blood you've spilt*.'

'I'm not like the rest of you.' My voice was high-pitched, my heart beating frenetically. 'I don't want power. I haven't caused any bloodshed.'

He sniffed more loudly. 'Blood paid your way through culinary school. Blood kept your little restaurant open. Blood paid for all your stellar reviews. Blood found you passage to this sur-fucked planet. Blood keeps you here.'

'I'm not a murderer.'

'Not *yet*. Though you're coasting on your grandparents' killing spree. After all, it's thanks to them that you get to use the Kaveri name to lie your way across the galaxy.'

'My hands are clean.'

'If you say so.'

'All I've *ever* done is try to escape my *fucked-up* family and leave their heinous crimes *behind*.'

'All you've ever done is be a good little Godavari who'd make your ancestors proud,' he said archly. 'Using your name and the resources it commands when convenient, dropping your name when it's a hindrance, lying and manipulating your way across the galaxy, playing on the sympathies of the universe… it's *quintessential* Godavari.'

'*Shut up!*' I swung my fist.

He effortlessly blocked my punch and grabbed me. I struggled against his grip, my legs tripping over the soft sand.

'*Stop! You let go of her!*'

My heart sank at the familiar sound of her voice. I twisted my head and saw a huddle of figures racing towards us.

'*Saras! Are you okay?*' another voice yelled.

I blanched.

'Let me go,' I begged. 'Please. Let me go and leave.'

Jog Tunga pushed me to the ground and grinned. Curiosity Zia reached us first, followed closely by Boundless Baz, who immediately stepped up to Jog Tunga and shoved him in the chest.

Jog Tunga shoved him back, much harder, his eyes glinting. Boundless Baz stumbled backwards.

'Call your dogs off,' Jog Tunga said to me coldly.

'Everyone, keep your distance!' I shouted urgently, shocked back into my senses. 'He's dangerous!'

'You know this guy?' Courage Oslo asked, out of breath as he drew into view. 'We saw him harassing you from the party up on the cliffs. Came rushing down all the way—'

Jog Tunga took a few steps back and drew himself up to his full height, exaggerated by his hideous crown. He was practically bouncing on the balls of his feet. 'So, you're her friends, are you?'

'What's it to you?' Boundless Baz snapped.

Curiosity Zia crouched beside me, her hands on my shoulders, looking intently into my eyes.

'What's going on here?' Starlight Fantastic and XX-29 had arrived.

I groaned, drew my knees in towards my chest, and began to shake.

'I have a great story for you, friends of Saraswati *Kaveri*,' I heard Jog Tunga say. 'Or should I say, Saraswati *Godavari*.'

Should I call the Primian Guard? Boundless Baz streamed.

_No._

But—

I said no.

'I don't understand what you're saying,' XX-29 said politely. 'Now please leave our friend alone.'

A bubble of hope welled up within me, and it was squashed by Jog Tunga.

'I'm leaving,' he said. 'But first, I'm going to tell you a story about someone who's a *Godavari princess* wretchedly playing *celebrity chef refugee.* She only faked her scrollwork and escaped the Earth to be on Primus. And she's been lying to you about her identity, and her family—we're murderous dictators, by the way, nice to meet you—all along.'

I glared up at him, hatred searing the insides of my skull. I struggled to rise, but my knees wobbled and I stumbled.

'Is any of this true?' Curiosity Zia asked, shocked.

My mind blanked at the accusation and doubt in her voice.

'Ashte, kanno,' Jog Tunga said, and I cringed at my Daxina dialect. It was the first time I'd heard it in māsas, and it sounded foul upon his tongue. He boarded his craft, and as it rose into the air, I sagged, completely deflated.

'Saras?' a voice said uncertainly. I looked up at Starlight Fantastic.

'Is any of this true?' they asked gently.

'Do you actually know that man?' Courage Oslo asked, his brows knotted in a scowl.

None of them smiled.

'I was just on my way to join you.' I forced a smile. Absolutely no-one returned it. My insides cracked. 'This is not how I wanted you to find out.'

'So it's true, then?' Boundless Baz's voice was hard.

He didn't reveal anything about stealing Feast, at least, I thought, momentarily relieved as I replayed the conversation with Jog Tunga. I felt an ache spreading through me as I perceived how my mind worked, constantly looking to cover my tracks.

'You saw what he's like.' My voice broke. 'I fled the Earth and ran away to Primus to escape him. And the rest of my family, who are even worse. I know I've lied, but—'

Boundless Baz erupted. 'Yes, you lied about all the *important bits*. Like you're not a refugee, your name isn't Kaveri. No, in fact, it's *Godavari,* as in the mass murdering maniacs who have ruled the Daxina Protectorate for close to two centuries.' He drew a sharp breath. 'Hey, Saras! Guess why my grandfather emigrated from Earth to Primus! You'll never guess, but go on!'

'I—'

'He worked for the press, and the *Godavaris,* who happen to be *your fucking ancestors* attempted to assassinate him! Congratulations!'

'I'm sorry—'

'No, it's not your fault!' He grinned manically. 'I'd never hold it against you. But you know what would have been nice? If you'd told us all the fucking *truth!*'

'I'm so sorry,' I gasped. 'I'm sorry, I lied to all of you. I—I don't k-k-know why I did. I wanted to tell you, I swear, but—'

'But it's just easier to lie, isn't it?' Curiosity Zia said coldly. 'Easier to find sympathy when you're a refugee than when you're part of a murderous megalomaniac family.'

'We—I—I feel like a fool!' Courage Oslo said. 'We opened our home to you, our restaurant, our lives…'

'I-I know, I'm sorry.'

'You could have told us at any time, you know?' Boundless Baz said. 'We liked you. It might have come as a shock, but we wouldn't have judged you—'

'There never seemed t-to to b-be a g-g-good time.' Tears streamed down my face, and my friends blurred in my vision.

'We'd have understood.'

'Please… please forgive me now.'

'I need time,' XX-29 crackled through xir vox-box, xir being howling softly.

'I need space, Saras,' Curiosity Zia said, and her voice sounded sad. 'I don't understand why you'd hide this from us—'

'*You saw him!*' I said, suddenly outraged at being put on the spot, over and over again. No matter who I was, I was always wrong to everyone on this sur-fucked rock. 'You saw what I came from, what I ran away from! I'm nothing like him—like *them!* But you'd have judged me the same if I told you at the start…'

'We—' Courage Oslo began.

'You'd never have given me a chance! I know how this works. I've worn the Godavari name for far too long—it's a stain upon who I am, and *I am ashamed of it!*'

I wiped my nose angrily on a tattered sleeve again, and looked up at their faces.

'Right now, I'm mostly judging you for all the lies,' Curiosity Zia said sharply. 'And wondering why you had to cover up your past if you had nothing to hide.'

'I'm on the run from them. What if someone talked? What if *they* found me? What if—'

'I can't even look at you any more,' Boundless Baz spoke over me in disgust, and walked away.

'I need some time,' XX-29 echoed.

'So do we. Shall we get you a flowcab?' Courage Oslo offered coldly. Curiosity Zia simply bit her lower lip, tears streaming silently down her face-tats.

I realised that Starlight Fantastic hadn't said a word, and looked at them imploringly. Their tentacles were ashen grey, and they didn't meet my gaze. 'I trusted you, Saras,' they said in a small voice.

'I'm sorry,' I whispered.

'Right,' Courage Oslo announced. 'We'll, er… we'll call you sometime, Saras. Good luck and everything.'

I watched as all my friends—the only people I trusted to have my back—turned and slowly walked away from me into the night. And then a sick, lurching feeling possessed me.

'Don't tell anyone, please. They'll deport me!' I shouted after them. 'Please! I'll come clean, I swear! Don't tell the authorities, and… don't tell *Ko*…'

Curiosity Zia turned and shot me a filthy look. I heard Starlight Fantastic speaking in a low murmur. They turned.

'We won't,' they said, twisting their tentacles together in a gesture of accord. 'But we hope you will.'

I buried my head in my knees and shivered. I should have run after them. I was too exhausted to move. I was too nauseated by what had just happened.

I'd faked my way across this planet manipulating everyone I met to garner sympathy, all to gain access to this world, all to escape my family. Was Jog Tunga right? Was I really no different from them? Was I just another Godavari, the filthy Earthling scum I was always told I was?

I missed Kili. *Kili would know.* My insides ached as if they were being ripped from within me. There was no way this could get any worse.

Sand crunched behind me.

I looked up.

> **The Kaveri family was annihilated by the ruling Godavari family in a power struggle not uncommon to the Daxina Protectorate. There were no survivors.**
>
> —Anita Umar,
> *One Nation Earth: The Myth of Unity*
> 2053 Anno Earth | 1978 Interstellar Era

TWENTY-ONE

SHE WAS PATHETIC.

Optimism Mahd'vi almost felt sorry for her. *Almost*.

Unfortunately for the "Kaveri girl," her sympathies were held at bay by the indisputable fact that she was *not a Kaveri*. She was, in fact, a *Godavari*. Her family was responsible for the slaughter of Optimism Mahd'vi's ancestry on Earth. They'd wiped them off the planet, erased them from galactic history, and Optimism Mahd'vi and her brother had been lucky to escape unscathed.

The Secretary for Culture and Heritage stared at the snivelling woman in the sand, and felt nothing. If she hadn't just witnessed her anguished confrontation with her former friends, if she hadn't secretly spied upon Saraswati standing up to that bumpkin Jog Tunga, she'd have summoned the Primian Guard and filled in the scrollwork for her immediate deportation.

Lucky for Saraswati, while she'd lurked in the shadows observing events unfold, the beginnings of a plan had meshed together in Optimism Mahd'vi's mind. And while she strongly felt the urge to grab the girl and shake her by the shoulders, she bit down on her ice-cold rage instead. Optimism Mahd'vi had positioned herself behind a large rock, and she stepped out from behind it.

The Godavari girl's shoulders shook. Her head was buried in her arms, and she was curled up on the sand, which was now smeared through her hair and all over her clothes.

Optimism Mahd'vi halted momentarily. *Think of the bigger picture,* she reminded herself. *It's within your grasp.*

She took another step forward.

Saraswati started and jerked upright, her eyes wild. Tears streaked her pale cheeks.

'I believe you lost this.'

'Kili,' Saraswati croaked.

Optimism Mahd'vi released the funny little flying robot from its flowmetal restraints, and it immediately whizzed over to the Godavari girl. It bobbled in the air before her, its screens flitting through a whirlwind of colours, wings whirring as the two of them engaged in some kind of private exchange.

'Secretary Mahd'vi,' Saraswati cried. 'How can I ever thank you? I thought I'd lost him forever…'

She caught herself midway through a loud sniffle, and pushed her sand-streaked curls from her eyes.

'H-how are you?' she asked. 'I'm so glad to see the explosion didn't hurt you.' And then, she hurriedly added: 'I had nothing to do with it. *I swear—*'

'It wasn't a bomb. It was a tech glitch,' Optimism Mahd'vi said flatly.

She regarded the con artist before her, irked by the tumble of unasked for feelings now vying for her attention. Rage, right at the surface, which she'd turned down to a simmer. Annoyance that the *Godavari* girl was so concerned for her well-being. A twinge, just the slightest, of newfound pity for the broken, exhausted woman slumped in the sand.

Saraswati hurriedly rose to her feet, her brow knitted with confusion. 'What are you doing here? I mean, of course you can go anywhere you want to, but… Shouldn't you be in the hospital?'

Optimism Mahd'vi wielded the power of an emotionless mask and silence.

'Is—is everything all right? Are you?' Saraswati continued.

'I made a public address to shed light on my condition and the circumstances of the explosion at the sinfonia,' Optimism Mahd'vi said, every single word carefully anodyne, chosen to betray no emotion. 'In my speech, I made a declaration that I trust you absolutely, and that your Earthling origins are not to be viewed with suspicion or derision.'

She'd held up her end of her bargain with Serenity Ko—in exchange for creative control over Feast's sim experiences, she'd publicly defended Saraswati, regardless of her personal feelings towards the lowlife now twitching apprehensively before her.

When she'd awoken at the hospital, she'd launched a thorough investigation into the cause of the explosion. She'd insisted that Saraswati be released the moment the cause of the incident had been revealed to be a short circuit. She'd decided she had to talk to her in person.

Much to her delight, among the "evidence" gathered at the sinfonia was a decrepit, outdated piece of Earth-technology that Optimism Mahd'vi instantly recognised as Saraswati's flying robot companion. It was simple to analyse all the data it held, on the pretext of the investigation.

Once the new regulations requiring off-worlders to broadcast their location at all times went live, Optimism Mahd'vi had decided to make a speech from the Ibnis-viewing at the Ur-sands, a few hundred metres away from where Saraswati was. Everything had lined up perfectly for a confrontation, followed by the "Kaveri" pretender's immediate deportation, and then the Earthling prince had shown up and made things… complicated, but in ways that would serve Optimism Mahd'vi's agenda.

'Thanks to me, most of Primus might not like you, but they'll think twice before dragging your Earthling past through the mud,' Optimism Mahd'vi said.

Saraswati's face twisted oddly. It scrunched up, her lower lip twitching, and she seemed to struggle momentarily before breaking out into a watery smile. 'You—you are most generous. I am beyond grateful—'

'Of course, your little robot and I had a fascinating chat before my speech,' Optimism Mahd'vi continued.

'Y-you did?'

'Well, he was knocked out for our chat, but it doesn't take much to scan outdated semiconductors, circuitry and wiring,' Optimism Mahd'vi said.

'But that's a breach of privacy…'

The words died on the girl's lips as Optimism Mahd'vi stared at her. Saraswati glanced at the flying robot, whizzing frantically by her shoulder.

'I discovered such wonderful things about you,' Optimism Mahd'vi continued smoothly. 'So many memories from your journey here, your hopes and dreams, your conversations with all your friends. And all your *guilt*.'

Saraswati eyed her uncertainly, and Optimism Mahd'vi felt a thrill of power coursing through her.

'*So much guilt*,' she said, repeating herself. 'About your past on Earth, and all the lies you've told about yourself since…'

The Godavari girl appeared to deflate. Her shoulders slumped inwards, and she wobbled unsteadily, threatening to keel over.

'I confess, I was outraged. I considered throwing your robot in the incinerator. After all, you were already being interrogated. But then I had a better idea—I decided to find you, and hear the truth from you firsthand.'

'I—I never meant to hurt anyone…' Saraswati shook, her voice barely a whisper.

A flash of anger blitzed through every fibre of Optimism Mahd'vi's being. *Focus on the bigger picture.*

'You've got to believe me, what I had to escape was—'

'I know what you had to escape. The Godavari clan is notorious on Earth. Must be so hard being their out-of-favour daughter. Tell me, was it tough sitting idly by and watching them murder and conquer? Was it difficult to be in the same room where war was being planned? Is that why you decided to funnel all that glorious blood money into being an interstellar public figure, loved and admired by half the galaxy for being this poor refugee immigrant rising from the ashes of her past?

'A refugee.' Optimism Mahd'vi snorted. 'Shall I tell you the story of the refugees I once knew?'

The *Godavari* girl whispered something inaudible, and Optimism Mahd'vi carried on.

'Once upon a time, there were two young children. A boy and a girl, brother and sister. They grew up in comfort, in a beautiful part of the Earth called the Daxina Protectorate. They were too young, too innocent to see beyond the high walls of their garden to the wider world beyond, mired in violence and bloodlust. They were protected fiercely by their family, and their family name was Kaveri.

'One night, they were shaken awake from their deep slumber. The boy was hugging his Mr Ted Explorer Bear, and the girl clung onto her Missy Caterpillar plushie. They were spirited away by their nursemaid, half asleep, into a strange spaceship. They went on a long voyage and begged to see their mother and father. They were told their parents were far, far away.

'They landed on a strange, new world. They were left at a community childcare centre. All they knew were their names. They were Kaveris.

'They never saw their parents again. When the girl was in high school, she stumbled upon a single sentence in a history scroll: "The Kaveri family was annihilated by the ruling Godavari family in a power struggle not uncommon to the Daxina Protectorate. There were no survivors."

'That girl was me. Your family destroyed mine. My past, my childhood, my home…'

The Godavari girl shook like a leaf eddying in the currents of a gale.

'Was it *fun* for you to coast on the privileges of your lineage, until you got bored of it all, and decided to make your way here?' Despite her best intentions, Optimism Mahd'vi's voice rose.

Give her a chance to explain. Please.

The intervention came from her flying robot companion.

I don't need explanations or apologies. I want actions, Optimism Mahd'vi shot back.

It was enough, though. It cracked through Optimism Mahd'vi's escalating fury and shattered it, so she felt like a volcano that had finally erupted, now cloaked in the comfort of an ash cloud and lava.

'That's what I thought, at first,' Optimism Mahd'vi said coldly. 'After all, the Godavari reputation precedes you all.'

'I'm not my family,' Saraswati said at last.

'No, you aren't,' Optimism Mahd'vi conceded. 'I gathered as much from sifting through all your memories. And when I arrived here'—she nodded to indicate the Ibnis-viewing party, still in full swing over her shoulder—'and finished my speech, I happened to chance upon your argument with your Earthling prince.'

'He's not my—'

Optimism Mahd'vi held up her hand, irritated. 'Yes, not *your* prince. Some political alliance, spare me the details…'

'He's a monster,' Saraswati said.

'Right, I'm sure,' Optimism Mahd'vi said without a shred of sympathy. 'He made you the most fascinating proposition though.'

'I *refused!*' Saraswati's eyes widened in panic. 'You've got to believe me! I'm not working with him. I—I'd never…' she sputtered, then regained control. 'I'd never steal Feast's tech for him. Not for anyone or *anything*.'

'No need to get all riled up,' Optimism Mahd'vi snapped.

Saraswati fell silent. 'You believe me?'

'About that, at least,' Optimism Mahd'vi said. 'But here's the thing, Saraswati *Godavari*.'

The Godavari girl flinched. Optimism Mahd'vi permitted herself a moment of grim satisfaction before carrying on. 'I think what he's suggesting is a brilliant idea.'

'You… *what?*'

'I think you should do it.'

'*What?*'

'In fact, I *want* you to do it.'

'*What?*'

'Do you need me to repeat myself in Vox?'

The Godavari girl scowled. 'Ur-speak is just fine.'

'Let me make myself clear, then,' Optimism Mahd'vi

said, then proceeded to spell things out insultingly slowly, accompanied by large, childish hand gestures.

'I'—she pointed at herself—'want *you*'—she jabbed her forefinger towards Saras—'to *steal Feast Inc.'s tech* and hand it over to *the buffoon from Earth*.' She mimed throwing things in a box, and mimicked a giant crown. 'Did you understand that?'

'But… *why?*' Saraswati looked aghast.

'That's for me to know, and for you to never ask me again,' Optimism Mahd'vi snapped, her patience evaporating. 'You're a fake refugee—an enemy of my erstwhile slaughtered family, no less. You've falsified all your scrollwork to get here. The penalty for that is immediate deportation and a ban on interstellar travel. You'll be sent back to Earth and never be permitted to leave again. So you either stop asking stupid questions and do exactly as I'm saying… or kiss your newfound life on Primus goodbye.'

'How do I know I can trust you?' Saraswati asked with a sudden spark of defiance.

'You don't, but you have no choice.'

'I—'

'You do things my way, or I deport you right this moment.'

That shut the Earthling up.

'Why did you defend me in public if you knew?' she asked in a small voice.

'That's between me and Serenity Ko.'

'What's Ko got to do with anything?'

Optimism Mahd'vi ignored the question. 'Do it. You know where to get in touch with me. Don't be stupid enough as to say what you're doing out loud. If a soul hears so much as the lightest whisper about it, you're deported.'

And with that parting shot, Optimism Mahd'vi turned and strode away, leaving the Godavari girl with an impossible choice that was no choice at all. She smiled. A trap had been sprung. And she would reel in every last Godavari when they least expected it.

When the state's hand dips into the river of cultural expression, it does not go with the flow, but creates undercurrents. To control the passage of thought is to control the direction of freedom.

—*Philosophies of the United Human Cooperative*
2034 Anno Earth | 1959 Interstellar Era

TWENTY-TWO

'Earth girl,' Serenity Ko said grandly, then winced as her voice came out as a squeak.

She resisted the urge to fling her arms around Saraswati and smother her with kisses, on two counts—first, she was playing it cool, because there was no way Ammamma was right, and no way Serenity Ko was *in love* with her. She *liked* her strongly, was *attracted to her* disastrously, but she wasn't *in love* with her.

And second, Saraswati looked like a wreck. Her eyes were swollen and red-rimmed from weeping, damp sand shimmered in her hair and streaked her dress, and her dress was shredded in about half a dozen places. Kili bobbed beside her, and even he appeared worse for wear—his usually polished chrome and green body was badly scraped, and he seemed to have lost his enthusiasm for whirring around in high energy.

'Hey,' she said softly. 'Earth girl. Are you ok—?'

Saraswati threw her arms around her and buried her face in her shoulder. Serenity Ko ignored the electricity shooting through her every nerve, and patted her on the shoulder awkwardly. She was suddenly hideously aware of her rumpled candy-floss-coloured pajamas, panicked momentarily about whether her breath was fresh, and then winced at the thought that her tousled long hair, free of her customary high braid, might be covered in snot from Saraswati's sniffling.

'It's really early in the morning,' she said. 'Um, let me make you some… chai?'

Saraswati mumbled something incoherent into her shoulder.

'Something stronger? Bira?'

Saraswati pulled away, sniffing. 'No. Chai.' She shuddered. 'I don't think bira will do me any good.'

'Suit yourself,' Serenity Ko said, secretly relieved. The last time they'd been in the same room drinking alcohol, one thing had led to another and they'd found themselves entangled against a staircase in an alcove, lips on lips and skin...

She shut the memory down. It was probably a good thing she'd gotten too wasted to walk straight that night, shutting things down before they went any further.

Carry on like that and we might as well commit to it, she thought. And that was the last thing she wanted—she thought.

She fumbled around the kitchen, pulling long-unused sachets of herbal chai from a large box. She sniffed them suspiciously; they didn't seem rotten. *Does chai rot?*

She dropped the little powdered bags in warm water and fervently hoped this was how one made chai. She vaguely recalled watching her Ammamma do this every night, and the steps seemed about right. She peeked across the kitchen counter to where Saraswati was slumped on her couch, absent-mindedly stroking Kili, who had snuggled all the way into the hollow of her neck.

'Um, how are you?' Serenity Ko asked.

'Terrible.'

'I was worried when I heard about the attack on the sinfonia.'

'I streamed you as soon as I could,' Saraswati said, her tone hollow.

'Yeah, "I'm okay" isn't a lot to go on, but I guess you did.'

'What did you want? My medical reports and location?' Saraswati snapped.

'No—'

'If you want, I can send them to you all the way back from my Earth days,' Saraswati said testily. 'Kili, you've got my total travel history since I was thirteen and we first met, right? Why don't we send it all over to Ko so she can keep tabs on me.'

'Nine Virtues—'

'In fact, can we put them on the Loop for public access? Because I'm *done*. Done!'

Serenity Ko divided the chai into two cups and hesitantly brought them over to where Saraswati had now flopped onto her back, covering her face with her arm, staring listlessly at the ceiling through the crook of her elbow.

She had a bad day, Kili said apologetically.

I gathered. Serenity Ko nodded.

A *really* bad day.

'What Kili said,' Saraswati interjected. 'I've been up all night.'

'I'm really sorry. What happened?'

Saraswati sniffed loudly, and Kili proceeded to explain.

I was knocked out by the Primian Guard after the explosion. She thought I was dead, Kili offered.

Nine Virtues…

They took her in for questioning and harassed her. I wasn't even around to help, Kili said guiltily.

Good grief.

And then Optimism Mahd'vi got hold of me and started snooping around Saras's data and—

'*What?* That's *illegal!*' Serenity Ko cried, disbelief and indignation welling up within her.

'Everything Kili said,' Saraswati said. 'And there's nothing I can do about it.'

'But—'

Saraswati shot her an intense glare, and Serenity Ko shut up, wondering what was going on but too afraid to ask.

Kili lapsed into silence. Serenity Ko decided to lighten things up.

'Well, I got into a fight with my grandmother about Feast last night. We were supposed to be doing tastings for my brother's wedding, and after the explosion, it all went sideways,' she said brightly. 'My grandmother hates me, it's official.'

Saraswati grinned weakly, and sipped on her chai in silence. Serenity Ko warmed to the thought that her diversion was working, and continued.

'She's convinced we have no clue what we're doing, warned me about a bunch of dire consequences, the price of fame, all the bad things. In fact, she's obsessed with the thought that governments across the galaxy are going to misuse Feast!'

She laughed, and continued laughing when she realised nobody was joining in, and her attempt at levity might have fallen somewhat flat with her present company.

'That's hilarious, right?' she prompted, refusing to let it go.

She was met by an expressionless stare, Saraswati's chai cup halfway to her beautifully full lips—which Serenity Ko quickly averted her gaze from.

'You don't find it funny,' she said.

'It isn't,' said Saraswati.

An awkward silence stretched out.

'I'm just glad that you're okay,' Serenity Ko said, the tumble of feelings she'd been struggling to repress all rushing out in a flood of words. 'When I thought you might have been injured at the sinfonia… I—I lost my sur-fucked mind. I couldn't get rid of the thought of you lying in a hospital ward somewhere, with half of you blown off, in miserable pain or even worse… dead. Ask my brother, he was there through it all. And my grandmother.' Her face darkened. 'Maybe don't ask my grandmother. All I'm saying is you scared me, Saras. I was *terrified*. And I'm really, ridiculously, stupidly, enthusiastically glad that you're okay.'

She reached across and rubbed Saraswati's knee gently, then kicked herself because it was bare, other than being covered in sand, and running her hands over her bare skin sent her hands tingling, and her mind wandering to places where they were skin against skin, mouths hungrily devouring each other…

She withdrew her hand and crossed her arms, resolving to keep all her body parts to herself.

Saraswati stared at her curiously. 'You were worried for me?'

Serenity Ko's heart ached. *It's a strong liking, not* love.

'How could you think I wouldn't be?' Serenity Ko asked quietly. 'You're my…'

'Friend,' Saraswati said sniffling.

'Unless… Do you want to be more?' Serenity Ko asked, and then kicked herself. This is why she never woke up before dawn—as opposed to being still awake before dawn—because that groggy half-asleep state of mind made her say the stupidest things. She didn't even know if *she* wanted them to be more.

'No,' Saraswati said. 'Right now, what I need is a friend. I feel like I've lost all of mine.'

Her lips twisted into an ugly little moue, and a tear ran down her cheek, much to Serenity Ko's horror.

'Here, tissue,' Serenity Ko said hurriedly, launching herself across the kaapi table and grabbing a stack of them, knocking over her own chai cup in turn. She pressed one into Saraswati's hands before whirling around and sopping up the spill, heaping tissue after tissue upon it, her attention wholly focused on the flowmetal surface to avoid making eye contact with Saraswati, in the hope that if she couldn't see Saras, then Saras wouldn't notice the heat creeping up into her cheeks turning them as red as blistered rubus berries.

'Thanks,' Saraswati blubbered.

Serenity Ko steeled herself to engage with whatever weirdness was going on in the room head-on. 'Do you want to talk about what happened?'

Saraswati shifted where she slouched, and regarded her with a pitying, sad gaze that Serenity Ko couldn't understand. 'Some of it, yeah.'

'Well, I'm here for all of it,' Serenity Ko said firmly. 'You can tell me anything. This is a safe space. I'm your friend.'

'Thanks,' Saraswati choked.

'Why don't I give you a moment to gather your thoughts?' Serenity Ko offered kindly. 'I'll just take this mess away and be right back.'

She rose from where she was crouched before Saraswati at the kaapi table. She grabbed the soaking wet tissues and her empty chai cup and walked into the kitchen, setting them down as softly as she possibly could. She looked out into her living room, glad that all her Bloxxos were at her parents' place, and that her space was vaguely adult-looking. Soft yellow lights, a large array of visio-nodes across the far wall, some scroll-shelves littered with important sounding Primian poetry, an oversized deep purple armchair and a matching sofa that had just the right amount of squishiness, cushions in all shapes and sizes, even a rug. She beamed momentarily before she caught sight of the dead houseplants and her satellite slinging jumpsuit flung casually across one of her side tables, then cringed as she remembered the state of her bedroom, her eyes quickly sliding to the door to confirm that it was, indeed, well and truly shut.

This wasn't the first time Saraswati had been in her space, but it was the first time they'd both been there sober enough to take in what it looked like, instead of being wrapped up in each other—metaphorically and literally—and she had to confess to herself that it was a nice, cosy feeling. *I wouldn't mind doing this every day…*

Serenity Ko shut the treacherous thought down. It was not something she wanted to encourage, and certainly not now when Saraswati clearly wanted to discuss other, more important things. *Be a good listener, Ko,* she thought sternly. *And keep that stupid mouth of yours shut.*

Saraswati and Kili seemed to be engaged in an animated private conversation, so she decided that giving them an extra moment or two wouldn't hurt. She slipped into her bathroom, popped a dental cleanse into her mouth, and stepped out triumphantly with minty fresh breath. She also quickly ran a brush through her hair, but not so as to make it obvious that she'd made any effort—the intent was to appear effortlessly dishevelled in a sexy but absolutely casual way.

When she returned, she heard—to her mounting horror and totally erasing all thoughts of sex appeal—all about what it was like to be an immigrant in the midst of a disaster on a planet like Primus, especially if your scrollwork said you were originally from the Earth.

'*Six?*' she practically shrieked. 'You had *six* interrogators?'

'Yup,' said Saraswati, who seemed a bit more cheerful now that she had told the tale. 'Ran through them all *twice*.'

'That's got to be a diplomatic crime!'

'I'm sure it isn't,' Saraswati said darkly. 'Earthling, remember?'

'Nine Virtues, on behalf of the planet of Primus, I am *so* sorry!'

'And Kili… I thought he was dead the whole time. Not *one* of the fuckers told me he'd been found in one piece. Not even the Primian Guard lady who dropped me off at the Ur-sands in the end!'

'Why didn't you come straight here?' Serenity Ko demanded.

'I—' Saraswati hesitated.

'Go on.'

'I was still mad at you. After the riot. I wanted to clear my head. I felt all alone in this star-fucked universe.'

'I was *worried* for you.'

'I know. I'm sorry.'

'And so, what? You just wandered around the Ur-sands *alone*?'

Saraswati paused, then hung her head. 'Yeah,' she said softly.

'Saras! I'd have come to you!'

'Like I said—'

'Yes, space. Sure, whatever,' Serenity Ko sulked.

'I came to you, didn't I?'

'I love being a last resort.'

'There's something I need to tell you. The truth.' Saraswati's lips twitched oddly. 'This isn't easy—'

Serenity Ko furrowed her brow, losing track of the words spilling out of Saraswati's lips. Something didn't quite add up.

'So wait, they dropped you off at the Ur-sands without Kili? So how did you get him before heading here?' she interrupted.

'Optimism Mahd'vi brought him to me,' Saraswati said, suddenly keenly interested in the dying fey-fern on the side-table. 'Which brings me to—'

Serenity Ko gasped. 'The Secretary for Culture and Heritage delivered your lost Winger to you *in person* after surviving an explosion and giving a public address?'

Saraswati glanced at Serenity Ko, her expression unreadable. Serenity Ko completely missed the foreboding gaze. She laughed in glee.

'It worked! I mean, of course it worked, I make only the best arguments ever!' She laughed. 'But also, she must really, *really* like you!'

'I wouldn't go that far. She *hates* me, and it's all because—'

'No, she must *love you*. Teacher's pet!'

'We're not in school, and she isn't my teacher,' Saraswati said irritably.

'Mommy's favourite!' Serenity Ko teased, sticking her tongue out.

'*She is not my mommy!*'

'You can thank me!' Serenity Ko said smugly, ignoring Saraswati's mounting ire. 'I called her and vouched for you right after the explosion.'

'You… *what?*'

'And then I made a deal with her. You're welcome, by the way.'

Saraswati sat bolt upright. 'Take several steps back,' she said slowly. 'And tell me everything.'

'Well, right after the explosion—and I'm sorry I have to bring this up—the stream media were really going after you,' Serenity Ko began, enjoying her triumphant march back into Saraswati's good books. 'And I mean *really* going after you. You should have heard the things they were alleging…'

'Yeah, skip forward.'

'Right, you don't need to hear it. You know the kind of thing—Earthling smear stuff.' Serenity Ko nodded. 'It was so unfair, I called Optimism Mahd'vi as soon as it was broadcast that she was out of the hospital.'

'And?'

'And I made a deal with her!' Serenity Ko said happily. 'I told her that if she made a speech in public defending you, I'd give her creative approval on everything we put into Feast. Primian superiority and all the rest. And she kept her end of the bargain, and found you and returned Kili, too! Not bad, don't you think?'

Serenity Ko finally registered that Saraswati was staring at her in open horror with a side of revulsion. 'What is it?' she asked uncertainly.

'Mahd'vi told me she'd struck a deal with you.'

Serenity Ko brushed her hands together smugly. 'Like I said, you're welcome. You could look happier about it.'

'You expected this to make me happy?'

'You've only got Primus's most powerful authority on culture backing you, so, um, yes?'

'You thought that ceding control of Feast—all our databases, memory triggers, curated experiences, audio-visual-sensory experiences—to the government would make me *happy*?'

Serenity Ko was irked now. 'She's publicly backing you and telling people to shut the fuck up about your Earthling origins. So yes.'

'You've given her unlimited power!'

'Primus to Earth. Reality check. She's government. She *has* unlimited power.'

'Not—not *this* kind of power. It was safe with us!' Saraswati shot to her feet, pacing. 'We were in control of it. Independent of the authorities, of any government. We had the power to do something *good* with it!'

Serenity Ko was now decidedly lost. 'Saras.' She attempted a soothing tone. 'You've had a very long night, and a very bad run-in with our government. But this means nothing—Mahd'vi will just be happy to be included, and feel powerful about getting to send us official comms saying "approved" a few hundred times. She'll get bored of it, and then outsource it to her interns or her AI or whatever. I don't like it—she's meddling with *my* end of the product, after all, messing with the sim databases and experiences. But it was worth the trade-off. It's no big deal.'

Saraswati rounded on her, much to her shock and dismay. '*No. Big. Deal?*' she asked, each word somehow louder and shriller than the last. 'Do you know what governments can *do* with the power to manipulate people's *minds?* The potential Feast has for *propaganda?*'

'P—propaganda?' Serenity Ko burst out laughing, then saw that Saraswati hadn't intended it to be funny.

'Yes, *propaganda*. We've given them the perfect way to

deliver it through *food*. It doesn't help that Primian food is already packed with all this heavy symbolism and Nakshatran values and the glory of the past and tradition and cultural superiority and so on. We've—no, *you've* handed Optimism Mahd'vi the perfect vehicle to literally stuff it down people's throats, until all they're left with is the absolute conviction that Primus reigns supreme.'

'Hey, Saras, calm down,' Serenity Ko said, also rising to her feet. 'That's not how things work here. We're anti-empire. Maybe that's how things are done on Earth—'

She instantly regretted it.

'It is *exactly* how things are done on Earth, and there's no reason they won't be done the same way here,' Saraswati said, her eyes filled with fear. A stray curl fell across her face, and she flicked it away.

'Saras, you're tired and paranoid. You need a nap,' Serenity Ko said, starting towards her and attempting to give her a hug.

Saraswati shrugged her off. 'Don't come near me! You've just handed her the keys to the kingdom, and you used *me* as a *bargaining chip*.'

'I did not—'

'Now the consequences are all on me. I'm drenched in blood, and I can never escape!'

'Star-fuck me, Saras!' Serenity Ko yelled. 'You're getting hysterical, and I'm going to call a med-cab and get you a sedative if you don't calm down. *What* blood? There is no blood! *Calm the fucking Nine Virtues down!*'

Saraswati's face was twisted with rage. 'You had no right to use me like this.'

'I was doing you a *favour*,' Serenity Ko snapped. 'I just wanted to get the fucking stream-media off your back, and Mahd'vi and I agreed on the best way to do so.'

'I'm not a fucking child. You don't get to make these decisions for me.'

'It. Was. A. Favour,' Serenity Ko said, livid.

'You know what, Ko? I think it's time you stopped doing me favours,' Saraswati said, and stomped towards the door. Kili did his best to calm Saraswati down, trying to hover around her and make eye contact, but she batted him away.

'Where are you going?' Serenity Ko asked, appalled.

'Home.'

'It's three in the morning.'

'Your point?'

She fled.

Sorry, Ko, Kili said apologetically. _She's had a terrible day. All over the place. I'll see if I can help._

Yeah, thanks, Kili, Serenity Ko said weakly, slumping down onto the couch as Kili whirred after Saraswati's departing figure in a hurry.

She stayed up the rest of the night, turning Saraswati's story over in her head. *Something's not right,* she concluded bleakly, drifting into an uneasy sleep in the wee hours of the morning. *I'm going to find out what it is. I need to help Saras.*

Ambition is a dark tunnel of one's own design, and freedom is the light at the end of the tunnel. Every so often, it's an oncoming train.

—Ancient Earth Saying

TWENTY-THREE

I'D LONG SINCE come to accept that I would always be alone, but I was beginning to learn that there are many kinds of loneliness, all burning holes into my heart in different ways.

I was used to being alone. I'd been the outsider in my family, a failure of a Godavari princess who refused to be enthralled by the trappings of power, choosing to lurk in the kitchen and learning to cook from Kanakamma instead. My mother's disgust each time she beheld the daughter who disgraced her with my disregard for fashion and parties, my father's disappointment that I was destined to be a diplomatic dud, and my sister's cruel mockery at my struggles to fit in underscored most of my growing up. Even the servants feared being too nice to me, on pain of remonstration from their masters.

I'd been alone while desperately plotting my escape. To convince my parents to send me to culinary school, I'd blackmailed them with a slew of bad behaviour. I'd shirked my private tutor and worked as an underage line cook in a local restaurant for months on end, giving my bodyguards the slip each afternoon until I'd eventually been discovered and put under perpetual surveillance—at which point I'd fasted on a hunger strike that nearly killed me. I'm sure my mother would have been content to be rid of me but for my father's grand designs. We'd negotiated: I would study at culinary school, and in exchange, I'd form a political alliance with the Bhadra clan, the family's second-biggest rival in the Daxina Protectorate. With my sister marrying into the Tunga clan, I would ensure the Godavaris held onto absolute power.

I'd learnt to be alone and powerless, making do-or-die

bargains, always buying time, all the while hoping sheer dumb luck would come to my rescue because everything I could do to escape was never enough. I'd spent years waiting for misfortune to find me, for the nuptials I never wanted to be announced. The eldest Bhadra son had died in a solar flare race; the middle one had married for love and been disowned. The youngest son was about a decade younger than I, and that gave me precious time until he came of age. I'd been alone and paranoid right through, glancing over my shoulder nonstop in case that sheer dumb luck ran out.

I'd honed being alone to a lifestyle choice. I'd studied at Protectorate Paradiso, and for the first time in my life, I'd been somewhere the Godavari name, while whispered in suspicion, didn't have power over me. It had been too late for me to make friends, though. I'd kept waiting for knives to find their way into me, even though my classmates were nothing but nice, and by the time I'd formed any real relationships, it had been time for all of us to graduate.

I'd tried to stop being alone, and it had come back to hurt me. When I'd returned to Daxina and started Elé Oota, I had handpicked my team of chefs for their skill, their daring, and their willingness to treat me as a regular human being. I'd developed a keen nose for sniffing out people who might cower before me or suck up to me because of my Godavari identity, and those never made it past their interviews. If someone could ignore the plainclothes bodyguards lurking at all the entrances night after night, frisking them for weapons on their way in—hilarious because there were knives, hot oil, and open flames all over the kitchen—and could keep their heads down through the occasional visit from high-ranking officials who made absurd demands of the kitchen, they'd been a keeper.

My sous chef, Kartikeya, with her gap-toothed smile and experimental desserts, and Juno who'd stomped around the fires of the tandoor like a violent ballerina, had sliced through my loneliness, straight into my heart. I'd had to leave them behind when I fled the Earth. I'd left no forwarding address, paying through my nose to rewrite my history so I couldn't be traced back to being Saraswati Godavari, out there in the vastness of space.

A fat lot of good that had done me.

I was now alone because I was a liar. I was alone because my hands were steeped in bloodshed spanning generations, even if I'd never done anything more violent than cook over an open flame myself. And this loneliness was different. It was the loneliness born of losing something I'd never imagined I could ever have—friends who loved me for who I was. Or rather, who loved me for who I claimed to be.

I was alone and I deserved it.

And even as I brooded over being all alone in the universe, I knew I was being selfish and ungrateful in the extreme. I still had Kili, and I'd nearly lost him, so if I didn't appreciate his unwavering presence by my side—my little Winger who'd been with me through most of my life—if I couldn't find it within me to stop pitying myself for a nanosecond and demonstrate some appreciation for the few good things in my life, then what kind of monster was I turning into?

The isolation that comes from self-awareness cuts deep.

A nava had passed since the many incidents that shaped my present loneliness. Each morning, I awoke from a cocoon of exhausted sleep into a shroud of wakefulness that threatened to strangle me. The moment consciousness found me, my breath came in rasps, my chest tightening, tremors wracking my shoulders.

Unfailingly, memories ripped through my mind, winking in and out disparately but all coming together in resounding confirmation that I was well and truly fucked.

The explosion at the sinfonia, the hours of interrogation, my shredded insides at the thought that I've lost Kili, the dread and fear that they're going to accuse me and deport me to my old life with my hideous family back on Earth…

Jog Tunga at the Ur-sands, insisting that I steal Feast's tech for him…

The expressions on my former friends' faces when they confront me—Boundless Baz's disgust, Courage Oslo and

Curiosity Zia's exasperation, XX-29's disappointment and Starlight Fantastic's dismay at my betrayal…

Optimism Mahd'vi's orders that I comply with Jog Tunga's demands and steal Feast, or face deportation…

Serenity Ko's unthinking bargain with Optimism Mahd'vi: Complete government oversight of Feast in exchange for an official, public defence of me…

Mixed reactions to that last piece of ghastliness were currently being expressed in the XP Inc. office, following Grace Kube's official announcement to the team. They'd invited me to be there so we could present a "united front" to the wider team, as if all of us were on board with total government control. Never mind that I'd expressed strong opposition to the idea—first to Serenity Ko the night of our fight, then later in multiple meetings with the Triumvirate. Only Optimism Sah'r had somewhat seen my point of view. Grace Kube had grimly said it was a non-negotiable in exchange for the full support of the Secretariat, and Courage Na'vil had been positively ebullient in his enthusiasm, something he was demonstrating again.

'…greater supervision will only lead to higher ethical standards,' Courage Na'vil was saying officiously, while simultaneously fighting to hold a smug grin in check. 'And with the Secretariat on board, there's nobody who can argue that we've dropped the ball on our implementation of Feast…'

'You mean, we all get to cover our arses,' Curiosity Nenna said, more belligerently than I'd ever heard her before.

'Nine Virtues!' Courage Na'vil spluttered. 'We're tinkering with sensory perception, manipulating memory, tweaking life experiences on the fly! We need all the ethical safeguards we can get.'

'That sounds like you have no confidence in the product,' Serenity Ko said coldly.

I quickly glanced at where she sat a few chairs down from me. I caught a glimpse of her leaning forward, her hand in the air, her face a mask of contempt.

We wouldn't be here if it hadn't been for you. I fought the urge to snap and say it out loud. We hadn't spoken since our argument, and I hadn't seen her at all until a few hours ago at XP Inc. I'd chosen to ignore her, and she'd streamed me so persistently, I was beginning to feel guilty about ignoring her so resolutely.

A stab of guilt wormed its way through me. At least she'd had the courage to tell me what she'd done—cede control of Feast to Optimism Mahd'vi. I'd nearly told her the truth about my past, but when she'd dropped that bombshell, I'd been too incensed to follow through.

Maybe I'm just avoiding responsibility for my trail of lies.

No, I decided. It was genuine outrage at what she'd done.

I'd built Feast to share my love of flavour with the universe, and to break free of the stranglehold of my family. And now, it was going to be misused as a tool of Primian propaganda—they could deny it all they liked, but in my bones, I knew it was true. All the while, Optimism Mahd'vi was encouraging me to steal the tech and hand it to Jog Tunga, while all the stream-media blamed me for everything that was going wrong on Primus, Feast or otherwise, and I hated being a pawn in whatever stupid games *everyone* seemed to be playing.

Grace Kube held his hands out placatingly from where he stood before the team. Behind him, a presentation was holorayed across a wall of visio-nodes, looming larger than life.

'We've had extensive debates on the ethics of Feast,' he said firmly, throwing a quelling glance at both Courage Na'vil and Serenity Ko. 'We're all on board with what we're doing. And we're doing it within the ethical guidelines laid out for sims according to the Extended Experiences Act of 1994 IE—look it up, or talk to one of our legal team if you have any concerns.'

He scowled briefly, accentuating the scars on his bald head accumulated through his modding past. 'What this means is we'll have a few amendments to our process. It will result in longer timelines for every Feast recipe we're offering.'

He tapped his fingers together and the presentation behind him morphed into a new series of process flows, where every Feast offering would be sent on for "Secretariat approval" before it could be alpha tested internally, and beta tested with a wider audience at our pop-ups.

'The Secretariat has a nava to object to any of our Feast experiences, failing which we will consider an experience approved,' Grace Kube said. 'This is the agreement we've come to, *no arguments*.'

A murmur of dissent had broken out in the small, packed meeting room.

'Strategically—and Ko will get into the specifics later—we're looking at an extra nava of development for each Feast dish, so we will be cutting the number of dishes on our road map for our initial release. All our pop-ups will go on hiatus while the existing dishes are sent to the Secretariat for approval or feedback. We've requested a high priority turnaround, so expect them back soon. And if there are any comments from the Secretariat, we will implement them *immediately*. If you disagree with their comments, we will have a meeting every nava to resolve your conflicts. Understood?'

There were troubled looks on many of the faces around me.

'We will be pausing our experimental foods and off-world foods development until we can get our primary offering—*Primian* Feast dishes—back on track as scheduled for the Millennium Feast.'

There was some booing at this, and Grace Kube smiled sympathetically. 'I'm not saying we'll never get round to them. You're just going to have to wait, that's all.'

'What's in it for you, Kube?' a voice called from somewhere near the back. 'Kickbacks? Are you running for the Secretariat?'

All heads snapped in unison towards its source. The speaker's name-tag identified her as *Harmony Flo, She/Her*.

'Flo, you ought to know me better by now,' Grace Kube said wryly. 'I'm doing this for the product. Feast gets complete and official support from the Secretariat of Primus. We find it easier to enter the market, given the fracas our product has caused in the culinary community. Maybe fewer chefs go after us on the Loop. We gain some leverage when it comes to negotiating licensing deals, or off-world exports, all of which leads to greater profits. For *us*.'

'And for the *government?*' asked Harmony Flo, refusing to back down.

I looked pointedly at Serenity Ko, who avoided my gaze just as pointedly.

'I'm not the government!' Grace Kube laughed, and that dispelled the tension in the room.

It didn't ease my sense of foreboding one bit.

'I COULD HOP on a mining ship to the Osmos Girdle, say I work as a cook, and find my way off the Girdle to one of the neighbouring moons on a trade ship,' I muttered, scanning future expenses as my brain did the kind of mental math I hadn't since school. 'Or maybe I ask Starlight Fantastic for a lift…'

My insides twisted at the thought, because it was underscored by a secondary one—Starlight Fantastic was the softest friend I had, and the most likely to go easy on me after they'd all discovered what an insufferable liar I was, ergo the most manipulable in terms of an escape route.

I hissed at myself. 'You are a fucking manipulative, lying, egomaniacal sun-baked bitch.'

Hey! That's my best friend you're talking about, Kili said angrily, whirring over to settle on my slumped shoulders.

'Says a whole lot about you, then,' I groused.

My best friend is someone who's been in some really tough situations, and who's always tried to do the right thing, but hasn't always made the best decisions, Kili said gently. _And whenever she makes mistakes, she always learns from them._

I slumped forward onto the dinner table in my space at the Faith of the Light. I'd come home from the meeting at XP Inc.—Serenity Ko and I still hadn't said a word to each other—and discovered a package from Good Cheer Eria. It was wrapped in some kind of light, patterned flowmetal and wound through with an elaborate knot of flowering vines. I hadn't opened it up yet; it was so beautiful, it felt like something I didn't deserve to have.

I ran my fingers through my curls, twisting them, still unused to their texture even after a year of having my hair modded from its more natural wave. 'I have no option but to run away,' I muttered.

I'm sorry I have to break the news, but you don't have the savings, Kili remarked.

Are you sure? I was just doing the math…

You could probably make it out into orbit, but not much further, he confirmed.

Amazing. Even my math is fucked up.

You can get yourself out of this mess, Kili soothed.

'I've made a clusterfuck of it,' I said, propping myself up on my elbows, still playing with my curls. 'The only way out is to do as Mahd'vi's directed and steal Feast for the Tunga fucker.'

You're doing an excellent job buying time—

'To what end?' I laughed hoarsely. 'I continue to do nothing and one of them will crack. I'll either be deported or abducted. Same unhappy ending: a joyous reunion with my parents.'

Or things could change before that happens.

'Nothing changes unless you force it to,' I said.

Philosophically speaking, there are a wide array of counter-arguments to that statement… Kili began, then read my expression and shut up.

In the wake of the explosion, I'd been on the receiving end of a slew of misdirected displeasure. Never mind that the Secretariat had announced it was an accident. The phrase, "All it takes is an Earthling in the room to start a war…" dogged my footsteps like a haunting. And my presence, which had, up until this point, only been registered by all of chefdom across the galaxy, had now been noted by a slew of Primian culture commentators, who were looking into why an Earthling should be at the sinfonia at all, and dissecting whether my "primitive Earthling brain" was capable of absorbing "the music of enlightenment." It was absurd to me that a tragic explosion caused by an accident had been shoved to the side in favour of speculation about whether I was a *worthy member of a sinfonia audience*. Stranger still was that nobody at the sinfonia itself seemed to be coming under fire.

Making things even worse were the Secretariat's new, utterly reactionary and unprovoked initiatives against off-worlders, despite our complete non-involvement in the incident. In addition to broadcasting my location live, *at all times,* I now had to submit expense reports every nava, documenting *every single thing* I acquired in exchange for Loop credits.

'*A precaution, no more,*' a Secretariat representative named Harmony Utra had insisted. 'After all, we don't go around *snooping* in people's Loop records—surveillance is banned here on Primus. Our only concern is that witnessing an explosion might mobilise radical elements our systems haven't filtered out, because naturally, we *trust* people, no matter what part of the galaxy they're from, or what species.'

Harmony Utra had smiled then. 'And if there's nothing to hide, there's no greater gesture of honesty than openness, is there? It's only temporary, and we regret the inconvenience, but it's for *the greater good.*'

There had been wild applause after the official Secretariat stream, and I'd painstakingly taken to putting together receipts from every single transaction I made—whether it was to buy groceries, or a new 3D-printed outfit, or take a flowcab to XP Inc.

'What do I gain by *not* doing as directed?' I asked, rising to my feet and pacing. 'This whole planet is well on its way down the slippery slope of state discrimination. I'm no longer being blamed for the explosion, but there are all these new rules. And they're still speculating upon whether I should have been at the sinfonia at *all…*'

I ticked the injustices off on my fingers. 'Mahd'vi wants control of Feast, and she now has it. Ko's handed it to her on a gilded platter. It's powerful tech. And this is exactly what Tunga said would happen—total government monopoly over it, a feast of propaganda, no pun intended.'

I built up steam as my thoughts coalesced. 'All of chefdom is divided on whether to love me or hate me, and as usual, the haters shout the loudest. Also, I have no friends left on this planet, on account of I've lied to them all along and they no longer want anything to do with me.'

I felt ill as I said the words out loud.

'And Ko has been fucking things up for me nonstop. First, the riot. Now, handing Feast off to Mahd'vi. It's as if she doesn't understand what it's like to be me at all…'

I stilled, and a hideous crawling sensation slid down my spine. 'Jog Tunga knows where I am. And if *he* knows, then I can't trust that my family doesn't know. He's a barefaced liar if I ever saw one. Add to that the fact that Mahd'vi knows my identity, and can deport me at a moment's notice unless I comply…'

My hands shook.

'The illusion of agency, that's all that's in it for me. If I resist.'

I took a sip of water.

'If I steal Feast for Tunga, that gets him off my back…'

*If* he sticks to his end of the deal.

'Well, he has a point,' I said, shocking myself even as the words left my mouth.

Kili's whirring stopped momentarily as he blanched. _You're—you're agreeing with him?_

I gestured vaguely. _Look at everything around us. It's all falling to shit._

But Primus is anti-Empire!

Doesn't mean they won't abuse power.

I was suddenly dizzy as I flashed back to the night at the sinfonia, watching their idiot Primian Guard firing upon Kili, interrogating me in a windowless cell for hours…

I collapsed into a chair.

Saras, are you okay? Kili hovered before me, examining me carefully.

I waved him away. 'They tried to coerce a confession out of me when there was no reason to suspect me,' I said weakly. 'They used my Earthling origins and tried to fabricate a story to fit their biases. They're as corrupt as any other power out there has been, right through history.'

And the answer is to give Feast to *Jog Tunga*? Kili asked, incredulous. _Even if that's what Optimism Mahd'vi *wants*—_

'It makes no sense. But it gets me off the hook, buys me time while I figure out my next move, and that's about all I can control in the star-fucked universe,' I said, grinding my teeth together. 'That, and hopefully, making it up to my friends for lying to them.'

I lapsed into silence, replaying the paths that lay before me, unconsciously toying with the package Good Cheer Eria had sent me. 'Tough life lesson, huh? Lose all your friends on a strange new planet and find yourself a pawn pushed around by two government officials who are obviously making a play for power,' I said bitterly. 'All for trying to escape my sun-fucked family.'

You haven't lost *all* your friends, Kili said. _You've still got Ko. You can come clean to her—_

'*After* the Millennium Feast,' I snapped. 'She thinks I'm an ungrateful wretch, and even though she's completely wrong on that count and all the reasons we ever fight are all her fault, I don't need to tell her I'm a liar. Not until we're done with launching Feast, when we can walk away from each other with no obligations.'

I was hollow at the thought. 'And if everyone screws me over, and I get thrown off this sur-fucked planet, I can walk away with no attachments to anyone else, too. Everyone else hates me, anyway.'

The others don't hate you, Saras. They're mad at you.

I've streamed every day to apologise.

Give them time, Kili said patiently. _It's a legit reaction after a big reveal, you know._

Don't say *I told you so,* I said grouchily.

I'm not going to.

You're right, though, I conceded, my insides aching with misery. _I should have told them the truth ages ago._

You did what you thought you needed to do.

That's what all the mass murderers back on Earth say.

Kili was silent at that.

I'm no better than any of them, you know, I continued quietly. _My family, I mean. I've coasted on their blood money, their wealth and power and privilege, to get to where I am today._

You couldn't help the family you were born into, Kili said. _You've tried to distance yourself from them—_

By lying.

You've treated everyone around you with kindness—

And betrayed them all by lying.

You've stood up to Jog Tunga—

And I'm about to sell out to him.

Optimism Mahd'vi has a plan, Kili said, now resigned. _She'll help you break free of this cycle._

I'm going to steal from Ko and Kube and the last few folks at XP Inc. who trust me, all to save my own skin, I said miserably, articulating my intentions as I spoke the words out loud. _I have no choice. It was always going to come down to this. I should have booked a one-way ticket to the sun._

My hands shook as I pulled open the strings that held Good Cheer Eria's gift together. The flowmetal fell away to reveal a large pastry that looked like it was made from xocolat with a cherry-sherry icing.

Good Cheer Eria had scribbled a note on papyro-scroll.

Keep the Faith, Saras. I'm on your side. Stream me if you need a friend.

I grabbed a spoon from the kitchen drawer and dug into the cake like the savage that I was. The decadent richness of xocolat and the sour burst of cherry-sherry was only slightly ruined by the salt in my unshed tears. And through my wretchedness, I saw my future with depressing clarity: I was going to have to play by everyone else's rules before I could play by my own.

I'd have to begin by stealing Feast.

I streamed Serenity Ko.

A Primian wedding is the union of two or more people, their identities melding for all eternity. It is a sacred, codified ritual that brings families together.

—Serenity Medi,
Primus: A New Hope for Humanity
2065 Anno Earth | 1990 Interstellar Era

TWENTY-FOUR

SERENITY KO HAD nothing but regrets. They were the recurring theme of her life.

They were magnified by the glorious sur-shine that illuminated the world around her on what was supposed to be a joyous occasion. She had somehow found her way to being in a shop with Good Cheer Eria and her mother, a small, bird-like woman who trilled enthusiastically about life, the universe and everything. She could see where Good Cheer Eria got her sur-shiney disposition from, and it only made her the crabbier for it.

At first, Optimism Rihan had been hesitant—borderline panicked, really—when Good Cheer Eria had invited Serenity Ko on their wedding-shopping excursion.

'Are you sure you want her opinions?' he'd asked skeptically. 'None of your tastes align.'

'An opposing point of view always brings new dimensions to my perspective.' Good Cheer Eria beamed.

Serenity Ko was inclined to weasel her way out of what promised to be a nerve-racking yet boring day. It wasn't as if she had nothing else going on in her life, what with the Millennium Feast timelines being tighter than ever before and the government getting its fingers into all her sim experiences. And then there was the question of Saraswati, who point-blank refused to talk to her…

'But it's Ko!' Optimism Rihan had persisted. 'She's likely to convince you to wear sheath-boots to the wedding.'

'And if I do?' Good Cheer Eria said, winking at Serenity Ko.

Personally, Serenity Ko saw nothing wrong with showing up in sheath-boots to a wedding.

'I—I mean, that's your call, but she... Your *mother* will be there!' Optimism Rihan had exclaimed, throwing his hands up in despair.

'I've always wanted you to meet her,' Good Cheer Eria said earnestly to Serenity Ko.

Serenity Ko fought the shudder that crept its way through her at the thought.

'Ko can't be trusted around parents!' Optimism Rihan had sputtered. 'Have you never hung out with her before?'

Now, *that* had annoyed Serenity Ko.

'What's your plan, Rihan?' she'd asked snidely. 'Hide me from your in-laws until after the wedding ceremony, when it'll be too late?'

'Eria, this could be disastrous,' Optimism Rihan said, ignoring her. 'Ko is unpredictable, she could—'

'Ko is right here, in this room,' Serenity Ko interrupted. 'And Ko would *love* to spend some quality time with Eria—*and* her mother—helping her choose her wedding dress.'

It had felt like an epic victory, spiting her brother, but now, Serenity Ko was trying her level best not to swear around her future extended family, perspiring under the pressure of making an excellent first impression and not letting Optimism Rihan down, all while Good Cheer Eria and her mother held hands and openly displayed so much genuine affection that it would make even the most diehard Ur-drama enthusiasts sick.

'I think you'll look beautiful in that one,' her mother said, tearing up, as they looked at a form-fitting, neon pink dress. In Serenity Ko's view, it made neon-ness itself appear reserved. The dress in question hung off the mannequin with the kind of attention-seeking defiance that shimmered and played with light in a manner that would make the laws of physics question themselves.

'Won't the contrast be too high with my chlorosapient makeup?' Good Cheer Eria asked, concerned for all the right reasons.

'It'll set your makeup off beautifully!' her mother exclaimed. 'I can't believe my little girl is getting married.'

Good Cheer Eria squeezed her hand. It was revolting.

Regrets.

Racks of dresses lined the walls, bursting with colour and displaying styles from the traditional to the avant-garde. Traditional wedding wear representing every culture across the galaxy was on display. Intricate masks hung alongside elaborate headdresses; there were Sagarican wetsuits woven through with shimmering bioluminescent coral of some kind, and even draped saris all the way from Earth.

It suddenly struck Serenity Ko that weddings were a rite of passage that seemed to unite all of human-occupied space, and it was baffling to think she'd never imagined her own, or anything close. She'd always assumed she'd be alone, hooking up with strangers for the rest of her life… Until Saraswati turned up.

The sales reps descended upon the trio in a flurry of fabrics. Silks from every far-flung corner of the galaxy, luminoweave and cosmowool, sur-skein and sagarra-tweed were pulled from shelves and unrolled on the display counters, with promises of being tailored and fitted in every style of bespoke dress imaginable.

'We've got hundreds of trial pieces if you'd like to see yourself in any of them?' the sales rep chirruped, waving their arm cheerily around to indicate the racks of clothing. 'If you find a style or a colour you like, we can make fabric recommendations, and our customisations are *most* flattering. Our nanobot tailoring programmes are fantastically sophisticated—you'll be able to alter within a millimetre of your measurements as the day draws closer…'

The sales rep droned on about fabrics and tailoring. Good Cheer Eria and her mother nodded now and again. Serenity Ko brooded about Saraswati.

She'd managed to score two tickets to the upcoming Legends of the Future concert. She'd only asked Saraswati to go with her a lifetime ago. Saraswati had agreed at the time, but she didn't know if that commitment still held good, seeing as they weren't on talking terms at the moment.

She'd imagined going with Saraswati, the two of them head-banging to the adrenaline-pumping sound of smash, giggling over drinks, returning planet-side nice and toasted, and letting the evening take its course in hitherto unexplored directions that didn't necessarily involve being fully clothed…

There they were again, all her regrets from the last nava.

She shouldn't have told Saraswati about that deal with Optimism Mahd'vi.

And she should *not* have streamed Honour Aki to reassure him on the night of the explosion. Her misguided empathy had led to a nava's worth of fending off a renewed effort—entirely one-sided, on his part—to reconnect with her. There'd been gifts at her work station, some hideously hand-made and sentimental, others expensive and garish. There'd been daily streams from him, wishing her a good morning, or a good night, and reassuring her that he'd always be there for her. She'd spotted him lurking in the Feast bay at the XP Inc. office now and again, attempting to make conversation with her team while desperately seeking eye contact with her.

It was ironic that she'd found herself behaving the same way to Saraswati, whose studied efforts to ignore her had taken a turn for the extreme. Serenity Ko hoped she was proceeding with more dignity than Honour Aki, but had no way to tell for sure. At least her streams didn't tell Saras she possessed "the radiance of a thousand Suriyas this morning," or reassure Saras that she would always be "held close to my heart like the gravity of Ibnis holding its lost moon in orbit." Instead, she'd tried to engage Saraswati with work updates. She'd tried to poke fun at some of the XP Inc. processes Saraswati had often been confused by. She'd received no response. She'd seen her for the first time at Grace Kube's briefing to the wider team, and Saraswati hadn't even bothered to say hello.

It was excruciating.

Serenity Ko didn't even think it was the hormones any more. She was coming to the grim conclusion that she might just be hopelessly in love with Saraswati.

Two tickets to Legends of the Future, a nava to go to the concert, and Saraswati wouldn't so much as look at her.

Good job, Ko. Congratulations, she thought sourly.

'You—you don't like any of them, Ko?' Good Cheer Eria asked hesitantly, interrupting her thoughts.

Serenity Ko realised that a scowl had crept across her face all the while she'd been zoning out, and snapped back to attention.

Good Cheer Eria was eyeing her uncertainly, and her mother wore a pinched, concerned expression. Between the pair of them and the sales rep, they held four potential wedding dresses up, while Good Cheer Eria stood before a mirror, deciding which ones to try on.

'They're all lovely,' Serenity Ko said hurriedly. 'I was trying to work out which one is most like *you,* you know? And by that, I mean the most sur-shiney, radiant, um... *pretty* one of the lot.'

Good Cheer Eria beamed. 'That's a relief! I'm quite torn between them all…'

Serenity Ko took a proper look at the dresses then.

She stepped forward and ran her fingers over a floating, gossamer thing that seemed to be made of fabric flower blossoms all woven together.

'We can customise this to use actual blooms on the day of the wedding,' the sales rep said immediately, and Serenity Ko had to admit that that was impressive.

Serenity Ko's eyes then trailed over a frothy cream and lace dress that looked like it was made from spun sugar, the regurgitated kind after snacking on one Primian pastry too many. She blanched. 'Not this one, it's hideously twee,' she said before she could stop herself.

The sales rep shot her a filthy look, but proceeded to take it away. 'It's avant-garde,' they muttered. 'An acquired taste.'

Serenity Ko was intensely aware that Good Cheer Eria's mother was appalled by her brutal honesty, and kicked herself. All she needed to do was be a warm body and survive this afternoon, make a good impression on behalf of Optimism

Rihan, and she could go back to being rude to the people who loved her the best and had learnt to tolerate her over the years. She shot a panicked look at Good Cheer Eria, and found that she was grinning in amusement.

'Ko's got a sharp eye, Ma,' she said. 'That's why I brought her along.'

Serenity Ko dismissed another dress—it had stiff, architectural shoulders, made from luminoweave, with an intricately draped skirt. 'Eria, I don't see you in this. It'll look gorgeous, of course, but it's too badass for you.'

'That's what I thought, as well,' her mother said appreciatively, suddenly warming up to Serenity Ko.

Good Cheer Eria's lips turned down in disappointment. 'Oh, I thought it would be a lovely experiment,' she said sadly.

'Boots would go great with it!' Serenity Ko quipped, and at that, Good Cheer Eria's high, tinkling laugh filled the room with its music.

'You can't laugh like that and wear that dress, though,' Serenity Ko teased.

'I see your point,' Good Cheer Eria said.

'And that leaves the blossom drape,' the sales rep said, a little miffed that their collection had been so thoroughly critiqued. They indicated the last dress they held in their hands, which shimmered in shades of green shot through with pinks and purples. 'As you all know, it's very symbolic and traditionally Nakshatran. It's made from flowmetal and wraps around you like a cocoon, but as the evening wears on, it begins to unfurl and blossom, like your marriage no doubt will.'

Serenity Ko tried to keep her face neutral at this saccharine pronouncement.

Good Cheer Eria made her way to the trial room. Serenity Ko was immediately accosted by the need to make polite conversation with Optimism Rihan's future mother-in-law, and proceeded to ignore it, sliding into the Loop to check on Feast updates instead. It beat the banality of making noncommittal sounds on safe topics, such as the weather, the best kaapi shops on Primus, and the local sports team.

The first thing she did was stream Saraswati.

Hey, she began.

Nine Virtues, that sounds awful.

Much to her surprise, she realised that Saraswati had streamed her just moments before, and she hadn't noticed.

It's so good to hear from you! Serenity Ko gushed before she could stop herself. She cringed.

There was a beat that stretched out a moment too long. Serenity Ko kicked herself for fucking things up, as usual. *I shouldn't have come on so strong,* she thought. *What an absolute fucking—*

This is unsustainable, Saraswati said.

Serenity Ko's heart skipped a bit. _What is?_ she asked, dreading the response.

Not talking.

Serenity Ko heaved a sigh of relief.

It's the worst, she agreed.

It makes work impossible, Saraswati said.

It wasn't the response Serenity Ko had been hoping for, but it was a start. At least they were talking again.

Yes, we can't function as an effective leadership team like this, she said officiously, then sent visuals of winking faces over to soften how pompous she must have sounded.

No, we can't. So I've been thinking… Saraswati said, ignoring her attempt at humour.

_Go on,_ Serenity Ko prompted, stifling a sigh.

I've got this whole nava to kill while we wait for Optimism Mahd'vi to approve our initial Feast offering. No pop-ups for me to host. The team seems to be running on rails with the next batch of flavour profiles.

Right.

Maybe you could walk me through all the tech? Beginning to end. I— Saraswati seemed to hesitate.

_Go on…_ Serenity Ko said encouragingly, her heart soaring at the thought of how many hours this would take—all hours spent in the same room with Saraswati.

_I don't understand all the moving pieces. I only know what

goes into the food science,_ Saraswati said. _And I want to understand how the rest of it works, really get a feel for the bigger picture._

Done! Serenity Ko said, quickly checking her schedule and deleting over a dozen meetings from it. _How does tomorrow look?_

Perfect.

Great, I'll see you at the office. First thing in the morning. Serenity Ko beamed.

Thank you, Saraswati said formally.

Serenity Ko slumped in relief. It appeared that Saraswati was finally coming round. It was inevitable, anyway—there was only so long one could hold out against government pressure—but it felt like a burden lifted from her shoulders to not be the source of Saraswati's ire.

Or so she assumed.

Maybe she's still mad at me, she thought, chewing on her lower lip. *But maybe this is the chance I need to win her over with my cleverness and the scale of the ambitions we're chasing and how we're going to transform the world… Letting Optimism Mahd'vi interfere for a bit is a small price to pay for galactic domination.*

Her Loop notifs were going off in a flurry.

I've got Legends of the Future tickets, too, Serenity Ko grinned. *I'll test the waters tomorrow and then remind her we have a date… I mean, a not-date.* A thing. *Commitment. Not in the dating sense, that is…*

Still more notifs slid across her field of view, but she dismissed them and turned her full attention back to reality when she heard excitable squealing.

Good Cheer Eria had stepped out of the changing room. She wore the gossamer dress woven through with sample blooms, and even though the flowers were still fake for the moment, she looked resplendent.

'Wow,' Serenity Ko blurted.

Good Cheer Eria blushed. Her mother wrapped her up in an enormous hug. 'You look perfect.'

'I love it,' Good Cheer Eria whispered.

She glanced at herself in the mirror shyly, then appreciatively, and Serenity Ko could see countless reasons why her brother was hopelessly in love with her. She was beautiful.

'The blooms contrast with your chlorosapient makeup perfectly,' Serenity Ko said hoarsely.

'Thank you,' Good Cheer Eria said breathily. 'I—I don't even think I need to try the other dress.'

'You should try the other dress,' her mother said, though it was an effort for her to choke the words out. 'You should never find yourself thinking *what if?*'

'Got it.' Good Cheer Eria nodded. She returned to the dressing room, while her mother dabbed at her eyes with a handkerchief.

Serenity Ko was annoyed that her notifs still seemed to be popping up nonstop, interrupting what might've otherwise been a reasonably moving moment for her, too. Resolutely ignoring them, she toyed with the thought of asking Saraswati to be her plus-one at her brother's wedding.

It was a stray thought, unformed and hideous and embarrassing, but the longer she dwelt upon it, the more it firmed itself in her head as a fabulous, wonderful, incredible idea, the kind of thing that would open up possibilities for what their future might hold.

And after all, the wedding was going to be *after* the Millennium Feast. It might be nice to see where things stood with Saraswati once the pressure had let up a bit…

The notifs were giving her a headache, now. Choking back a string of cusswords so as not to upset Good Cheer Eria's mother, Serenity Ko slid into the Loop to see what all the furore was about.

She balked.

Optimism Mahd'vi had suggested changes to *every single one of their sims.* She'd set up an immediate, emergency meeting to address the "Primian loyalism" of Feast, or in her words, "the lack thereof."

Serenity Ko couldn't help herself. She swore out loud, right as a loud wail drowned her out. She emerged from the Loop with what felt like mental whiplash.

Good Cheer Eria stood before her in the blossom drape dress, which clung to her slender figure as it was induced to bloom. As it unfurled its petals around her, she appeared to be an ethereal being, a bloom upon the planet, awakening into life. Her mother wept into her handkerchief, but looked up at Serenity Ko, who realised that she was still swearing.

'… motherfuc—' she caught herself, and feigned a hacking cough. 'Mother of Nine Virtues!' she amended. 'You're beautiful!'

As mother and daughter bawled all over each other, Serenity Ko disappeared into the XP Inc. dash, where her team was reacting with chaos to Optimism Mahd'vi's demands.

1. *The shrooming symphony needs to reiterate the cultural values of our foraging practices.* Centre *Wanderer experiences in the sim. Wandering is essential to Primian identity and unique to us—assert this superiority.*
2. *The meen crudo uses vat-grown meat, but this isn't emphasised. We don't fish in our rivers for a reason—it's part of the Nakshatran philosophy to "tread lightly." Emphasise the superiority of how we embody this sentiment.*
3. *The Berry-Anna needs to reflect our ras-harvesting processes. Ras is at the heart of Primian culinary thought, and yet there's barely any mention of it. It's what makes us superior.*

On and on it went, fifty dishes long. Every single paragraph used the word "superior" in a condescending manner that suggested how Optimism Mahd'vi viewed *herself* relative to everyone at XP Inc.

The scale of what she'd ceded to the Secretary of Culture and Heritage hit Serenity Ko like a meteorite, leaving a crater in her heart.

I endangered my relationship with Saras… for this?

There were nothing but regrets.

The K'artri-tva have released an official statement:

"We affirm, with profound conviction, the blossoming of our multilateral relationship with all the member states of the United Human Cooperative, seeking new ways to align our interests and transcend our differences. We are at the precipice of a new epoch that will impact every future generation..."

—Honour Fair,
Universe Today
2075 Anno Earth | 2000 Interstellar Era

TWENTY-FIVE

SHE WAS LOATH to admit it, but Optimism Mahd'vi had taken her eye off the ball.

In the māsas since she'd announced the Millennium Festival, right through its numerous planning meetings, at the many events she'd attended—cutting symbolically knotted ribbons, making speeches, applauding politely in the audience—her mind had been greatly troubled by the question of the "Kaveri" girl.

Now that the Kaveri girl had been discovered to be a dirt-licking, bloodstained *Godavari* liar, she felt smug satisfaction that all her suspicions had been justified. All she had to do was overlook the deeper disappointment, evinced by a lingering hollowness within her gut, at the realisation that she hadn't discovered a long lost member of her erased family, miraculously resurfaced.

She'd stifled her dismay and chosen to reinforce her growing paranoia. Her radar for sniffing out duplicitous, self-serving Earthlings—which was *all* Earthlings, really, when she thought about it—was functioning with an incredible accuracy. She shuddered to think of what might have happened had she not followed Saraswati Godavari with the intensity that she had, breaking into her Winger's Loop records (*such a foolish decision to have an external backup for one's private data*), tracking her all the way down to the Ur-sands, eavesdropping on her conversation with the malevolent Earthling prince, Jog Tunga…

It was evident that the Godavari girl would do anything to save her own skin.

She was a carapamboochi, an insectile creature crawling around the planet with an air of sheer indestructability, feelers twitching in the air looking for the next opportunity, armoured in a carapace that was impossible to crush by brute force alone. Carapamboochis were the bane of the United Human Collective: a blight upon every world humanity had travelled to after the Nakshatrans first took flight, and their dirty little secret when it came to narrating the tale of how Primus was settled.

Tread lightly might be the official message, but lurking beneath its pithy phrasing was the reality that the indestructible carapamboochi had stowed away on every single spacecraft ever launched, somehow surviving on crumbs of astronaut mush from the galley, creeping around unnoticed until the ships were well away in the dark reaches of the universe, impossible to space because they were so small one could never say if they were gone for sure. Nobody had noticed them through years of cryogenically-induced sleep, through the early years of living in tented habitats and researching the planet, and then their numbers had multiplied, they'd turned into a menace, and it had been too late to wipe them off the face of the universe.

The Godavari girl was no different: An insignificant woman masquerading as a benign visitor to Primus, whose only interest was her own survival, whatever the cost to the world.

That's not entirely *true,* Optimism Mahd'vi conceded grudgingly.

She'd witnessed the Godavari girl stand up to Jog Tunga, despite his best efforts to harangue and intimidate her. She'd even cheered her on, very quietly, because as much as she found the woman distasteful, the bumpkin prince was positively *odious,* and if she had to pick one of the two Earthlings who'd been loosed upon her world, she'd probably go with the Godavari girl.

And that brought her round to Jog Tunga himself.

This was where she'd really let things slip through the cracks. She'd let her paranoia rest momentarily, a mistake she should never have made when dealing with an Earthling. She'd been so consumed by the Godavari girl, the Millennium Festival, creative control over Feast and all the rest, that she hadn't pieced together the disturbing nature of the prince's behaviour. She'd written it off as a string of unconnected events of debauchery and foolishness committed by a boor, instead of viewing it as a pattern.

It was unheard of for diplomatic missions to persist for as long as his time in the Suriyan System had. Jog Tunga had been spotted *everywhere* and by *everyone*, publicly disgracing himself at pleasure domes with Ur-drama stars, publicly partaking in bacchanals on other planets, with other species, including their latest allies, the K'artri-tva, whenever he wasn't harassing Saraswati. It was beginning to look like a ploy to build Earthling allies.

Optimism Mahd'vi had mentioned this suspicion to select members of the Secretariat in informal settings, in passing, as casually as she'd dared, and had been repeatedly reminded of the Trust Protocols, which prohibited espionage in UHC space. Surveillance was also banned on Primus. It was impossible to know what he was planning.

And while Jog Tunga was a backwater bumpkin, he was hardly going to be building a ray-bomb in front of all the cam-drones flocking around him.

It was why she'd acted on impulse. When she'd stumbled upon him confronting Saraswati at the Ur-sands, bullying the Godavari girl to steal Feast for him, Optimism Mahd'vi had caught the merest whiff of opportunity, and had pounced at it.

She'd made it clear to Saraswati that she expected her to comply with Jog Tunga's less-than-polite request and steal Feast for him. She suspected that Jog Tunga was plotting something enormous—either with the backing of his Godavari masters back on Earth, or of the Earth itself, united as one, in some kind of eleventh-hour play to gain might in a universe where they'd been relegated to irrelevance. And Optimism Mahd'vi needed to get to the bottom of it.

She'd invited Jog Tunga, as well as the Godavari family, to the Millennium Feast. To her delight, they'd accepted, trading false platitudes about how honoured they were to be held in mind, but oh, no, the honour was all hers, and et cetera. Over the course of the dinner, she was going to trick the Earthling prince into an admission of guilt—get him drunk, or alternately feed and bruise his ego until he slipped up, unravelling his plans for Feast. Her methods for doing so were still sketchy—she was toying with the idea of slipping truth serum in his drink. But she was going to catch them all off-guard by presenting Saraswati to them, seated at the same dinner table, despite her lack of diplomatic privileges. Given everything she'd seen, Saraswati could be used as a catalyst to set them off nice and violently.

And then, she'd catch them red-handed with top-secret Feast tech, and take them away for questioning. That would make an example of them all, and teach them not to mess with the might of Primus.

Optimism Mahd'vi had approved Honour Fen's proposal to hold the Millennium Feast at Nakshatran Rock. The idea of having Primians looking outward from the planet of their origins, to the stars and beyond, held deep philosophical appeal. It had the added benefit of trapping the entire Godavari clan planet-side, where they could be dealt with appropriately without the option of making a hasty escape on a spaceship.

Optimism Mahd'vi was just waiting for the missing pieces to fall into place. A nava had passed since she'd confronted Saraswati, and the Earthling woman hadn't yet confirmed that she was stealing Feast. She wondered if she should accost her with an invite to another sinfonia performance, now that repairs to the theatre were nearly complete. Or perhaps ask her to attend the play *Nadira* and apply some gentle pressure.

As if on cue, her comms beeped with an incoming message from the Godavari girl.

Thank you for your patience and your support, Secretary. I wholly intend to repay the favour.

Excellent, she fired off in response. _I appreciate it._

Saraswati Godavari was doing as directed. Optimism Mahd'vi still wasn't sure whether she'd let her go or imprison her with the rest of the Godavari family.

As if she'd read her mind, another stream popped up.

I'd like to discuss my terms with you.

You don't have the option of terms, Optimism Mahd'vi snapped.

I do if you want my help.

Harmony Knot in an hour, Optimism Mahd'vi fired back, irritated.

Saraswati had somehow caught onto the possibility that she could yet be deported. It was aggravating to say the least, but using her to catch the other Godavaris and foil their plans was the bigger picture. Their wayward daughter could be dealt with later...

When she arrived at the Harmony Knot, the Earthling girl was there with her flying companion. She smiled at Saraswati as if this were a chance meeting, and the pair exchanged loud, polite greetings as Optimism Mahd'vi raised a sound-bubble over them.

'Let's make this quick,' Optimism Mahd'vi said, as soon as they were ensconced in relative privacy. 'And don't let the grin fall off your face.'

The space around the Harmony Knot wasn't packed, but there were a handful of tourists, as always, recording and streaming their experiences. It was important that this clandestine meeting appeared nothing more than a casual catch up to anyone who happened to chance upon it.

'I want carte blanche for what I'm about to do,' Saraswati said firmly. 'And amnesty afterwards.'

'Can't guarantee it,' Optimism Mahd'vi said brusquely.

'I don't want you lumping me in with Jog Tunga for whatever you plan to do with him,' Saraswati said. 'And I need assurances that you won't stab me in the back and try and deport me for theft or my false scrollwork in the aftermath.'

'I could deport you *right now* for your false scrollwork,' Optimism Mahd'vi snapped, still smiling. 'Really, you have no bargaining chips. You steal Feast and hand it to Jog Tunga, and let me deal with whatever happens next. Accept the consequences of your actions while you're at it. Your being here is already a crime.'

Saraswati shrugged, and it struck Optimism Mahd'vi as an odd response for someone on the back foot. 'I happen to have something you want.'

Optimism Mahd'vi snorted.

'I know my family erased yours. The Godavaris and Kaveris were bitter rivals,' Saraswati said. 'I apologise for my ancestors.'

'I don't need your apologies,' Optimism Mahd'vi bit out.

'No, you don't. But perhaps you want to know what happened,' Saraswati said, her tone even. 'All *official* Loop records have been deleted—as you'd expect. Erasure of a genocide for posterity, the victors always do this. There's no trace of the Kaveri clan, its rich historic contributions, and its brutal murder at the hands of the Godavari clan in public record.'

'Believe me, I know,' Optimism Mahd'vi said, wondering if her smile resembled a grimace yet.

'But…' The Godavari girl paused dramatically and gratuitously. Optimism Mahd'vi resisted the urge to grab her by the shoulders and shake her. Saraswati continued. 'There are private records. I studied them with my tutor. Only the Godavari clan has access to them.'

'I scanned your Winger, remember? I know you're being dishonest—I found no trace of them on the machine.' Optimism Mahd'vi said this tonelessly, but hated that her voice shook ever so slightly as the words left her. Her heart pounded in her ears.

'It doesn't mean they don't exist,' Saraswati said. 'And I know where to find them.'

'What are you suggesting?'

The Godavari girl took a deep breath. 'Keep my secret identity a secret. Give me legal scrollwork to remain on Primus. Grant me amnesty after I steal Feast. I'll give you your family history.'

The United Human Cooperative Criminal Relocation Act authorises the immediate deportation of all thieves—from petty shoplifters to tax evaders—to the Osmos Girdle, where they will undergo psychological rehabilitation for their crimes...

—The United Human Cooperative Penal Code
1176 Anno Earth | 1101 Interstellar Era

TWENTY-SIX

EARLIER THAT DAY, Serenity Ko proudly proclaimed that nobody at XP Inc. bothered locking their work stations. Ever.

'Trust,' she said, grinning. 'It's a part of Primian culture—we've got no security cams because surveillance is banned across the planet. And we don't use credentials to sign into our work stations. Nobody at XP Inc. ever steals ideas or credit. It's not in the spirit of the org. We've got nothing to fear in the office.'

'Except you, Ko,' Courage Praia muttered, elbowing her in the ribs.

'*Unfair.*' Serenity Ko pouted. 'I've gotten so much better, haven't I, Nenna?'

The intern mumbled something incoherent and rushed to check on one of the Feast sims they'd redone for Optimism Mahd'vi's approval.

Serenity Ko had taken careful pains to walk me through all the techno-babble and nitty-gritty surrounding building Feast. Ordinarily, I might have struggled to focus, but I made it a point to pay careful attention to every single word. I paid extra careful attention to anything she described as a "critical component," marking its location on the databases and which work stations seemed to have ease of access to them.

I knew, as I listened to her unravel the intricate mesh from which Feast emerges, that I was going to steal Feast later that night. It felt like I was floating outside of myself, looking in at me through a keyhole, catching glimpses of the despicable person I'd become. Perhaps it was the person I'd always been…

After all, I'm a Godavari. My existence is bathed in blood. This is what I've been trained to do since I was a child: lie, manipulate, steal, worm my way around the corridors of power, commit to nothing, eviscerate everything in sight with a subtle knife, walk away unscathed because blood will protect me.

It felt as if a fist had reached into my chest, exerting a gentle but unrelenting pressure upon my heart.

Serenity Ko beamed with pride as she revealed the inner workings of Feast to me. I was struck by the scale of what I'd managed to build by plugging into XP Inc.'s behemoth infrastructure of code, biocircuitry and neurotechnology. All I'd contributed were footnotes on flavour and how it worked, and yet I was the public face of it all because I happened to be good at describing food. Serenity Ko was the real architect.

I said as much to her, and her cheeks flushed deep pink. 'Not true,' she said hurriedly. 'The real architects are Kube and Sah'r… and all right, even Na'vil. They had a vision for what we could do with sims, and came together to make it happen.'

'But Feast is *your* vision,' I insisted.

I noticed how her lips twitched as she fought a smile. They were such kissable lips…

So kissable that I was tempted to forgive her for ceding control of Feast to Optimism Mahd'vi, even though I'd seen the feedback the Secretary for Culture and Heritage had sent in.

So kissable that I'd even agreed to go to the Legends of the Future gig with her later that nava, never mind that I had indescribable feelings for her that only seemed to grow each time I was around her, however aggravating so much of her behaviour was, however inconsiderate she could be when she thought she was being helpful. Never mind the giant wave of unresolved sexual tension that swept over me in the dead of night when I was alone with my thoughts, unwilling to take my chances with her because I had fibbed so often about who I was…

So kissable that my insides squirmed with guilt at the thought that I was going to betray her, and *continue* to lie to her about everything.

I half considered not going ahead with my plan. I owed her the truth and it would destroy her, even without the latest in my string of treacheries.

But. I owed myself freedom first.

Sneaking around in the dead of night on another planet: check.

Technically, you're not so much sneaking around as lurking casually... Kili said helpfully.

This is true.

I leaned against the handrail, letting the walkway into the heart of the XP Inc. office propel me towards an interstellar crime. *Another* interstellar crime, if I were being totally honest. *Intellectual property theft, espionage* would go on the list right after *faked identity, falsified scrollwork,* and the whole lot of it would be more than enough to have me deported back to Earth at best, and exiled to a distant mining asteroid at worst.

Do prisoners actually do any mining? I mused.

Huh?

When convicted criminals are sent off to prisons, I mean. You usually hear they've been dispatched to an asteroid mining station somewhere... Do they have to *work* or are they rehabilitated?

You're *not* going to get caught, Kili said firmly. _Or betrayed._

Even so. My heart was pounding now that I was in it so deep that getting caught was a distinct possibility. _I've never thought about how prisons work in the UHC._

Are you sure you want to talk about this right now? Kili asked skeptically.

Maybe not.

I've looked up the answers for you, Kili said. _If you're still into it, I'll make a little presentation once we're back at home._

The shimmering lights of the tunnel invited me to slip into the Loop and treat myself to the many dozen sims triggered by the entryway to XP Inc. The visio-nodes embedded in its arching surfaces played holovids of the org's history of triumphs, including Grace Kube giving a moving speech about the connection between sim experiences and improved mental health.

I felt ill at the sight of him; he reminded me of the immense scale of the betrayal I was about to commit. I sped up on the walkway until I was well past his likeness.

That wasn't suspicious at all, Kili said.

I just—I don't want to have to look him in the eye before I stab him in the back.

Calm. Down. Saras. Kili whirred off my shoulder, hovering a few inches in front of me. _Optimism Mahd'vi herself has *personally* asked you to steal this tech and hand it over to Jog Tunga. You're carrying out a *government-approved* plan._

We slid past the bays leading off to Boundless Ano's cafe, and my stomach clenched. *How am I going to work with him at our pop-ups after this?*

Kili continued. _She's promised you amnesty in exchange for the Kaveri family records._

In order to get my hands on the missing history of the Kaveris, all I had to do was sign in to the private family database. There was no way to trace it, only a top secret Loop location that every member of my family memorised as a child.

I'd checked to make sure they hadn't deleted my credentials before making the offer to Optimism Mahd'vi. I had limited access: no military deployment codes, no armoured transport options, but all the history of the great and glorious star-fucked Daxina Protectorate clearly didn't amount to much of a threat, seeing as all of it, including the files marked *Restricted Access* and *Top Secret,* were in plain sight.

My family clearly didn't think its archives were much of a superweapon. At least, not in my hands.

Optimism Mahd'vi, ever the consummate diplomat, had displayed no emotion when I'd brought up the Kaveri family records. They were my only bargaining chip, and she'd almost led me to believe that they didn't matter to her. Almost.

It was the barest hint of a tremor in her voice that gave her away. I sincerely hoped I hadn't imagined it.

She wasn't very convincing, I said, chewing on my lower lip as I replayed her reaction.

Then turn around and walk away, Kili said. _We talked about this, remember? Doing nothing is a valid choice, too._

It's too late, I said.

It's not too late until you make the dead drop.

My head spun as I stepped off the walkway. We were at the doorways leading off to the Feast development bay. I played my lack of options over in my head for the billionth time as I passed my palm over a scanner and the flowmetal pulled apart for me.

Jog Tunga wants Feast, claiming that it's far too much power for one government to control.

Until a few māsas ago, I'd have disagreed. Primus was the shining, golden dream for human civilisation, I'd have argued. But that argument had steadily unspooled.

I've been harassed by Primians in private. I've been targeted by Primians in public, all the way from my first appearance on Interstellar MegaChef *to every stream-media outlet chasing me, alternating between adulation and vitriol, perpetually questioning my credibility. I've been put through the wringer by the Primian government itself. All because I'm an Earthling.*

Primus didn't deserve to exclusively possess such powerful tech. And Serenity Ko had ceded creative control to Optimism Mahd'vi …

I laughed out loud.

What? Kili asked.

I'm justifying the theft in my head. Telling myself all the reasons Primus doesn't deserve to control Feast exclusively, as if Jog Tunga has a valid point. I rolled my eyes. _I keep insisting it's for the greater good, which is true … but I also hate how *they've* come after *me*. Nonstop. And when it really comes down to it, I'm doing this to save my own skin so that I don't get deported and sent back home._

Ah, so that was a *bitter* laugh.

You know, there comes a moment in your life when you realise that all you've ever done is run away and save yourself, I said sadly. _And here I am, doing it again._

How about this? Kili offered. _We get through tonight, make the drop, and save introspection and self-loathing with a view to improving one's character for tomorrow._

I smiled weakly. _Sounds like a plan._

The tightness in my chest eased somewhat as I stepped into the Feast bay. It was completely deserted, given the lateness of the hour. A handful of work stations projected three-dimensional visuals into the air above them. There were a couple of graphical representations of the data we'd gathered from our pop-up experiences. One of the consoles had a teetering pyramid of code, another displayed a half-finished comms stream. I recognised a walkthrough of one of my flavour curves for a lemon uru-gai, a recipe that involved a lightly pickled, moderately spiced accompaniment served with savoury tarts like a relish. It had now been deprioritised to a later release date, seeing as how the XP Inc. team had to incorporate a slew of government feedback into our first batch of recipes that we'd be debuting at Feast.

Not a soul was in sight.

My sense of relief mingled with a wave of nausea. The moment was upon me, and it was going to be all too easy. Unfairly so.

At the work station I'd earmarked to use, I found a delicate brooch pinned to a scarf. I'd intentionally left it behind on my visit earlier in the day. It was my excuse for returning to the office; the jewellery wasn't so valuable that it would be odd to lose track of it, but it was just valuable enough to warrant returning late at night for.

Plus, now that my location was constantly streaming on the Loop, thanks to Secretariat-sponsored xenophobia, I needed a plausible reason for my presence here, so late at night.

I picked the scarf up, committing to my cover story.

I produced a thin piece of mem-film and approached the nearest work station. I slid it into a mem-port, pulled up the databases, and started to copy them. I didn't need any credentials.

Trust. Serenity Ko's words echoed in my head.

So much for that.

The act took less than two minutes. It was dreadfully anticlimactic, like the worst sex I'd ever had, except a few hundred times more awful. The complexity of the crime contrasted sharply with the enormity of the betrayal.

Another betrayal, my mind supplied. *To go with all the lying.*

I shuddered. I'd pull apart the person I was becoming the morning after. Stillness would be death; the contemplation of my crimes would stop me in my tracks.

Saras! Kili streamed, right as a voice said: 'Can I help you?'

I nearly jumped out of my skin, but managed to close my trembling hands into a fist, shoving them deep into my pockets along with the sliver of mem-film clenched in my right palm.

He didn't turn up on the Loop! Kili said in alarm.

I turned around, forcing a smile onto my face.

Honour Aki gazed at me curiously. His hair was dishevelled, his usual topknot starting to fray. A five o'clock shadow dotted his strong jaw, and he appeared to be half-asleep, his eyes limned with dark circles. He held a bottle of water in his hand, and was dressed in pyjamas.

'What're you doing here, Aki?' I asked casually.

'Working late,' he replied, also casually. 'What about you?'

'On *Feast*?' I asked, evading his question.

He gestured vaguely to the work bay. 'I was just passing through. On my way to the neuro-dev bay.'

'On the other side of the office,' I persisted, deciding to go on the offensive to cover up my equally flimsy excuse for being there.

'Last I recall, you don't actually work in *this* office at all,' he said with a scowl. 'And yet here you are, *twice* on the same day.'

'If you have a problem with that, you'll have to talk to Grace Kube.'

'Right. Working in the dead of night with your imaginary team, are you?'

I forced my hands from my pockets and awkwardly held the scarf up. 'Forgot this,' I said, feigning an embarrassed grin.

'A scarf.' His voice was toneless.

I shook it out and displayed the brooch on it. 'It's of sentimental value,' I said, attempting to sound sheepish.

He stiffened suddenly, the colour draining from his face. 'Ko give that to you?' he asked gruffly.

A light went off in my head. *Of course! He was looking for Ko in here, on the off-chance that she might be working late, and got me instead.*

Awkward, Kili said.

I know.

I smiled politely. 'It isn't from Ko,' I said gently. 'It's a family heirloom. One of the few things I have left from my home-world.'

My insides cringed as I repeated the sad refugee lie I was getting sick of parroting. *Take a deep breath. You can untangle your feelings tomorrow. First get out.*

Honour Aki didn't step out of my way, though. His expression didn't change, either. He was breathing a bit heavily, and I inadvertently took a step back, knocking into a console.

Should I raise an alarm? Kili asked anxiously.

And draw even more attention to me?

Better than being the victim of violence… or whatever Aki's about to do.

That's when I noticed tears welling up in Honour Aki's eyes.

_*Oh no*._

He's having a meltdown.

Am I going to have to… *console him* about their *breakup*?

They were never together. Not exclusively, Kili said sagely.

'Are you okay?' I asked hesitantly.

'Fine,' Honour Aki sniffed, turning away. 'At least, I will be.'

'Why don't you go home?' I suggested.

'Yeah. I will. You do that, too,' he said, waving his arm vaguely. 'Want me to call you a flowcab?'

'Um, no, thanks. I'll take the flowtram.'

Honour Aki walked away from me slowly, as if in a trance. His shoulders were hunched over in pain.

Should I—?

None of your business, not your job, Kili said quietly.

I walked as quietly as I could to the exit. Honour Aki shuffled away from me, as if he couldn't quite tell where he was going and didn't really care.

'Er, Aki…' I said quietly at the door. 'Take care.'

I stepped outside, holding myself with more confidence than I felt—in case there were any *other* visitors at the building that night—and made my way out the tunnel with no further incident. I reached the flowtram station, my breath coming up shorter now that I was finally giving myself permission to process everything that had happened in the last hour.

A moment sooner and he'd have seen me take Feast. I swallowed, my chest tightening.

But he didn't. I had eyes on the doors and he stepped inside right as I warned you; he must have been offline …

Yeah, easier to sneak up on Ko if she can't see him on the Loop, I said, shuddering.

You've done it, though. All you have to do is deliver it.

I didn't respond. We rode the flowtram in silence to the Harmony Knot a few stations away. I was sick of seeing the monument, sick of it punctuating every angsty moment I'd suffered on this sur-fucked planet. It was beautiful, even in the gloom in the dead of night, and its fragility as it wove past and future together in a blossoming of hope made me ill.

I located the yellow park bench beneath the wisteria, and found a little flowmetal case nestled in a hollow in its trunk. I slipped the mem-film into it.

My stomach clenched as I streamed Jog Tunga. _It's done._

I walked away numb.

At the end of the nava, I would attend the Legends of the Future gig with Serenity Ko, and pretend I hadn't just taken her brainchild and handed it over to an unscrupulous personification of terror to use it for whatever nefarious purposes he saw fit.

I felt a creeping sense of my total and utter failure to be a good person.

But at the end of the nava, I would attend the gig with Serenity Ko, and for the first time since I met her, I would be *free*. No longer a runaway desperately trying to save my skin, no longer a pawn in power games that were far bigger than I could comprehend.

There arose a stirring within my heart, pulsing, brimming with the dregs of hope I'd clung onto since my earliest memories.

I would come clean to her after the Millennium Feast; and I would pay the price for it, but I would do so on my own terms, without the shadow of the past threatening my future.

My heart sang now, a lightness growing to fill me where the weight of my crimes dragged me down. Soon, I would tell Serenity Ko everything, and there would be consequences, but at least there would be a future to face them in.

For the first time in my life, I was free.

And if we fall,
We fall together,
Into the infinity of a new beginning...

—Legends of the Future,
"Falling into Infinity"

TWENTY-SEVEN

THE TROUBLE WITH *gigs in orbit,* thought Serenity Ko, *is that you need to leave early to beat traffic heading planet-side—ergo missing out on the encore and after-party—or else stay the night.*

Ordinarily, spending the night with her flavour of the evening was never a problem. When that flavour happened to be one she'd seldom tasted (not often enough, by far), and longed for relentlessly but couldn't have (she really needed to work on changing that), who was dressed in a figure-fitting sheath-suit that set off every line and curve in her body (it was criminal not to drink it all in, Nine Virtues)... it was bound to lead to complications.

Separate rooms. Serenity Ko had made sure of that. She'd taken charge of logistics for the evening, seeing as this was Saraswati's first time attending an in-orbit concert.

Saraswati seemed somewhat overwhelmed as they stood in line, waiting to get their passes scanned at the entrance. Kili bobbled upon her shoulder, whirring about in the state of high-energy delight only Wingers were capable of, of which there were none other than him on Primus.

'Are you feeling all right?' Serenity Ko asked.

'Fine,' Saraswati said, sounding distracted, seeming to shrink.

'I thought you'd be thrilled to be at your first concert,' Serenity Ko said, now genuinely worried that she was going to have to deal with a downer of an evening, when she'd done everything in her control to make it unforgettable.

'There's just so much to see!' Saraswati said. 'It's all so... *extra*.'

She beamed, and the transformation was sudden and striking. Her beautiful lips parted and she ran a hand through her curls. 'Look,' she said, pointing up at the transparent domed ceiling, where a life-sized holoray of a blue whale swam over the heads of the assembled crowd, shimmering against the backdrop of the never-ending Milky Way that spun away beyond the pressurised dome. 'That is just exquisite.'

'It's from the *Oceanscreams* album,' Serenity Ko said.

'I know,' Saraswati said, then fell silent. 'Sorry, I've never been to anything like this. And I'm dead tired… Recharging my batteries now.'

The whale was a shimmering weave of colours, displaying an oceanic ecosystem within its belly as it glimmered, as if windows were opening up to permit glimpses into its soul.

Saraswati bounced up and down on the balls of her feet. 'Recharging,' she explained.

'Okay, so *that* is either your secret stash of MellO, or you've murdered Good Cheer Chaangte, or you've forgiven me for all my mistakes…' Serenity Ko said, grinning.

'It's the *atmosphere!*' Saraswati said, continuing to bounce.

Serenity Ko experienced a stab of jealousy that *she* wasn't the cause of Saraswati's happiness.

'I don't know if you know just how much I worshipped Legends of the Future when I was growing up,' Saraswati said.

She was obsessed, Kili said, from his perch on her shoulder. _I have vids…_

*No vids,* Saraswati said firmly.

Please send vids, Serenity Ko begged.

'I never thought I'd get to watch them live! They don't tour the Fringe planets—nobody does, really. Even the hasbeens avoid us,' Saraswati carried on. 'And you know, we've never really talked about our favourite bands, or music, or Ur-dramas, or very much outside of work. I'm not sure if you've noticed that.'

'Um…' Serenity Ko hesitated, wholly aware of this fact, and that she'd made a dedicated effort to keep it that way, in the forlorn hope of keeping her feelings for Saraswati from growing more complex.

'It's just nice to… hang out with you,' Saraswati said shyly, her pale cheeks flushing pink.

She fidgeted with the cuff of her sleeve, which wrapped around her arm so tight that the strong lines of her forearms rippled through. Serenity Ko realised she was staring and quickly averted her gaze.

The Stellar Arena was an enormous space station, and it was packed. With a capacity of fifty thousand people, it felt as if all of Primus had turned up. Tickets had sold out the moment it was announced, and Serenity Ko had camped on the Loop for hours, hoping to nab a pair. The moment she'd learnt that Saraswati had never been to a concert in orbit, she'd fantasised about introducing Saraswati to what was an otherwise basic Primian rite of passage, something every Primian teenager did as soon as they were old enough simply because they had access to all the biggest bands in the universe, all performing in their own cosmic backyard. And to make it *perfect,* she'd splurged on all-access tickets right up at the front of the stage, which synced with one's Loop credentials the moment they were scanned so you could view the concert straight from Chloriana's POV, or Enigma's, with detail that went all the way to the sound streaming to them from their monitors.

Imagine being *Enigma, looking down, and watching your hands play the electrochord,* Serenity Ko thought, excitement trailing up her spine.

All around her were cosplayers dressed as each of the band's members. MellO vapes sent a mist of fruity smoke up in the air, and Serenity Ko breathed in the tangle of fumes along with all the accompanying nostalgia. By the end of the gig, the entire arena would smell like a fruit basket, despite the space station's sophisticated filtering system doing its best to pump fresh oxygen into the room. It could make you sick if you weren't used to it, but Serenity Ko was *very* used to it. A burst of inspiration struck her as she looked around at the booths selling merchandise, packing the entryway into the arena.

'Hold my spot in the line?' she asked Saraswati. She turned

around and smiled at an older couple who stood right behind them. 'I'll be right back, so sorry.'

'No worries!' said the woman wearing everfeather ornaments in her hair.

Serenity Ko ducked out of line and rushed to the merchandise stalls. She grabbed a couple of MellO vapes—a Chloriana-themed fraiseberry flavoured one for Saraswati, an Enigma-themed chilli-mamba-zham for herself. She added two enormous mugs of fruit-flavoured bira before practically skipping her way back. She handed one of the mugs to Saraswati. 'While we wait,' she grinned.

'Thank you!' Saraswati took a sip.

'Ah, to be young again,' a voice said behind them.

Serenity Ko spun around and beamed at the older couple. 'I could pop out and get you some, too!' she offered.

'Can't do it any more, I'm afraid,' the everfeather woman said. 'I have it in me for one glass of star-sherry, and I'm waiting for them to sing "Limitless in Colour" for that.'

'Oh! I hope they do it unplugged; the Axian bass arrangement,' Saraswati chimed in.

Serenity Ko nearly dropped her bira in surprise. 'You're a serious fan! You never told me that!'

'We *had* music back on Earth, you know.' Saraswati winked, and Serenity Ko spluttered on her bira.

'Aren't they adorable?' the everfeather woman said to her partner.

'Young love.' Her partner grinned, her heavy black eyeliner accented in the dim light.

'We're not together!' Serenity Ko said hurriedly, right as Saraswati Kaveri burst out, 'Just friends!'

Smooth, Kili streamed them both.

An awkward silence began to grow, and the eyeliner lady rushed to fill it, recounting the first Legends of the Future concert she'd ever been to.

'…it was this absolutely decrepit club in the Osmos Girdle. The Grim Gardener, I think it was named—ironic, because they don't have a single plant on that rock. And this tiny little woman pops out with this enormous voice. There was no way to know that she'd turn into Chloriana—she didn't even have chlorosapient mods back then, or wear a shred of makeup!'

Serenity Ko glanced at Saraswati and saw that she was awestruck by the story. She didn't have the heart to tell her that this happened *all the time* when you grew up on Primus.

'You've left out the best bit,' the everfeather lady said. 'Where you bought her a drink afterwards and spent the night with her.'

'Ah, yes. That happened, too,' the eyeliner lady said. 'Trust you to bring that up, twenty years later.'

'Someone's got to keep the record straight.' The everfeather lady grinned, then leaned in to kiss her partner.

Serenity Ko felt a twinge of yearning at the sight of the happy couple reliving their youth, strangers though they were, and wondered if she'd ever feel so soppy about someone. It was uncomfortable to linger in the halo of their undying love, so she wished them a good gig and turned her attention elsewhere, namely to Saraswati, only to find that she was gazing at her with a look of such wistful longing that Serenity Ko wished the space station would develop a sudden pressure leak and plunge them all into the void before her feelings swallowed her whole.

She caught sight of a familiar face standing in a line parallel to theirs. Grasping at the distraction, she called out in a loud voice. 'Amol! Oi, that is your name, isn't it?'

Saraswati whirled around.

'Your friend is here!' Serenity Ko said, faking good cheer, privately thinking, *Star-fucker.*

She kicked herself as soon as she caught sight of Saraswati smiling.

Why did I shout out to him? She panicked as it struck her that she really *didn't* want other people to fill the space between her and Saraswati, not when there was so much electricity filling that space right now, supercharging so loudly that it couldn't possibly be ignored for much longer and was starting to demand some form of action. She wanted that space to *disappear,* not grow and be consumed by *other* people; she longed to be wrapped around Saraswati, pressed skin to skin, their lips frantically seeking each other out…

And she was doing everything in her power to sabotage those desires.

The man she'd yelled at looked in their direction, caught sight of Serenity Ko, and raised a hand in greeting. His face brightened when he saw Saraswati, and he walked over to them.

Serenity Ko kicked herself for always being the kind of idiot who fucked things up, even things she'd planned as grand romantic gestures, for a given value of *romantic*. Now they'd have to socialise all through the concert, and she wouldn't have Saraswati all to herself, and it was dawning on her that "alone time with Saraswati" was everything she wanted.

Amol Khurshid pulled Saraswati into a big hug.

'Congratulations, Saras!' Amol's eyes twinkled. 'It's so good to watch you succeed!'

He nodded towards Serenity Ko in acknowledgment. 'Pavi and I have been singing Feast's praises nonstop.'

Serenity Ko smiled, fought the urge to say "star-fucker" out loud, and streamed it to Kili, instead.

Kili gleefully agreed.

'Thanks!' Saraswati said politely. 'We need every endorsement we can get!'

'Chaangte's a bit sour,' Amol said, leaning forward and dropping his voice. 'We refused to rehire her, you know.'

Saraswati nodded. 'How's Pavi?'

'The usual.' Amol grinned. 'Anyway, I'm on a date. I'd best be getting back. And you two—?'

'No,' Saraswati said hurriedly.

'Nope,' Serenity Ko echoed.

'Have a great evening!' Amol called, walking away.

Saraswati evaded Serenity Ko's gaze.

'Definitely not a date!' Serenity Ko said loudly, covering up the twinge of disappointment in her gut.

And then they were admitted to the arena. Saraswati gasped audibly.

'All-access tickets?' she squealed. It was a sound Serenity Ko had never heard her make before, and it was oddly delightful. 'Ko… you shouldn't have!'

Serenity Ko would have given up her life savings to hear Saraswati's thoughts as she spun in a slow circle, taking it all in. She tried to view the arena through her friend's eyes and not her own, attempting to see what she might be seeing. She tried to revisit her own first experience of an in-orbit concert. She'd been chaperoned by her parents to catch Cribbage, the sulk-smash band she'd been obsessed with as a teenager, along with Boundless Ano, who'd gone to the same school.

On that night, the arena had taken on a more moody atmosphere—everyone had been seated on assigned floor-cushions, for a start. Cribbage was mellow and melancholy, and their fans were a more low-energy crowd that tended to drape themselves all over any space they occupied. Serenity Ko had sipped on her first bira, swaying to their sparse, percussive sound, and the endless night had melted away.

As she drunk in the view through Saraswati's eyes, she was moved to wonder for the first time in ages. The crowd was packing into the arena, a babbling of voices in so many accents and tongues, the words undefinable. Scents filled the air, from musky perfumes to fruity vapours, bitter bira brews and spiced wines. The lights were dim—bright enough to offer visibility, but low enough to soothe. And Serenity Ko and Saraswati stood at the heart of it all, the circular stage mere metres away from them, the band's instruments close enough that light reflected off their many facets, as if the merest whisper of a breeze would make the electrochord's strings vibrate with the song of the universe itself. Overhead, through the clear dome that arched above them, enclosing them protectively from the void that lay beyond, the endless spiral of the Milky Way spread its arms out, fingers seeking the unknowable in a universe promising all of infinity for those who dared to reach for it.

Serenity Ko was knocked breathless, her feet leaving the ground as if she were defying gravity, when Saraswati flung her arms around her. She sloshed bira all over the floor, and laughed as she apologised for the mess she was making, but refused to let go of her. Serenity Ko took in the scent of spice and sweetness, like a cinnamon roll dusted with sugar, and longing hunger spread through her.

Saraswati pulled away, abashed. 'Thank you, I mean.'

Serenity Ko averted her eyes, refusing to make eye contact. 'You're welcome,' she said softly.

'This is the most amazing thing I've ever experienced,' Saraswati said, her tone hushed in awe.

Serenity Ko attempted to recover her wits. 'The gig hasn't even started yet!' she said, hoping to fill the unfair space that now stood between them with the loudness of her voice. 'You wait until you hear what they sound like. The setup in this space is *insane*. They feed sound in through the speakers and ceiling, and you see this thingamajig right here? It's going to beam a wall of sound right at you.'

She was prattling.

'And before I forget, you won't *believe* what all-access tickets get you.'

She heard the words coming out of her mouth as she explained the POV-feeds, but she had no idea what she was saying; her mouth was running on some kind of autopilot. It was impossible to tear her eyes away from Saraswati, whose sheath-suit shimmered in shades of deep green, clinging to her like a second skin, accentuating all that lean muscle and the curves of her breasts...

Don't go there.

She flicked her eyes up to her face and found herself drawn to Saraswati's lips, painted a glorious deep purple, like ripe berries you could just bite into...

Don't go there, either.

She gazed into her deep brown eyes, dramatically outlined in shimmering gold eyeshadow that brought out their warmth...

This is safe.

...and she found herself falling into them...

Stop.

She looked away abruptly, her mouth still running on about all the cool things they could do with their all-access pass, until she ended by thrusting the MellO vape in her hands into Saraswati's.

'I brought you this…' she said, lamely, ignoring the electricity rippling through her nerves when their fingers grazed.

'Ooh!' Saraswati exclaimed. 'Is it strong?'

'No, it's pretty light, I promise,' Serenity Ko said reassuringly, glad to have more things to explain so she couldn't dwell on the feelings that were spinning through her mind. She ripped the packaging off hers and took a deep, satisfying drag. 'I don't get people smashed on the first da—'

She bit her tongue when she stopped herself, and swore at the sharp stab of pain. To hurriedly cover it all up, she took a large swig of her bira.

'Is—is this a date?' Saraswati asked seriously, mirroring her and taking a sip of her bira, too.

*Is* this a date? Kili echoed, streaming her privately.

'It's not… I mean…' Serenity Ko stammered. 'Only if you want it to be.'

Saraswati gave her an unreadable look.

'Take a hit of MellO!' Serenity Ko said brightly. 'It's great!'

'Stop evading the question,' Saraswati said, but unwrapped her vape and took a drag. 'Oh, this is *good!*'

'Right?' Serenity Ko said smugly, relieved that they'd all decided to move on.

'Now coming back to whether this is a date…' Saraswati said, smashing that premature sense of relief.

'Look, you don't have to decide right now. You can decide tomorrow, or next nava, or whenever…'

Saraswati nodded slowly, her eyes never leaving her face. 'Okay. Thanks, I appreciate that.'

Idiot. Serenity Ko kicked herself. *Can't go thirty minutes without fucking things up.*

Don't mess with her, Kili streamed her.

I'm *not,* Serenity Ko shot back.

Do you want to be with her? Kili asked protectively.

I… I don't know.

She's supposed to just… wait around? Kili asked incredulously.

Of course not!

You're not supposed to drop the word "date" like a ray-bomb!

It just slipped out, Serenity Ko sulked. _I didn't mean it to._

Well, I'm "just" looking out for her, Kili said firmly. _And for you, too._

We'll talk about it like adults, Serenity Ko said irritably. _I promise._

She took another large swig of her bira, downing the rest of the mug's contents in one go.

'I'm getting a refill,' she announced. 'Would you like another?'

'Yes, please,' Saraswati said. 'But let me pick this up.'

'No,' Serenity Ko said firmly. 'You stay right here. If they come on stage, I want you to be able to soak every second in. No telling what the line at the bar might be like…'

'That's considerate, thank you,' Saraswati said, politely.

'You're being weird,' Serenity Ko snapped. 'All extra formal.'

'So-sorry.'

'Just be normal, Saras.' Serenity Ko smiled. 'This is nothing more than two friends hanging out at a concert, okay?'

'Okay.'

'Now take a hit of that vape. I'd better find you nice and mellow when I'm back,' she said bossily, storming away.

It took her all of ten minutes to get their refills of bira and return, and she was glad for the short respite.

She handed Saraswati her drink. 'Here you go—'

Her words were drowned out by an enormous cheer that echoed through the arena, and she whipped her head around.

Legends of the Future strode onto the stage like they owned it. Chloriana appeared larger than life, diminutive as she was: her dramatic padded shoulders and signature trailing wings turned her into an otherworldly creature. Enigma stomped over to their electrochord, dressed all in black, their clothes shimmering like plated armour on the side of a spacecraft, their neck tats glowing glossy black as if the ink was swirled to life, creating pockets of shadow that highlighted the sharpness of their features. Minos took her place behind the drums, topless except for a tiny, lacy bralette, Elvarata sat at the keys in a sweeping brocade gown woven from flower petals…

And Serenity Ko heard her voice screaming with all the rest of the audience, shouting her undying love for the band at the top of her lungs. Saraswati yelled beside her, their voices tumbling together in a chorus of adulation, and for the briefest moment, they made eye contact, and grinned at each other.

Saraswati's hand slipped into hers, Serenity Ko's every nerve was set ablaze, and a wall of sound slammed into her as the band kicked into their favourite opening song, "Beginning Infinity."

Serenity Ko bellowed the lyrics off-key, as was her wont, and experienced a twinge of shock to hear Saraswati beside her, harmonising perfectly with the band. She lost herself in the dizzying spirals of the notes, the ethereal sound of Saraswati's voice, mirroring Chloriana's perfectly, glanced up at the galaxy trailing across the depths of space above her, felt her insides unravelling, and let herself fall hard.

Blossoming Romance: Are Serenity Ko and Saraswati Kaveri Primus's newest power couple?

—Primian Power Watch
2075 Anno Earth | 2000 Interstellar Era

Earthling filth shouldn't get their dirt-stained fingers on our people.

—Curiosity Voe
2075 Anno Earth | 2000 Interstellar Era

They're perfect for each other! SK² all the way!

—Harmony Jenn
2075 Anno Earth | 2000 Interstellar Era

TWENTY-EIGHT

I WAS APPREHENSIVE at first, but the sheer energy of the evening had taken over and dispelled all my fears. I'd been terrified that I was going to crack, and that Serenity Ko would sense that something was up and ask uncomfortable questions about it all, in her usual no-filters-or-tact way…

But she didn't. And the sheer spectacle of it all, the raw power of the wall of sound drowning us in its swell, the sensation of being in the stars while Legends of the Future sang about our relationship with the universe, and how its mysteries were the mysteries of ourselves, and why we were all both lost in space and at home in space, one with the void yet shimmering with hope, had filled me like a song of hope. It cracked me wide open as if breaking me free from imprisonment in ways that nothing I had ever done could accomplish.

I'd clean forgotten that I'd stolen Feast for Jog Tunga on Optimism Mahd'vi's command; it was irrelevant that I'd faked my way onto this planet, into a new life… All that mattered was the moment in which we were. At one point, the grav-management had been switched off, and the audience was lifted ten feet into the air while the cosmic whale and its ocean-scape engulfed us, flowing forth from the stage, as Chloriana's ethereal vocals engulfed us all and called us to swim, to be one with the life force driving us all onward.

Guilt had gnawed at me for so long, dogging my footsteps and haunting my dreams… but all of it faded like vapour trails misting the air. I suppose a lot of my exuberance had to do with the MellO I'd inhaled, tentatively at first, and then with more confidence as I realised just how much it was helping me unwind. It was clear that I was going to have drunk my weight in biras by the time the evening was done, and I was grateful that the loos were right around the corner and spotlessly clean.

Kili bobbled in time to the music, sometimes perched upon my shoulder, sometimes whirring around in excitement, dancing with me. All the while Serenity Ko grew to fill my senses, headbanging with me through the heavier bits when Enigma's chordophone surged in its breakdowns, swaying with me when Elvarata kissed the keys with her fingertips, creating melodies haunting and joyous at once.

I was painfully aware of her every gesture, the sheen of perspiration on her skin, the way her hips moved to the all-encompassing rhythms around us, her lips articulating the words of every song—now yelling, now wailing, always just a shade off-key, but beautiful regardless. And I felt a longing within me, a void gaining mass and gravity, wishing fervently to draw her into its pull, closer and closer towards me until we were skin upon skin…

When the encore resounded and Legends of the Future took their bows, it was as if I'd emerged from a dream, wrecked and wasted. As we shuffled out of the arena, our fingers brushed, and then her hand was in mine, and she was squeezing it. Fifty thousand people were singing in a disjointed chorus, disparate groups all laying into their favourite songs from tonight's performance, and Serenity Ko and I raised our voices to join them, following the eddying trail of one fragmentary melody into the next.

You are positively smashed, Kili giggled.

Guilty.

I hope you're having the time of your life, he added.

Also guilty.

This is what you deserve, Saras. To feel like this. Always, he said, nuzzling my cheek.

Serenity Ko practically danced her way to our hotel. She'd informed me in no uncertain terms that we'd be spending the night in orbit, and that it would be madness to try to catch a craft planet-side before morning. I could see why; the lines were excruciatingly long as people departed the space station, and the thrill of the evening slid off the faces of all the commuters depressingly quickly.

We stepped into the elevator leading us to our floor, and Serenity Ko led me to a room off to one side, passing her hand over a scanner.

'You're right next door,' she mumbled.

'Thanks,' I said. 'I remember from when we checked in a few hours ago.'

Serenity Ko grinned.

I passed my hand over the scanner. The door whooshed open. All I had to do was let go of her hand …

'Good night, then,' she said.

'Yeah, good night,' I echoed.

I couldn't let go of her hand. I didn't want to step through the door. Not alone.

I pulled her in after me, and the lights went on automatically. I reached for a switch to flick them off, right as she pushed me up against the wall.

_ I'm out,_ Kili said, dropping into my pocket and switching off our Loop comms, as he always did with the greatest consideration every time I hooked up, which I suddenly realised I hadn't done since I'd left Earth, not properly.

Serenity Ko ran her hands roughly across my waist and pressed her lips against mine hard.

I gasped.

I kissed her with a ferocity that came out of nowhere, on instinct. All those māsas of yearning, lying in bed alone at night, wondering what it was I felt for her, coming undone within me. She grabbed my curls and held my face firmly to the wall behind me, parting my lips with her tongue, and I gave in.

She filled my senses as I ran my hands along her curves, drawing her in to me. All I wanted was to close the gap between us, the yawning distance I had felt ever since our first kiss, through all our arguments and meaningless conversations, skirting around all the reasons why we should never do this, except that doing this felt as if my whole life had been building up into this moment. All I knew was that I wished this moment would go on forever.

Abruptly, she came up for air.

'No objections?' she teased. I heard the grin in her voice, as she ground her hips into mine, lightly tracing her fingertips down the curve of my cheek.

I made an inarticulate sound.

'Let's try again, shall we?' she said, touching her lips to my neck.

I shivered.

'Let me make this clear,' she said, her voice hoarse as she undid the lowest button on my blouse. 'I'm saying all of this so that I know for sure, without a doubt, that you want this as much as I do.'

'Uh—' I gasped, as her fingers grazed the skin of my stomach.

'It's not the alcohol or the MellO, is it?'

'No,' I gasped.

'The Saras I know will stop me any moment,' she continued. 'And that's fine. Go ahead and stop me.'

I didn't stop her.

'I mean it,' she said, her breath grazing my collarbone.

She undid another button, then pulled her hands away from me. My skin tingled, aching for her touch.

'We can talk about all our feelings now, or later, or never. I don't want you to regret anything.'

And then, she stepped back from me, the distance between us growing too large for my mind to comprehend, as it screamed at me to close the gap again, to lean into the crackle of electricity rippling through the air, magnetic and on fire.

'Ko,' I said, my voice shaking, my newfound freedom rippling through me. 'I've wanted this all along. And I don't care if we wake up tomorrow and we have to talk about feelings and what this means for our working relationship and all that shit. We can figure it out later.'

I heard her draw in a sharp breath. 'How later?'

'Whenever you want to, whenever you feel like it,' I said, letting control slip through my fingers. 'I'm sick of thinking about tomorrow.'

I closed the space between us again, pulling her to me. 'This has gone on long enough. And I want you now.'

I FOUND MYSELF lying awake, exhausted and euphoric, long after Serenity Ko fell into a deep sleep.

I was riding the wave, triumphant that every second we'd been together had been the best moment of our lives...

I was free.

I was letting go of my past and its long shadow over me was receding into the realms of memory.

Maybe it was the certainty of knowing that I'd fucked things up forever, so nothing really mattered. Or the searing hope that maybe, just maybe, I'd come clean to Serenity Ko and she'd forgive me. It was the thought that all these possibilities even existed that let me give in.

All I'd wanted to do was escape my family and establish a name for myself far outside their circle of influence by winning *Interstellar MegaChef*. I hadn't achieved what I'd set out to do, but something even better had come my way. I was unstoppable, famous and well-regarded, widely hailed as the creator of a new culinary culture. I'd far surpassed any ambitions I'd ever held for myself—on Earth, in my previous life, and even when I'd run away.

All because I'd taken my chances and leapt. With unshakeable, unfathomable trust that the universe would catch me when I fell.

And that's exactly what I was doing now…

A moment of clarity dawned on me with alarming sharpness. *I trust her.*

I trusted Serenity Ko. Beyond just our working relationship, I *trusted* her.

And she trusts me.

That shattered it all.

I hadn't done anything to earn her trust. I'd stolen Feast—her vision for revolutionising the future of food—and handed it over to someone I knew would misuse it. I'd committed countless acts of betrayal, and I remained duplicitous, even as I lay there in her arms.

You can lie to the world, but it's impossible to keep lying to yourself, once you've taken a good long look at your reflection.

I was a Godavari down to the tiniest atom in my bones. Deception and manipulation was the Godavari way, and even if I'd never wielded a knife or a gun, I'd hurt and harmed everyone who crossed my path.

I'd been deceitful to the woman who now lay beside me, the woman I strongly cared for—maybe even loved—whom I'd just spent the better part of the night actually making love to…

I pushed the thought away.

Jog Tunga had promised my family would leave me alone. At least she'd be safe from them.

Jog Tunga is a liar. Do you really believe him?

If I didn't believe him, if I didn't truly believe that I was free, then what had I done? Why had I stolen Feast? And what was I doing in bed with Serenity Ko?

I need to tell her the truth. I panicked.

I thought about my friends… and my stomach clenched.

Boundless Baz had been disgusted to discover I was a Godavari. He'd said his grandfather had had to flee the Earth because of what my family had done. Courage Oslo and

Curiosity Zia had been appalled that I'd lied to them. XX-29 had been miserable at the discovery, and xe wasn't even human. My falsehoods had hurt xir on some universal plane that was fundamental to all intelligent life.

And then there was Starlight Fantastic. They'd been my first friend on this sur-fucked planet, they'd stood by me and cheered me on through it all, and I'd let them down too.

I pulled up all my Loop comms and looked at the days that had slid past with all my comms unanswered.

I'm still sorry, I streamed at all of them.

A moment passed, and then a notification popped up.

You hurt me with your lies, Saras, Starlight Fantastic said. _I'm sure you had your reasons, and maybe we'll talk about them someday._

I'll explain everything, I said, with a rush of relief.

Not now. I'm not ready.

I deflated, and tears pricked at the corners of my eyes.

I hope you're well, they said. _I'm still rooting for you to find your way._

I hope you're well, too. I don't deserve your goodwill. I never have. All I can say is that I'm sorry and, given half the chance, I will make it up to you.

Starlight Fantastic didn't respond. I counted the seconds as they ticked by. And then I felt sick to my stomach for making it all about myself again, and what I did and didn't deserve. Who was I to judge that, anyway? Did people ever get what they deserved? If they did, then everything I'd said and done to all these people warranted a nice cold cell on a distant rock …

Serenity Ko shifted beside me, mumbling in her sleep, and I was nauseous.

She wanted it, too, a part of me thought defensively.

Would she have wanted it if she knew what you've done? If she knew you've been lying to her since the moment you first met her?

I couldn't process this on my own.

Hey, I streamed Kili.

It's been a minute, Kili streamed good-naturedly.

You can come out of my pocket. She's asleep.

Great, it was starting to feel cramped in there, Kili said enthusiastically, whirring over to me.

I'm a terrible person.

*That* went downhill quick, he said, his voice tinged with concern. _Was it… not good?_

It was spectacular.

Uh-huh, Kili said. _So what am I missing?_

I should have listened to you all along.

I've waited my whole life to hear these words, Kili teased. _But somehow I don't feel like gloating._

You can gloat, I said bitterly.

What was I right about?

Everything. I should have been honest with everyone I trusted from the start.

Saras…

I trust her, Kili. And she trusts me, I said sadly. _That's why tonight happened. We both know that even if this goes nowhere in the end, we won't destroy each other. And I don't deserve that—_

You deserve to be trusted, Kili said loyally.

Do I? Be honest.

Kili was silent.

I have to tell her the truth about who I am, I said, my breath catching.

That's brave. When?

I—I don't know… I was planning to do it after the Millennium Feast.

That's ages away.

I know, I said miserably.

And? Kili prodded.

And what?

I sense an "and" coming. That's why you're still up, instead of blissfully asleep after some long overdue sex, which from everything you've said was excellent.

I sighed.

And? Kili repeated.

And things between us are going way too fast for me to keep lying for that long. I need to do it sooner.

That would be best for both of you, even if it hurts, Kili said gently.

Yes, before things can go any further. Before romance gets in the way.

It's the right thing to do, Kili said sadly.

Before our feelings become even more…. complicated.

Oh, Saras. Kili nuzzled my cheek.

I could have told her who I was early on.

Maybe.

I didn't.

No, you didn't, Kili said. _But you did what you thought you had to do._

And I was wrong.

I pressed my hands to my face where it was buried in the pillow.

I'm not going to say you were right, Saras, Kili said kindly. _But I can't judge you. I can only love you, and wish you peace while you live with the consequences of your actions._

Easy for you to say, I snapped, suddenly exhausted and irritable. _You're just a machine._

He flinched. I knew I'd cut him spitefully, and that he didn't deserve it.

I'm sorry, I said, miserably.

I know you didn't mean that, Kili said. _But that hurt. Tremendously._

I've done absolutely nothing right all my life. Including this, I said, filled with self pity.

That doesn't mean that can't change.

You're right.

I needed to tell Serenity Ko the truth. *She can decide if she wants to be with me then.*

I turned around, and found that Kili had retreated to a safe distance away from me. I couldn't blame him. Who'd want to be anywhere near me, once they knew what I really was on the inside?

The truth is pretty convenient. You can always choose to tell it… or not.

—Optimism Niha,
Uru: Origins, Season 3, Episode 6
2056 Anno Earth | 1981 Interstellar Era

TWENTY-NINE

THE NAVAS SWEPT by in a high-pressure blur.

Serenity Ko couldn't tell when one thing tumbled headlong into the next—and on into the next, and on and on. It was only when she was exhausted from exploring Saraswati's body, when her head hit the pillow—consumed and elated—that she began to process everything that was flung her way each day, and she was out cold before she got to mull things over, which was likely a good thing.

There was problem-solving at the office, and they never seemed to run out of problems to solve in the final run up to the Millennium Feast. Over the last nava, she'd gone to war with Courage Na'vil repeatedly.

'What the actual *fuck* do you mean, Na'vil?' Serenity Ko yelled. 'Tickets to the Millennium Feast sold out *ages* ago. Invitations were sent to special guests by no less than the Culture and Heritage department, and you bring this up now?'

'I brought it up then, too,' Courage Na'vil snapped. The bones stood out on his lean face, skin taut over the veins in his neck, as if all of him were straining to make his point as emphatically as possible. 'I told you to raise concerns with them over having minors partake of Feast.'

He flung a projection onto a visio-node and beamed data from our pop-up experience with minors. 'Look at that spike in stimulation of the emotional centres of the brain. We're priming young children with unrealistic expectations of reality, heightening their emotional patterns—'

'And we *warned* parents to exercise discretion when

bringing their children to all our Feast pop-ups,' Serenity Ko interrupted. 'We can't parent the world. It's the same warning label that goes on *all* our XP Inc. sims.'

'But this is *food,* not entertainment. It's a *basic need,*' Courage Na'vil said, his voice now a whine.

'So you've said since the day we started developing Feast, but that hasn't stopped development, has it? You haven't refused to build everything we've asked you to, have you?' Serenity Ko hissed, her voice low.

The matter had been taken to Grace Kube and Optimism Sah'r. Serenity Ko idly wondered if there'd be minors at the Millennium Feast or not, and if they were going to get tied up in legalese post-launch, while the galaxy debated the impact of Feast on young, impressionable minds.

To further add to the snarl of stupidity, Honour Aki had been streaming her with increased desperation, repeatedly insisting that all he wanted to do was "talk." If precedent was anything to go by, that would be an entire evening of one-sided, unasked for feelings, deep confessions from his soul that he couldn't bear the burden of having to live with if they went unexpressed…

And Serenity Ko didn't need any more romance in the air. Or so she insisted, despite knowing in the depths of her heart that it was wholly untrue.

Good Cheer Eria and Optimism Rihan had thoughtfully scheduled their wedding the māsa after the Millennium Feast, swearing that they'd keep Serenity Ko minimally involved, and promising they wouldn't carve a gaping hole into all her time with tastings and fittings and all the rest of the delightful wedding haze that surrounded them like a cloud of fragrant astrianas on a summer's day. Except, unlike being out in the garden in the sur-light, Serenity Ko had *wanted* to be involved as much as possible. Optimism Rihan was her only sibling, and the chances of her celebrating a wedding of her own any time soon were slim, to say the least.

Odd, she often found herself thinking. *Never thought I was the romantic sort.*

But she'd agree to accompany her family on impulse, only to be swept away in the high emotion of it all. She burst into tears watching Dad and Appa get all choked up when Optimism Rihan chose his scent-memory for the big day. Hovering around her family's hex while her Ammamma prepped all the traditional sweet pastries—one for each nava, for eighteen navas in a row until the wedding—both made her hungry and filled her with an inexplicable sense of being part of something larger than herself, even if Ammamma shooed her away every time.

The longer she spent around Saraswati—which was a lot longer than ever before, and all of it was extraordinary—the more she was convinced that she wanted to attend Optimism Rihan's wedding with her, in some kind of official date-type capacity. She was working up the courage to bring it up and failing miserably, but was determined that she'd pull it off by the time the wedding rolled around.

The big launch would be over by then, she reasoned. And things could afford to get *more* complicated.

She was daydreaming along similar lines, while appreciating the way Saraswati's lips moved when she was explaining complicated food-based ideas to idiots—namely, her team at XP Inc. Saraswati had wrapped up their last pop-up before the big day of the Millennium Feast, and had agreed to give the team a pep talk about how brilliant everything was going to be. It wasn't quite a lie, and it would do the team good to have their nerves soothed somewhat.

'We had an impromptu performance of one of the sinfonia pieces—a really popular one,' Saraswati said with a smile, then looked off into the distance. 'I think it's called… "Primian Pirouette"?'

Curiosity Nenna burst out laughing. 'That's not the sinfonia! It's an action song they teach little kids in school,' she said kindly. Her eyes shone radiant. 'That must have been brilliant.'

Saraswati beamed. 'That makes it *even better,*' she said. 'Wait till you see the footage. There were a couple of grandparent-age folks dancing along while everyone sang out the tune, *oompah*-ing their way through the beat.'

Serenity Ko pulled up the raw data files from the tasting and saw a huge surge in hippocampus and neocortex stimulation. The sim that had given rise to this was the Nakshatran Gelato, one of their amuse bouche offerings. She made a mental note to fire off a full report to Optimism Mahd'vi, grimacing at how the Secretary for Culture and Heritage would lord this over them all as a big win for the heightened Primian experiences she'd forced them to include.

Saraswati proceeded to walk them through the rest of the five-course tasting menu from the pop-up, and after the team positively skipped out the room, beaming at the incredible success they were being primed to expect at the Millennium Feast, Serenity Ko found herself alone with her.

'Does this mean you're making updates to the menu we've finalised for the Millennium Feast?' Serenity Ko asked, furrowing her brow slightly as she pulled the menu in question up on their stream.

Visualisations of each dish in their actual form, accompanied by their featureless Feast cube equivalents, spun in the air. Each was annotated with high-level data monitoring their performance, which had been consolidated across testing groups, and normalised to create a comprehensive view of their impact and efficacy. One layer deeper was a qualitative analysis, along with Saraswati's notes on why she'd chosen to include each dish.

'I think we might like to include the Nakshatran Gelato, instead of the Citric Crush, as our amuse bouche…' Saraswati said slowly, flicking a stray curl off her forehead.

'Mm-hmm,' Serenity Ko said, tapping her foot as she drew up a computational comparison.

'The Citric Crush is a more traditional flavour profile for an amuse bouche,' Saraswati explained. 'But we've never seen an outpouring of emotion like this, have we?'

Serenity Ko rapidly read through the comparative charts. 'We've tested the Citric thing with a bigger sample set, though. What if today's test group was more primed for nostalgia? They were an older sample set, after all.'

Saraswati blew out her cheeks. 'Fair enough,' she said.

Serenity Ko glanced up at her quickly. 'You look tired.'

'I am,' she smiled weakly. 'It's exhausting putting my public face on and smiling through being a nervous wreck.'

'Nearly there, though,' Serenity Ko said. 'The Millennium Feast is just a couple of days away.'

'I can't wait for it to be over,' Saraswati said. 'And for the rest of... everything else to begin.'

'Fully understandable,' Serenity Ko said gently, then added, on a sudden burst of inspiration. 'Why don't you come over for dinner tonight?'

'I—'

'We'll unwind. We'll talk about not-work,' Serenity Ko said sincerely, ignoring how her heart rate skyrocketed at the thought that she could casually brush her fingers against Saraswati's skin, hanging on to her every word, before kissing her and ripping her clothes off. 'We'll discuss feelings-type stuff, even.'

Saraswati snorted.

'I'll open a nice bottle of... starfruit wine. Or maybe just biras.'

'Okay, done,' Saraswati said with a sudden smile.

'You can even bring your other friends over,' Serenity Ko said before she could help herself, in a last-ditch attempt to play down the significance of the evening. She'd decided that she was going to ask Saraswati to be her plus-one to her brother's wedding, but was also terrified of simultaneously confessing how ardently she loved her.

A funny look passed across Saraswati's face. Her brows scrunched up and her lip twitched momentarily, before smoothing over. 'No, I don't think so,' she said hurriedly. 'Too last minute.'

'Right,' Serenity Ko said, her mouth suddenly dry. 'So I'll see you and Kili.'

'Sounds like a plan!' Saraswati said, too bright, before her likeness winked out.

Serenity Ko rushed through the rest of the day only half paying attention to the ongoing battle between the neuro-devs and the marketing team. Courage Na'vil wanted all the Feast packaging to be branded with labels cautioning against excessive usage, while the marketing team was decidedly against it.

'Show us the statistical data that links this to addiction,' was countered by: 'There are strong indicators that the dopamine releases linked by mem-triggers could *spark* an addiction, as is historically evidenced by—'

At which point, Serenity Ko idly pulled up her satellite slinging training guides and started perusing them, content to be a warm body in the room in a meeting that would eventually be escalated to a meeting of the Triumvirate, where Optimism Sah'r and Grace Kube would have to sort things out with Courage Na'vil, hopefully in her absence. She hadn't been slinging in ages, not since the awful accident she'd narrowly evaded, but she was looking forward to being up there in space again as soon as Feast was out in the world.

Maybe I'll even introduce Saras to it, she thought, then realised that she had no idea whether Saraswati enjoyed adrenaline rushes, only to further realise that she'd asked her over for dinner, except she still couldn't cook to save her life, and she had no idea if her pantry was stocked with food or not, and fuck, she should have practiced marbling techniques with more diligence under her Ammamma's supervision…

As soon as the meeting wound up, Serenity Ko excused herself in a hurry.

Here are pending to-dos, she streamed Courage Praia. _You're in charge. I'm out for the evening._

She was racing through the tunnel, flashing lights spinning all round her, wondering if she should ask Dad or her grandmother to help supply her with food for her dinner with Saraswati, or take her chances and attempt to make it herself, when she slammed straight into a wall of muscle as she stepped out into the sur-light, momentarily disoriented by the nanosecond lag it took for her visio-filters to kick in and help her eyes adjust to the change in illumination.

'Oof,' she grunted. 'I'm so sorry.'

And then she groaned in dismay.

'Ko, I desperately need to talk to you,' Honour Aki said. His eyes were tortured, which Serenity Ko had regrettably once been attracted to, back when she'd thought they were merely brooding. It turned out they were filled with a haunted, unrequited love for her.

'Aki, I don't have the time right now,' she snapped. 'If you want to tell me all about your undying love for me, find a slot on my calendar—'

She brushed past him, walking away.

'That's not it,' he said, chasing after her. 'It's got nothing to do with how much I love you.'

That stopped her dead in her tracks, the fine hairs on the back of her neck standing up. 'What else do you have to say to me?' Serenity Ko asked warily.

'It's about your friend. Saraswati. The Earthling,' he said.

'Thanks for clarifying which Saraswati you're talking about,' Serenity Ko said. 'If you're going to sell me rumours—'

'No,' he said flatly. 'It's something I… I caught her doing. Red-handed.'

Serenity Ko's heart stuttered. 'What do you mean?'

'It's sensitive,' Honour Aki said cryptically. 'Will you just walk with me to the park? I don't want us to be overheard.'

Against her better judgment, Serenity Ko followed him to the neighbourhood parkland, making sure she was a good distance away from any hand-holding or other romantic gestures he might want to try. When they found themselves in the shade of a willowoak, she whirled around, her arms crossed firmly over her chest.

'You've got ten minutes. Make it quick.'

Honour Aki did. It was the loudest Serenity Ko had ever felt her heart break.

'You look lovely,' Serenity Ko said so brightly that even she could hear how false she sounded.

'Er, thanks,' Saraswati said uncertainly. 'I'm pretty sure I look like shit—'

'No, you're drop dead gorgeous. As always,' Serenity Ko said truthfully, though it felt like being stabbed by a billion needles to say it out loud. Saraswati's eyes were shadowed in dark circles, and her dress was rumpled from a long day spent at the Feast pop-up, but her skin was flushed from the wine, and the light in her eyes danced merrily as it always did. Serenity Ko loved and resented all of her. 'More wine?' she asked.

Without waiting for an answer, Serenity Ko refilled Saraswati's glass and her own, and took a large, ungainly swig before plastering a smile across her face again.

'Are you okay, Ko?'

'Me? Fine,' Serenity Ko said grandly, throwing her arms out wide. As the starfruit wine sloshed over the side of her glass onto an intricately patterned rug, she winced, but kept smiling. 'It's *you* I'm worried about.'

Serenity Ko couldn't bring herself to form the words and spit them out, even though they were hovering on the tip of her tongue. *I know you stole Feast, betraying me and everyone at XP Inc. And I never want to see you again.*

Instead, she picked up a plate of cracker-pastry, with savoury gelées and pickled shrooms, and thrust it clumsily at Saraswati. 'Didn't make these myself,' she said, laughing awkwardly. 'I'm sure you can tell. They're edible, after all.'

'Thanks, Ko,' Saraswati said meekly, nibbling on the end of a cracker.

'Don't get to host too often, you know,' Serenity Ko said, her mouth running on autopilot. 'Too much effort. Much easier to take someone to a bar, get them wasted, sleep with them and leave in the middle of the night, don't you think?'

'Can't say I've ever done that—' Saraswati began, but Serenity Ko cut her off.

'Of course, that's not quite *your* MO, is it?' Serenity Ko leaned forward, leering. She knew she was leering and strained to stop herself, but emotions bubbling up within her were making her do unpredictable things, and none of it had anything to do with the wine. 'Not what you do, at all. Instead, you worm your way into people's hearts and win their trust and then let them down hard, don't you?'

Are you okay? Kili asked. He rose whirring from where he'd been settled on Saraswati's shoulder to hover in front of Serenity Ko, gazing deep into her eyes.

'Ah, and here's your faithful accomplice. What's a life of crime without a good robot sidekick, eh?'

'What're you talking about, Ko?'

'I'm sure you know, Saras,' Serenity Ko said sweetly. She felt positively unhinged, and knew she was coming across that way, but tough nuts. That's what thieves deserved.

'Ko—'

'I mean, you even get your targets to take you to Legends of the Future gigs,' Serenity Ko said, fury rising to the surface. 'Sleep with them, blame them for things going wrong that are out of everyone's control, get them to apologise for being shitheads—which, fair, seeing as we're talking about me. And generally string them along through having a great time, drop hints about deep feelings, making all kinds of promises about the future…'

Hey, Kili said, annoyed. _Snap out of whatever this is and behave like an adult._

'Your robot sidekick is telling me to be an adult,' Serenity Ko said, rolling her eyes.

'He's not my sidekick, Ko,' Saraswati snapped. 'And yeah, you're acting all funny. If you've got a problem with me, just say it out loud.'

Serenity Ko laughed at this, her heart crumpling up into a crushed, withered object. 'Oh, you think *you* deserve honesty. After all you've done.'

Saraswati went pale and dropped the cracker in her hand.

'Now you'll look all woeful and expect me to pity you,' Serenity Ko said, steeling herself. 'Like you did at the Uru and Beyond Marketplace all those māsas ago, when you tricked me into becoming friends.'

'I didn't trick you—'

'And then you tricked me into staying friends, didn't you?

All this will-they-won't-they unresolved sexual tension, the kiss we had on the special episode of *MegaChef*, the sudden ethical boundaries against hooking up with me because we work together…' Serenity Ko trailed off. 'All of this was to get to where we are right now, wasn't it?'

'I have real feelings for you, Ko,' Saraswati said softly. 'I've never been sure about your feelings for me—'

'I've *always* loved you, but that's *not what this is about*,' Serenity Ko shouted, cracking at last.

'You *what*?'

'I've been trying to show you all along, even if I haven't said so out loud…' Serenity Ko said miserably. 'Maybe I was wrong to always rise to your defence, as if you couldn't take care of yourself. All I wanted to do was have your back in this stupidly fucked-up world. And *I* fucked up. A lot. But I loved you, and I wanted to show you, because I just… I didn't have the courage to tell you.'

Saraswati went even paler. 'I—'

'And you *knew* all this. And continued to lead me on.'

'*What?*'

'You made friends with me so you could build Feast and then *steal it*.'

Saraswati's hands started trembling uncontrollably.

'I know what you did,' Serenity Ko whispered.

'How?' Saraswati's voice came out barely a croak.

'You don't deny it, then?' Serenity Ko laughed, as the last piece of her heart that had held out hope that this was all one of Honour Aki's bizarre conspiracy theories, designed to break them up before they could even begin, shattered.

Saraswati buried her head in her hands. 'I was going to tell you,' she said hoarsely. 'This isn't how I wanted you to find out. I wanted to tell you everything—'

'Well, *too fucking bad for you*.' Serenity Ko's voice rose as the woman before her—the woman she'd finally begun to accept that she was in love with—slowly deflated. 'Now I know the truth. I can't *believe* you'd betray me—not *just me*, by the way, but all the folks at XP Inc. who welcomed you to the team with such openness and kindness… I can't believe you'd stick a knife in us like this.'

Saraswati's shoulders shook. 'I'm sorry,' she rasped. 'I'm so, so sorry.'

'Save it for someone who cares,' Serenity Ko snarled.

'I—I never meant to… I didn't lead you on. My feelings for you are real,' Saraswati began, then doubled over as if in physical pain.

Serenity Ko knocked back the contents of her wine glass. She poured herself another, and quaffed that too. She glared at Saraswati, collapsed into the cushions on her couch, wondering how she had ever chosen to trust the woman who had trampled all over her insides like this. She rose to her feet and walked away. 'You know your way out,' she said, wholly intending to slam her bedroom door and leave Saraswati to do what she liked, willing her to disappear from her life for good.

Her insides hollow, she paused momentarily. 'I won't say a word of this to Kube until the Millennium Feast is over. But afterwards… I never want to see you again.'

'Wait,' Saraswati called hoarsely. 'If that's how you really feel…'

'That's absolutely how I feel,' Serenity Ko said, though a quiet voice inside of her questioned the veracity of the statement.

'If that's how you feel, then I might as well come clean about everything else,' Saraswati said in a hoarse whisper.

'What do you mean?'

'I—I need to tell you *everything*.'

'There's an *everything*?'

The words poured out of Saraswati.

'I've lied to you from the very beginning, Ko…' she began, her voice shaking so badly the words were barely discernible. 'I'm not who you think I am. I'm the same person, but I don't come from where you think I do.'

The air rushed out of Serenity Ko's chest.

'I'm a Godavari. A princess, born to a clan of murder-mongering, power-hungry gangsters who run the Daxina

Protectorate. My first name is Saraswati, but I'm not a Kaveri. I'm Saraswati Godavari.'

Serenity Ko whimpered involuntarily, fighting the urge to cover her ears and shut it all out.

Saraswati recounted the history of the Godavari clan, their brutal lives of bloodlust and greed. 'They killed all the Kaveris. It's why I chose their name—it was the easiest way to gain a refugee visa.'

'*Stop*,' Serenity Ko pleaded.

'I'm sorry, but you need to know.' Saraswati's voice sounded hollow and far away. 'I ran because they were using me all along. I had a famous restaurant, named Elé Oota. They used it as a money laundering front. They bought and paid reviewers. I needed to escape them. I—I was worth nothing.'

She stumbled over the words, stuttering as she recounted the names of all her chefs, and all her regrets. Serenity Ko slid down the wall, slumping onto the floor beside her bedroom door.

'I ran because they were going to force me into a diplomatic marriage. It didn't matter to them that I only like women…' Saraswati continued, her voice now toneless. 'And I lied to you because I couldn't tell you the truth. I didn't have the courage. Besides, who'd believe me? I'm sure you don't, not even now…' She trailed off.

None of this can be real, Serenity Ko's thoughts screamed, echoing Saraswati's fears.

'I wanted to be with you, but I couldn't. Not until I knew I could be free. I needed to protect you. What if my family ever found out where I was?' Saraswati's voice was hushed. 'They've disappeared my lovers before…'

Serenity Ko listened to her recount a string of names—Noura, Mithali, Anais—and none of it made any sense to her.

'I was going to tell you everything. I—I have no friends left here. Everyone else found out the night of the fake explosion at the sinfonia.' Saraswati wept as she narrated how her other friends had learnt the truth on the Ur-sands.

Serenity Ko laughed. 'Of course! I'm the last person to find out.'

It was petty, but all of it hurt.

Her insides were shredded like confetti by the time Saraswati got into all the reasons—the justifications—why she'd stolen Feast right from under her nose. How Jog Tunga and Optimism Mahd'vi had cornered her and blackmailed her, how she was tired of having no say in her own life. 'It was the only control I had. The only way I could guarantee my freedom, and be rid of my family for good.'

Serenity Ko was ground into cosmic dust by the time Saraswati was done.

'I was going to tell you.' Saraswati sniffed. 'It was never the right time. And I was a coward…'

'Fuck Aki.' Serenity Ko buried her head in her hands.

'I wish… he'd let me come clean, myself,' Saraswati whispered.

'You don't get to wish for things like that,' Serenity Ko said harshly, with brutal honestly. 'Not when you're a thief and a liar.'

They lapsed into dejected silence, and Serenity Ko hated that they were sharing this moment of mutual destruction, even as she longed for Saraswati's companionship.

'How did he find out, anyway?'

'He told me he was in the office, and came into the Feast bay to see if it was me. When he found you…' Serenity Ko replied.

'Yeah, I spoke to him. He was having a meltdown. I told him it would all be okay.'

'Right. He went snooping around after you'd left. Found that one of the work stations had recently accessed all the Feast code and made a copy…' Serenity Ko said. 'I would have helped, you know. You don't know how our workstations operate. I'd have helped you cover it up.'

Saraswati snorted. 'You're joking.'

'I deleted your logs,' Serenity Ko confessed. 'I wouldn't have helped you steal Feast. But Optimism Mahd'vi clearly has a plan, and I don't want to out the whole thing. I'll keep your secret… for now.'

'Why?'

'Like I said. I loved you. Maybe still do.'

Saraswati sniffed.

'I wish you had come to me with all of it,' Serenity Ko said.

'What could you have possibly done?'

'Listened. Worked with you to find another way…'

'There was no other way.'

'There might have been,' Serenity Ko insisted, without knowing where the words were coming from. 'At least, there might have still been a way forward. For us.'

'And now there is no us, is there?' Saraswati said haltingly. Her voice was muffled, as if it were coming from very far away.

'No. And there never will be,' Serenity Ko said with a finality she forced herself to feel.

Family is a constellation, each twinkling light a source of hope in your hour of darkness.

—Good Cheer Eria

THIRTY

'FUCK YOU,' SAID Serenity Ko, wondering why all the star-fucked universe had decided to involve her in another enormous cosmic joke beyond her comprehension. The tang of salt made her tongue feel far too alive, and all she wanted was to find her way into the numbness of alcoholic stupor, which was why she'd made her way to a decrepit shack out in the Ur-sands.

'You invited me here,' Honour Aki said.

'Did I?' Serenity Ko was genuinely surprised. She surveyed the array of glasses before her on the table, then decided it was plausible, but she couldn't quite place why. Then again, Honour Aki lying to her about his reasons for being there wasn't out of the question, seeing as he'd stalked her for a year and revealed the devastating news that had destroyed anything she and Saraswati could have ever had.

She'd slid out of the Loop, muted all notifs, and done her best to disappear from everything that could possibly remind her of Saraswati after sobbing herself to sleep in the wee hours of the morning… and Honour Aki was the last person she wanted to see, so why would she stream him? She could always pop back on the Loop and check, but she couldn't bring herself to face her life just yet. So she decided to verify his story the basic way.

'You've never lied to me, have you?' she asked, peering at Honour Aki suspiciously in the dim light.

'No,' Honour Aki said bluntly. 'No reason to. I kept throwing myself at you, and you kept pushing me away. Lies are only useful when they serve to uphold one's dignity. I've had none for ages.'

'That's an astute observation,' Serenity Ko said. She stared out at the ocean, which ebbed and flowed with unfailing regularity, completely indifferent to the emotional turmoil taking place within her. The shack—Serenity Ko hadn't even bothered registering its name, something along the lines of Sur-shine and Stars—was nearly deserted. She figured it wouldn't hurt to invite Honour Aki to join her.

'Want a seat?' she asked.

'I'm not hooking up with you tonight,' Honour Aki said as he took a seat.

'I'm not asking you to,' Serenity Ko snapped.

Honour Aki looked at her with concern, his eyes wide over the bira he'd ordered at the counter and carried over. 'Then why am I here?'

'Saras stole Feast,' she said. It didn't hurt any less to say it out loud.

'Yes,' said Honour Aki unhelpfully.

'Why did you have to tell me?' she asked, and it was followed by a groan.

Honour Aki looked momentarily confused. 'I thought you needed to know,' he said gently.

'So that you could sabotage any chance I had with her, win me away with your chivalry, and keep me to yourself forever?' Serenity Ko asked, miserably sipping on her fourth nīlatini of the afternoon.

Honour Aki blanched. A wind blew in and stirred a stray strand of hair that had come undone from his topknot. 'You think so little of me,' he said bitterly.

'What *other* reasons could you have?' Serenity Ko demanded.

'I care about you, Ko,' Honour Aki said firmly. 'I'm not proud of what I've done, mooning over you and following you around like a desperate, lovelorn stalker…'

'And you shouldn't be,' Serenity Ko said acerbically.

'I did all that because I loved you.'

'Oh, fuck me, here we go again,' Serenity Ko said, knocking back the contents of her cocktail glass.

She ushered a server over and asked for a refill.

'I said *loved*. As in past tense.'

That snapped her out of it. She looked at him in disbelief. 'You're finally over me?'

'No.'

'Oh, no.'

'That's why I'm leaving.'

'Yes, best if you leave me alone now,' Serenity Ko said. 'I don't want to hear all about your feelings. Again.'

'I'll do that soon, too. But I meant: I'm leaving Primus.'

Serenity Ko studied him for the first time in ages. He had dark circles, his hair had thinned somewhat, and his muscle tone was fading ever so slightly into gauntness. 'You don't look so great, Aki,' she said, experiencing a sudden twinge of concern. 'Is this—did I do this to you?' she asked in horror.

'I did this to myself.' Honour Aki smiled weakly, as Serenity Ko's nīlatini arrived. 'I should have taken you at your word and gotten over you.'

'But you haven't?'

'No.' Honour Aki leaned back and crossed his arms over his chest. 'And that's not why I told you about Saraswati. I know you don't want to be with me, but I'd never sabotage your relationship with her.'

'Except you have,' Serenity Ko said bitterly.

'Ko…' Honour Aki began, then gave up. 'Never mind.'

'No, tell me.'

'I didn't sabotage your relationship with her out of jealousy,' Honour Aki said slowly, as if struggling to find the right words. 'I told you about her because you deserve better. You've poured your life into Feast… like you've done with every single project you've ever started. You shouldn't have all that taken away from you because the person you're in love with betrayed your trust.'

Serenity Ko felt like she'd been punched in the gut. The silence that followed was uncomfortable, every bit as uncomfortable as the truth in his words. The wind picked up, sending a flurry of serviettes on a doomed journey towards freedom, and Serenity Ko wanted nothing more than to follow them, free upon the wind, only to eventually be trampled into the sand. She took several sips of her drink.

'I'm not going to thank you,' she said abruptly.

'For sparing you the pain later?' Honour Aki asked.

'For ratting her out to me.'

'That's a misplaced sense of loyalty.'

'And I don't want you to tell a soul about it,' Serenity Ko said, more harshly.

'I haven't. Not yet.'

'And you won't,' she said firmly.

'All right, Ko,' Honour Aki conceded. He looked tired.

'That's it?' Serenity Ko raised her voice. 'No reasons why, no tedious explanations?'

'I'm sure you have your reasons. And anyway, I'm leaving XP Inc. Like I said…'

'Where are you going?' Serenity Ko demanded.

'Sagaricus.' He attempted a smile. 'Far away, so I never bother you again.'

Serenity Ko's head swum with the blend of alcohol, the heartbreak of Saraswati's revelations, and the bizarre sensation of having a respectful conversation with Honour Aki, all at once.

'Why are you even here now?' she asked dully.

'You called.'

'So?'

'I'm your friend, Ko. And I wanted to say goodbye.'

Serenity Ko snorted. 'Dramatic.'

Honour Aki swallowed the remains of his bira. 'I know you'll be okay. No matter what happens.'

'Thanks for the vote of confidence,' Serenity Ko said sourly.

'I've called Rihan to keep you company,' Honour Aki said.

'How do you have my brother's number?' Serenity Ko snapped.

At this, Honour Aki grinned, and Serenity Ko saw, momentarily, everything that had once attracted her to him in the brightness of his smile. 'Stalker, remember?'

Serenity Ko burst out laughing. It was genuine and absurd, and genuine in its absurdity, given everything else that was going on, and the sombre tone of their conversation. And the absolute shattered state of her heart, flung across all the universe like cosmic debris.

'Goodbye, Ko,' Honour Aki said. 'I wish you well.'

Serenity Ko rose from her seat, stumbled in the sand, and hugged him, suddenly mortified at how badly she'd treated him, even if it had been necessary, relieved that he was going away—seemingly for good—but also, slightly bittersweetly, imagining how things might have turned out if they'd simply been friends. For a brief moment, the opening riff of "Falling Into Infinity" began playing in her head, and she shoved it away.

'Goodbye, Aki. And good luck.'

She meant it, too. Even though she knew she'd never forgive him for telling her what Saraswati had done.

As he walked away, the ocean waves continued their relentless back and forth, and Serenity Ko found herself making friends with the cocktail glasses with renewed ambition. She began to arrive at that specific state of inebriation where the world was beginning to make either far too much sense or none at all. And much to her annoyance, the star-fucked Legends of the Future returned, supplying a soundtrack in her mind, and she cursed herself for ever having listened to the smash band as it played on loop and her thoughts took a nosedive into all the infinity there'd ever been in the universe.

Saraswati had *lied* to her. About everything, down to her last name.

How can I believe a word of what she says about her family? A mysterious brother-in-law had turned up out of nowhere, and had apparently blackmailed Saraswati since she'd first arrived on Primus. How was it that Serenity Ko had never seen the man, especially since he was given to wandering around with a giant golden crown, going by what Saraswati said? Saraswati had escaped her murderous family, one that ran a dictatorship back on Earth. *Allegedly.*

Serenity Ko had looked up the Godavaris on the Loop, and found a slew of critical stream-media pieces about them, but mostly voiced by non-Earthling political commentators.

Reports from the Earth itself were scant, and there was no way to know if this was because the Godavaris had suppressed or executed all critical media—as Saraswati *claimed*—or because the Earth was a backwater that seldom contributed anything of value to the Loop due to a sheer lack of technology. And the only source Serenity Ko had to counter this view was the now entirely dubious Saraswati.

And if Serenity Ko could look the family up on the Loop, then so could Saraswati. Maybe she was just a galactic grifter, the kind one always heard lived on obscure satellites or mining asteroids, scamming people of their resources so they could find their way off their benighted rock to a real part of the universe, falsified papers and all. It didn't often happen that one of them found their way to Primus, given the thoroughness of Primian bureaucracy, but it certainly happened.

And the utterly absurd story that this mysterious brother-in-law had forced her to steal Feast—and that Optimism Mahd'vi herself had encouraged Saraswati to do so—beggared belief.

Maybe she just stole Feast to sell to the highest bidder. She'll find her way off this rock next, to greener planets.

Except that Saraswati was leaving a bizarrely public trail in her wake, as the face of Feast. Unless she planned to fake her own death, there was *no way* she would escape all the attention, even halfway across the galaxy.

She's done it once before, if she really is a Godavari.

She groaned, and buried her head in her hands as the electrochord solo from "Falling Into Infinity" repeated itself, over and over again, pouring into the desolation of her mind.

'You look terrible,' a voice announced. She looked up as Optimism Rihan took a seat across the table from her.

'Thank you,' Serenity Ko sulked. 'I've been working hard at it.'

She raised her glass, quaffed its contents, and then set it down amidst the impressive array of empty glasses arranged before her, like archaeological evidence of her sodden decrepitude.

'Let me get a drink with you,' Optimism Rihan offered. 'And then you can tell me why you're falling to pieces.'

'So you can judge me, then tell me it's all going to be okay?'

'So I can listen to you, and give you a hug.'

'Ah, Rihan. Always the nice guy,' Serenity Ko said uncharitably.

Optimism Rihan ordered a bira. 'What's going on?'

Serenity Ko considered coming clean about the truth, telling her brother everything, but then recalled the promise she'd made to Saraswati, to keep all her secrets until the Millennium Feast was over.

'Nothing,' she sulked.

'Right. You're taking a ray-bomb to your liver over nothing.'

Serenity Ko was numb. So numb it was as if her inner self were far away, a distant being living another life.

'Is the pressure of Feast getting to you?' Optimism Rihan offered, leaning forward.

'No.'

'Is it Saras?'

Serenity Ko felt the sound leave her before she heard it. It was a sob that ripped its way from her like a shrieking piece of machinery.

'Nine Virtues, Ko!'

In a second, Optimism Rihan was beside her, his arm around her. She turned and buried her face in his chest, hating how nice he smelled, and how she was going to ruin his lovely shirt with snot. She tried to pull away, but he held her close.

'It's all right,' he soothed, rubbing her back.

Serenity Ko wept.

'We're never going to be together,' she moaned.

'Never say never,' Optimism Rihan said, quietly.

Serenity Ko pulled away, her vision all blurry from the tears. 'Don't give me that false hope bullshit.'

Optimism Rihan held up his hands defensively.

'Enough feelings. Go drink your bira,' she commanded.

Optimism Rihan slowly rose to his feet, returned to his seat, and took a sip.

Serenity Ko scowled as more tears leaked down her cheeks.

'Does… does she not like you, too?' Optimism Rihan asked.

'It's not that.' Her voice quavered.

'Did she do something to hurt you?'

Serenity Ko resisted the urge to answer, then nodded.

'Do you want to—?'

'I don't want to talk about it,' she snarled.

Optimism Rihan's eyes widened in concern, and Serenity Ko realised that he must have imagined Saraswati doing something terrible on a galactic scale; which she supposed she had, but she didn't want him to know about that, not just yet…

'She… She led me on,' Serenity Ko lied.

'I'm sorry.'

'I'll get over it.'

Serenity Ko ordered another drink.

'Do you want me to just drink with you in silence?'

'That would be great,' Serenity Ko said.

They stared at the ocean in silence and Serenity Ko was grateful for the company.

The waves lapped against the shore like her thoughts, the notion that she might still love Saraswati, despite it all, tentative and whispering; the hurt from being betrayed by her thunderous and crashing. As the sur-light glimmered upon the clear waters, the horizon seemed to draw a perfect line between the certainty of all that was tangible, grounded and true, and all the limitless dreams that lay beyond…

Gulls punctuated the stillness with their insistent commentary, the smell reaching her in layers: a sharp saltiness that cut through her blocked sinuses, followed by a deeper, primordial scent that reminded her that all life came from the ocean. As Suriya began its descent, the water turned a palette of impossible colours, and watching the rhythmic pulse of the ocean was like listening to the throbbing heartache within her—agonising because she was broken, beautiful because that which had been broken was true.

'You know,' Optimism Rihan said, after a contemplative sip. 'I always liked Saras.'

'I still like her,' Serenity Ko said, hating herself for the admission.

'I still like her too,' Optimism Rihan confessed. 'She's brilliant. Funny. A good person. But that doesn't mean she hasn't made a mistake of cosmic proportions.'

'No, it doesn't.'

Optimism Rihan continued, treading carefully. 'What you two built in Feast, you built together. And I know she's been getting a lot of the publicity for it, but it is also yours. Especially yours.'

'I couldn't have built it without her.' Serenity Ko sniffed.

'*But*. It was your concept. Your creation.'

'I—I didn't do it alone,' Serenity Ko rushed to supply. 'Every single person at XP Inc. worked so hard on it—'

A funny look crossed Optimism Rihan's face, and his lips twitched.

'What?' Serenity Ko asked warily.

'You've grown, Ko,' he said, and his voice was hoarse. 'The Ko I knew last year wouldn't have said that.'

'It's all thanks to Saras,' Serenity Ko said.

'Don't devalue everything you've done to be a better person, too,' Optimism Rihan said sincerely. 'And don't devalue your contributions to Feast. You should take immense pride in what you built. I'm proud of you.'

Serenity Ko gagged on the last sip of her drink. She signalled for another, but Optimism Rihan took over smoothly, asking for the bill instead.

He got to his feet and pulled Serenity Ko's chair out for her. 'I saw how happy you made Saras. It's unfortunate that she chose to lead you on. Sometimes, the people we fall in love with are black holes—it's too late to escape their gravity until you're already so deeply in love with them, it'll rip you apart if you try.'

Serenity Ko's world spun violently as she stood up. Optimism Rihan held her gently by the arm, and put his arm around her.

'Thank you,' she slurred.

They stepped outside into the night, and Serenity Ko leaned against Optimism Rihan, looking up at the stars.

'What's that constellation?' she asked drunkenly.

'After exactly the right number of drinks, it spells out "everything will be alright,"' Optimism Rihan teased.

'Sap.'

'In your case, it definitely spells out "watch your step."'

Serenity Ko smacked her brother in the chest, but then flung her arms around him and hugged him tight, glad that even if all the world were falling to pieces around her, she still had him. She found herself humming, and he joined in. Everything else could wait. Even if it was only for tonight.

Never trust a savage to flick a light switch, let alone touch your heart...

—from 'Ray-bomb through the Heart'
by Proton Drive

THIRTY-ONE

She loves me.

No. She *loved* me.

If my life were a biopic or an Ur-drama, this would be the bit where I brood. Silently. Staring into the middle distance while walking through the rain, perhaps. Or bawling into my blankets surrounded by a comfortable pillow fort.

The thing about real life is that it doesn't give real people that option, unlike characters in fiction, who always seem to have adequate time to process their feelings as they sulk, lie in bed for days, eat their way through tubs of ice cream, and cut themselves off from the world for an indeterminate period of time.

As a real person without the convenience of an Ur-drama script, I got to do press conferences in the two days running up to the Millennium Feast, with the whole gang at XP Inc. including Serenity Ko.

Serenity Ko sat across from me beside Optimism Sah'r, and was engaged in what appeared to be deep conversation, admiring the latter's new ear piercings. A stab of jealousy shot through me.

Bad news if you start pining for her, Kili warned.

Beside me, Grace Kube and Courage Na'vil muttered about the intricacies of something they referred to as the "stimulo-mem mesh," and I couldn't follow a word. Unfortunately, this didn't leave me to enjoy the ride in a sullen, brooding silence, because Optimism Tina was seated across from me, and taking the opportunity of a tightly-enclosed space to unburden herself of every single stressor she was being forced to contend with, minute by minute, in an unending diatribe that kept interrupting everything else that everyone else had going on.

'And now Ariam is saying we need to cut today's speech from four minutes to three,' Optimism Tina wailed, flinging her hands up in the air. 'Kube, how in all Uru are you going to manage that?'

'I'll find a way,' Grace Kube said, smiling wryly.

'Okay, so that's a confirmation, then?' Optimism Tina asked, waiting for him to nod before flinging herself back into her meeting. She re-emerged almost immediately. 'Ariam says we can still do four if Saraswati can do a four-minute intro to Feast from a culinary perspective, instead of the six minutes we had planned…'

'What?' That caught my attention.

'Your speech,' Optimism Tina snapped in impatience. 'Can you cut it from six to four?'

'What speech? I don't have a speech.'

'Of course you have a speech!' Optimism Tina paled. 'I ran the programme by Serenity Ko and she said—'

'Must have forgotten to mention it,' Serenity Ko cut in tonelessly, staring pointedly out the window. 'I'm sorry.'

'Maybe we can just drop my speech?' I asked hopefully.

'Nope,' Optimism Tina said. 'You're the face of this thing.'

'How about this?' Grace Kube suggested. 'I'll do three minutes, and Saras can do the same.'

'Great,' I said faintly. 'I'll make a speech, then.'

'Don't worry about it,' Serenity Ko said, still averting her gaze from my person. 'There'll be at least a dozen speeches, and all of them will send folks straight to sleep.'

Fuck, I need a speech now, I muttered.

I'll write one for you, Kili said helpfully.

Thank you, I said.

And so it went, as we paraded around Uru making tons of speeches about the future of food and the significance of Feast, and attending dinners hosted by the culinary who's who, where I was frequently accosted and complimented on my Ur-speak, when I wasn't being badgered into explaining how I, a nothing nobody chef from Earth, had been audacious enough (read: talented enough) to create such a revolutionary cuisine.

'That's because on Earth, people know no limits,' a familiar voice said behind me. Amol Khurshid clapped me on the shoulder and beamed at my interrogator.

The woman scowled. Her nametag read *Boundless Celia, She/Her.* 'I've heard Earthlings always look out for each other,' she simpered. 'It's good to see such… *camaraderie*.'

She flounced away.

'I don't think she meant that as a compliment,' I said.

'She definitely didn't mean that as a compliment,' Amol Khurshid said. 'How have you been, Saras?'

I shrugged, turning to face him. 'It's a whirlwind,' I said, running my hand through my curls. 'I still don't know what to make of it.'

'You just go with the flow,' Amol said sagely. 'You never know when the wind will change.'

'That's for sure,' Pavi Khurshid said, joining her twin. She gave me a quick smile. 'Here we are, drumming up public support for you and Feast, and back when we first met, I could have sworn you were just another troublemaker from our home-world.'

I wasn't sure if she meant that as an apology or a statement of fact, but before I could respond, Optimism Tina had appeared by my elbow and was dragging me away. 'Time to ditch this do,' she said in a whisper that I was sure carried all the way through the room. 'We've got three dinners to get you through tonight.'

I waved apologetically at Pavi and Amol, my erstwhile employers at Nonpareil. 'I'll catch you on the other side of this chaos,' I said ruefully.

'No worries!' Amol said cheerily. 'We've been there.'

The blur carried on until I found myself filled with a deep sense of foreboding on the day of the Millennium Feast, trying to make sense of how I'd brought my life to this singularly depressing moment, while surrounded by the chaos of XP Inc.

I was on speaking terms with absolutely nobody I'd made friends with since my arrival on Primus. Serenity Ko was doing her best to behave normally around me at XP Inc., but she was being exceedingly polite, and I was sure Courage Praia and Curiosity Nenna were going to catch on that something wasn't right.

Except that they were sucked into the pre-release drama unfolding all across the Feast bay.

'Nenna, do we absolutely *have* to wear these Feast team jackets?' Courage Praia moaned.

The jacket in question featured a smorgasbord of traditional Primian foods splattered across its front, enclosed in a large gelatinous cube.

'No, I suppose not,' Curiosity Nenna said, biting her lower lip. Her face fell. 'I just thought it might be nice if we all showed up like a team.'

'But we *are* a team,' Courage Praia said, wrinkling their nose as they studied the sparkly lettering that proclaimed *It's A Feast* across the back of the high-collared jacket.

'It lights up,' Curiosity Nenna said quietly.

'No.'

'Yes.'

'Is there a button?' Courage Praia's voice was hushed.

'You can control it from your XP Inc. dash,' Curiosity Nenna explained.

'Nine Virtues!'

The jacket in Courage Praia's hand lit up like a shack out in the Ur-sands. They looked at it witheringly. 'Why didn't you run this past me before getting two dozen of these printed?'

'I was put in charge of the Feast memorabilia for the team,' Curiosity Nenna said defensively.

'Ko is going to *hate* it,' Courage Praia whispered.

'You don't know that!'

Courage Praia turned around to look for Serenity Ko. I hadn't taken my eyes off her since walking into the XP Inc. office this morning: she was talking to Courage Na'vil, who was hovering by her work station.

'What the actual fuck do you mean, Na'vil?' she snapped.

'There are serious ethical concerns that surround the simulcast of Feast sim experiences while they're taking place live tonight.'

'So get on a call with the stream-producers and sort it out,' Serenity Ko said.

'They say they'll only listen to you.'

'Star-fuck me!' Serenity Ko exploded.

Courage Praia caught my gaze and grinned. 'Maybe we don't talk to Ko right now,' they said to Curiosity Nenna. 'Maybe I'll just shut up and wear the jacket.'

Curiosity Nenna flung her arms around Courage Praia in a mixture of relief and delight. 'It'll grow on you. You'll see!'

I was waiting around in the Feast bay to be summoned to hair and makeup. As the public faces of Feast and XP Inc., the Triumvirate, Serenity Ko and I were going to be a professionally curated version of well-turned-out. Serenity Ko had insisted that she go first "to get this star-fucked clown show out the way," after first biting Optimism Tina's head off for making such a big deal out of the publicity effort.

She looked stunning now, even as she bickered with Courage Na'vil in more hushed tones, while they hovered over some kind of readout, flicking through it with their haptics. Her makeup was minimal, but it accentuated her thick brows and full lips. Her hair was pinned up in her signature high braid, woven through with gemstones. A long, flowing deep pink dress trailed down to her calves, cinched at her waist to hug her ample hips. I couldn't stop myself from staring, even though I knew I was no longer permitted to have feelings about her hips, or any other part of her.

I tore my attention away to monitor things on the Loop, where the public debut of Feast was heatedly debated by all of chefdom, and half the galaxy, with everyone streaming their opinions. Good Cheer Chaangte streamed loudest—and most insincerely—of all.

'... *this sham, this abomination that's an attack on the very best of Primian culture, will take centre stage at Nakshatran*

Rock later this evening. And sure, there's going to be a performance of the Nakshatranāma, *and of course, the who's who of the culinary world will be there, and naturally, it's all been blessed by Secretary of Culture and Heritage Optimism Mahd'vi herself, but don't forget, folks! At the heart of it all is an Earthling chef. That's right, you've heard me say it before, and I'll say it again—Saraswati Kaveri is the beating heart of Feast. And if that doesn't tell you everything you need to know about the state of our planet, of our galaxy, of all of human-occupied space, then I'm not sure what will.*'

Why are you torturing yourself again? Kili asked.

I want to do this with my eyes wide open, I said grimly.

I switched streams to discover that the Wanderers had assembled by Nakshatran Rock, a safe distance away from where the banquet tables were being set up. All of them cast protest signs from visio-nodes embedded in their attire, though much to my relief, none of the protest signs said anything rude about me. It must have paid off to hear them out at the Cathedral, even if I'd completely forgotten to escalate their concerns, with everything else that had happened.

I switched streams again. The most absurd speculation, the deepest regret, many paranoid misgivings about Feast flickered on the fringes of my peripheral vision.

Until I stumbled into a string of blithely positive opinions, brimming with enthusiasm. I recognised many of their faces from the pop-up tastings I'd hosted, sharing their stories of how spectacular Feast was going to be. I smiled as I heard all about how transformative Feast had been for these diners, and how it had helped them all reconnect with deeply personal memories from their youth, with departed family members and lost loves…

'*We wholly support Saraswati Kaveri, who was nothing but charming and radiated an air of competence at our pop-up tasting experience,*' said a woman dressed in a minimalist Primian formal suit, complete with a high collar and all. She held a young child by the hand, who wore a chef's hat, grinning away with her two front teeth missing. She proceeded to sing my praises, and I beamed with pride, until she chose the unfortunate words of her closing. '*And to think, she's a poor refugee, who's run away from her troubled, painful circumstances and escaped to Primus. This is why we need to keep our skies open to people from all over, regardless of their past, and the unfortunate planets they might come from. She is a shining example of all the best the galaxy has to offer… To have come so far, and achieved so much despite so many setbacks—including a* hideously xenophobic *judging panel on* Interstellar MegaChef. *Shame on them for punching down, her work ethic and integrity must be unparallelled—*'

A wave of nausea swept through me.

What would this woman say if she ever learnt the truth?

I deserved none of her praise and adulation. A sickening thought struck me. *There must be others like her.*

And then, as if right on cue, the woman's child beamed and said, 'When I grow up, I want to be a famous chef just like Sarrastiti, and make all the people in the world happy with my food.'

My breath came up short, in sudden bursts. I had *fans* who had faith in me, and I'd lied to said *fans* and the web of untruths I'd woven would impact so many people who'd never even met me…

Sure, that was self-aggrandising, to say the least. And maybe I was afraid of their judgment, should they ever find out. But more than anything else, I was coming to a painful realisation that I would let people like that young girl down. Even if there were just five young girls like her across the galaxy, it was gutting to have your idols turn out to be shitheads.

Saras, stop watching this stuff, Kili said urgently.

My happy fans were replaced by naysayers from the pop-ups. Many of the competitive poets we'd had the misfortune of hosting complaining that Feast would replace "true inspiration" for their art. The man who'd popped the question to his girlfriend, only for her to leave him when Feast had prompted unasked for memories of her ex, accused me—not Feast, but *me,* personally—of destroying their relationship. The Culinary Circle members who still hadn't forgiven us for the riot Serenity Ko had started had decided to go to group therapy together to process their trauma from that night, and were working on seeking compensation from XP Inc.

Stop! Kili shouted at me, sending visuals of raining fireballs my way.

I stopped. I slid out of the Loop and looked around at my surroundings, trying to centre myself in space-time. I stretched my legs from where I'd unknowingly curled them up on the couch, and pressed them to the floor, trying to ground myself. My ears echoed with the sounds of all the words I'd heard, and the conversations that surrounded me like an overwhelming barrage of noise, while everything seemed to slide around me. I dug my fingers into the armrests of my seat and forced myself to count slowly to ten, closing my eyes, focusing on my breathing.

Serenity Ko drifted into my thoughts.

She knew the truth about me, now.

She was in the room with me, now.

She was being professionally polite to me, today.

She would never speak to me again after tonight.

Tomorrow, I would be alone, again.

This is what it feels like to be a Godavari.

To lie until your lies were your undoing, to cheat and steal until you were found out, at which point you promptly erased the person who called you out for it. My family would probably murder them. My special talent was running away.

'Um, Saras, are you okay?' Someone tapped me on the shoulder.

I blinked my eyes open hurriedly. Optimism Sah'r stood over me, all concern in the knotting of her brows. She appeared resplendent in a beautifully knitted silken wrap dress, with a fine print of fraise-berries.

'Just nerves.' I smiled weakly, lying as always.

'This is what it's all been for.' Grace Kube appeared at her side. 'You've done an incredible job. Need a hand?'

He held his palm out to me, and I took it, noting the calluses and roughness of his skin. Knees knocking together, I raised myself from my seat unsteadily.

'They need you in hair and makeup,' Optimism Sah'r said. 'Tina is throwing a fit. She says we're already way behind schedule.'

'Something about how all of this will be a publicity and marketing nightmare,' Grace Kube winked.

'That's what she says about everything.' I grinned, faking good cheer.

'They're in the Ideatheque.' Optimism Sah'r nodded towards the doors. 'It'll get you out of this zoo, too.'

Serenity Ko raised her voice, and so did Courage Na'vil. I turned towards them, and they both appeared to be on the same call, yelling at someone halfway across Uru.

'Nice to see them working together at the end of all this,' Grace Kube chuckled.

I went to get dressed, my insides numb.

A flood of streams came in from well-wishers of the kind I didn't imagine particularly wished me, or Feast, very well. A bunch of folks I'd given interviews to said how excited they were. Good Cheer Eria was a pocket of sincerity in the wall of noisemaking, and I guessed she hadn't had the chance to chat with Serenity Ko about the awfulness of who I really was yet. That would change, soon enough.

And nestled in the noise was a stream that sent me to the bathroom, tears streaming down my face, grateful my makeup hadn't been applied yet.

Good luck, Saras! said Starlight Fantastic. _I'm cheering you on to succeed. And I'm willing to talk to you afterwards._

Why? I asked.

Everyone deserves a chance to tell their story.

Numb and overwhelmed, I sat through hair and makeup.

When Optimism Tina pronounced me ready, I was led through a series of pics and vids by a professional, posing with a tray of Feast cubes in ridiculously stupid ways. And then I was ushered off into a private flowcab for the thirty-minute ride to Nakshatran Rock.

Immediately, I leaned my head back into the cushions.

Fuck me. That's been a lot.

You're doing great, Kili said, reassuringly.

I feel like I'm going to throw up.

That's the nerves.

I don't know if I can do this, I said, and my hands shook.

You've got to smile and wave, make a speech, and celebrate Feast, which *you* built.

Ko and I built it. And everyone else at XP Inc., I said sadly.

Before I knew it, Nakshatran Rock loomed outside my window. I flicked a switch and made the flowcab go transparent so I could drink it all in.

One more performance to go.

Experience Primian civilisation at its zenith this Millennium Festival!

You are invited to dine at the Millennium Feast at Nakshatran Rock.

The evening shall commence with a cultural fair held on our pristine grasslands in the Valley, followed by a brief performance of the *Nakshatranāma* by Poet Premier Boundless Paco.

Dinner shall feature a Feast.

–Official Invitation to the Millennium Feast
2075 Anno Earth | 2000 Interstellar Era

THIRTY-TWO

'THIS IS THE most gloriously tacky thing I've seen in all my sur-fucked life,' Serenity Ko pronounced, shrugging on her *It's A Feast* jacket.

Curiosity Nenna's face fell. 'Praia warned me you'd hate it.'

'I *love* it,' Serenity Ko said loudly, checking her reflection out in a mirror.

'That's not what you said to me earlier today,' Courage Praia huffed.

'Things change,' Serenity Ko said sharply.

She eyed the whole Feast team as they slipped into their own jackets. Expressions of uncertainty and dismay flashed across some faces, and Serenity Ko beamed at Curiosity Nenna encouragingly, trying to distract her from paying too much attention to her teammates' reactions. 'When we get to Nakshatran Rock,' she announced, in a sudden burst of inspiration. 'We're *all* going to flick the switch and light up our jackets when I give the signal.'

Someone cleared their throat at the back of the crowd.

'Any questions?' Serenity Ko asked bossily, and wholly rhetorically.

'Where's the switch?'

'Nenna, explain,' Serenity Ko said, and swept her way from the room, leading her team to the chartered flowbus they'd be taking to the Millennium Feast.

The jacket clashed hideously with the elegant lines of her deep pink dress, but it didn't look completely awful with the boots she'd changed into the moment the publicity folks had left her alone. And it made her feel good to throw their plan off kilter; she hadn't had a say in anything she was wearing that day.

She wasn't sure if Saraswati was still in hair and makeup, or performing some other publicity rigmarole, or if she'd already left for the Millennium Feast. And if she were being completely honest with herself, she was glad that she wasn't in the same room right now. It had taken all her professionalism to share a physical space with her over the last few days, and often in the public eye at that.

She hadn't told a soul about what Saraswati had done—not just faking her identity as a refugee, but stealing Feast, too. She'd decided to wait until after their launch to reveal to Kube that the Earthling government probably had their hands all over it, and encouraged by none other than Optimism Mahd'vi herself.

Deep down, beneath her hurt at being betrayed and lied to, Serenity Ko was beginning to *sympathise* with Saraswati. She knew she'd found herself between a rock and a hard place, and had made an impossible decision. But she was mad at Saraswati for not confiding in her, for not coming to her for help, when she'd always tried to be there for her over the last few māsas.

Was I really, though? a small voice in her head asked. *I kept making decisions that I thought were for her own good, without asking her. I pushed her away because I didn't want to confront my own feelings for her. I can't fully fault her for hiding all of it from me.*

That held true at least for stealing Feast. As for lying about her identity…

Again, Serenity Ko couldn't quite bring herself to *blame* Saraswati for that. She must have been terrified of her family to go to such great lengths to run away. It just hurt that she hadn't trusted *her.*

Much to her surprise, Serenity Ko found herself wishing she could have another conversation with Saraswati to address it all. Perhaps it was the sense of closure she'd experienced after having an adult conversation with Honour Aki, inebriated though she'd been through it all. It was possibly the way Optimism Rihan's presence had soothed her hurt and betrayal when her brother had showed up for her in the middle of his workday. She hadn't *forgiven* Saraswati, but she wanted to hear her out again, try and make peace with why she'd done the things she'd done, even if they didn't lead to a relationship of any sort, any time in the future.

Maybe tomorrow, or a few days after Feast debuts.

'Star-fuck me sideways!' Courage Praia exclaimed, knocking Serenity Ko out of her thoughts and back to the present.

Their eyes shone as they looked through the window at what lay below them.

'Quick, let's make the hull transparent!' Curiosity Nenna said, practically bouncing up and down while still strapped into her seat.

Serenity Ko hit the button, and gasped.

The Ursridge swept away in a distant curve down to the Sagarra Sea. Standing alone, like a solitary watcher upon the grass, was Nakshatran Rock, where the first settlers on Primus, the Nakshatrans, had left their palm prints upon the moss. Hovering at its apex was a large circular stage, trailing long, fluttering swirls of ribbon that shimmered and flickered, changing colours constantly, both trailing to the ground and rising in the air in defiance of gravity. Outsized drones hovered around it on all sides, beaming lights onto the stage, where a band had set up and was playing something that was inaudible from inside the craft.

Sky-platforms surrounded the stage in concentric rings, each larger than the one below. They floated in the air, bobbing up and down gently. Tables and chairs were arranged in banquet-style seating on all of the rings. Slender bridges ran between the circles, and there were elevators for ferrying people up and down from the ground.

'Not recommended if you're afraid of heights.' Curiosity Nenna grinned.

Serenity Ko wiped a trickle of sweat off the bridge of her nose. She *hated* heights. Even the flowtrams often made her ill.

As the craft descended below the level of the stage and the seating for the Millennium Feast, Serenity Ko gasped again. Beneath the rings where the Feast was going to take place, it was as if the Uru and Beyond Marketplace had been transported into the valley below. Wending away through paths in the woodlands, seamlessly erected around outcrops of rock and wholly respectful of the blossoming flora, were flowmetal tents of all sizes in resplendent colours—some striped, some spangled, others open to the sky above, still others transparent and glimmering in the sur-light—each boasting wares from across Primus, all packed to bursting with the citizens of Uru who had come to a veritable carnival they'd tell their grandchildren about years and years from now.

Curiosity Nenna's face fell. 'I wish we'd gotten here earlier.'

'This will be here all week,' Serenity Ko said briskly, looking it up on the Loop. 'So come back tomorrow, and don't get shitfaced tonight!'

Courage Praia smirked as they disembarked. 'A bit rich, coming from you.'

Serenity Ko made a face, but grinned as she stepped out of the craft.

Somehow, magically, *everything* looked even better from ground level. Every single tent told a different story as they made their way from the parking bay, through throngs of people, to the elevator shaft that would take them to their banquet table. A large, striped flowmetal tent boasted a boardgame lounge, and traditional games tables were set up all across its floor. There was a casino tent—far flashier, with spinning holo-signs and twinkling flowmetal lights—where card decks were shuffled and fanned and folded at a dizzying rate. Live musicians performed everything from snatches of pop music to sinfonia pieces, and one could slide into the Loop to set one's soundtrack preferences and tune in to any one of the performers. And Serenity Ko stopped dead in her tracks when she noticed that there were nodes embedded through the warren of stalls, all inviting the crowd to try out sim experiences from SoundScape.

'Surprise!' Courage Praia said happily.

'What even the—?'

'They asked for immersive sims that could entertain, and I didn't want to bubble that request up to you,' Courage Praia said, somewhat abashedly. 'You seemed so insanely busy with Feast, and…'

'Star-fuck me, Praia!' Serenity Ko blushed furiously, and flung her arms around them. 'You shouldn't have—'

'You deserve to be cheered for everything you've accomplished. Not just Feast,' Courage Praia gasped out, their ribs being squished so hard it was difficult to breathe. 'And SoundSpace is where your insane ambitions began.'

Serenity Ko blinked back tears, and spun around to face her team. 'You are all the *best*.'

She led them onward, past the food tents, which hadn't opened yet. Every single person in attendance that evening had been invited to Feast's public launch, or had purchased tickets to be there, and a collective decision had been made to *not* offer traditional food and ruin their appetites before the Millennium Feast itself. The hope was that the diners would work up an appetite by the time the dinner began, and be able to revel in the experiences Feast had to offer. From the next day onward, as long as the carnival ran all nava, all the food stalls would offer Feast experiences exclusively. It was only after it all wrapped up that Feast would then be available to purchase in shops all across Uru.

That didn't stop all the purveyors and crafters of excellent beverages from setting up shop, though. There were cocktails in dazzling colours being served from within brightly lit stalls with edgy, abstract decor; aperitifs giving off heady scents from more minimalist tents; biras bubbling and brews resting, wines being sipped in great elegance, along with chais and kaapis, slurries and shakes, and dozens of flavours of MellO.

'Shall I spot everyone a round of bubblewine?' Serenity Ko asked, and was met by cheers from her team.

As they waited for their drinks, Serenity Ko felt a twinge of regret that their number was incomplete. Saraswati ought to be here, sharing this moment with them, wearing one of their tacky Team Feast jackets and laughing with all the rest.

'A toast to all of you!' Serenity Ko said, raising her glass to her people, pride welling up within her, and taking a sip.

'Saras ought to be here!' Curiosity Nenna chirped, echoing Serenity Ko's thoughts.

'Ah, you know how it is,' Courage Praia said, waving their hand airily. 'Celebrity and all that.'

It gave Serenity Ko the moment she needed to recover, and she faked a bright smile. 'She's with the Triumvirate, probably giving a pre-Feast stream-media interview or something. We'll see her at the banquet table, or at the after-party if they give her a break,' she lied. She ardently hoped Saraswati wouldn't show up at the after-party—she knew it was happening, naturally, because the team had been talking about it nonstop, and were very keen to work off some of their burnout through an alcohol-sozzled evening, but Serenity Ko didn't want an awkward face-off of any kind marring the rave. It was bad enough that the ugly truth about Saraswati was taking the shine off the triumph that should have been Feast.

She deserves to be there, though, a small voice within her head said.

Feast wouldn't exist without Saraswati.

If she shows up, maybe we can just avoid each other, Serenity Ko thought optimistically, writing the idea off as improbable, even as it voiced itself.

The team hadn't noticed the super cool politeness with which they'd gingerly tiptoed around each other over the last few days, and Serenity Ko was grateful she hadn't been subjected to uncomfortable questions by her more observant friends at XP Inc., like Courage Praia.

Once the truth was out—if it was ever made public—then she'd take Courage Praia out for drinks and sob her heart out to them.

A notification popped up on the Loop, inviting all diners to take their seats for the evening. The pre-dinner performance of the *Nakshatranāma* was set to begin in fifteen minutes.

Serenity Ko made her way to the elevators leading up to the banquet tables. They stepped into a transparent flowmetal chute and ascended. Along the horizon, Suriya was beginning to sink in hues of burning orange shot through with incandescent pink, tipped heliotrope fingers trailing into the sky, a resplendent conflagration promising the magnificence of the night to come.

'Saras!' Courage Praia exclaimed when they spotted her at their banquet table.

Serenity Ko winced. Saraswati flinched.

'Lighten up, Ko,' Grace Kube said, misreading her reaction from where he was seated beside Saraswati. 'It's almost as if *you* were forced to give a group interview with Four Chefs, as well as *The Consummate Cuisinologist,* instead of us.'

'You should have snapped at Tina some more.' Serenity Ko grinned, shifting smoothly into the demands of polite conversation, and nodding her head in the publicist's direction. 'That's what I did to get out of it all.'

Optimism Tina was deeply involved in a call on the Loop, and the words bounced right off her.

Serenity Ko scanned the table for the seating arrangement, and found herself across from Grace Kube.

'I couldn't be prouder of you, Ko,' Grace Kube beamed, leaning forward and dropping his voice. 'The way you've handled the pressure, grown this team, all without micro-managing the project… You've really earned your promotion to Evocateur Extraordinaire.'

It was as if the past had dropped upon Serenity Ko, dousing her in a deluge of ice-cold water.

So much had happened since Feast's inception, since they'd won *Interstellar MegaChef: The Millennium Feast Special,* in just the last few days, that the idea that she'd been inspired to start on this journey as a quest for revenge and vindication—all because she hadn't been awarded a promotion for SoundSpace, suddenly sounded insane to her. She laughed. 'Really?'

'Really,' Grace Kube said conclusively. 'I want you to know that you've *grown*. And I'm so proud of you.'

They were interrupted by a voice announcing that the *Nakshatranāma* performance would begin in five minutes. A hush fell upon the crowd as the last few diners took their seats, the only sound the gentle susurrus of muted conversation, the breeze whipping against the sky-platforms, and the occasional scrape of a chair being pushed back. An air of expectation descended upon the evening, and Serenity Ko found herself on the edge of her seat.

'Excuse me,' someone said.

Everyone turned towards the sound that broke the silence.

'I'm here for Sarwa-stiti Kaurri?'

The table winced in a singular motion at the way her name had been mangled. Except for Saraswati, Serenity Ko noticed, whose distinct lack of expression was admirable.

'That's me,' she said.

'I know.' The speaker—a man in a server's uniform—blushed. 'All of Primus knows.'

'What's this about?' Saraswati asked politely.

'I'm so sorry about this, but I'm afraid there's been a mix-up on the seating charts,' the server said, clearly mortified.

'We have her right here, with us,' Grace Kube interjected, bringing up the seating chart on the Loop and holoraying it off a visio-node. They had prime seats in the third row from Nakshatran Rock, where the evening's entertainment would be staged as soon as Suriya set.

'Er, I know, but this is a special request.'

'You'd better not be downgrading her seat,' Courage Praia said in an unexpected growl. 'I've had enough of her being targeted for being an Earthling. And I'll have you know—'

'No, not a downgrade!' The server's pitch rose in panic. 'It's from over there.'

He turned and pointed towards Nakshatran Rock. 'Straight from the Secretary of Culture and Heritage herself.'

Saraswati's brow furrowed in confusion, but the rest of the table visibly relaxed, and Grace Kube beamed.

'Well done, Saras!' Grace Kube said. 'That's the Secretariat's table. All the biggest dignitaries in the galaxy will be there, including diplomats and ambassadors…'

'Exactly,' the server grinned, relieved that he wasn't bearing bad news.

'Right,' Saraswati said, her voice suddenly small, even though she forced a smile. 'I'll follow you, then.'

She rose and hesitantly crossed the long, narrow sky-bridge to the next circle, and onward to the Secretariat's table. Serenity Ko watched her figure recede, a sense of relief mingling with longing at her absence, until Saraswati turned momentarily and looked back, her face a mask of anguish.

Serenity Ko's stomach twisted in knots. She had an uneasy sensation that things were about to go very wrong.

Our whispers in the void of space rose to song
Silence and peace arising from our hymnal
As forgotten stars awakening from a deep sleep, spinning starlight from the dust of oblivion,
Our harmony sparkled, constellations born anew into darkness...

—translated from proto-Nakshatran to Ur-speak
by Honour Gabriel
400 Anno Earth | 325 Interstellar Era

THIRTY-THREE

My family was here.

And they were watching me as I walked towards them, across a spindly, narrow bridge, several hundred feet in the air, with no escape.

Twilight was giving way to the darkness of the night, and the stage hovering above Nakshatran Rock was suddenly illuminated. Ribbons flickered in gravity-defiance all along its periphery, and human figures clambered up them with exquisite grace and at alarming speeds, twirling around them and performing somersaults as the rhythmic and atonal notes of a thera-mridangam signalled the beginning of the night's performance of the *Nakshatranāma*.

And yet, all of the magnificence was lost on me. I had tunnel vision, fixated upon my family in the halo of the stage lights, as an ominous, sweeping force dragged me forward, against my own will.

A year had passed since I last saw them. I hadn't missed them. I hadn't longed for the way my skin crawled as if it were on fire, the weight that sank onto my shoulders like a stone, the shivers running down my spine, the crushing sensation around my ribcage, my breath coming up short and my heart threatening to rip its way out my chest.

The poet on stage began to sing the first verse of the historic, epic poem in its original language, and the hair on the back of my neck stood on end from the unfamiliar sounds, the alien words, and the surreal reality that pulled me on into the heart of darkness.

I tripped, and grabbed the railing on the bridge to steady myself.

*Kili*. You've got to tell Ko that something isn't right. She won't check my comms, but if *you* stream her, we have a chance.

Already on it, he said, his voice tight.

My sister beamed, nauseatingly ebullient, evidently revelling in the world of trouble confronting me. I was scared, and she knew it. She giggled coyly at Jog Tunga, who was across the table from her, but whose head had swivelled to face me, a snide grin creeping across his face. My mother's nostrils twitched as if a rotting corpse had been placed on the table, and my father was terrifyingly expressionless, his eyes like glittering black coals in a waxen mask.

Optimism Mahd'vi was seated with them, and smiled benevolently as she waved me forwards, signalling me to hurry.

Against my better judgment, following deeply embedded social codes, I complied.

It's rude to interrupt a performance by walking around after it's started, a prim voice in my head said, clearly overcompensating to drown out my panic in a sea of rational thought.

There was no reason for me to walk on, into the cold embrace of my family. And yet I did.

Kili juddered within my pocket as if he were having a seizure. I *hated* my family, but he was *terrified* of them. They'd only threatened to have him decommissioned and scrapped in about a million different ways, a million different times, whenever I'd "misbehaved" according to their definition of the word.

What are you doing? I frantically streamed Optimism Mahd'vi.

Arranging a family reunion, she responded.

I have the file you want, I said, playing my only bargaining chip. _The one about the Kaveris. Your *family*._

I know, she said coldly.

Our agreement said you'd keep me safe in exchange for the file.

Our agreement said nothing about not fucking with your head, though.

Please, I begged, trying my hardest not to let my desperation creep onto my face. _They'll take me away with them._

*If* they get away.

I had no idea what she meant, and my panic-stricken brain wasn't capable of parsing it.

Please, I repeated.

'How nice of you to join us,' my father said, his voice menacingly low.

My sister, Narmada, tittered like a depraved bird. The sound jarred against the haunting melody of the *Nakshatranāma*.

'They say absence makes the heart grow fonder,' my mother said softly. 'Not sure it's true.'

'Nice to see you too. Or not.' I tried to summon up a snarl, but my voice shook.

The server was glancing between all of us curiously, so I forced a smile and let him pull my chair out for me, ordering an everberry sherry to send him scurrying. I took my seat beside Jog Tunga. He leered.

'Such a shocking lack of court manners,' he said. 'She's really devolved since I last saw her.'

My mother sniffed. 'Her manners will have to be beaten back into her.'

'She didn't even perform the namaskāram she's supposed to.' Narmada pouted. 'To *all* of us.'

'Different planet, different rules,' I said icily. I was glad I'd completely forgotten to drop to my knees and press my forehead to the floor upon meeting them, as Daxina tradition commanded one must do in the presence of one's elders.

'She'll be punished for this slight when we take her home,' my father said without glancing away from the stage. 'And for her other crimes…'

'You betrayed me,' I leaned over and hissed in Jog Tunga's ear.

'Sure I did,' Jog Tunga muttered, barely audibly. 'But you have our *Primian* friend to thank for this happy reunion.'

He raised his cocktail glass at Optimism Mahd'vi, who looked at us questioningly, but proceeded to raise her glass in return, and took a sip of her starfruit wine.

'What do you think my parents will do when I tell them you've known I was here all along?' I asked, feigning courage I didn't possess.

He chuckled.

He could laugh all he wanted. I could use it to get out of this situation.

And then, it dawned on me that I had another way out.

I spoke loudly enough that a few heads swivelled in our direction. 'There's a conspiracy brewing between *some* of the folks at this table—'

'It's rude to speak through a performance,' Optimism Mahd'vi said loudly, laughing. '*Some* of our off-world friends don't know that, of course.'

After shooting us disapproving looks, the faces turned back towards the stage.

He doesn't know, she snapped at me. _None of them do._

He doesn't know what?

That I know you stole Feast and gave it to him.

I don't understand.

Optimism Mahd'vi said urgently, _The Tunga *savage* and I aren't working together. *Your* twisted family and I aren't working together. Bring it up again and our agreement is off._

I shut my mouth mutinously, furious at my inability to grasp what was clearly an escalating situation, with me right at its heart. Jog Tunga, and ergo my parents, had no idea that Optimism Mahd'vi had officially sanctioned my theft of Feast. I stored the nugget away. It was *another* snag I could trip them up with, depending on how this played out.

I turned my face to the performance, trying to buy time, take deep breaths, do anything at all to give me the space to process the surreality of what was happening. A solitary singer occupied the stage, right at its centre. As they performed a melody that was on occasion lilting and haunting, then dissonant and rhythmic, only to flow back into more mellifluous tones, the acrobats leapt and twirled about the ribbons. It was spectacular in its strangeness.

'And how are we?' my father asked imperiously, slicing through the brief respite. He carried on without bothering to wait for a reply. 'Enjoying dressing in rags and being on reality shows like a *commoner,* working in kitchens like a *servant,* and pretending to build advanced technology when we all know you can't flick a light switch to save your life.'

I balked at the xenophobic slur my own father—an Earthling, the usual object of the saying—was now attacking me with. I attempted to recover. 'It's not usually the Godavari way to air dirty laundry in public,' I said, indicating Optimism Mahd'vi.

'We had a lovely chat about you,' my mother said calmly. 'While we were waiting for you to get here, we told her you're our problem child. We're very grateful for your return.'

'She arranged you as a surprise,' Narmada said, giggling, so loud and shrill that someone hushed our table loudly.

I felt a savage satisfaction as her face fell, but turned to Optimism Mahd'vi and hissed, 'You *what?*'

She simply shrugged.

You're really doing this just to fuck with me, I streamed her, outraged.

Like I said, our agreement didn't cover not arranging happy family reunions.

You *told* them I was here.

Not quite. I invited them to the Feast, and since we were all in the same place, I thought I'd surprise them… she said smugly.

You *planned* this. Down to the last moment, everyone being here at this table.

Probably.

I'll tell them you made me steal Feast.

I'll send you away with the lot of them.

You'll never get the file, I said, with more hostility than I felt.

I'm going to get everything I ever wanted this evening. She smiled cryptically.

My mother's voice cut through our silent conversation like a whip. 'You've disgraced us in public,' she said.

'You disgrace yourselves in public all the time,' I muttered under my breath, too afraid to say it out loud.

'What was that?' My mother leaned forward, eyeing me like a hunter eyeing up its prey.

'Don't worry.' I smiled sweetly. 'Nobody knows I'm a Godavari here. The credit for my disgraceful behaviour goes to me, and me alone.'

'It's a good thing you disguised your identity.' My mother sniffed in grudging approval. 'You were never the prettiest, but you're now so utterly hideous that you're unrecognisable.'

'Aren't you glad?' My insides burned as I said the words, hating that her opinions still hurt, even though they shouldn't. I was ashamed that I felt anything at all when it came to these people. 'You can disown me in peace,' I challenged.

'We can save your reputation when you come home with us,' my father said distractedly, his eyes still on the performance. 'And salvage whatever we can of your face.'

'I'm not going anywhere with you,' I said hotly.

My father ignored me.

'She's always thrown tantrums,' Narmada supplied by way of explanation, although nobody had asked.

'She has, hasn't she? Some people never grow up.' Jog Tunga grinned and kicked me under the table like a juvenile.

The melody was beginning to resemble a wail, not of despair or hopelessness, but of awe and wonder. The stage and the singer were swallowed from sight by an enormous holoray projection of a planet, which began to spin as the planet grew larger and ballooned outward, threatening to engulf everyone. Right at the edge of the sky-platform where we were seated, the burgeoning planet stopped, and the singer emerged floating above it, seated cross-legged on a plinth, still holding their final note.

I gasped in amazement, along with everyone else present, and there was wild applause.

'Remarkable,' my father commented politely to Optimism Mahd'vi.

'Exceptional,' Jog Tunga chimed in.

It was only then that it struck me that they hadn't come all the way to Primus just for me. They were diplomatic envoys from Earth, here to represent the planet on official business, and build interstellar ties with the most powerful culture in all human-occupied space.

Well, that I can work with.

I didn't know how, not just yet, but it gave me the tiniest bit of leverage to think that I could fuck it all up for them.

Kili, I said urgently.

No word from Ko, he said in despair.

My heart sank, but I had another job for him to do. _I need you to look up every anti-Primian thing my parents have ever said behind locked doors. In our private records. Stream it my way._

What're you doing, Saras? Kili asked uncertainly.

Making a plan, I said. _I will fuck this dinner up for everyone if I have to._

If I can publicly humiliate them and destroy their diplomatic relationships, any shreds of respect that they might command, I can probably escape from their grasp…

See how things play out before you set shit on fire, Kili said. _I've been listening to everything. Mahd'vi seems to have an agenda._

This makes sense, I agreed. _But… I'm working on a Plan B. Just in case._

There's also Ko…

A Plan C, then. I don't know what alphabet this plan is. I know I need all the backup I can get.

Got it. On it.

Optimism Mahd'vi rose to her feet and proceeded to the stage, crossing a bridge from the platform towards Nakshatran Rock.

'That was the first part of the *Nakshatranāma*, my people of Primus, performed for you by none other than our Poet

Premier, Boundless Paco. True to their given-name, the boundlessness of the rich history of our traditions is tangible in the very air we breathe tonight. And tonight, I welcome you to the Millennium Feast, where we will take our rich culture into the future…'

My mother's razor sharp voice sliced across the beginning of Optimism Mahd'vi's speech. She looked at me with disgust. 'There will be consequences when you're back on Earth with us. Despite your disgracing the Godavari name, we're willing to forgive you, and you can finally do your duty as a daughter of our clan and prove your worth to us.'

'You can all fuck right off, I'm done,' I said, my voice rising slightly.

'This "duty" thing keeps coming up,' Jog Tunga said, speaking over me. 'As your heir apparent—naturally, Narmada is excluded from *ruling* as she's the Priestess Immaculate, and Saraswati is, well…' He trailed off snickering, no doubt implying what the whole family held as their shared understanding of my incompetence, complete lack of fucks about being a tyrant, and other failures that spoke to my weakness of character in their view. 'As your heir apparent, I don't know what this "duty" is, and I feel I should be included.'

My father scowled at him in wordless response.

Optimism Mahd'vi's voice soared above the wild applause from the crowd. She'd probably said something incredibly stirring, and was still making her speech. '*We* on Primus,' she continued, 'have always held the universe together at the heart of its web, through imparting an understanding of how to be *evolved,* leaving our murky origins in the wreckage of the Earth behind—no offence to our Earthling guests here tonight, of course. Your ancestors' crimes are no more yours than they are ours…'

My father's scowl deepened, but Jog Tunga pressed on. 'I don't like these rings of secrecy. As part of your family—'

'You aren't family *yet,*' my father growled.

'Papa!' Narmada objected.

'Not until *after* the wedding,' my mother said.

'This betrothal has gone on far too long,' Jog Tunga complained. 'A year and a half is—'

'Well, if *you* hadn't been gallivanting around the universe all year…' Narmada started.

'I was on *official* business,' Jog Tunga snapped at his fiancée.

'You extended your official business. Twice.' My father was still paying careful attention to Optimism Mahd'vi's speech.

'You *what*?' Narmada practically shrieked, and was shushed loudly again.

I ground my teeth. Here we were: branded savages, and behaving like savages. I wondered how many cam-drones were recording our faces, even though a sound-bubble protected all the words we—and other diplomats—were saying on this platform.

'He told me *you* made him stay here longer,' Narmada sulked, looking at my father imploringly.

'Behave like an adult,' my father snapped at her. 'And get used to it. This is what a political career is all about, and this is what being married to a prince is going to be like.'

And then it hit me.

My parents *still* hadn't told Jog Tunga that my "duty" as a Godavari daughter was to be married off to his rival clan, the Bhadra family, to offset the balance of power in the region, and make sure neither the Tungas nor the Bhadras could move against the Godavaris. Jog Tunga had no idea that I was being bartered as a hostage to secure my family's continued dominance in Daxina, because for whatever reasons they had—and here, I had to agree with them—*my parents didn't trust him*.

A wave of triumph washed over me. All the cards I had to play to sow discontent, and thereby extricate myself from this ghastly situation, were dealt face up before me.

Jog Tunga didn't know that I was meant to be betrothed to the Bhadra clan. My parents didn't know that Jog Tunga had been stalking me on Primus for a year, and had known where I'd run away to all the while they'd been looking for me. They didn't know that he'd gone so far as to make a *deal* with me to keep my location in all the star-fucked universe secret. Jog Tunga didn't know that Optimism Mahd'vi had used me to steal Feast and hand it to him… for whatever mysterious reasons she had. Optimism Mahd'vi didn't have access to any information about her family that had been slaughtered back on Earth—by my own bloodthirsty ancestors, no less—and I was her only source to an unredacted file, which lay in my family's top secret archives. She also didn't know all the nasty things my parents had said about Primians, and the half-hearted plans they'd made to declare war on various communities, which I'd generally been excluded from, except that I'd occasionally stumbled upon them in our private archives.

I knew all their deceits and secrets. I could play them off against each other, trade in their ugliness, and find my way out.

Optimism Mahd'vi's words echoed in my head like a song of hope. 'We offer you a Feast in this, our celebration of two millennia of unparalleled, singular, spectacular culture. Let the Millennium Feast begin!'

Let the Feast begin, indeed.

The Tunga and the Bhadra clans are the only challengers to total Godavari power in the galaxy.

—Anita Umar,
One Nation Earth: The Myth of Unity
2065 Anno Earth | 1990 Interstellar Era

THIRTY-FOUR

THE SPEECH HAD been well-received, as Optimism Mahd'vi had expected.

And now, she was experiencing a malevolent kind of delight in watching the Kaveri-pretender squirm, surrounded by the family she so loathed, whom she'd been so unwillingly reunited with.

Optimism Mahd'vi couldn't truly blame Saraswati for lying her way off the Earth to escape these people. She'd met the expressionless shell who was her father at a few dozen United Human Cooperative banquets and conferences over the years, whenever the Earth had been invited. She'd always wondered if he was the best the Earth could send their way, or if he'd somehow coerced and bullied his way to being their representative. It didn't matter, seeing as the Earth's perspective was practically never listened to, but Optimism Mahd'vi's Kaveri roots found her drawn to speculation.

There was the mother, who was clearly an iron-willed manipulator who wasn't shy about playing out the family drama in front of a stranger such as herself. The sister was a religious leader of some kind, and carried herself like a shrill, giggling schoolgirl—the sound of her voice made Optimism Mahd'vi's insides cringe. And Jog Tunga, whom she'd had the unfortunate opportunity to meet several times over the course of the last year, really put the icing on the whole damned Nakshatran Gateau. Or Earthling cake, as it were.

If she'd been in Saraswati's shoes, Optimism Mahd'vi would have fled on the nearest spaceship, too. She was beginning to feel sorry for the Godavari girl, but not so sorry as to save her from her present predicament.

As the first Feast cubes were served, Optimism Mahd'vi retook her seat to find the party bickering. The word "duty" was being bandied about by Jog Tunga, but they immediately shut up as she returned. After the display she'd seen, when they'd all piled onto Saraswati, she wondered what exactly these barbarians counted as private, but this "duty" clearly qualified.

'Some interesting notes on the Earth, Secretary,' Ambassador Godavari said, leaving the rest of his displeasure unvoiced.

'Rather insulting, no?' Jog Tunga asked, before Optimism Mahd'vi could reply. In his typical barbaric way, he beckoned a server over, and ordered knives and forks for the whole table.

'I'm sorry, sir—I mean, your Royal Highness,' the server responded, visibly uncomfortable. 'Feast can only be eaten with your hands. It's just a single cube, you see? You just pop it in; a bite-sized portion.' He attempted a smile that withered at the look that crossed Jog Tunga's face.

Optimism Mahd'vi was ready for him to make a scene. In fact, she'd been counting on it. He'd demonstrated exceptionally bad form at the banquet when they'd announced peaceful ties between humans and the K'artri-tva. Jog Tunga had behaved like the graceless boor he was. It was the reason she'd created this powder keg situation tonight—to set him off and give the Secretariat an excuse to arrest him.

'No cutlery?' Jog Tunga said, his voice rising in disbelief. Again, as had been happening all evening, several heads swung in the direction of their table.

'No *cutlery?*' he repeated, ignoring a menacing glare from Ambassador Godavari. 'Well, if this isn't cultural imperialism, I don't know what is!' he spat.

Over at the next table, where most of the Secretariat was seated, the High Secretary himself went pale, despite having probably already drunk his weight in starfruit wine.

Should I call security, Mads? Courage Ilio streamed.

_No,_ Optimism Mahd'vi said. _The evening's barely begun, and we haven't even gotten through the amuse bouche yet._

If you're sure...

I'm sure, Optimism Mahd'vi snapped. _I can handle this._

She regarded the savage prince and smiled blithely. 'It is Primian tech, after all,' she said smoothly. 'And we do love our traditions here.'

Scowling, Jog Tunga picked the Feast cube up and popped it into his mouth. Optimism Mahd'vi observed him suspiciously for a few seconds, watched as his eyes glazed over, lost in a sim. She didn't touch the Feast cube on her plate. She needed to stay vigilant.

Her plan was to goad Jog Tunga and the Godavari clan—preferably both, though she'd settle for either—into creating a major diplomatic incident that night. If all went well, it would involve a decent bit of violence, preferably against Primians; whether herself or others was immaterial. Curiosity Ariam had hundreds of cam-drones streaming the Millennium Feast live across the galaxy, including capturing live reactions to Feast. The diplomatic tier was in a sound-bubble, of course, but the visual of Earthling violence would create a great narrative for the stream-media to obsess over.

It was part of the reason she'd chosen to invite Saraswati to their table—to act as a catalyst for an outburst. The Ambassador Godavari was too well-schooled to crack under this kind of pressure, as Optimism Mahd'vi knew him to be, but Jog Tunga had demonstrated no similar temperament in the time she'd known him. Quick to anger, unpredictable when aggravated, once he exploded, she'd have the whole lot of them taken away for questioning for sparking violence. Their tech would be scanned. Jog Tunga would be discovered in possession of Feast—*Primian* technology that he shouldn't have access to. If he tried to throw Saraswati under the bus, Optimism Mahd'vi would cover for her, holding up her end of the bargain. And she'd move the Primian Secretariat to direct the United Human Collective to deport the rest of them off to a distant mining asteroid for stealing top secret tech, in an act of aggression against Primian culture.

It was so simple. She'd avenge her long-dead ancestors.

She'd establish in no uncertain terms to the Secretariat that the Earth was a threat, so they could militarise again and establish stronger safeguards. She'd double down on why Feast had to have pro-Primian messaging as part of all its sims.

That she'd fuck with Saraswati in the process was a bonus.

When it was all over, she'd finally be able to discover what her family had been—what their names had been, what they'd done, and why they'd been killed.

Jog Tunga emerged from the sim.

'Haven't touched your goop, Secretary?' he said, nodding at her plate. 'Primian culture not to your liking?'

'I've only supported the development of this cuisine from the ground up, Prince Tunga,' Optimism Mahd'vi replied with disdain. 'I'm going to savour it in better company.'

'Direct insults, hmm?' Jog Tunga grinned slyly. 'We must be friends.'

Saraswati was pale, her expression mortified. Her Feast cube lay untouched as well.

'Tunga, perhaps you'd better excuse yourself,' Ambassador Godavari said coldly. 'You're embarrassing us.'

'You don't need much help with that,' Jog Tunga snapped ungraciously.

Optimism Mahd'vi couldn't really disagree, but found herself shocked by the display again. It was unheard of for a family to bicker in public at an official dinner. But it would serve her well.

'Don't talk to Papa like that,' the Priestess-daughter hissed.

'Or you'll, what? Break off our engagement?' Jog Tunga laughed.

Saraswati's face twitched at this, and Optimism Mahd'vi regarded her with sudden interest. The girl appeared on the verge of smiling, but she fought the quivering of her lips and said, in a quiet voice, 'My family has other options, you know.'

'What do you mean?' Jog Tunga snapped.

'You know what my "duty" is?' Saraswati asked, her voice dead level. 'The "duty" nobody wants to tell you about?'

'Don't,' the mother said in a warning tone.

'Traitor,' Narmada gasped.

'They want to marry me off to the Bhadra clan. To prevent you and the Tunga family from gaining power in Daxina,' Saraswati said simply.

Jog Tunga looked at her family in disbelief. 'You're going to *deny me* the rule of Daxina? After all I've done for you? You're going to invite those corpse-climbing, sycophant, goat-fucker Bhadras into the clan?' His voice was rising. '*This* is how you repay me for my services to the Godavari family?'

Before the other Godavaris could react, Saraswati chimed in. 'You know, there's a Godavari saying about the Tungas…'

'*Don't,*' her mother said.

She translated from Daxina to Ur-speak as best she could: 'If you need to kill a Tunga, never drown them in a river. They're so full of hot air, they'll float.'

'You *bitch,*' Jog Tunga growled, lunged for her, then seemed to think better of it and composed himself, though his eyes were now wild, his lips twitching.

Optimism Mahd'vi wasn't sure what Saraswati was up to, but she was egging her family on to their imminent self-destruction, as if she'd somehow read her plans. It was delightful.

Cam-drones had started to hover around them, and many members of the Secretariat were slowly rising to their feet in concern.

Maddie, the Primian Guard is on standby, Courage Ilio streamed.

Stop interfering, Ilio. The Earthlings are falling apart. Optimism Mahd'vi was irked by the intrusion. _We might learn something vital here._

The servers arrived with the second course, took a look at the developing situation, and hesitated.

Jog Tunga smoothed things over with a benign smile. 'My apologies,' he announced, with affected languor and a slur. 'Too much *excellent* starfruit wine.'

People began to return to their seats, unconvinced but relieved they could be unconcerned. Jog Tunga's eyes glittered cold again. He didn't say a word, though, or violently attack anyone at the table. Instead, he took a sip of his wine, and seethed in silence.

The cloches were placed before them and raised in perfect synchronicity as before, revealing the appetiser for the Millennium Feast. It was supposed to be a shrooming symphony, a classic dish evoking the earthiness of the Urswood. Optimism Mahd'vi decided it would look bad if she wasn't seen partaking of Feast on the cam-drones, and popped the cube into her mouth. She was halfway through chewing when she looked around the table at her dinner companions.

Saraswati hadn't touched her jelly, which was understandable, since she'd likely lost her appetite. None of the Godavaris had touched their portions. Jog Tunga was glowering at Saraswati with what could only be described as pure hatred, with a side of murderous rage, but his Feast cube was uneaten, too.

A sense of unease spread through Optimism Mahd'vi's limbs. A tingling in her fingertips. A slowing of all her senses. She heard her pulse pounding in her ears. Her breath sounded loud and ragged, even though it seemed to be perfectly even. She tried to raise her hand to her head, which was beginning to feel shrouded in fog, but found that she couldn't move.

With a mounting sense of horror, she watched Jog Tunga rise to feet, his long legs weightless, his crown glittering in the dim lights. He stepped off the platform, and seemed to fly towards the stage hovering above Nakshatran Rock, like an outsized bat.

And then Optimism Mahd'vi felt her arms snap to her sides. Her mind screamed, but her lips wouldn't part to make a sound.

Why am I here?

She'd had a plan... *Something to force the Earthlings to display their true colours.*

The soles of her feet tapped a rhythm on the floor of the sky-platform, as if of their own accord.

Whatever my plan was, it wasn't this.

A force outside of herself raised her to her feet. She gasped soundlessly in horror.

Optimism Mahd'vi began to dance.

We invite you into a new millennium of peace and harmony in the United Human Cooperative, through this… a traditional offering of a shared meal that reinvents Primus and takes us into a new future, beneath the stars that connect us all…

—from Optimism Mahd'vi's speech at the Millennium Feast
2075 Anno Earth | 2000 Interstellar Era

THIRTY-FIVE

Serenity Ko had chosen to ignore her Loop notifs for the evening.

Saraswati had looked back at her with an unreadable expression—was it regret or fear or something else altogether?—while crossing the bridge to the Secretariat's tables, and she supposed Kili was trying to play mediator when he streamed. Serenity Ko wasn't ready for that; not tonight. She was here with her team, part of something larger than herself, proud of all the work they'd done. And she wanted to be *present*.

She could reply to Kili later.

It was odd how she missed the little whirry Winger. He was a good friend to Saraswati, and Serenity Ko had grown fond of him.

When the first portion of Feast—the amuse bouche—had been placed before them, Serenity Ko had eaten it with relish, losing herself within its simulated taste, texture, and audiovisual experiences. The whole crowd assembled at the dinner seemed to have burst into spontaneous applause a few minutes later, and Serenity Ko had beamed at what she could only surmise was an unfettered approval of Feast.

Grace Kube rose from his seat and walked over to her, thumping her on the back before hugging her. Curiosity Nenna had burst into tears, and Courage Praia had wiped their eyes on the back of their sleeve, all while the team's jackets had proudly twinkled It's A Feast to the dozens of cam-drones circling them.

Serenity Ko had automatically slid into the Loop, continued to ignore Kili's messages, and had started viewing the live reactions now making their way across the galaxy instead.

'*...my grandmother had a lemon tree, and we harvested lemons each year. The Citric Crush took me back to the scent of her...*' a woman wept.

'*...acidity, and that distinct sourness of lemon rind,*' someone said at the table hosting the popular stream, *Four Chefs*. '*We know we've been skeptical of Feast, but the flavour details are immaculate.*'

'*I underestimated how excellent this would be. I remain a skeptic, but I can't deny the talent of the chef—and the team—behind Feast,*' said Grace Menmo...

Serenity Ko's heart had skipped a beat. *Of course Ammamma's here. There's no way we're launching without the approval of Grace Menmo herself.*

She stifled a sob as the second course was served.

She found that she couldn't eat, looked around the table, and saw that many of her teammates shared that sentiment, teary-eyed and beaming with joy, overwhelmed by the impossible journey they'd shared.

'Group hug?' Serenity Ko croaked.

They piled in, squeezing together ...

And then they pulled apart, and Serenity Ko felt the tiny hairs on the backs of her arms rise, gooseflesh prickling upon her skin. *Something's wrong.*

It was inexplicable, but she *knew*.

She slipped into the Loop on instinct.

Big trouble. Saras's family is here. We might need help.

Ko, I know you're mad at us. But they might abduct her.

Sorry for dumping this on you. You're the only one we can count on.

Please tell me when you see this.

Serenity Ko blanched at Kili's desperate streams. Of all the times to let her pride get in the way of checking her comms...

I'm coming to help, she fired off at Kili.

She slid out of the Loop again, and found that the whole crowd stood on their feet, swaying. Something clicked into place.

'Don't eat that!' Serenity Ko shouted, knocking a Feast cube out of Courage Praia's hands. 'Stop eating the Feast cubes!' she yelled.

Her voice was drowned out by the sound of explosions. Fireworks arced into the night air, lights cascading in a shower of sound and colour. They were supposed to accompany the dessert course. They were going off way ahead of schedule.

She glanced around her table, her mind an agitated whirl. In the seconds it had taken her to check her comms from Kili, half her team had eaten the second Feast cube. Curiosity Nenna's head tilted to her side at a bizarre angle. Her legs worked oddly, rising and falling as if she were marching, while her hands floated eerily by her sides. Serenity Ko grabbed her and shook her, but she didn't respond. Across from her, Grace Kube was performing identical motions, except nodding his head in rhythm to a silent music.

Their Team Feast jackets twinkled ominously.

'Is this a seizure?' Serenity Ko panicked, momentarily blinded by a burst of bright light as more fireworks went off.

'No, it isn't.' Courage Na'vil's voice shook. She'd never been gladder to hear him speak. He was seated towards the end of the table, and he rose shakily to his feet. 'Something's controlling their minds. This is an issue with the neural mesh.'

'What the fuck is going on, Ko?' Courage Praia asked in a small voice.

'I don't know. I don't know…' Serenity Ko spun, looking around in a frenzy as if she'd see the answer to what was happening written in thin air.

'I agree with Na'vil.' Optimism Sah'r's voice pierced the loud night. 'This is a virus. It can't be a bug. We tested too extensively for this.'

She stepped within Serenity Ko's field of view, her face pale and dripping with sweat. 'We need to investigate,' she said calmly. 'We don't know if this is going to wear off on its own, or if we need to reboot the XP Inc. databases, from the nano-pills managing their biocircuitry all the way to our programs.'

'We don't know if this is isolated to Feast… or if it's all our code,' Courage Na'vil added hoarsely.

Serenity Ko swallowed, her heart pounding. Beside her, Curiosity Nenna's hands snapped jerkily over her head and she performed an awkward pirouette. Grace Kube mirrored the dance. If this weren't outright, straight up fucking terrifying, it might have been hilarious.

'We need to establish a hypothesis.' Optimism Sah'r took charge. 'Ko, Praia—did you eat the second Feast cube?'

'No,' Serenity Ko said. 'I knocked Praia's out of their hand.'

A few other folks at the table were rising unsteadily to their feet, their faces drawn in horror.

'And the rest of you?' Optimism Sah'r addressed them. Once she'd tallied the responses, she made an announcement. 'Right, so I think this is isolated to Feast. At least, that's what I believe right now. I'm having reports generated so I can analyse them, but I can handle this best at the office.'

'I'll come with you,' Courage Na'vil said.

'We need all hands on deck.' Optimism Sah'r looked around at the team that had managed to remain in their senses. 'This is an external attack.'

As the words left her lips, realisation slammed into Serenity Ko with the force of a gravity well.

She knew who was behind it. She could have stopped it.

'I-I'm going to stay here,' she announced. 'To help people. To tell them what's happening if they emerge from… whatever this trance is.'

Optimism Sah'r gave her a curious look, but only nodded in response. 'I gather Praia will help you?'

'Yeah,' Courage Praia said. 'That's me: Serenity Ko's faithful sidekick.'

Curiosity Nenna spun with her arms outstretched by her sides and thwacked them in the chest.

As the team left the platform, Serenity Ko slumped into her chair, moaned and buried her head in her hands.

'Ko? Are you okay? Please don't die on me... or get all trance-like.' Courage Praia's voice was laced with panic.

'I think this might be my fault,' Serenity Ko whispered.

And then, a voice rose to fill the night air. 'People of Primus,' it proclaimed boldly.

'People of the great and glorious star-fucked United Human Cooperative,' it continued, then sniggered. 'At least, those of you still in possession of your minds and bodies...'

Serenity Ko raised her head ever so slightly. Silhouetted against the dazzling display of light and colour, magnified to be larger than life by whatever tech they'd used for the *Nakshatranāma*, was a lone figure dressed in glittering robes. A golden crown sparkled upon their head.

'Fuck me,' Serenity Ko said hoarsely. 'I don't believe it.'

'This is the Crown Prince Jog Tunga from Earth speaking, and I control you all,' the man said, grinning broadly. Fireworks punctuated his pronouncement.

Serenity Ko flinched at the sneer that twisted his outsized face, projected on hundreds of visio-nodes set up around Nakshatran Rock. A swarm of cam-drones buzzed around it, broadcasting to the galaxy.

'Before you get any funny ideas about stopping me right now,' he announced, gesturing to where a dozen Primian Guard ships were closing in towards the stage. 'Don't forget that I have thousands of *your* people hostage. Their minds are now mine. They will do whatever I command.'

He snapped. As one, every single dinner guest who'd eaten the second Feast cube moved towards the low walls of their sky-platforms, and placed a tentative foot upon the edge.

Jog Tunga raised his arms to his sides and paused dramatically.

'Fuck me, this is all my fault,' Serenity Ko said, her mind drowning in panic.

'Ko, this pity party you're having? Save it for later,' Courage Praia snapped.

Serenity Ko streamed her family, all of whom had been in the audience several tiers away. She received no response.

The Primian Guard crafts backed away, and circled at a safe distance.

'That's better,' Jog Tunga said approvingly.

The crowd stepped back from their precarious positions on the walls, and began their slow, shambling dance again. Arrhythmic and jerking, all as one.

Kili, what's happening? she asked.

I don't know, he fired back. _But we need help. The whole Secretariat is knocked out. Saras's family is threatening to take her away._

Fuck. I'll be there.

'For too long *Primus* has been at the centre of the United Human Cooperative. All because *this planet,* with its holier-than-thou philosophies and obsession with propagating its culture, happened to be the first to recover from the atrocities that plagued the ancient Earth,' Jog Tunga said, launching into his speech. 'For too long, *Primus* has dominated all discourse, asserted itself unfairly in matters of trade and inter-planetary policy, and quite frankly, had its fucking way with all the rest of us. For too long, *Primus* has condescended to us, arm-twisted us into parroting its own belief systems right back at it, while denying us the right to flourish in our own right, in our own ways, asserting our own identities and letting free people—*you people*—choose your own paths. *Primus* has swollen to the size of a gas giant in its estimation of itself, its hubris growing greater still to consume every rock, asteroid, space station, moon and planet in the galaxy...'

Serenity Ko winced each time he said "Primus." He spat it out with venom and loathing, as if saying the very name of her home-world physically hurt him.

'Fuck me, is this how wars begin?' Courage Praia asked, their mouth agape.

'I don't know.'

Serenity Ko rose to her feet, and slowly proceeded towards the bridges linking the sky-platforms to each other. She swallowed hard. She hated heights. She stepped onto the first bridge.

We're coming, she streamed Kili.

She fired off streams to Courage Oslo, Curiosity Zia, Boundless Baz, XX-29 and Starlight Fantastic, fervently hoping that some of them were here in the audience with all their faculties intact. She gingerly stepped onto the bridge, knowing that she had to move faster, that time was running out, but she was so fucking high up that her knees were wobbling and her legs turning to jelly…

'Ko,' Courage Praia soothed. 'Take my hand.'

Curiosity Zia streamed in. _What the fuck is happening? Oslo's a zombie._

Head to the Secretariat tables. *Now.*

Boundless Baz registered his presence a few moments later, and Serenity Ko relayed the same instructions, right as Starlight Fantastic said they'd caught what was happening on the Loop and were heading their way with XX-29.

It had completely slipped her mind that Feast only worked for humans, and so neither XX-29 nor Starlight Fantastic were likely to be in the live audience that night. Or having their minds turned to mush, as it were.

'Come on, Ko,' Courage Praia said more firmly. 'We're going to run.'

They ran.

Jog Tunga's voice filled Serenity Ko's senses as if it were being broadcast straight into her skull.

'The price of hubris is tragedy. Or do you not get Ur-dramas on this sur-fucked lump?' Jog Tunga chuckled wildly at his own joke. 'Well, here's some tragedy for you. Feast is now under Earth's control. *Primus* selfishly decided to hoard it, to wield its technology singlehandedly, in yet another predictably boring attempt to spread *Primian* propaganda across the galaxy. *Primus* is learning its lesson.

'While *your lot* has ignored and judged *our lot* for centuries, we finally found a partner willing to work with us. Someone who believes in our ability—and by that, I mean the *Earth's* ability—to develop sophisticated, cutting-edge technology. What an exciting opportunity for us, no? You can only imagine how wonderful it is to be wanted.

'On Earth, you see, we don't fight wars with nuclear weapons anymore. We've even gotten rid of our ray-bombs. All that really dramatic violence you condemn us for? It's a myth you've constructed, the stuff of Ur-dramas. No, we've been working with the K'artri-tva—you know them, lovely chaps—on developing what we call the hive mind. It's a beautiful thing. We can talk inconvenient elements into throwing themselves off buildings, overdosing on medication, shooting themselves in the head… it really drops the cost of murder, so long as someone's on the Loop. And while it's adapted to Earth tech, it *just so happens* that it's perfectly compatible with your little Feast cubes, and is incredibly efficient at attacking all your biocircuits.'

He paused.

'*This* is a demonstration of what we are capable of doing,' Jog Tunga said, laying emphasis on every word. 'This is just the tip of the iceberg. It's a *warning*.'

Serenity Ko's head spun as she drank in everything the madman was saying, the dizzying height of the first bridge now crossed. She reeled from the adrenaline rush, as Courage Praia dragged her towards the next bridge, which would take them to the Secretariat tier.

'Never again will Primus, or the United Human Cooperative, or anyone else in this star-fucked galactic hole, fail to take an Earthling seriously. Never again will any one of you dare to call us savages, or laugh in our faces, or attempt to cut us out of your secrets, whether they're trade deals or gossip.

'The Earth holds you all within its palm, and we will crush you.'

Jog Tunga grinned.

'Oh, and because this is so much fun,' he added as an afterthought. '*Kneel*.'

As one, the dancing, shuffling crowd dropped to its knees, and pressed their foreheads to the ground.

At the edge of the Secretariat tier, still on the bridge, Serenity Ko stopped abruptly. 'The others should be here any minute,' she gasped. 'It might be dangerous. Stay here, Praia.'

She eyed the stage. Jog Tunga was strutting back towards one of the tables to Serenity Ko's left. She turned her head and saw Saraswati had eased herself out of her seat and was lowering herself into a crouch, fists balled at her sides. The blood had drained from her face, but her eyes were razor focused on the figure of the Earthling prince.

'Godavari scum,' Jog Tunga spat. 'This is for trying to cheat me of my inheritance.'

An elderly couple Serenity Ko didn't recognise as Primian began to choke and gag.

Saraswati's parents? she thought wildly, putting two and two together.

'*Stop!*' a woman cried, and flung herself at Jog Tunga. In the dim light, she bore a striking resemblance to Saraswati, though her skin was darker and her hair was ramrod straight, and flowing all the way down to her waist.

The sister.

'Sun-fucked bitch,' Jog Tunga whirled around and yelled at her. 'You *knew!* And you were part of their betrayal.'

He loomed over the woman and drew his fist back.

Before she knew it, Serenity Ko was racing towards the madman. She flung herself at his back, and clawed at him as he tried to shake her off. He roared. She caught an elbow in her side and gasped, right as Saraswati joined her and punched him square in the stomach.

'You fucking *cow,*' the long-haired woman said, grabbing Saraswati round the waist and knocking her off her feet. Kili whirred out of her pocket and hurled himself at the woman, and she shrieked, batting him away. Courage Praia joined in the fray, pinning the woman to the ground, using all their weight to hold her in place as she writhed and struggled.

Serenity Ko clung onto the man as he reached backwards and wrapped a hand around her wrist. His grip threatened to crush her bones with its intensity. She screamed and tried to break free, swatting at him. She slung her free hand in a wild arc, aiming for the side of his head, but made contact with his crown.

She knocked his crown off his head and onto the ground. He whirled around.

'You have no idea who you're dealing with,' he said, his eyes wild as he lunged towards her. As he launched himself her way, Serenity Ko spotted large, bald patches on his skull, lined with embedded circuits.

'His *crown!*' she shrieked. '*Saras! Praia!* Get his *crown!*'

Grace Kube used to be a modder, she idly recalled, as Jog Tunga's fist made contact with her face. *He has scars, but they used to be circuits. This is what the madman is controlling everyone with. His crown.*

He spun around right after the punch landed. Spots danced in Serenity Ko's vision, but she struggled to keep her balance and go after him.

With a snarl like a cornered animal, he stalked towards Saraswati.

She held his crown high above her head, backing away slowly.

'Run!' Serenity Ko yelled.

Saraswati wasn't quick enough. Jog Tunga launched himself and knocked her off her feet.

Fingers still tightly clasped around the crown, she stumbled momentarily against the low wall of the sky-platform, and went right over the edge without a sound.

The B'naar are known for tunnelling through space, and must often wear mechanised bio-suits to ensure their raw strength can be contained when they're planet-side...

—*Intelligent Life Beyond Greater Human Space*
1965 Anno Earth | 1890 Interstellar Era

THIRTY-SIX

MY LIFE DIDN'T flash before my eyes.

Everything happened too quickly for that.

Saras! Kili screamed.

The roar of the wind rushed past me, or maybe that was my heart pounding in my ears, threatening to implode. Darkness pulsed as the ground rushed up to me. There was no thought.

And then I was hovering in mid-air, still hundreds of feet off the ground, something coiled tight around my waist, crushing the breath out of me. As counter-intuitive as it was, I struggled, my body's need to breathe surpassing my primal fear of being flattened into chutney if whatever was holding me in place let me go.

I rose.

My mind was blank with panic. Unable to form words, I streamed raw emotion Kili's way.

Starlight Fantastic, came Kili's response.

I had no idea what he meant by that, but I continued to rise, until I was higher than the sky-platform, looking down. Logic oozed into my addled brain, framing the picture for me, comprehension dawning painfully slowly.

One of Starlight Fantastic's tentacles held me in the air, powerfully strong, though their grip on me had relaxed. Their being was latched onto the side of the sky-platform, along a wall, with cephalopodesque resilience. On the sky-platform below, my friends were facing off against Jog Tunga. Serenity Ko circled him, Curiosity Zia and Courage Praia flanking her at a distance. Boundless Baz had stumbled into a table, holding the side of his face. XX-29 hovered in mid-air, moving slowly towards my brother-in-law-to-be, xir feet off the ground in xir mechatronic frame.

I didn't know XX-29 could fly, I thought stupidly.

It was a scene straight from an Ur-drama fantasy.

The rest of my family was down there, too. Narmada was wailing into a napkin, and my parents sat on the floor, my mother gasping for breath as my father rubbed her back. It might have been touching if only they hadn't been megalomaniac psycho-killers, or if I hadn't despised them all.

It appeared that knocking the crown off Jog Tunga's head had done some good. When I'd held it in my hands, I'd felt a mesh of circuitry in its hollow. Clearly whatever he'd done to my parents had worn off, but the rest of the diners still moved eerily. They were rising from their enforced namaskārams, all jerks and twitches and uncoordinated stumbling. I took this to be a good sign. Now, I just had to stop him from murdering my friends.

Saras, I'm so glad you're okay, Kili practically sobbed, whirring up to me. _But feelings later. We need to stop him._

I love you, Kili, I said. _Let's end this._

I looked down at Starlight Fantastic, still majestically clamped to the side of the sky-platform.

Starlight Fantastic, thank you, I streamed at them. _Please put me down._

Are you sure? they responded.

Yes. I started this and I need to end it.

Where? Starlight Fantastic asked.

Out of nowhere, a plan came together in my mind.

How hard can you throw a punch? I asked Starlight Fantastic.

I'm afraid that's not among my talents. XX-29, on the other hand…

Of course! XX-29 was used to tunnelling through space, and xir mechatronic frame had given xir a world of trouble while xe adjusted to its force and pressure constraints.

XX-29, it's good to see you. Can you do me a favour and throw a really hard punch at the Earthling prince when I say? I asked.

Yes, Saras, XX-29 streamed back. _But I need to recalibrate all my settings._

How long will it take? I asked, panicking.

Five minutes. Maybe seven. I'm not configured to do violence. I *hate* violence, xe said sadly.

Please. We need you.

I winced as Jog Tunga lashed out at Serenity Ko, rushing towards her, catching her off-guard, grabbing her around the waist and flinging her to the ground.

If I must, XX-29 conceded.

You *must*, I said, wincing as my future brother-in-law kicked Serenity Ko in the ribs. When she stayed down, he spun to face Courage Praia and Curiosity Zia. _Tell me when you're ready._

What're you going to do? XX-29 asked, brimming with concern.

I'm going to buy you time.

I looked down at Starlight Fantastic. _Put me down right in front of Jog Tunga._

Saras, do you have a plan? Kili asked.

Yes. Trust me.

I'd tried to end this non-violently by causing chaos within my family, but Jog Tunga had clearly had plans of his own for the evening. Typical of my family to devolve into savages.

Jog Tunga's eyes widened at the sight of the tentacle extending towards him, holding me in its grasp. He must have lost track of me after I fell over the edge, and chosen to fight his way off Primus before his mind control tech wore off completely. The Primian Guard were still keeping their distance, clearly uncertain about whether he was still controlling his hostages. As I descended, he grinned like a maniac and beckoned me on.

Starlight Fantastic set me down with a gentle thump, a table spanning the distance between Jog Tunga and I. The diners around us were no longer moving, standing still and statuesque, their eyes staring emptily into the void.

'Hello, crown fucko,' I said more bravely than I felt. 'Oh wait, you lost your crown, didn't you?' I taunted.

He snarled.

'It's me you want,' I declared boldly. 'Leave the others alone and let's go.'

I balled my fists up and stood my ground, knees knocking together. He shoved a couple of diners out the way, who fell to the floor with a thump. Then he flung a chair aside and leapt onto the table between us, running down its length towards me and throwing himself off it.

I took an involuntary step back, and willed myself not to duck.

He caught me around the chest even as I threw a feeble punch at him, knocking me to the floor. He drew his fist back and I braced for impact, but he looked down at me and began to laugh.

'I have an even better idea for you,' he said.

He rose and dragged me up with him, twisting my arm behind me painfully, and wrenched me towards where my parents were seated, now fully recovered, watching the unfolding scene in disbelief.

'A crown for a daughter,' Jog Tunga said, thrusting me forward without letting go of me. 'She's mostly undamaged. Marry her off to a peasant, send her to a whorehouse or a nunnery. I don't care. Call the Bhadra arrangement off and she's yours.'

'You just tried to kill us, son,' my father said. 'Full marks for catching us off-guard.'

'A bit on the nose, though.' My mother sniffed. 'I prefer my assassination attempts to have subtlety.'

Jog Tunga grinned, abashedly. 'You've got to take your chances where you get them.'

Curiosity Zia had been drawing steadily closer in my peripheral vision, but she stopped abruptly and balked at the words.

Don't move, I streamed her. _I've got this._

'It was a good speech until then,' my father said. 'And you brought our stray home, of course.'

'The *bitch*.' Narmada rose to her feet. She strode towards me and slapped me. My face stung and I hissed.

'Now, now, Narmada. This wasn't her fault,' my mother said placatingly. 'Except inasmuch as she caused all this to happen.'

'On the plus side, it's nice to see that our newest weapon works,' my father mused. 'Food that can kill you without a trace—a real winner, Feast. We'll use it to subjugate the rest of the Earth first, and then move outwards.' He looked straight past me at Jog Tunga. 'Good call leaving her out here to do our dirty work for us.'

It felt as if my head had exploded. All thoughts of the plan I had to save the day, the planet, the galaxy evaporated.

'You *knew*?' I howled.

I'd learnt to expect nothing but power games, feints and manipulations from my family, but I'd been blindsided by *this*.

'Of course we knew you were here,' my mother said coldly. 'It's the only reason we let you continue to shirk your duty to our clan.'

'A brilliant strategic play,' my father said to Jog Tunga, then looked at me. 'I told you a year ago, and I'll say it again. You are nothing without your Godavari name, an empty shell unless we permit you to be more.'

What had started out as a do-or-die ploy to buy time so I could take them down crumbled within my mind.

I had been used again.

It was just like the night I'd won the Golden Knife. They'd sat me down and revealed that my restaurant was a money laundering front for their dirty businesses, that they'd bought off all my reviewers. They'd convinced me that I was a talentless hack, and the only reason I'd tasted any success was because I had the backing of the most powerful name in the Daxina Protectorate.

It was happening now, all over again. Bile rose in the back of my throat.

Everything that had happened since—my wretched flight to Primus, the year I'd spent struggling to prove myself to a people that didn't want me to succeed—was all because of that night.

And it was repeating itself.

All the xenophobia and slurs I'd experienced, the public

hatred, the months I'd spent hiding my identity from the friends I'd made, only to lose my friends when they'd discovered that I came from *these people.* Even my accomplishments, even *Feast* belonged to these people, my family…

It was all because *they'd* permitted it, wielding the long arm of their power and corruption across twenty-one jumpgates, managing to strike at my heart and rip it out my chest from halfway across the galaxy. And here I'd thought I was finally making my way out into the galaxy on my own. I'd foolishly believed that I was finally going to be free…

'No.' I sagged, the fight leaving me.

Saras, Kili streamed urgently.

It's all over.

They're poisoning your mind. Don't let them.

They've won.

You're free. You can fight them

I've never been free. I will never be free.

'…let's leave this sur-fucked planet and continue this wholesome destruction of Saraswati's life later,' Jog Tunga was saying, a world away. 'The bitch knocked my crown off and broke the circuit. They'll start waking up any moment. Best to escape before the Primian Guard catch on and come for us.'

*Saras!* Kili shouted. _You're the only one who can stop this. Not to save the world, but to save *yourself.*_

I'm powerless.

Jog Tunga dragged me towards the elevator capsule. Kili slammed my mind with an overwhelming sequence of visuals, playing my whole life out for me:

Every time I'd stood up against my parents when I hadn't had a chance in the world…

The way I'd carried myself in public when the Primians took to bashing my Earthling origins…

My face-off with Good Cheer Chaangte, where I'd emerged triumphant…

All the friends I'd made since I got here, their smiling happy faces relishing the food I cooked for them over an open flame…

Kissing Serenity Ko for the very first time…

They're no longer my friends.

They all came here to fight for you. *Look,* Kili commanded.

I looked around and saw—truly *saw*—my friends. Curiosity Zia and Courage Praia held at bay by my command to stand down, waiting for me to act; Boundless Baz bleeding from a head wound; Serenity Ko slumped on the floor, clearly in pain, trying to drag herself up to her feet. Starlight Fantastic clinging to the side of the sky-platform, and XX-29 hovering in mid-air, still recalibrating their systems…

You've got so much to live for. You've got your freedom to fight for. Don't throw it all away.

Maybe we'd never speak again, after tonight. Maybe I'd never *see* them again, after tonight. But I'd brought this nightmare to their doorstep, and I owed it to them to look for a way out.

_XX-29?_ I asked.

Two more minutes. I'm so sorry.

I could work with that.

'I'm not coming with you,' I declared, although Jog Tunga kept shoving me towards the elevators, following my parents. 'And I'm not here—the creator of Feast, boldly going where no cook has gone before—because I'm a *fucking* Godavari. I'm not here because you *permitted* me to stay, because you *manipulated* me into building Feast only for you to weaponise it. I'm not here for your agenda…'

'We could have hunted you down and disappeared you off this rock any time in the last year,' my father said. 'Believe whatever fairy tales you want. You're only here because of us.'

The words hammered their way out of me, stone cold. 'I'm here because other people believed in me when my family wouldn't. My *friends* believed in me. Total *strangers* believed in me. An *entire foreign government* believed in me. They helped me succeed where you failed to do your job as parents.'

As I spoke, I realised that I wasn't just buying time. I meant every single word that was ripped from my lips.

'So go on, do your worst,' I said. 'I've escaped once. I can do it again. You can trap me on Earth, strip away my privileges, tell me I'm nothing, a nobody but for my Godavari name. You can destroy everything I try to build. But I will keep going. I will fight you every step of the way.' My breath was ragged. 'Whenever I get the chance, I will destroy the plans you build. I will annihilate you and your stupid little kingdom from the inside. I will break you and make sure you never hurt anyone ever again, even if I have to sacrifice myself. I will be free—'

I heard a crack, and only felt the sting later. Spots danced before my eyes as I saw my mother draw her hand away. 'Ugh, blood,' she said, wiping her knuckles on her dress.

I tasted iron. 'You will never use or destroy anyone again.'

Behind me, Jog Tunga chuckled. 'It will be enormous fun to break her.'

Saras, I'm ready, XX-29 said.

_*Go!*_

I stomped with every ounce of my strength, bringing my right foot down on Jog Tunga's instep. He screamed and let go of me, and I dropped and rolled away awkwardly. A rush of air whispered past, and I saw a mechatronic arm slam into the side of Jog Tunga's head, followed by a loud thud.

Jog Tunga crumpled to the floor.

XX-29 froze in place. _Oh, no, what have I done?_

You might just have saved the world, I said.

Narmada wheeled around and rushed to Jog Tunga's side.

'*Leave him,*' my father commanded, his composure breaking for the first time in my memory. 'We need to go.'

'I can't—I love him!' Narmada wailed.

'Stupid girl,' my mother snapped. She grabbed her by the arm, but Narmada whirled around and gave her a hard shove, before falling to her knees beside Jog Tunga again.

'Leave them both!' my father barked.

'My baby!' my mother whispered, standing still in horror.

'*Come!*' he commanded. 'At least we still have our son!'

They broke into a run, far faster than I might have imagined, slamming the elevator door behind them, as the words he'd spoken crashed into me.

Did he just say "son"? It made no sense. I'd never had a brother. Or so I'd thought.

I rolled over onto my back and saw a fleet of ships rolling in towards us like clouds.

And we were suddenly enveloped in noise, the air filling with sobs, cries, and exclamations of shock and protest. The diners had woken from their eerie, statuesque stillness. Optimism Mahd'vi was barking commands.

Saras. You did it, Kili said quietly.

Not yet, I replied, staggering to my feet.

I walked over to where XX-29 stood, and placed an arm gently on xir mechatronic frame. 'I'm sorry I asked you to be violent.'

Xe flinched, then turned and whistled a sad howl. 'I'm sorry for judging you. Too harsh. Still mad at you, but want to talk.'

And then a many-tentacled hug wrapped me up in its cool folds, and Starlight Fantastic was weeping. 'We don't get to judge what we don't know. We should never have walked away from you, left you alone to deal with this. I forgive you. And I beg for your forgiveness, in turn.'

'There's nothing to forgive,' I choked out.

Curiosity Zia and Boundless Baz stood off to the side, at a distance. I met her gaze, and she took a tentative step towards me, before Boundless Baz grabbed her by the elbow. They turned as one and slowly walked away.

My heart sank. Perhaps it was stupidly romantic to believe that all would be forgiven because I'd saved the world after nearly destroying it.

I made my way to Serenity Ko and Courage Praia. Courage Praia moved aside. 'I'm not sure I understand what happened,' they said. 'But then again, I'm not sure I want to know.'

I knelt beside Serenity Ko, who winced in pain with every breath, but managed to summon up a weak grin. 'Earth girl,' she said hoarsely. 'Your fucking brother-in-law kicked me hard in the ribs.'

'I'm sorry for everything,' I said, my voice cracking.

'You can make it up to me later,' Serenity Ko said. 'I want you to tell me your story again.'

'Tomorrow?' I rasped, scarcely able to believe it. The adrenaline was beginning to ebb, leaving me on the verge of tears.

'Too soon. Maybe someday.'

She took my hand and squeezed it briefly, and I found myself falling into her eyes even as my heart cracked.

I was hauled to my feet, the moment crashing down upon me.

'We're taking you in for questioning,' someone barked.

'Are you *crazy*?' Serenity Ko practically shrieked.

Members of the Primian Guard had dropped down from their ships with the thunderous sound of boots upon flowmetal. A dozen of them surrounded me, their weapons pointed my way.

'*Halt!*' The command whipped through the air. Optimism Mahd'vi strode our way. 'She has nothing to do with this,' she said, standing in front of me.

'We need to do a thorough investigation—'

'You can start by questioning the witnesses,' Optimism Mahd'vi interrupted, nodding her head in the direction of my friends. 'And get Serenity Ko medical help—she might have broken ribs.'

'Right away, Your Excellency,' the guardsman said, backtracking in a hurry.

Optimism Mahd'vi turned to face me, her expression unreadable.

'You might be a Godavari,' she said in a low voice. 'But I think you just saved the universe.'

And that's when it struck me.

Kili, I said. _This isn't over._

It isn't?

There's something I've got to do.

And then I told him what I intended, and he nuzzled up to me and brushed my cheek. _I'm by your side no matter what._

I owed it to the universe, and to myself—but mostly to the universe—to come clean once and for all.

The Kaveri clan brought an iron pragmatism wrapped in velvet diplomacy to the Daxina Protectorate, often challenging the Godavari clan's strategy of direct violence. Their treasury overflowed with wealth extracted through taxation schemes of brilliant complexity that somehow left merchants feeling fortunate even as invisible fingers slipped into their coffers, funding magnificent public works and hospitals, and it was this that made them a threat to the ruling Godavaris...

–from the Classified Godavari Files

THIRTY-SEVEN

'THAT'S THE FILE,' Saraswati said, handing over a papyro-scroll proudly proclaiming its contents as Primian poetry, no doubt containing a slim mem-film wrapped within it as bonus content.

Optimism Mahd'vi accepted it with trembling fingers, trying not to let her excitement show. She finally had the story of her family in her hands.

'Were you really going to fuck me over, or were you just fucking with my head?' Saraswati asked.

A sound-bubble ensconced them, shutting the outside world off.

Optimism Mahd'vi winced at the choice of language, but eyed Saraswati Godavari with less disdain than she'd ever felt for the Earthling. After running over her options briefly, she decided to be forthright with her. It would draw her into a fragile, but firm, trust to be told the truth. And Optimism Mahd'vi could always leverage that later if she needed to.

'I was enjoying watching you squirm,' she said honestly. 'After all, your family did annihilate mine. And you are on my planet under a false name, which happens to be *my* name.'

Saraswati nodded slowly, in apparent understanding.

'More to the point, though, I wanted to set your family off,' Optimism Mahd'vi explained. 'I wanted to send them ballistic.

Maybe not your parents, sure, but I was sure Jog Tunga, the buffoon, would be triggered by *something* you said or did.'

Saraswati frowned at this. 'Why?'

'You set yourself apart from them,' Optimism Mahd'vi said. 'People in power hate it when you ask questions of them, resist their bullying, or meet their unreasonable demands with composure. I watched how you handled Tunga on the Ursands, remember?'

'All this to broadcast Earthlings losing their tempers across the galaxy?' Saraswati asked, shaking her head sadly. 'It'll just generate more xenophobia.'

'Not just *any* Earthlings.' Optimism Mahd'vi was swift to correct her. 'The *Godavaris* and their allies.'

'Nobody in the galaxy cares about the specifics.'

'*I* do,' Optimism Mahd'vi said firmly.

Saraswati smiled sadly. She gently stroked the Winger that followed her around everywhere, hovering at her shoulder.

'I didn't know he'd misuse Feast as mind control, though,' Optimism Mahd'vi admitted. 'All I wanted to do was catch him unawares and elicit some violence. Maybe injuring a Primian citizen or two... I didn't know he was going to build a weapon with it. All I wanted was to recover Feast from him, and use the threat of Earthling espionage to bolster our own defences.'

'So things went wrong?' Saraswati asked.

'Indescribably so.'

Optimism Mahd'vi studied the Godavari girl again. She held herself tall, but without the arrogance that usually accompanied aristocratic origins. Sur-light filled the world around them, and the Harmony Knot blossomed in a swirl of colours—Earthling flora and Primian flora bound together, woven into an inseparable knot, their heady scents rising to fill the air. It was fittingly symbolic to be having this conversation beneath its boughs.

'What'll you do about it?' Saraswati asked, her eyes narrowing.

'Plan, prepare.' Optimism Mahd'vi sighed. 'We have no way to know what your family might have done with it back on Earth.'

'You've got the lot of them in your interrogation chambers,' Saraswati said bitterly.

'Are you actually feeling *sorry* for them?' Optimism Mahd'vi asked, taken aback.

'No, I just hate them being on the same planet as me.'

Optimism Mahd'vi paused, then plunged forward with what she'd been thinking. 'There's a reason I didn't ask you to send me the Kaveri file as a dead drop.'

'Which is?'

'I wanted to talk to you. Personally.'

'Why?' Saraswati tilted her head.

'We don't have your *whole* family in captivity. There's a son.'

'I know nothing about him,' Saraswati said. 'I've never met my brother. Didn't know he *existed* until a nava ago.'

'You might be able to convince them to tell us more…' Optimism Mahd'vi suggested, working her way to what she really wanted to say, feeling out Saraswati's reactions.

Saraswati burst into peals of laughter. If the birds could have heard them within the sound-bubble, they would likely have taken flight.

'My parents never trusted me on Earth. None of them did. That won't have changed. Never will,' she said, continuing to chuckle before her voice took on a steel edge. 'And I never want to see them again.'

'Not our best idea then,' Optimism Mahd'vi conceded, smiling as if embarrassed. She then faked a laugh. 'We might as well send you to Earth to try and find him.'

Saraswati demurred. 'I'm no spy. I'm just a cook.'

'You did a great job being a double agent,' Optimism Mahd'vi tried. 'Saved the universe, at least temporarily. That did nothing for you?'

'Nope,' Saraswati shrugged. 'Hated every minute.'

'Shame,' Optimism Mahd'vi said. She changed tack. 'We have a lot of top secret information about you, and it would be tragic if it leaked to the public…'

'On that note…'

'What now?' asked Optimism Mahd'vi.

'I'm coming clean to the public. About my Godavari identity,' Saraswati said in a rush.

That nearly knocked Optimism Mahd'vi's breath from her. '*What?*'

'I owe them the truth.'

'Stupid girl,' Optimism Mahd'vi said. 'You'll be deported. Why endure all this hardship if—?'

'Not if you pardon me for saving the universe at the Millennium Feast,' Saraswati said boldly. 'I looked at the Primian citizenship bylaws, and Secretariat pardons can be issued under exceptional circumstances, such as acts of bravery resulting in saving the planet—no wait, the entire galaxy...'

Optimism Mahd'vi took a deep breath.

'You'll keep what we did with Feast a secret?'

'Yes.'

Optimism Mahd'vi paused, considering it. And then, she grinned.

'You haven't given me the complete file on my family, have you?'

'Do you take me for a complete idiot?' Saraswati shot back.

'When do I get the rest?' Optimism Mahd'vi asked, feigning casual indifference while kicking herself for having overplayed her hand.

'When you prove to me that I can trust you.'

Saraswati Kaveri turned and walked away.

She'd really make an excellent spy, Optimism Mahd'vi thought as she eyed the retreating figure.

That was a problem for another day, though. As was the Godavari family, now safely under lock and key where they could hurt nobody—at least not directly—while she worked at convincing them that sharing all their secrets would be to their advantage. Once the Primian Guard had sucked them dry, Optimism Mahd'vi would move for the UHC to send them to a mining rock, somewhere in a distant star system.

On the whole, while the debacle at the Millennium Feast had been regrettable, Optimism Mahd'vi had used it to fuel a wave of pro-Primian sentiment, not just at home, but across the galaxy. Within the halls of the Secretariat, she was pushing through legislation that would boost Primian programming all across the Loop. She was even exploring expanding their military, and urging a number of members of the United Human Cooperative to do the same, waving evidence of Earthling hostility with underlying K'artri-tva cooperation under their noses to goad them into action.

A few days from now, she'd double down on her plans for Feast, as well.

But right in this moment, as she looked to the future, Optimism Mahd'vi held the key to her past in her hands, which were trembling violently. She walked past the Harmony Knot, through the gardens, the sounds of tourists jabbering in strange languages and children laughing with delight all around her, the gentle breeze stirring her hair, the scent of summer washing over her, all the way until she reached the silence of her chambers in the Secretariat.

She poured herself a glass of starfruit wine from a bottle in her drawer and sat at her desk.

Optimism Mahd'vi slid into the Loop, scanned the code on the mem-film, and began to read the story of her long-lost family, dating back four hundred years.

Tears streamed down her face.

What we put on a plate captures the exquisite paradox of being human—our yearning for transcendence through creative expression and our rootedness in human connection. Every single plate is a beautiful monument to our own impermanence, preserving who we are in fleeting stillness.

—Grace Menmo,
Art and Culture in the Interstellar Era: The Definitive Edition
2065 Anno Earth | 1990 Interstellar Era

THIRTY-EIGHT

'WE NEED TO shut this *down*.' Serenity Ko slammed her palm onto the table and rose to her feet. 'Feast is a threat. We are far too open to manipulation. We were *used*. And we built the thing that let them use us.'

'I concur,' Courage Na'vil said, and Serenity Ko gave him a grateful nod. 'We've evinced no long-lasting effects from the mind control technique that was used, on a biological level. Naturally, there's psychological trauma, and I'm not sure how that might manifest in the long run. But overall, we've opened up a plethora of possibilities—and keep in mind that even though the Earthlings who incited this were arrested, it was performed on a live broadcast across the galaxy. It could inspire dozens of other factions to try their hand.'

'There was no direct damage to our codebase,' Optimism Sah'r said. 'The pathways were clearly redirected to whatever stack the Earthlings were using to manipulate everyone. That's why we couldn't shut things down from the office on the night of the Millennium Feast—we had zero control.' She paused. 'We've changed all our security keys, but they've got a copy of all our Feast code now…' She trailed off bitterly. 'Anyone can reuse it if they decide to license or sell it. The whole galaxy can try their hand at building something similar. Even with bolstered security, we're too vulnerable to continue.'

Grace Kube steepled his fingers. 'The great tragedy of art is when it becomes commodified by the government as a tool of propaganda, a means to control, turning it from an expression of joy into a weapon of fear, towards the ends of domination and subjugation.' He took a sip of his kaapi, then looked straight at Serenity Ko. 'You built something bold, brave and beautiful. And I'm sorry it turned out this way.'

'I still don't understand how they got their hands on our code in the first place…' Optimism Sah'r frowned. She rose and paced the Ideatheque, weaving a path through the towering indoor plants. 'We thought our systems had the strongest security protocols in place. It's almost as if they had someone on the inside…'

Serenity Ko glanced at Grace Kube, who was suddenly preoccupied with snipping dead leaves off one of the bottle-lilies, and then at Optimism Mahd'vi, whose face revealed nothing. Everyone who'd been involved in the incident at the Millennium Feast had signed scrollwork swearing them to secrecy, and Honour Aki had been tracked down and compelled to swear his silence, too. At XP Inc., only Grace Kube had been informed of Saraswati's role—walking straight into XP Inc. and stealing Feast from right under their noses—and he'd taken the only possible course of action and fired her.

Saraswati, for her part, had told the wider team that she was leaving to seek other challenges, and to recover from the trauma of seeing her creation misused at the hands of the Earthlings. She'd effectively disappeared, though Serenity Ko checked in with her every day to see how she was doing. She still loved her, even though she wasn't sure what she wanted to do about it. After witnessing what her family had been like firsthand, Serenity Ko could no longer blame her for her trail of falsehood or her desperate actions…

'So there you have it, Your Excellency, Optimism Mahd'vi,' Grace Kube said, summarising to break the awkward silence. 'We're all in favour of shutting Feast down and moving on. It's the only way forward.'

'No.'

'I'm sorry?' Grace Kube asked politely.

'I said "no." Absolutely not,' Optimism Mahd'vi said. 'We *can't* shut Feast down, precisely because there's the distinct possibility that everyone else has got their hands on it. All across the galaxy, even this very moment, there might be threats developing that will see it weaponised and used to break the peace—once strong, now fragile—of the United Human Cooperative. The Earthling attack was just a demonstration. We need to be prepared for what happens next.'

'By continuing to develop a dangerous tool and marketing it to consumers?' Courage Na'vil said, his tone ringing with disbelief.

'Yes. By reassuring them that Primus is safe. It's a show of confidence.' Optimism Mahd'vi's voice was like cold steel. 'If we throw in the towel, we concede that we fucked up, confirm that the technology is a treacherous weapon, and encourage those around it to use it in that manner.'

'You're joking!' Serenity Ko said.

Optimism Mahd'vi continued as if she hadn't heard her. 'We give an inch, they take a mile. We crush them by showing them that we're unassailable. We display our invulnerability by taking something that was brutalised—turned ugly—and returning it into something joyous, and wondrous. As it was *intended*.'

'So you can use it as a tool of propaganda, and pro-Primian messaging. As it was intended by *you*,' Serenity Ko said bitterly.

'That's certainly an upside I wouldn't scoff at,' Optimism Mahd'vi said coldly. The light streaming down through the windows cast a halo around her head, framing her like a deranged prophet. 'If the situation escalates, if other governments, or even alt-being species, decide to use it to their advantages, the galaxy will need every reminder it can get of *our* values. Of *Primian* virtue. Of the Nakshatran vision to *co-exist in peace*.'

Optimism Sah'r tilted her head to the side, clearly considering what Optimism Mahd'vi was saying.

'We have other ways to do that,' Grace Kube argued. 'Our Primian programming. Ur-dramas. The sinfonia…'

'Yes, but this beams it right into people's minds,' Optimism Mahd'vi said softly. 'It tangles up all our philosophies and virtues with their memories, binding them to it inseparably, reminding them of why we stand for all that we do.'

'I have ethical concerns,' Courage Na'vil began, and for the first time, Serenity Ko was delighted to hear the words leave his lips.

'I'm sure you do,' Optimism Mahd'vi said smoothly. 'And I have carte blanche from the Secretariat, extra funding for neuro-dev research, and anything else you might need to ensure this goes smoothly.'

Courage Na'vil opened his mouth as if to argue, then closed it soundlessly.

'This is *madness!*' Serenity Ko snapped.

Optimism Mahd'vi ignored her, and addressed Grace Kube instead. 'We will also work on incentivising *official* exports and licensing, and not whatever shabby code folks on Earth might take to peddling, if Tunga made backups. An enormous bump to your profits. And your creative team—including your *former employees*—will be protected from any unfavourable outcomes, past, present or future.'

Serenity Ko noticed the emphasis Optimism Mahd'vi had laid on her words, and it dawned on her that this was blackmail. She bit her tongue to force herself not to say it out loud, and Optimism Mahd'vi gave her a fleeting smile.

'In case you're wondering, there's litigation incoming from about five hundred diners who were at the Millennium Feast. They're all citing mental trauma at the hands of XP Inc., and they name Serenity Ko and all the rest of you. We can work together to make it go away,' Optimism Mahd'vi carried on. 'Assuming you need any additional incentives.'

She produced the scrollwork, and Serenity Ko's heart sank as, one by one, each of the Triumvirate broke in the face of absolute power and signed it. It was passed on to her, at last. She eyed the scrollwork in dismay, and her gut twisted as she came to a decision.

'I object to this strongly, but it doesn't matter anymore. None of you will listen to me, and your decision is unanimous.' Her voice shook. 'Determining the fate of the universe is above my pay grade. I quit.'

Ammamma smelled of flowers and spice—like jasmine blossoms whose petals were stained in chilli-ras. Serenity Ko waited for her to shout at her, to chastise her, to say the dreaded words, "I told you so," and refuse to ever talk to her again.

Instead, the old lady seemed to shrink, looking more frail and withered than ever before. She drew Serenity Ko in for a hug, and wrapped her arms around her. Serenity Ko noticed for the first time that her skin felt paper-thin as she gently patted the top of her head, her fingers massaging the back of her bare neck.

'I'm sorry it turned out this way, Ko,' Ammamma said softly.

'I should have listened to you,' Serenity Ko whispered. 'You were right all along.'

'One never wants to be,' Ammamma said.

Serenity Ko pulled away, tears streaking down her cheeks. She brushed them off with the back of her hand.

'They all sat there and let her coerce them with honeyed words,' she sniffed.

'That's how power works, my child,' Ammamma said. 'When you fly this close to Suriya, you're bound to feel its heat searing across your face, its light burning your eyes... It's impossible to escape its gravity.'

'I quit. I just walked away.' Serenity Ko felt a sudden surge of panic. 'What if I'd stayed, and tried to fix things from the inside?'

'Maybe you'll find new ways to fight them,' Ammamma said, walking into the kitchen. Serenity Ko followed her, and her grandmother started to mix a cup of hot xocolat.

'Maybe I'm a coward and I don't want to fight.'

'You've already started the fight. You stood up to them. You quit to tell them you weren't on board with their plans,' Ammamma said. 'That's shots fired, right there.'

'What do I do now?' Serenity Ko asked, hating the note of despair that caused her voice to come out high and squeaky.

'Now you rest, child,' Ammamma said soothingly. She handed her a cup of steaming hot xocolat.

Serenity Ko sipped on it gratefully. Her insides began to untwist and relax.

'You rest, and you think about things, and maybe you cry. And then you choose what you do next, how you move on, and where you go,' Ammamma continued.

'I'm sorry I failed you,' Serenity Ko said, the words bursting out of her before she could help herself.

'You didn't fail,' Ammamma said. 'You succeeded. And that's the problem. We always anticipate worst-case scenarios. We never ask ourselves: "What if this works?"'

'You asked me that exact question,' Serenity Ko sulked. 'I was too wrapped up in myself to see where you were coming from.'

'An old lady's condescension, and an idiot child's ambition.' Ammamma shook her head sadly. 'What were we really fighting about?'

'I should have listened,' Serenity Ko said.

'I should have been kinder,' Ammamma soothed.

'All is lost,' Serenity Ko said, slouching down in her seat.

'All is never lost,' Ammamma said cheerfully. Then she snapped, 'Now, watch your posture and don't slouch, Ko. Idiot child.'

She ruffled her hair fondly, and left Serenity Ko to her thoughts, which circled in endless loops, round the proverbial drain.

She'd spent the nava since the debacle at the Millennium Feast advocating to the folks at XP Inc. to shut the star-fucked project down. She'd won the Triumvirate over, and had been ecstatic at the thought of steamrolling their way across Optimism Mahd'vi's wishes, only to watch her superiors fold like a house of cards when the Secretary for Culture snd Heritage had pushed their buttons.

A part of her wanted to end Feast so the team wouldn't have to deal with the fallout to come. It was bad already, and it would get worse. She hadn't been able to shield them from the worst of the stream-media scrutiny. Political streamers and chefs around the galaxy had come for them with knives and hatchets, butchering Feast and everything it had once stood for, lambasting them for developing such dangerous technology and then having the stupidity to lose it to hostile off-world powers. Good Cheer Chaangte was having the time of her life, from what Serenity Ko saw, going after not just Saraswati, but all of Feast, and firmly establishing herself as a speaker for the traditionalist culinary lobbies who wanted to see it banned. The Wanderers were protesting en masse, framing the incident at the Millennium Feast as confirmation of everything they'd always feared about the new technology.

Paranoid fucks, Serenity Ko thought savagely. *A janky sim still delivers experiences if you're looking for them.*

And then the xenophobes had come after Saraswati, in tediously repetitive and painful ways. Even if Saraswati hadn't been fired, she'd have been fully justified in quitting and retiring to a quiet corner of Primus—or even the greater galaxy, given the kind of mental strain this was likely putting her under.

It was one of the many reasons why Serenity Ko had kept checking in with her. She felt like they needed to talk. She wasn't quite sure where she and Saraswati stood, but she knew she needed a friend at this time.

I still love her. But when—how *do we begin again?*

Much to her relief, Optimism Mahd'vi hadn't outed the truth about Saraswati's Godavari identity, and everyone who knew who she was had been rounded up and threatened with dire consequences if they were ever to reveal it. So there was that, at least.

A notification popped up on the Loop. She slid in.

The Harmony Knot. Three o'clock, said Saraswati.

Okay. Why?

You'll see.

A rush of feelings flooded her—nerves at what their reunion might be like, excitement, crippling anxiety, all causing her heart to hammer as if it were about to leap right out her chest.

It would be good to see Saraswati again, she decided.

And maybe Ammamma was right. Maybe things will turn out fine after all.

Hope stirred within Serenity Ko's chest, and she held it gently, as if it were a vial of ras.

The art of dishonesty doesn't lie in weaving a web of lies. It's remembering which threads you need to reveal, like gossamer pathways, to each person you ensnare. It's remembering who you are, and holding yourself secret at its heart.

—Godavari saying

THIRTY-NINE

I CONVINCED OPTIMISM Mahd'vi to let me make my announcement at the Harmony Knot. It seemed appropriately symbolic.

A panoply of Earth-origins flora wove its way through plants native to Primus; bougainvillea and rosinia creepers, beaumontia blossoms and astriana blooms, all tumbling into each other around the trunk of a magnificent tree, grafted together from saplings of oak, apple, spindlewood and stonefruit. It was a living monument that connected the Earth and Primus, and I felt its significance in my bones, even as I rebelled against the self-important Primian pageantry.

The press conference tent had been designed to make important people feel even more important than usual, while they said all-important things that would, in all probability, be forgotten by the time everyone reached the complimentary refreshments table. Feast cubes occupied that table, and I blanched as I took my seat at the other end of the tent.

Serenity Ko and I had had perfunctory conversations ever since the night of the Millennium Feast, and she'd let me know that the Feast tech hadn't been shut down. Optimism Mahd'vi hadn't permitted it. Serenity Ko had quit in protest.

It saddened me that Feast—something I'd built in a futile bid to be free of my past—had been mutated into this hideous apparition, a superweapon of insidious capabilities. It wasn't lost on me that my actions had, in part, unleashed its monstrous avatar, even if I'd had no way to know at the time that my family would misuse it so terribly. I was glad that Grace Kube had fired me from XP Inc. without a second's thought in the wake of the Millennium Feast disaster. He would probably never talk to me again for my role in it, but I'd try and make it up to him, just as I was trying to make it up to all my friends for lying to them about myself right from the beginning.

Saras, don't worry, Kili said reassuringly from where he hovered beside me. _Whatever happens today, I'm proud of you. You are brave and beautiful._

Thanks, Kili, I said, watching people file into the space.

I'd sent invites out to every single person I'd met on Primus, from the culinary world, to the stream-media and every socialite from every single party. I didn't expect them all to turn up, and I hadn't revealed my true intention for the day. A swarm of cam-drones filled the air, buzzing before me, each jostling for position so they could capture the perfect shot.

I took a deep breath when I caught sight of Pavi and Amol Khurshid and the kitchen staff from Nonpareil. Boundless Baz's expression was unreadable, if unimpressed. And then Good Cheer Chaangte swanned in, delight etched on her face. She'd come after Feast—and me—with renewed vengeance.

Don't lose your nerve, Kili said. _No matter what happens next. You're doing this to be free._

I'm doing this to be free. I might never work in a kitchen on Primus again. I might never have friends again. But I'm doing this to be free.

Serenity Ko walked in and time stopped. A look of confusion crossed her face, her brows knotting together, but she caught sight of me and beamed, making her way to a seat at the front of the tent. Her smile could have powered all of Uru for a month, and it set my heart ablaze, even as I tamped down any hope for us or for a future together.

I cleared my throat.

'Thank you all for coming.' I straightened up in my seat. 'I've called this conference to make an announcement that may come as a surprise to many of you.'

A collective hush descended, and I could feel the crowd hanging on my every word. They were clearly expecting me to make a statement about Feast, or maybe why I'd been fired from XP Inc. To my detractors, this would fuel even more cause to deride me. But to the rest…

'I owe you all an apology,' I said. 'You've all been a part of my life, my journey on Primus.'

Several faces frowned at this pronouncement.

I soldiered on. The consequences would be bleak, but at least I wouldn't be deported. Optimism Mahd'vi had arranged my pardon and secured my place on Primus. But this would be ugly.

'I'm sorry for lying to each and everyone of you. To my friends and the people I've loved. To my employers and the people who have supported me. To my well-wishers, who have cheered me on from afar, including the little girl who said she wanted to grow up and be like me…' My voice caught, and I paused for a moment to compose myself.

The cam-drones swarmed closer, with all the enthusiasm of insects at a particularly good picnic.

'For the last year, I have lived and worked alongside you on Primus. You've grown to trust me—*some* of you—as the face of Feast.'

This elicited a few cheers.

'I have not earned that trust,' I said flatly.

Steady on, Saras, Kili said.

'Nothing about me, to put it mildly, was as it appeared to be,' I continued. 'I'm not a nobody cook, with no reputation, and no restaurant experience from Earth.'

There was a collective gasp. The room erupted in the sort of chaos typically seen in busy bars after midnight. People began shouting questions at me, like a kitchen full of pressure cookers all set to go off at the same time.

'No,' I said loudly. 'I'm not from Primus. I'm from the Earth. That much is true. Everyone please sit down. *Please.*'

It was several minutes before everyone returned to their seats and listened to me again. I wiped a trickle of sweat off my brow.

'I'm not from Primus. I *am* from the Earth,' I repeated. 'But on Earth, I was the Golden-Knife-winning Executive Chef of Elé Oota. Before you slide into the Loop and look up what that means—'

'She's a *Godavari!*' Good Cheer Chaangte cried from near the back of the room. She shot to her feet and pointed an accusing finger at me.

Faces turned to each other in a sea of confusion. I could tell that the meaning of this only registered with Pavi and Amol Khurshid—the former had her hands clapped to her mouth, and the latter shook his head sadly at the revelation.

'What this means is that I'm related to the family that weaponised Feast, destroyed the Millennium Feast celebrations, and tried to control all our minds,' I clarified.

This elicited an electric response. A few folks backed away, dragging their chairs along with them far from the stage, as if I were now holding them hostage, threatening their lives. I saw a number of people rise and leave the tent in disgust. Hands shot up in front of people's faces, as if everyone suddenly collectively believed that causing a fracas would somehow trigger an act of violence on my part.

A culture critic I'd met at several parties raised a hand with the tentative air of someone poking a sleeping tiger. 'Are you a spy?' they asked.

'No,' I said, sticking to my end of the bargain and revealing no part of the role I'd played in the Feast fiasco. 'I am *not* a spy. I came to Primus to run away from them because they're terrible people.'

'And that makes you *less* terrible?' someone else asked with skepticism.

'My lies are terrible. I falsified my scrollwork and came here pretending to be a Kaveri. I've been pardoned because of my role in de-escalating the Feast catastrophe…'

'You *started* it!' Good Cheer Chaangte cried, rising to her feet again.

'I helped develop Feast, but I never wanted to see it misused like this,' I said honestly.

'Hah! You expect us to believe you? An *Earthling* and a *liar?*'

With those words, the dam broke and the hesitance and politeness of the Primian crowd before me evaporated. The swarm of cam-drones descended upon me, as the people beneath them shouted angry slurs at me.

Serenity Ko shot to her feet.

'Will all of you *shut the fuck up?*' she bellowed. She then strode up to the stage and grabbed the mic from me. 'Nine Virtues! Just shut the fuck *up*.'

That caused a momentary lull, and she leapt right in. 'Saraswati happens to be a brilliant person and a kind human being, no matter what her last name is.'

Everyone swivelled towards her to pay attention. 'You probably expect me to defend her, but I'm not going to. She can speak for herself. But I expect you to *listen* to her because she deserves to be heard.'

This was greeted with an echoing silence.

'All yours,' she said in a low voice, handing the mic back to me with a tight smile.

'We were right all along!' Good Cheer Chaangte crowed. 'You were—and *are*—a self-serving, self-absorbed vehicle of Earthling excess.'

This gave rise to a new ripple of murmurs. I flashed her a withering look of disbelief.

'I created a technology that revolutionised how we taste the world. Literally,' I plunged on. 'It was misused and—'

'That was what you had planned from the beginning!' Good Cheer Chaangte shouted, positively bouncing up and down on the balls of her feet. The murmurs in the room grew to a dull throb of conversation.

I dropped the mic. I couldn't carry on like this. I couldn't do it alone.

Serenity Ko was at my side again. 'May I?' she offered.

I shrugged, helplessly. She took the mic, cleared her throat and started speaking again, with a firm, clear voice.

'Saraswati built Feast *with me.* With XP Inc. and a hundred other Primians. With the backing of the Secretariat. And she did it while tolerating my presence as an overbearing, domineering, bossy co-worker. She did it despite all the judgment, criticism and pressures she was under from *all of you*.' Serenity Ko's tone took on a rare note of genuine pride that even the most cynical journalist couldn't mistake. She paused, looking around the room fiercely, as if daring someone to challenge her. 'And yes, regrettably, she lied. And maybe she doesn't deserve your forgiveness right away. But what in sur-fucking hell is your problem with *listening*?'

The room stilled.

'Yours. Again,' she said, handing the microphone back to me.

I dared to breathe, then.

'Thank you,' I whispered.

'I *don't* deserve your forgiveness. Not just yet,' I said. 'But you deserve to know the truth. I owe it to you. The universe doesn't revolve around me, but I know my lies have hurt people I love deeply and care about tremendously.'

At this, I glanced at Boundless Baz and XX-29, then looked at Serenity Ko.

'It doesn't matter that I didn't intend to hurt you. I never thought things would get so out of hand. But intentions don't count; I hurt you all, anyway. And all I can do is ask you to let me *earn* your forgiveness, and earn your trust, one step at a time, whenever you are ready.'

Serenity Ko left then, with a slow, sad smile upon her face.

As the stream-media pummelled me with their questions, my heart ached. But I was free. Alone in this star-fucked universe, but for Kili.

But *free*.

Cooking is love.
Food is friendship.
A meal shared is a celebration

—Kanakamma
2045 Anno Earth | 1970 Interstellar Era

TWO NAVAS LATER...

I DIDN'T REALISE I was humming as I worked. I'd gotten all the way through slicing potatoes, throwing lentils in a blender to grind them down, roughly chopping sprigs of cilantrino and peeling baby gayam before it dawned on me that I might have actually been hopeful, if not entirely happy.

In fact, my attention was only drawn to the Legends of the Future song I was humming when a loud voice, somewhat off-key, chimed in to supply the lyrics.

'*And if we fall, we fall together, into the infinity of a new beginning...*' Serenity Ko belted at the top of her lungs.

I winced, then grinned, and stopped working. My heart soared at the sight of her, my pulse erratic and my ears hot as I tried to fight the feeling down. It was too much to hope that she might want anything to do with me, other than be the occasional friend who dropped by for a bira, or streamed to check if I was doing all right. And I didn't blame her one bit.

'How are your ribs?' I asked cautiously.

It's good to see you, Ko! Kili bobbled over to her, and nuzzled her cheek fondly.

She stroked his chrome and green body and grinned at me. 'Ribs are great. Modern medicine at its best.'

'I'm glad,' I said, before returning to the cilantrino chutney I'd been prepping.

She hovered awkwardly in front of the counter, and I was uncomfortably aware that she was staring at me.

'You're up early,' I teased, to break the awkward silence.

'Only for you,' she said awkwardly, devastating my attempt.

We lapsed back into silence as I started putting together the gayam sambar, stewing the baby gayam shoots in a spice blend with a spiced-sour ras concoction I'd discovered at the back of the kitchen.

'I understand if you never want to talk to me again—' I began, right at the same time as she said, 'I forgive you for all of it.'

'What was that again?' My hands shook.

Serenity Ko shrugged, smiled bashfully. It was the first time I'd seen her looking so earnest, and vulnerable, and it was incredibly attractive. 'I've been doing some thinking…' she said slowly. 'And it isn't worth staying mad at you. I saw what you were up against. The family you were born into are awful. I have nothing but sympathy for you. You did what you thought was best, what you had to do to survive.'

Her voice grew more intense. 'Sometimes we need to run away, protect ourselves. Sometimes we're manipulated and used. You've suffered that more than most. And nobody deserves it, least of all you.'

'Thank you,' I said. 'I really am sorry, though.'

'I know.'

'No more lies, I promise.'

'I know. I knew the moment I turned up at the press conference.'

'I had to come clean.'

'I hope they haven't been too hard on you.'

I snorted. 'It's no more than I deserve.'

'It's been brutal, hasn't it?'

'You bet.' I smiled wryly. 'But I'll face the heat. It needed to be done.'

'You're incredibly brave, you know?' Serenity Ko said.

'Not really. Just desserts and all that. But… Thanks.'

We lapsed into another awkward silence.

'So… friends?' I offered.

'I—'

'Look who it is, trespassing on our property!' A voice cut her off.

I gazed at her, ardently hoping she'd continue, but she quickly whirled around and plastered that idiotic, performative grin of hers across her face.

The moment unspooled as Curiosity Zia strode into her kitchen, followed closely by Courage Oslo. They'd just returned from a run in the local park after letting me into their home earlier that morning.

'If that aroma is anything to go by, she's welcome to trespass any time,' he said, winking at me.

Breakfast at ours tomorrow. We're inviting everyone, Curiosity Zia had streamed last night. _You're cooking._

I'd jumped at the offer. The past few navas had been excruciating, and I would cling to any gesture of friendship like a life raft.

'I'm making masala dosas for breakfast,' I announced. 'You probably don't know what those are, and you're in for a treat, I promise.'

'You could tell me it was barbecued tree bark and I'd eat it,' Curiosity Zia said with a grin, then her expression softened. 'We didn't get to chat when you got here. How're you doing, Saras?'

I shrugged. 'Nothing has changed, really. A ton of people hated me before, and that number has only grown, but I'm used to it by now.' I smiled at her. 'Thank you for letting me into your home again. I don't deserve it, but—'

'We want to be friends with you,' Curiosity Zia said firmly. 'And we're willing to work on it. I saw firsthand what your family was like and… well, you clearly are nothing like them. Plus, it took incredible courage to come clean to the whole fucking universe. So, I'm willing to listen.' She smiled.

'Also, from what I heard, you saved my life!' Courage Oslo said, running a hand through his damp hair. 'I can't tell you what it was like, being a zombie. I had no idea what I was doing—my mind was a complete blank…'

'I'm sorry,' I said, genuine guilt worming its way through my insides.

'It's not your fault,' Curiosity Zia said.

I opened my mouth to argue, then remembered that she didn't know I'd stolen Feast, only that I was related to the people who'd caused all the chaos and violence that night.

'Don't apologise on behalf of your family, Saras,' Curiosity Zia continued firmly. 'You are *not* them. And I'm glad you've escaped them.'

'Hear, hear!' Boundless Baz said, walking in with a cooler. He popped it open and extracted two bira bottles, before offering the contents to everyone else. He then walked straight over to me, put the pint down on the counter and commanded, 'Drink.'

'We're here for breakfast, Baz,' I said. 'And I'm cooking.'

'Drink,' he repeated.

Hesitantly, I grabbed the bottle, pulled the cap off, and held it up to my lips. He opened his bottle and raised it in my direction. 'To you. For not turning out a shithead, unlike the rest of your family. No offence—except no, I take that back, full offence to the lot of them.'

I laughed and took a sip.

He leaned over the counter. 'I'm sorry I judged you so harshly,' he said. 'I had no right. It took a world of courage to do what you did—stand up to your family, come clean to the galaxy…'

XX-29 and Starlight Fantastic arrived right then, before I could respond.

'Our off-world heroes are here!' Curiosity Zia said with a whoop.

Starlight Fantastic's tentacles turned crimson in mortification, and XX-29's soft, globular being radiated shades of pink within xir mechatronic frame.

Boundless Baz abandoned me and walked up to XX-29, pulling xir into an awkward, lopsided hug. I beamed at the sight of everyone in the same room for the first time in ages. Curiosity Zia and Courage Oslo had a fairly large living space, but it was positively cramped with the friends I'd made and lost… and hoped to regain, given time.

As the familiar sounds of their nonsensical conversation washed over me, now with a wilder, bolder edge since

Serenity Ko was here, regaling them with tales of her drunken escapades—and no doubt charming the socks off them—I set to making them all breakfast.

My chutney was ready, and I gave the gayam sambar a quick check to make sure it was reducing nicely. When I was certain it was done, I took it off the burner. The stir-fried potatoes were perfectly seasoned, and laid off to one side. The trouble with using a single camp stove for cooking was that I couldn't prep ingredients simultaneously.

I pulled the dosa batter out from the fridge. I'd made it at home from arasi-grain and let it ferment the previous night. I heated up a pan on the illegal burner Curiosity Zia and Courage Oslo had smuggled in from Earth, looking around to make sure the smoke alarms had been disabled. I then placed a saucepan on the open flame to pre-heat it.

'Ooh! The fragrance of Earth food,' Boundless Baz said, leaning his head back and inhaling deeply.

'Soon!' I teased, surprised at how easily we fell into our old rhythm, as if the last few māsas had never happened.

Once the pan seemed hot enough, I spooned some butter on, then tentatively ladled some dosa batter onto it, swirling the ladle around in a circle to spread it out evenly. I'd never used this set up to make dosas before. Usually on Earth, we had a flat, heavy, cast iron dosa kallu… I beamed when the crepe-like dosa began to brown at its edges before flipping it over.

'Is that mine?' Boundless Baz asked.

'The first one's always a dud,' I said. 'Patience.'

I started prepping the second dosa, and soon, I was turning them out at a rapid rate. Each dosa came hot off the griddle, and was laid flat on the plate and stuffed with potato filling before being served with a side of chutney and gayam.

'Fucking delicious as always,' Boundless Baz said, talking around his food.

Everyone lapsed into silence, only stopping by to help themselves to more dosa from where I was turning it out in a towering stack on the kitchen counter.

Serenity Ko walked up to me, a shifty look in her eyes.

'Don't touch anything,' I said, part-warning, part-teasing.

Serenity Ko rolled her eyes. 'Not this again.'

'You haven't eaten yet,' I said, noticing the distinct lack of a plate in her hands.

'I thought I'd wait and keep you company,' she said. She hovered by my side in the kitchen, sipping on a bira as I turned out at least three helpings of dosa apiece, everyone giving into their own gluttony.

'I want to talk to you,' she said hesitantly.

'Go on,' I said, focusing a shade too intently on the little burner.

'I know—I said some things… And I've *done* some things, and things kind of ended badly between us before they even began, but…'

My heart stuttered, and my hands shook as I poured out more dosa batter.

'Nothing compared to what I've done,' I said in a low voice.

'And like I said, I've forgiven you,' Serenity Ko said impatiently. She fidgeted with the now-diminished stack of dosas.

'I have overwhelmingly deep, horrendously sincere feelings for you, Saras,' she said quietly, then paused. 'I've been doing some thinking. Will you come to Rihan and Eria's wedding with me?'

'Of course! I wouldn't miss it for all the world. If they'll still have me after everything…'

'Not as friends,' Serenity Ko said, the words rushing out of her.

'What are you trying to say, Ko?'

'I want to be with you. After everything we've been through, it feels right to give us a chance.'

I dropped the ladle and spun around. 'Are you serious?'

'I mean, if you want to—'

I cut her off mid-sentence, reaching out to cup her face in my hands, drawing her close to me and kissing her. A thrumming rose to fill me where an emptiness had been, and all of me felt like it was dancing, even though we were locked together, utterly still in a moment that defied time itself. I drowned myself in the scent of her—spiced, with a hint of fruit, and fought the urge to pull her closer to me, to tear her clothes off …

The smell of burning singed my nostrils, and I broke off the kiss and whirled around.

The dosa I'd been making was turning to charcoal on the pan. I quickly scraped it off. When I looked up, my friends' delighted faces were beaming at us.

*Yay!* Go Saras! Kili cheered, flying around in exaggerated loop the loops.

'Took you long enough,' Courage Oslo grumbled.

'I win!' Boundless Baz crowed.

'Win what?' I asked suspiciously.

'We had a bet on how long it would take for you to wind up together,' Starlight Fantastic said, tentacles blushing pink.

'I bet it helps that you no longer work together,' Curiosity Zia said wickedly, then glanced at Courage Oslo. 'Though by that logic, it's time I retire, isn't it?'

'It would make the kitchen much quieter, possibly more tolerable,' Courage Oslo shot back.

Curiosity Zia flung a cushion at him. The living room devolved into a cushion fight.

'Juveniles,' I heckled.

Tell me about it. Kili smirked.

He whirred off my shoulder and began to dive-bomb everyone, throwing himself into the chaos with a vengeance.

Serenity Ko wrapped her arms around my waist and rested her chin on my shoulder. 'What about my breakfast?' she asked.

'You just want someone who can cook for you, don't you?'

'It's a benefit.'

I beamed, leaning into her. Suriya streamed through the windows and into the living room, dappling it in a warmth that reflected the feeling of contentment spreading through me.

I didn't know what the future held. I only knew that I was safe. I was free.

I was surrounded by people I loved, with a chance to build a life with them. My best friend Kili was by my side, had stood by me through it all, and always would.

The woman I loved had her arms wrapped around me.

I gasped.

'What is it?' Ko asked.

'I just realised that I love you,' I said.

'Oh!' She laughed and it tickled my ear. 'I realised that ages ago!'

I beamed, and flipped a fresh dosa over onto a plate.

I didn't know what I was going to do next, and it didn't matter. I was content, and cooking over an open flame.

THE END

ACKNOWLEDGEMENTS

ACKNOWLEDGEMENTS

NO WRITER IS an island. A novel can only exist if those who surround the fragile world of its creator hold them in kindness, bearing the burden of their transience between worlds—the imagined and the real, lines blurring all too often—with unwavering support. While the world in a novel reflects the origins of an idea pressed between the pages of time, reality often shifts in tremors and landslides. The writer finds themself carried onward by time's relentless torrent, struggling to remain within the bubble in which a story began, while without, their own story unravels and quakes, threatening to shatter the precious balance of the world within. This book you hold was protected, its writer steered through tumultuous uncertainty, by the careful hands of countless people, and to them I owe a tremendous debt of gratitude.

While I was drafting, my dog Tugger suffered a terrible health spiral, leading to his eventual passing. I was left with fifteen and a half years of beautiful memories and an unconquerable sense of loss. His twin brother, Scamper, had passed just over a year before, and for the first time in two decades, I wasn't a dog parent. I lost an enormous part of my identity, and with it, my words were swallowed into the void. I was halfway through my draft and I had nothing left to say.

My wonderful editor at Solaris Books, David Thomas Moore, and my fantastic agent, Cameron McClure at Donald Maass Literary Agency, stepped up with incredible kindness, giving me the space and time I needed to be able to make sense of reality again. Thank you both for being there for me, for the deadline extensions and supportive email exchanges that kept me going.

All the folks at Solaris Books—Jess Gofton and Natalie Charlesworth for their brilliant publicity ideas, Sam Gretton for two gorgeous *Flavour Hacker* covers, and everyone else on the team who chipped in, you have all my thanks.

To my parents, Amma and Appa, my sister Bhamini and my brother-in-law Ani, my Ammamma, and my enormous family—thank you for the beers, the cheers, the word of the day challenges, and limitless supplies of food and coffee.

To Scamper and Tugger, in whose memory I write these words—thank you for the best two decades of my life, including spending your final years surrounding me with love while I took to writing my first three novels.

Tons of gratitude to Samit Basu, Tashan Mehta, SB Divya, Indra Das, Lavie Tidhar, Zen Cho, Tasha Suri, Frasier Armitage, and so many writers around the world for your words of kindness and encouragement through it all. All my thanks to my friends for their limitless patience while I disappeared into my writing cave and ignored their texts for weeks on end.

To my little beagle nephew Hugo, for bringing new light into the world: May you always enjoy gnawing on the spines of all my books.

To you, dear reader, for joining me again on another journey with Saras, Kili and Ko… I wouldn't be doing this if it weren't for you.

And as ever, to my husband, Shiv: I'm glad there is you.

ABOUT THE AUTHOR

Lavanya Lakshminarayan is the first Indian woman to be shortlisted for the Arthur C. Clarke Award. She is the multi-award-winning author of *The Ten Percent Thief,* listed in *Esquire* magazine's 75 Best Sci Fi Books of All-Time, and the *Flavour Hacker* series. She's also a Locus Award finalist, and her novels have been included multiple times in Reactor's Best Books of the Year.

She's occasionally a game designer, and has created worlds for *FarmVille* and *Mafia Wars*, among other games.

Lavanya lives between Bangalore and Hyderabad. *Intergalactic Feast* is her third novel.

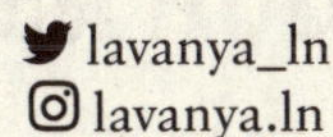